SPEEDSTER'S
SPARK

BOOKS BY JAKE TYSON

JAKE TYSON

THE VINDICATORS BOOK FIVE

SPEEDSTER'S SPARK

THE SICARAN WAR

Ambassador International
GREENVILLE, SOUTH CAROLINA & BELFAST, NORTHERN IRELAND

www.ambassador-international.com

Speedster's Spark

©2025 by Jake Tyson

All rights reserved

Hardcover ISBN: 978-1-64960-884-0
Paperback ISBN: 978-1-64960-432-3
eISBN: 978-1-64960-571-9

This is a work of fiction. Names, characters, and incidents are all products of the author's imagination or are used for fictional purposes. Any resemblance to actual events or persons, living or dead, is entirely coincidental. Any mentioned brand names, places, and trademarks remain the property of their respective owners, bear no association with the author or the publisher, and are used for fictional purposes only.

All Scripture used is taken from the King James Version of the Bible. Public Domain.

Cover design by Hannah Linder Designs
Interior Typesetting by Dentelle Design
Edited by Sydney Witbeck

AMBASSADOR INTERNATIONAL
Emerald House
411 University Ridge, Suite B14
Greenville, SC 29601
United States
www.ambassador-international.com

AMBASSADOR BOOKS
The Mount
2 Woodstock Link
Belfast, BT6 8DD
Northern Ireland, United Kingdom
www.ambassadormedia.co.uk

The colophon is a trademark of Ambassador, a Christian publishing company.

TEAM ROSTERS

The Vindicators:

- Carter Jonson/The Crusader—Son of Wyatt Jonson, the first Crusader, nineteen-year-old Carter has taken up his father's mantle and his mission to protect the Brooks.
- Jarrett Mercer/Yeoman—Jarrett is a former member of U.S. Special Forces and an active agent of CLOUD. He lives on a farm outside Wichita, Kansas, and protects that city as a crossbow-wielding vigilante.
- Patrick Omer/Spright—The youngest member of the Vindicators, Patrick has super speed and lives in California. He is a recent high school graduate, preparing to attend college.

The Opera Mask Gang:

- Anton Coleman/Negator—The oldest of the Coleman triplets and the force behind their criminal activities. Anton has destructive power when he draws on negative emotions.
- Darius Coleman/Infuser—The most passive of the Coleman triplets, Darius does not wish to be a criminal but goes along with Anton's plans to keep the family together.
- Zoey "Zee" Coleman/Sensory—Zoey is a political activist and agitator. She has no interest in crime but follows her brothers because of their mutual need for money.

The Sicarans:

- Roland Demirci/Keskin—Formerly an apprentice of the assassin Kane McCrory, Roland has been tasked with recruiting superhumans to the Sicarans' cause.
- Adranis—A mysterious Sicaran with wealth and luxury who lives in the United States.

Others:

- Alexa Patel—A Pakistani student attending a Christian college, Alexa is a fish out of water who likes to keep to herself.
- Asher Lincoln—A good friend of Patrick's, Asher attends a nearby college and is supportive of his friend's superhero identity.
- Bryce Emerson—Bryce is Patrick's roommate in college and has a brilliant mind for technology.
- Janet Mercer—Janet Mercer is a renowned biologist and the wife of Jarrett Mercer. She also gained superpowers during Ashcroft's attack on Washington, D.C.
- Joey Paxton—Joey is Asher's roommate. Although heir to a fortune, Joey does not know what he wants to do with his life.
- Lucy Carmichael—Patrick's girlfriend, Lucy, is an aspiring journalist. She attends college with him and supports his heroic endeavors as Spright.
- Shannon Weeks—A girl from Asher's college he meets at a party. She is interested in him, but Asher's curiosity is piqued by Shannon's mysterious past.

PROLOGUE

The corner office of a business complex was hardly the typical workplace of a Sicaran. It was too opulent for Roland Demirci's tastes. It stank of pleasure and ease, an atmosphere contradictory to the tenets of the Sicarans. They carved out an existence of simplicity in order to focus on the betterment of the world. But to further that cause, some Sicarans took on lives that better reflected those outside their organization. The man across the desk—known among the Sicarans as Adranis—was famous for it.

Roland, dressed for once in a tailored business suit rather than his comfortable black assassin's attire, sat in a plush chair across from Adranis. A few weeks earlier, Roland—known to his fellow villains as Keskin—had received his first assignment as a full Sicaran rather than merely an apprentice. His task was daunting, and he would need help to accomplish it. Adranis' position of power and influence made him ideally suited to assist Roland.

Roland was tasked with finding people with extraordinary abilities—*superpowers*—and recruiting them to the Sicarans' cause. Most known superhumans were either superhero vigilantes fighting crime and likely to oppose the Sicarans or common criminals using their powers for selfish gain. Neither type was suited to the life that the Sicaran elite would expect.

"I'm glad you came to me, Keskin." Adranis leaned against his desk. "In fact, I have been working several leads in this field for quite some time now. Give me a few weeks to test my candidates. I may have some options for you."

"Your assistance is appreciated." Roland rose from his chair and extended his hand to Adranis. "Call me when you have something. In the meantime, I will continue my search elsewhere."

He turned for the door. But as he crossed the office, Roland paused. Without looking back over his shoulder, he spoke again.

"Adranis, it is critical that the Sicarans' involvement should not be discovered here. If any of the so-called superheroes interfere, I expect you to deal with them before they unravel our plan."

"Understood." Roland heard the wicked grin in Adranis' voice. "It will be my pleasure."

CHAPTER 1

Patrick Omer steadied his breathing and prepared for the intense onslaught of projectiles about to come his way. His senses, heightened by superspeed, slowed the world around him as adrenaline flowed through his system. Patrick's muscles coiled, ready to spring the moment the first projectile approached.

Standing across the room from him, his opponents sized him up. There were six of them, a variety of sizes and ages, male and female. Several of them wore a garish uniform, while others were clad in subtler street clothes. The uniformed subjects were the greater threat. They had more experience than those in street clothes. They knew what they were doing, and they knew Patrick was still learning.

He decided to engage the woman on his left first. She was lean and athletic, wearing one of the uniforms; she was probably the biggest threat in the room. There were others bigger than her, more threatening; but she had a cunning, intelligent look in her eyes. If Patrick didn't watch her, she was going to take him down.

A skinny young man to Patrick's right prepared to unleash his projectile.

Patrick danced aside as the blue dodgeball sailed past him.

He turned as the dangerous-looking girl hurled her ball. Extending his left hand, he caught the ball, eliminating her from the game. Groaning in frustration, the girl threw her hands in the air and stomped off the basketball court. Patrick grinned and knelt, using his right hand to pick up the blue dodgeball that the skinny boy had thrown. As his remaining five opponents pressed in, Patrick looked around the room. Nearly a hundred other young adults shouted and cheered. Some were rooting for Patrick, while others dared his competition to eliminate him from the game.

It was orientation week at Echelon Bible College. The uniformed men and women were older students who had volunteered as welcome staff. They all wore bright red shirts with white lettering that couldn't be missed, even across the campus. During orientation week, the welcome staff hosted a variety of games and events for the freshmen, such as dodgeball. In this game, Patrick was the last man standing on his team.

There were two remaining welcome staff members on the opposing team. If he took them out, he should be more than capable of handling the three freshmen. Juggling his pair of dodgeballs, Patrick prepared to throw. He could probably implement his superspeed so subtly that no one would notice and throw the balls so hard and fast that the opposite team would never dodge them. But that wouldn't be fair. Patrick wouldn't use his powers as an unfair advantage, even to make himself look good at a new school. It was tempting, though.

His eyes widened, and he jumped over a yellow dodgeball. At the apex of his jump, Patrick hurled the dodgeball in his left hand, striking one of the freshmen—the skinny kid who had launched the blue ball—in the shoulder. The guy groaned and stormed off the court to watch from the sidelines.

Patrick's feet touched the ground, and he raised his blue dodgeball to block an oncoming green sphere. He hurled his ball at the thrower, one of the two remaining welcome staff, and snaked out his left hand to grab the green ball. The welcome staffer, a Latino guy a few years older than Patrick, dodged, but the ball grazed his ankle.

Three left.

Patrick stood in the center of his half of the court, waiting for his opponents to move. He wasn't even breathing heavily. Running and jumping at normal human speeds were like tiptoeing for him. He could have played dodgeball all day without breaking a sweat. But he had to give the other team a sporting chance, too. He spun and hurled the green ball, and it struck a red ball midair. Both bounced harmlessly to the floor. Patrick looked around for a new ball to arm himself with, but there were none on his side of the court. Seeing an opening, his remaining opponents pressed in.

"You're dead now, Your Highness!" one of his opponents shouted.

Patrick rolled his eyes. *How original.*

He couldn't count on all his fingers and toes how many times his bright red hair had earned him nicknames like Prince Harry or Ron Weasley. The freshman who had shouted the quip, a thick-framed boy with pale skin, brown hair, and the peach fuzz beginnings of a mustache, grinned at his own joke and prepared to hurl his dodgeball as did Patrick's other two opponents.

They're going to throw them all together.

Patrick could tell they didn't believe there was a way for him to dodge all three balls at once. They were wrong. He didn't even have to use his superspeed to do it. He narrowed his eyes and rushed forward as the balls sailed through the air. He jumped and spun between two of the balls, reaching out to catch the third.

It wasn't there.

The ball struck him square in the chest. He dropped to the gym floor, smacking his backside on the hard surface. Half the gym cheered, while the other half moaned and headed for the exit. Blinking in surprise at his own failure, Patrick struggled to figure out what had happened. His superspeed allowed him enhanced perception, so he closed his eyes and thought back.

The third opponent had not thrown her ball at the same time.

They had all wound up together, making him think they would throw in unison. The welcome staffer and the jokester kid had done just that; but his final opponent, a freshman girl—brown-skinned, with dark hair in a bob—waited until Patrick was midair, already dodging, and then threw her ball. Patrick had been paying so much attention to where he expected the balls to be that he had not noticed where they actually were.

"Wow, so graceful."

Patrick looked up. His girlfriend, Lucy Carmichael, stood over him, hands on her hips. She grinned down at him and shook her head. Patrick shook his head and smiled ruefully. His overconfidence had earned him a moment's humiliation in front of the girl he loved. Lucy held out a hand, which Patrick gratefully took. Lucy pulled him to his feet. He rubbed the back of his head.

"Is everyone mad?"

"Oh, yeah." Lucy laughed. "I'm sure you'll have quite the reputation now."

"Oh, come on. I lasted a lot longer than everyone else, didn't I? I feel like I should earn points for that alone."

"Only if you'd won, apparently." Lucy shrugged. "Come on, it's dinnertime."

Patrick followed Lucy out of the gym. They stepped out into the hot August air of New Echelon, California, and strode toward the cafeteria, falling in line behind dozens of other students. As they did, the girl who had eliminated Patrick from the game stepped in next to them, brushed a lock of hair out of her face, and extended a hand.

"Hi," she said. "I'm Alexa. Alexa Patel."

Based on her skin tone and last name, he guessed she was Middle Eastern. He had not met many people of her ethnicity in the area, let alone at a Bible college. He wondered how she had ended up there.

"Patrick Omer." He shook her hand. "This is my girlfriend, Lucy Carmichael."

"Nice to meet you," Lucy said.

"That was quite a throw," Patrick told Alexa. "Honestly, I'm not sure how you got that past me. I have pretty quick reflexes."

Lucy concealed a giggle behind her hand.

That's an understatement, he could almost hear her saying.

"Hard to react to something when you're already paying attention to another threat." Alexa shrugged. "Thought about it at the last second. Wasn't sure it would actually work."

"Clearly, it did." Patrick chuckled. "I'll probably be the butt of jokes on my team for a while."

"Sorry about that." Alexa glanced at a group of girls walking by and waved to them. "I'll see you later, Patrick and Lucy. Nice to meet you both!"

As Alexa bounded away to meet with her friends, Patrick turned his attention back to the line in front of him. He was hungry; a speedster's metabolism required a lot of nutrition.

"She seems nice," Lucy said.

Patrick nodded. "Maybe we can be friends. Once orientation week is over and we're not mortal enemies anymore, of course."

Lucy laughed. "Yeah. After that."

It was hard for Patrick to believe he was starting college already. The past year and a half had flown by in a blur—between becoming a superhero, moving from San Francisco to Sojourn City and then back to San Francisco, fighting an army of supervillains and saving the world, and being in his friend and mentor Gideon Turner's wedding, it had been a crazy time. He'd also started dating Lucy, and his parents had converted from Orthodox Judaism to become Messianic Jews. But maybe with college starting, things would slow down.

That was unlikely, though. He was a speedster. Nothing ever really slowed down.

Later that night, Patrick, Lucy, and half a dozen other freshmen sat in the student lounge, playing cards and getting to know one another. Patrick's roommate, an ebony-skinned guy named Bryce Emerson who wore thick, black hipster-style glasses, sat to Patrick's left; and Lucy sat to his right. Bryce reminded Patrick a lot of Dean Sterling, the Vindicators' resident tech expert who went by Drifter. Bryce had the same energy as Dean, as well as his good nature. Patrick expected to get along well with Bryce.

Bryce slapped the table. "Doubles. My hand."

Lucy rolled her eyes as Bryce scooped up all the cards on the table and prepared to start the next round. Patrick gave her a small smile and put a hand on her knee. Across the table from Lucy, Alexa scrunched her nose as she watched the game. She had never played before, but she seemed to be picking up on the rules.

"So, why did you come to EBC?" Bryce asked.

"Music scholarship," Lucy said. "I'm majoring in journalism, though. One day, I'm going to be a reporter."

"Nice. I'm majoring in church administration—a new technology-in-ministry degree they started recently."

Patrick placed a card on the table. "I'm here for youth ministry studies. I came to Christ because of a youth event that Lucy invited me to. I want to be able to provide the same service for some other kid someday. Particularly other Jewish kids."

Bryce glanced at Alexa. "You?"

Alexa smiled sheepishly and studied her cards. "I don't know what I want to do here yet. My parents and I are immigrants from Pakistan and only recently became Christians. They wanted me to come to a school that taught the Bible. I don't know what I want to study here, but I know it's where I am supposed to be."

The others nodded or murmured their understanding. As Bryce played his next card, Patrick glanced up at the TV mounted in the corner across the lounge. The news showed a live feed of a trio of police cars racing through the city streets, chasing after a speeding vehicle.

"A carjacker has evaded police pursuit for the past half hour," the anchor said, "leading them on a chase through New Echelon. Barricades and checkpoints have been set up. The owner of the stolen vehicle has said—"

"Hey, Patrick," Bryce said. "Your turn."

Patrick slapped a card down on top of Bryce's and looked at Lucy. She nodded. Patrick rose, muttered an excuse about needing to go to the bathroom, and wove his way out of the lounge. As soon as he was out in the hallway, he looked both ways to make sure no one was looking and then sped out the door. He ran to his car, where he kept his super suit in the trunk, changed into it in an instant, and zoomed down the street toward the chase.

These guys have no idea what's coming for them.

The criminals in San Francisco had come to expect Spright's intervention, and thus, crime rates had dropped. But New Echelon didn't have a superhero—or at least, it hadn't, until Patrick had started college. He was going to put as much effort into cleaning up New Echelon as he had his hometown.

Spright wove through the streets, avoiding cars that moved less than half his speed. He passed through the business district and caught a glimpse of police lights ahead. It was only seconds before he caught up to them. He darted between two of the cruisers and approached the fleeing car, which was headed toward an interstate on-ramp. Spright slowed, so he was pacing the car. The back seat was full of large bags of money.

It's not just a stolen car; it's a getaway car.

Spright angled in closer to the vehicle, grabbed the handle to the driver's door, and jerked it open. Grabbing the driver by the collar, Spright pulled the man from the stolen vehicle and sped over to the sidewalk. He deposited the driver on the curb before rushing back to the car, leaping inside, and grabbing the steering wheel.

The world around him resumed normal speed as he slowed to turn the wheel without flipping the car. He hit the brakes and pulled the car to a stop on the roadside. The pursuing police cars slowed to surround him. Spright darted out of the car and went back to the curb where he'd dropped the thief. The man stood and turned to flee.

Spright ran past him, turned, and stopped in front of him. The man blinked in surprise and tried to stumble to a halt. Spright stepped in and slammed his fist under the man's chin. A pair of police officers rushed up.

"Who are you?" one of the officers asked.

"Spright. Don't tell me you've never heard of me."

The officers exchanged glances. "Thought you were in San Francisco."

"I was." Spright backed away. "But you've got a nice city. I think I'll stick around for a while."

CHAPTER 2

One month later . . .

It was strange that the most freedom Ty Vickers had known in his life was found behind prison bars. Since childhood, Ty's life had been in turmoil. When his parents had died and he was adopted by his godfather, Chin Liang, Ty had felt like a prisoner. Liang was a cruel taskmaster, determined to turn Ty into a warrior. Although Ty's real father, Shiro Watanabe, had trained him with a disciplined regiment, he had been a kinder teacher . . . gentler.

When he had turned eighteen, Ty—under the adopted name Tao Liang—could not get out from under his godfather's roof quickly enough. He had set out on his own, met a girl named Rachel Sellers, and applied to the police academy using his birth name, Taro Watanabe. After he and Rachel had married, they'd had a daughter named Emi.

But things had turned sour when Ty's godfather was outed as a criminal. Ty had left the police academy in shame and changed his name from Taro Watanabe to Ty Vickers. Shortly thereafter, his godfather was believed dead in Luca Serban's Uprising.

For a while, Ty's life had been difficult but happy—until Rachel died. Devastated and unable to care for his precious Emi alone, he'd turned to a life of crime. Joined by Rachel's sister Joanie and his friends Ned and Richie, Ty had become a criminal mastermind, using the superpowers granted to him in a monster attack earlier that year.

The string of events that followed led to Ned's death, Liang's reemergence into the public eye, and a battle with an assassin named Kane McCrory. McCrory was called Mac Tíre—The Wolf. Liang insisted that Mac Tíre had killed Ty's birth parents, but Ty had learned that Liang was responsible for Rachel's death. Mac Tíre had claimed with his dying breath that it was Liang who had betrayed Ty's parents.

Ty had been determined to kill his godfather but was forced to flee the scene, thanks to the vigilantes known as the Crusader and Stonewall. It was the Crusader who had convinced Ty to turn himself over to the authorities in the hope that he could be released one day and eventually have a relationship with Emi. In a last act of kindness, the Crusader had left Ty a Bible that he should read while in his cell.

Although there was much about the Bible Ty did not understand, he was doing his best to read it. The Crusader—Carter Jonson—had done all right by him. He had ensured that Emi was put in a good home with a man named Silas Rockwell, and he had delivered word to Ty that Joanie was not facing prison time. The least Ty could do was skim the small, leather book.

The words offered comfort. However, Ty's sense of freedom came not just from the Bible but also from knowing that his godfather was in prison and could not lay a finger on Emi. Ty was not bound to secret identities or hiding from the police anymore. And though that meant he faced years in prison, he was willing to accept that. When he finally got out, he would be truly free.

Free of everything except Mac Tíre's ominous words: *Let me end Liang, boy, and then I'll explain the truth.*

What truth had Kane McCrory wished to impart on Ty? Was it merely about Liang's involvement in the Watanabes' death, or was there something more? Ty would never know now. He had killed McCrory to avenge Ned's death. That action would stay with him for the rest of his life, he knew, but those haunting words would stick with him even more closely. What was the truth about this mysterious organization, the Sicarans, and their bitter rivals, Charybdis, that the assassin felt compelled to share with Ty?

It would be just as well if he never knew. Once he served his time in prison, got out, and had his daughter back, he would be content.

The outer wall of Ty's cell exploded inward. Ty cried out as he slammed into the unforgiving steel bars and slumped to the floor. A sharp ringing filled his ears. Dust and debris were everywhere. He coughed and struggled to sit up. His head felt like it was filled with static as he struggled to figure out what was happening. Ty caught sight of a small, black shape on the floor and instinctively reached for it. He snagged the Bible from the floor and tucked it beneath his prison uniform.

A quartet of dark-clad men stormed into his cell with automatic rifles at their shoulders. The leader of the group stepped up to Ty and knelt next to him.

"Taro Watanabe?"

Ty furrowed his brow. "I'm Ty Vickers."

"We know who you are." The leader gestured, and two of his men grabbed Ty by the shoulders. "You're coming with us."

"What? No." Ty struggled against their grip. "I'm not—"

A fist cannoned into his face. Then Ty's world went black.

* * *

I'm late. Late, late, late!

Lucy Carmichael snagged her backpack from where it hung over the back of her dorm room desk chair, slung it over her shoulder, and rushed for the door. While still pulling one Converse sneaker on, she grabbed the doorknob and yanked it open. She hopped down the hall until her shoe was fully on her foot and then sprinted for the door to the stairs. Lucy nearly toppled into a pair of girls chatting quietly at the end of the hallway. Murmuring an apology, she yanked open the stairwell door.

Of all the days she could have overslept, her body had chosen the morning of her biggest test of the semester. It was only September. This did not bode well for the rest of the school year. Lucy bounded down the stairs and reached into her backpack for the flashcards she had prepared. At the bottom of the stairs, she pulled open the door and cycled through her flashcards as she power-walked across campus.

Music theory. Of all the classes to be late for, why did it have to be music theory?

If only her superfast boyfriend could whisk her across campus. That would be nice. She wished she had Patrick's gifts at times like this. Considering he didn't have a class until next period, he was probably sleeping—and would continue to do so until a minute before class started, at which point he could superspeed into his clothes and across campus and still make it with time to spare.

Lucy tugged open the door to the Masterson building and rushed down the hall toward the music department. She checked her phone as she ran. Lucy made a right turn and entered the music department, passing the professors' offices and a handful of other classrooms before finally reaching the correct room. She darted inside and dropped into her seat with less than a minute to spare.

Dr. Andrews raised an eyebrow. "Cutting it close, Ms. Carmichael?"

"Sorry, Dr. Andrews." Lucy brushed a strand of blonde hair out of her face. "Uh . . . but I got here in time, though. Right?"

"Yes, indeed." Dr. Andrews gave her a small smile as he moved to close the door. "All right, class. It's time to begin. Put your study materials away, and I'll pass out the test."

Alexa leaned over to whisper in her ear. "Stay up too late talking to Patrick?"

"Something like that, yeah." Lucy blushed and removed a pen from her backpack. "But it's fine. I made it."

Lucy *had* been up late talking to Patrick the night before, but it was not typical significant-other, mushy talk. She had been coaching him as he raced through New Echelon to stop crime. Because of his speed, Patrick was able to handle more crime as Spright than the average police officer or even superhero could in several days. Unfortunately, the more crime he stopped, the more he thought he could push his limits. In the past twelve hours, he had shut down a weapons shipment and rescued a shipping container full of trafficked women. It had to be burning him out. Helping him navigate the city was certainly burning Lucy out.

Patrick's biggest focus was a group of amplified thieves known as the Opera Mask Gang. The trio got their name from the gold masks they wore, each emulating an emotion—happy, sad, and angry. The gang used their powers to cut a crime spree through New Echelon; but so far, Patrick had been unable to find them. Lucy wondered if they had noticed the speedster's arrival and decided to lay low.

She took a deep breath, struggled to clear her mind, and focused on the work in front of her as Dr. Andrews put the test down on her desk.

An hour later, she left the classroom and trudged down the hall toward her next class. Her brain was fried; and her confidence in her results was shaky, to say the least.

I've got to talk to Patrick about going to bed sooner.

She loved that he wanted to help everybody and stop all the crime that he could, but he had other priorities, too. Such as schoolwork. Such as *her.* Lucy didn't want to be selfish with him; but she missed spending time together as boyfriend and girlfriend, not as hero and hero support staff.

Another problem was that the only place Lucy could coach Patrick from was her dorm room. When Alexa was there, that was difficult to do. How the other girl did not suspect Patrick was a superhero by now, Lucy didn't know; but sooner or later, something was going to go wrong.

We need to figure out a new system.

Patrick's best friend, Asher Lincoln, was also in the know about Patrick's secret. But since he went to Echelon University across town, he could only help out via conference call. There had to be some way to balance the hero's life with college and social life.

Of all the things Lucy had to worry about at this point in her life, she didn't think Spright's activity should take as much of a priority as it did. The crime in New Echelon was minimal. Nothing the police couldn't handle. Patrick was often going all the way to San Francisco to find crime to fight; and while she admired his enthusiasm, it was getting to be too much. She loved him. She just wanted to see more of him.

* * *

Patrick rolled out of bed and ran a hand through his hair. He could tell by the tangles that it had been well-mussed by sleep. He would have to do some work to tame it. But he had plenty of time, as long as he didn't get overzealous in combing it at superspeed. He had learned long ago that if he wasn't careful, he could pull a lot of hair out doing that.

Another good night's work.

Patrick had stopped an arms deal, sex traffickers, and even a few convenience store robberies the night before. Spright was finally gaining recognition as a hero in these parts, just as Gideon had as the Seraph back in Sojourn City, and as his successor, Carter Jonson, was achieving as the Crusader. Patrick wasn't a sidekick, or just another member of the Vindicators anymore. He was a superhero in his own right—a superhero who also had a youth ministry class to get to.

He pulled on a long-sleeved, white-and-blue striped polo shirt, a pair of black jeans, and blue tennis shoes. He brushed his teeth, and worked furiously at his hair, wetting and combing it until he finally beat it to submission. A few weeks before, he had gone to the barber and had his hair cut several inches shorter. Now, he combed it back and to the side, rather than down in his face. He studied his reflection, nodded in satisfaction, and strode out the door with ten minutes to get to class. Whistling to himself, Patrick casually strolled down the stairs to the dorm lobby and then out the door and toward the Masterson building.

Once there, he wound his way through the halls and mounted the stairs to the second floor. He tilted his head in search of Lucy as he climbed. He usually ran into her on his way to class. Their schedules intertwined, so one of her classes ended as his began. Maybe she had been let out early or decided to skip. He didn't see her as often as he would like to, so between-classes rendezvouses were nice. But at least they still got to talk while he was out in the field as Spright. That made up for it a little bit.

Patrick pulled the classroom door open and stepped inside. The classroom contained three tables that ran the length of the room from side-to-side, which left walking room only between the table and the walls. Each table had space for ten students. A whiteboard, a podium, and a projector screen dominated the front wall of the classroom. Rick Walker, a local youth pastor and the adjunct teacher of Patrick's class, stood in front of the board. Rick was in his mid-fifties; and he had closely cropped dark hair, which was slowly fading to gray. He wore thick-rimmed glasses that reminded Patrick of depictions he had seen of Superman. Rick smiled and nodded as Patrick entered the room.

"Morning, Patrick."

Rick and Patrick had connected over the past month. Although Rick tried to remain impartial with his students, he had already discussed the possibility of Patrick interning with his youth ministry in a few years. Patrick appreciated the special attention. It motivated him to study harder.

"Morning." Patrick took a seat at the middle table next to Brandon, the Latino student he had battled in dodgeball during orientation. "How's it going?"

"How are you so cheerful in the morning?" Brandon asked.

Patrick shrugged. "Guess I'm a morning person."

"Brandon's just mad because I gave him grief over his project idea." Rick winked at the older student.

Brandon rolled his eyes. "Yeah, whatever."

Patrick raised an eyebrow. "What's your idea?"

"He wants to study the effects of living near the beach on Christian teen mentality." Rick shrugged. "Probably just an excuse to spend all day at the beach, right, Brandon?"

Brandon crossed his arms, leaned back in his chair, and didn't respond. Several of the other students in the class laughed in chorus. Patrick chuckled good-naturedly but patted Brandon on the shoulder. It was possible that his idea was borne out of the intent to hang out at the beach with college girls, but Patrick preferred giving people the benefit of the doubt. There was some merit to Brandon's idea.

"Don't sulk, man." Patrick leaned down to unzip his backpack. "Do it right, and I think it's a great idea."

Rick cleared his throat. "How about you, Patrick?"

Patrick blinked. "Hmm?"

"What's your project idea?" Rick asked. "It was due today, remember?"

Patrick's heart thumped. He had completely forgotten to plan for the project. Between speeding around the city and trying to find any extra minute to spend with Lucy, the assignment had slipped his mind. He smiled sheepishly and averted his gaze.

Brandon chuckled. "At least I had an idea."

"I'm sorry. I've been . . . busy. The project's not due for another two weeks, right? Give me until the end of the day, and I promise I can come up with something."

"Sorry, Patrick." Rick scribbled on a sheet of paper in front of him. "The rule was, if you didn't have a project idea picked out by today, I'd assign you one. Don't worry, I'll try to make it as dreadfully boring as possible."

The rest of the class laughed. Patrick grimaced and scrambled frantically for an idea. He hadn't given it any serious thought, so he didn't even have a fragment of a concept to latch onto. Sometimes, being a superhero was so inconvenient.

Or was it?

"Wait! I've got it."

Rick stopped writing. "Do tell."

"I'll study the effects of superheroes on today's generation." Patrick drummed his fingers on his desk. "Think about it. No other generation has grown up in a world with superheroes. Will that make them more likely to believe in the supernatural stories of the Bible or less? How does it affect the concept of salvation? Will teens still respond to a need for a Savior when real, visible heroes are all over the news?"

"You just came up with that on the fly?" Rick laughed. "I'm impressed. All right, Patrick. Your assignment is to study the effect of superheroes on the average teenager in the church. You got lucky, kiddo."

Yeah, I did. Patrick sighed in relief. *Man—I've really got to remember these things.*

* * *

It was not often that Carter Jonson, the Crusader, was in the business of helping criminals. In this case, though, he felt it was warranted.

Days ago, a team of mysterious masked men had broken into Stone Gate Penitentiary and taken Ty Vickers from his cell. The prison warden and the police believed it was a rescue. With his ability to phase through solid material, Ty could avoid detection easily outside the prison and could be anywhere in the world by now. Carter had a different theory.

After working his shift at the front desk of Sterling Enterprises, he took the maglev train from Sojourn City's lake-bound Platform to the Brooks. The basement of a local establishment there—known as Pop's Gym—hid his secret lair. He was still breaking in the lair. It had been a gift—as well as a show of good faith—from Carter's friend and mentor, Silas Rockwell. Silas had recently revealed that he was a secret agent for the government organization CLOUD. Carter's initial reaction to the news had been fiery, to say the least. However, Silas had shown his allegiance to Carter and his friends by joining their fight against Vickers, his criminal gang, and the Red Dogs. Now, Silas was a vigilante going under the codename Stonewall, and he helped Carter patrol the streets of Sojourn City at night.

Silas was also caring for Ty's daughter, Emi, while the criminal served his time in prison. Emi was the reason Carter was sure that Ty would not risk an escape attempt. He would never be able to have a life with his daughter if he was on the run, and he had made no move to visit her or try to kidnap her from Silas' home in the month since the breakout. Carter was certain of one thing: whoever had attacked the prison and taken Vickers from his cell had not done it for the purpose of rescuing him. It had been a kidnapping.

He suspected he knew the culprits—the mysterious sect of assassins known as the Sicarans. Vickers' father and godfather had both been members before the latter betrayed the organization. A Sicaran assassin named Kane McCrory had come after Vickers' godfather, but Ty had killed McCrory. The Sicarans were probably out for Ty's blood—in which case, he had probably died the same day he was freed from prison.

Carter was not giving up hope, though. Tracking the assassins was next to impossible; but until he knew with absolute certainty that Vickers was dead, he would not stop pursuing them. He wanted Emi to get her dad back someday—or at least to be able to tell her what happened to him, once she was old enough to understand.

Carter strode through Pop's Gym to the basement door. He entered the access code and descended the stairwell, making sure the door latched behind him. It would not do to have some kid waiting for boxing lessons stumble onto the lair of Sojourn City's vigilantes. With all the money Silas had spent on the lair, they could not afford to move it somewhere else.

"There you are." Raina Watts, Carter's girlfriend, looked up from the lair's computer. "Have a good day at work?"

"Same old, same old." Carter leaned down to kiss her on the top of her head, crowned with curly brown-and-blonde hair. "Any news on Vickers?"

Raina spread her arms. "I wouldn't know where to start looking. Silas has CLOUD's spy satellites hooked up to the lair's computers, but I don't know the first thing about running them. We need a real expert helping us with this."

"Right. Happen to know one?"

Not waiting for Raina to answer the rhetorical question, Carter opened one of the desk drawers and removed a sheet of paper scribbled with instructions on how to access the CLOUD satellites from the computer. Silas had dumbed down the IT lingo enough that Carter could get his head around it. He handed Raina the sheet. Their hands met briefly. He ran a thumb across the back of her hand, which was two shades lighter than his own dark brown tone. Then he kissed her again, this time on the cheek, before striding across the room to the rack full of weapons stationed on the east wall. Taking a *bo* staff from the rack, Carter stepped into the center of the practice mat laid out on the floor and started working on a series of drills.

"There is one tech whiz who would probably be more than willing to help us look for Vickers," Raina said.

Carter paused mid-swing and tilted his head. Did she mean who he thought she meant? No. She couldn't. That would mean giving a cyber-criminal access to government technology, and that had disaster written all over it. They were desperate, but not that desperate. Were they?

"You mean Joanie Sellers." Carter ran a hand over the dark hair atop his head. "Bad idea, Raina."

Joanie was Vickers' sister-in-law, and she had been part of his criminal gang. A hacker extraordinaire, Joanie had blacked out the security cameras to the buildings Ty broke into. She had also created a code that could crack the encryption in the federal reserve. Joanie was smart, no doubt about it—smart enough to be dangerous.

"Oh, come on. We can monitor her, make sure she's not doing anything illegal. And as soon as we find Ty, she's out. We don't even have to bring her to the lair. Maybe we could set up at a neutral location, only meet her when you and Silas are in costume, and let her run wild. She has to be worried about Ty, Carter."

He sighed. "Let's talk to Silas about this before we go ahead with anything. But I will consider it."

"That's all I'm asking."

Was his need to find Ty really so urgent that he would risk this? Yes, it was. He could not explain why, but Vickers was important to him. He could easily imagine himself having fallen into the same lifestyle if he had been in Vickers' position. Ty was not a bad man. He just needed a chance to make things right. Carter was determined to give him one.

CHAPTER 3

Joey Paxton had everything a guy could want—fame, money, fast cars, girls. Everything. As the heir to the Paxton family fortune, Joey had it made. Unfortunately, he found that getting whatever he wanted just because he wanted it was boring. There was no challenge to it, no adventure.

So he had decided to take a risk. Rather than following his father's footsteps and continuing in the family business, Joey enrolled in Echelon University. He was determined to make a name for himself on his own merit. He could do anything he wanted. With his wealth, the world was his to explore. He only needed to decide what he wanted to do. Become a lawyer? He had the resources to go to the most expensive law schools. Achieve greater fame as a sports star? His athletic ability was exceptional. Joey could make whatever he wanted of his life. There was just one problem: college was hard.

He had failed two of his five classes his first semester, another his second semester; and his sophomore year looked equally grim. It was not that he didn't want to do well or didn't have the ability, but there were so many more fun things to do in college than study. Dorm parties, campus activities, off-campus activities—the list was endless.

The only person who was doing anything to keep him accountable (and the only reason his grades were holding on by a thread this semester) was Asher Lincoln. Joey's new roommate was a good guy, an average guy. He had grown up in a neighborhood that, in comparison to Joey's, was dirt poor. But he didn't care about Joey's wealth. Asher was his friend just to be his friend. It was the first time Joey had felt that from someone.

Joey stared down at his algebra homework. He could certainly cross mathematician off his list of potential careers. He did not understand why he had to go through this algebra course. He was never going to use it, anyway. As he rapped the end of his pen on his desk, Joey wished math would just fall off the edge of the world.

His phone buzzed. Joey put down his pen and picked up the phone. It was a text from Maddie, one of the girls on the softball team:

Party at Riley's house tonight! Be there? ;-)

"Oh, yeah." Joey stuffed his homework away.

"Where do you think you're going?"

Joey looked up. Asher was lying on the top bunk, typing on his laptop.

Aw, great, got to get past the homework police.

Joey appreciated Asher's attempts to keep him on the right track. But at times, it could be a real pain. Joey wanted to be his own man, but he wanted to have fun, too. Algebra was no fun.

"Uh . . . a party. Come on, man. I've been doing this homework for . . . "

"Fifteen minutes." Asher sat up. "I'm not your babysitter, Joey. You want to go to that party, go ahead. I won't stop you. Just remember this when you're sitting in class wondering why you're about to fail your next test."

Joey sighed. "Yeah, whatever. Why don't you come with me? You do homework all the time. I'm sure you're studied up. You could use a little downtime, right? Besides, a freshman like you could use a party. You need to get to know who's cool on campus. All I see you do is study."

Asher rarely partied. When he did come with Joey, he would hang out and talk to people; but he never got into it. He did not seem to want to make friends. He certainly never let loose. Joey had tried to invite him to come with him before, but Asher—responsible as ever—always refused.

What he really needs is a fun girl to loosen him up.

Asher sighed. "I'm good, man. You go on ahead."

"Come on, Ash. Homecoming's on the way, and you don't have a girl. Maybe tonight you can make a date. You'll have your pick of the lot—the whole softball team will be there, and they probably invited, like, half the campus."

Asher pursed his lips.

I've almost got him.

"I know you miss your friends from over at that Bible school; but if you can't see them, why not make some other friends? Let's go, dude. No reason for you to stay here all by yourself, is there?"

"Guess not." Asher hopped off the bed. "But I'm driving; and when I say it's time to go, we go. Got it? I'm not letting you ruin your already-slim chances of passing that test by staying up all night and waking up with a hangover."

* * *

Asher had been in college for over a month, and he did not understand college students. He loved to have fun as much as the next guy. When he was around Patrick and Lucy, he was the carefree one who balanced out Lucy's studiousness and Patrick's nobility. Every friend group needed a carefree quipster, and that was Asher. But on his own, without the two of them around to achieve that balance, he had to take care of himself. He had learned to be studious and put aside the jokes when seriousness was necessary.

But the students of Echelon University seemed to think life was one big party. If Asher had to guess, he would predict that 75 percent of the people at the party were using generative AI to pass their assignments.

Joey, for his part, had wasted no time stripping down to swim trunks and leaping into the pool. Asher liked Joey. His desire to make something of himself beyond his family fortune was admirable. The problem was, Joey was so used to a life of luxury that working for what he wanted was still foreign to him. Asher wanted to help him, but he could only do so much. Joey had to help himself, too.

Asher's phone buzzed. He glanced down at it. Patrick was calling. Stepping as far away from the pool as he could without entering the house full of dancing college students, Asher put his phone to his ear.

"Hello?"

"Ash? You there? I can barely hear you."

"Yeah, I'm—" Someone whooped and cannonballed into the pool. "I'm here. Sorry, just some idiots being louder than common sense dictates!" Asher shouted the last five words, hoping his raised voice was heard by all around him. "What's up?"

"Just wondering if you wanted to come over and hang with us tonight, but it sounds like you're busy."

"I wish I could." Asher sighed. "I've got to babysit my roommate. Besides, get real. You aren't going to hang out tonight. Ten minutes in, and you'll be out on the streets, am I right?"

Patrick's nonstop dedication to being Spright was admirable. When Asher had learned that his best friend was a superhero, his head had nearly exploded. That was the kind of thing teenagers dreamed of. The downside was that it did not leave Patrick with much time for fun. Asher missed his best friend and not just because they went to different colleges. They were in the same town. They could get together anytime they wanted to. With his speed, Patrick could reach Asher's dorm in under a minute from almost anywhere in the city. The problem was, Patrick didn't seem to want to.

"Aw, come on, man," Patrick said. "Don't be like that. You know what I do is important. You and Lucy are the only ones who understand when I run off. Alexa and Bryce think I'm crazy. Do you know how hard it is to hide this from my roommate?"

"Yeah, we do understand. But you shouldn't take advantage of it. Look, I've got to go."

"Oh." Somehow, Patrick made the word sound like it came from a wounded puppy. "Okay. See you later, then."

"Later."

Asher hung up and stuffed his phone in his pocket. He wasn't angry with Patrick. Asher felt like he had to bear some of the blame for Patrick's single-mindedness. He had been eager to be a part of Spright's support team back when Patrick had first revealed his powers. Having a superhero for a best friend was cool, and being part of a superhero team was even cooler. It started to feel like work, though, when it took up all their time. Patrick had become dangerously obsessed. In particular, he seemed determined to catch the fabled Opera Mask Gang, even though they had not shown their gold-shrouded faces in the past month.

Maybe he'll find a balance after a while.

Surely even a speedster would get burned out. Asher shook the thoughts of his best friend away and moved over to the snack table set up on one side of the pool. He filled a plate with cookies that looked store-bought and found an empty lawn chair. No sooner was he seated than a beautiful girl in a swimsuit, a towel wrapped around her waist, dropped into the chair next to him.

"Hi," she said. "Asher, right?"

Asher blinked and studied her. Her dark eyes, framed by wavy brunette hair, threatened to suck him in. Her tanned skin looked flawless under the oranges and purples of the evening sky. And for some reason, she was talking to him. Asher realized the silence was starting to carry on too long to be comfortable.

"Yeah, nice to meet you. You are?"

"Shannon Weeks."

"That's a pretty name." Asher took a bite of one of his cookies to give himself a moment to think. "You go to Echelon U, I guess?"

"That's right. I'm studying political science." Shannon crossed her legs and rested her hands on her knee. Then, she giggled. "We have biology together."

"Wow, I . . . wow." Asher looked around. "This doesn't seem like the typical crowd a poli-sci major would hang around with. No offense."

"None taken." Shannon laughed. "We're not all pressed-suit snobs. Some of us just need to burn off our stress, just like anyone else."

"Okay, fair enough. So why did you come over to talk to me?"

"Because you were sitting by yourself." Shannon leaned forward and smiled. "And I think you're cute."

"Uh . . . really?" Asher stammered. "I . . . uh . . . thanks. You, too. I mean, I think you're cute too."

His mouth was going into overdrive, and he couldn't stop it. "Do you have plans for homecoming?"

Oops.

What was he doing? He knew practically nothing about her. They might be polar opposites. Political students tended to be all-or-nothing in their beliefs; and if she was not a Christian, then she might become instantly repulsed when she found out Asher was. Still, she was pretty and interested in him. Both of those were wonderful qualities. It couldn't hurt to pursue the dangling thread and see where it went. Then again, asking her to homecoming outright was brash, even for him.

"I don't if you don't." Shannon held out her hand. "Give me your phone. I'll put in my number. You can call me, and we'll figure something out."

"Oh . . . okay. Here you go."

Shannon took the phone, entered her number, and then angled the phone up to take a selfie. She snapped the picture, typed again, and handed the phone back to him. Asher looked down at the screen. She had set the selfie as her own contact image in his phone.

He should have invited her to church. Her reaction to the invitation might tell him all he needed to know about her stance on faith. Unfortunately, his mouth was suddenly dry as he tried to wrap his mind around the fact that a girl like her was interested in him. He blinked twice at her and struggled to form words.

"Don't wait too long to call." Shannon stood. "I'll be waiting."

Asher looked up at her.

"Okay, I'll—" A flicker of movement from inside the house caught his attention. "Hey, what's going on in there?"

The heavy beat of music and the bright flash of LED lights were still going, but the partying had stopped. Everyone was sitting or lounging, seemingly at random. Some were on the couch, some on the floor, others on top of furniture. Asher crossed the back patio toward the screen door, Shannon following in his wake. No one in the pool seemed to have noticed yet. Asher slid open the door and stepped inside . . . And was struck by a wave of calm.

He stumbled and reached out to lean against the wall. He smiled drowsily. No wonder everyone was so relaxed in here. He looked back at Shannon and saw the same happy, sleepy expression on her face. She leaned her back against the wall and slid down it until she was sitting on the floor.

Wow . . . this is nice.

All Asher's stress melted away in an instant—worries about his classes, Joey's studies, Patrick's obsession with his powers, his upcoming date with Shannon—all of it was so small and insignificant. Asher slumped to the floor next to Shannon and looked up at the flashing blue lights that illuminated the wall. A man walked through the living room. Why was he walking? He should've been resting like everyone else. He wore all black except for a gold mask decorated with a deep frown. As the stranger made his way through the room, he occasionally reached down, removing a piece of jewelry or a wallet from one of the relaxed partygoers.

Opera Masks . . .

But as Asher tried to sit up, another wave of calm washed over him, so powerful that his fingers and toes tingled.

Why don't I just go to sleep?

Asher leaned back against the wall and rested his head on Shannon's shoulder. His eyelids drooped; and for a moment, he struggled to keep them open. Then, he surrendered to the peaceful embrace of sleep.

* * *

When Ty was taken from his prison cell by a squad of armed mercenaries, he had not known what to expect. A quick death? Torture? A trial before a court of Sicarans set on judging him for Kane McCrory's death? Outside the walls of his cell, he should have been able to escape easily. His superpowers allowed him to phase through any solid matter. He could have phased free of his rescuers—or captors, as the case might be—and taken off running. Even if they opened fire on him, their bullets would have passed through his incorporeal body harmlessly.

But no sooner had they dragged him from his cell than someone struck him across the back of the head, rendering him unconscious. When he came to, he was lying on the floor of a van; and his hands were bound by a pair of the same dampening cuffs that the prison used for its amplified prisoners when they had to leave their cells.

Whoever had taken him had access to advanced technology, then. It would not surprise him to learn the Sicarans had that kind of resource. And so, he prepared himself for the worst.

But when they arrived at their destination after so many hours of driving that Ty lost count, they did none of the things he had expected or imagined. Instead, one of the captors threw a blindfold over his head and dragged Ty from the van into an air-conditioned building and down a flight of stairs. There, he was chained to the wall, and his blindfold was removed. Ty found himself in a dark, dank basement right out of a thriller movie. Dripping water, puddles of unidentifiable liquid—all of it was incredibly theatrical.

And that was where Ty remained. A guard visited him occasionally to bring him food and water; but outside of those visits, Ty never saw anyone. By counting those visits, Ty figured he had been in the basement for a few days. He had no idea why he had been taken. Why had his captors exchanged his prison cell for another one? They had to have some purpose for bringing him here, but they were taking their time revealing it.

Is anyone even looking for me?

He had to imagine they were. But whether they would find him was another story. After so many hours driving, there was no telling what state—or even what country—he was in.

I'm sorry, Emi. I will try to find my way back to you.

The one upside was the Bible Ty had managed to sneak inside his prison uniform. There was just enough light from the dim yellowish bulbs to read it. He would remove it at times when he was sure no guards would come, usually after his meals, and scan the pages. There was much he did not understand, but he took comfort in some of the words he found in the ancient book.

"For the LORD heareth the poor, and despiseth not his prisoners,[1]" Ty whispered.

He did not know if he believed in God yet. Maybe God wasn't anything more than a distant Watcher. Maybe He didn't care about people like Ty. But the verses he read gave him hope. Maybe, if God did love him, He would send someone to rescue him from prison.

Ty would hold onto that hope. He had to. It was all he had left to believe he would see Emi again one day.

---

1 Psalm 69:33

CHAPTER 4

Patrick—along with Lucy, Bryce, and Alexa—sat in the student lounge, gathered in a half-circle of comfortable chairs and bean bags, watching *Lord of the Rings* on the TV in the corner. Other students milled about the lounge, playing pool or foosball or cards. It had been a calm evening, and Patrick found himself grateful that he had taken the night off from fighting crime. He needed this.

"Are we sure it's okay to watch this movie?" Alexa asked. "My parents said it was full of magic and evil."

"*Lord of the Rings* was written by a Christian," Bryce replied, "and it's full of Christian themes, if you pay attention. It's a story of redemption, sin, and hope."

Lucy nudged Alexa with her shoulder. "Bryce is right. They're my youth pastor's favorite movies."

Alexa pursed her lips. "All right."

Patrick's phone trilled. *Great.*

He looked over at Lucy and shrugged apologetically. Pulling the phone from his pocket, he stepped away from the group and checked the screen. *Asher?* Patrick's best friend had seemed irritable when they had talked less than an hour ago. Maybe he was calling to apologize. Patrick answered.

"Hello?"

"Hey, Patrick?" Asher's voice sounded hoarse, almost scared. "Do you think you can get down here? I've got kind of a situation."

"Send me your address. I'll be right there."

Patrick hung up the phone and walked over to Lucy's side. He bent down, so his lips were nearly pressed against her ear.

"Asher had an emergency. I've got to go."

The disappointment was evident on her face as she turned to look at him, but she inclined her head toward the door before turning back to the movie. Patrick turned and strode away from his friends.

"Where's he going now?" Bryce asked.

Patrick didn't hear Lucy's reply. He rounded the corner, stepped outside, and sped away from the student center. After making a brief stop to his car to retrieve his suit, he ran down the road. He keyed his phone's GPS to the address Asher texted him and double-timed it across the city. The house was only a few blocks from Echelon University. Asher must have been at a party. He had said he was babysitting his roommate. Where else would he be?

What could happen at a college house party that would lead to Asher calling a superhero?

Spright skidded to a stop outside the suburban home and looked around. Dozens of cars were parked around the house and down the street. Everything looked calm. There was no fire, no sounds of screaming or chaos. Was there really an emergency? It was not like Asher to prank-call him. Patrick's best friend was prone to hysterical exaggeration sometimes, but he knew how seriously Patrick took being Spright. He would not abuse the privilege he had of knowing his best friend's secret identity. Spright stepped up the steps to the porch. Did he knock or just go in?

A shadow moved in the living room window, and the front door opened as he approached. Asher stepped out. His eyes were sunken as though he had not slept in days, and he kept looking around as if he expected something to pop up out of nowhere. He pulled his black bomber jacket tightly around himself and stepped closer to Spright.

"Thanks for coming."

"What happened?"

"You should see for yourself." Asher motioned for him to enter the house. "Come on."

Spright stepped inside. Dozens of college students filled the living room and the back yard beyond it, which was visible through a sliding glass door. None of them were partying, though. They all sat in a daze, as though every one of them was hungover.

"Is everyone okay?" Spright asked.

Several of the partiers went wide-eyed when they recognized him, but none of them jumped up to greet him or even said his name. He frowned beneath his mask. What was going on here? Asher pulled him away from the others.

"They started acting like this while I was outside. I came inside to investigate and . . . I don't know. It was weird—like this happy, drowsy feeling washed over me. All I wanted to do was go to sleep. I sat down; but before I passed out, I saw a guy in one of those gold opera masks. He was going from person to person, stealing stuff. He got my wallet . . . must have been while I was asleep."

Patrick's blood ran cold. *The Opera Mask Gang.* The amplified criminals had not been active since Spright's arrival in New Echelon. He had searched for them, but to no avail. Maybe they had finally decided they could risk coming out of hiding. A house party was an incongruous-enough setting for them to avoid notice and still make a tidy profit off rich college kids. It was a cunning scheme, but Patrick wasn't about to let them get away with it.

Asher pointed at the backyard. "None of them were affected until he went outside. Whatever was happening to us, I think he was the one doing it."

"We haven't identified the Opera Mask Gang's powers for sure, only that they can alter people's emotions. This one must have the power to put people to sleep, or at least cause them to feel relaxed and restful. How long ago did this happen?"

Asher looked at a clock on the back wall. "I called you . . . what, five minutes ago? That was at 9:30. But I got to the party at 8:00, and I hadn't been here for more than half an hour when it happened. We were out for at least an hour."

Spright shook his head. "Which means by now, the thief is long gone."

* * *

Teeth chattering, Joey wrapped himself in a blanket and trudged inside Riley's house with the other numbed-out partiers. He wasn't sure what had happened. He had been swimming in the pool with Maddie for a while before they had decided to go inside. As the two of them approached the door, Joey had been hit with a wave of extreme calm and relaxation. He and Maddie had settled down outside, still in their wet swimwear, and fallen asleep. When Joey woke up, everyone else around him was yawning and stretching, too. Joey went to get his stuff and found that his wallet and watch were gone, as were everyone else's valuables.

Now it was like he had a bad hangover—but a mental and emotional one, rather than a physical one. Trying to think about anything felt like swimming through a thick soup. His brain was sludge. But even so, he had the presence of mind to recognize the purple-and-black getup of the famous superhero Spright when he entered the house. Unfortunately, he was too drained to react. All he had been able to do was sit and listen while Asher, who was uncharacteristically dull, explained the events of the night to the speedster.

"Is that Spright?" Maddie mumbled.

Joey nodded. "Yeah."

"He looks . . . skinnier in person." She frowned. "He looks so macho and buff on TV."

Joey studied the superhero. Yeah, he was lean, even if his purple suit's padding added some mass to his frame. He wasn't the ripped wall of muscle that superheroes were portrayed as. But maybe that made sense. He was a runner. He didn't have to be jacked because he didn't get in straight fights a lot. He just ran around and used his speed to take out the bad guys before they could ever touch him.

"What do you think he looks like under that mask?" Maddie asked.

Spright's mask was predominantly black and shrouded his entire head. A pair of purple-tinted goggles covered his eyes, and they were just translucent enough to see through; but Joey couldn't get a good look. Why would he cover his whole face, though? Most other superheroes, like the Seraph, wore those eye masks.

Although, he supposed, it hadn't worked so well for the Seraph, since his identity leaked pretty quickly. Maybe that was why Spright wore the full mask.

"Probably an average-looking middle-aged dude."

"Yeah . . . probably." Maddie rubbed her temples. "Ugh . . . I need a pick-me-up."

"I need to sleep for twelve hours." Joey stood. "I think it's time for me to head back."

Asher glanced back at him. "I'll be ready in a minute, Joey."

Spright put his hand on Asher's shoulder. "Go ahead. I'll wrap things up here and call the cops. They can take a full report on everything that's missing."

"Thanks."

Asher sure seemed chummy with Spright. Joey wondered how the superhero had known to come to the house if the cops hadn't been called yet. But trying to puzzle it out made his head hurt. He nodded to Asher and walked toward the door.

What a night.

So much for enjoying some downtime to avoid worrying about his test. The party had turned into one big robbery. Maybe he should've just studied, after all.

* * *

Carter balanced on the fire escape outside the one-room apartment building Joanie Sellers was renting in the Brooks. A soft fall rain pattered against the building. Droplets beaded on the red plating of Carter's armor and ran down his mask's blue-tinted visor. He wiped them away and scanned the streets below. Joanie had not returned from work yet, but she should be here anytime now. He glanced upward and caught a glimpse of Silas's form, clad in gunmetal-and-cobalt armor, on the fire escape above.

"Are you sure this is a good idea?" Carter asked. "She's a criminal, remember."

"I've met Joanie a couple times," Silas said. "She has come to visit Emi. She's a good girl. Yeah, she has an edge to her, but I don't think she would have taken to crime if not for Ty. She deserves the same second chance you gave him."

Carter sighed and drummed his fingers against the fire escape railing. Silas was right on that score. He had opened himself up to the possibility that Ty could be redeemed. He should do the same for her. It was not that he thought Joanie was some terrible person. Many of the low-level criminals he put away only committed crimes out of desperation. He did not know Joanie, though. How did they know she would not take this opportunity to steal government secrets?

Unfortunately, it looked more and more like she was their only option. Detective Jolie Turner had managed to use traffic cameras to track a van fleeing the prison until it made it to the interstate. After that, it vanished. It was very unlikely that Ty was still in Sojourn City. Either his rescuers had taken him somewhere far away, or Ty had escaped and fled. Or he was dead.

But if his rescuers actually wanted him dead, they could have shot him in his cell. They had taken him from the prison, which meant he was more useful to them alive than dead. Carter clung to that hope.

Silas cleared his throat.

"Here she comes."

Carter's gaze dropped to the sidewalk. Sure enough, the girl was approaching. She had warm brown skin and dark hair braided into dreadlocks. She wore a pair of black jeans and a blue polo shirt—probably the uniform for wherever she was working. Joanie climbed off a rickety bicycle, chained it to a rusty bike rack outside the apartment building, and hurried inside. A few moments later, the light inside the window next to Carter flicked on. He nodded to Silas and slid open the window, stepping into the apartment.

Joanie, who had been looking at her phone, spun to face him and yelped. She backed toward the door, but Carter held out a hand.

"Joanie Sellers. Don't worry, we're not here to hurt you."

She trembled. "W-we?"

Silas climbed in the window behind Carter. "I'm Stonewall. You probably already know the Crusader."

"I know." Joanie looked between them. "Are you here to arrest me?"

Carter felt a pang of sympathy and regret. He wanted the Crusader to be a symbol for hope to the innocent, and here was this poor girl frightened out of her boots to see him. This was not how he wanted to be seen—except by hardened criminals who deserved it.

"No, we're not. We're here to ask you for help." Carter gestured to Silas, who withdrew a laptop from a shoulder bag he was carrying. "This is about your brother-in-law, Ty Vickers."

Joanie's eyes widened. "You know where Ty is?"

"No, we don't," Silas said. "That's why we need you. Do you want to help Ty?"

"Yeah, of course." Joanie frowned. "What can I do?"

Carter held out a hand slowly and guided her over to a paint-flecked chair next to her dining table. "We're going to give you access to a government-controlled satellite feed. We're not exactly tech experts, but you are."

"You want me to use the feed to look for Ty?"

Carter nodded. "If anyone can do it, it's you. Can we trust you?"

Joanie's fear was gone, replaced by a steely gaze. She eased into the chair and popped her knuckles.

"Absolutely."

CHAPTER 5

Patrick slipped back into his dorm room and closed the door behind him as quietly as he could. With any luck, Bryce would already be in bed. The last thing Patrick needed was for his roommate to ask questions he couldn't answer. He ducked into the bathroom to buy himself a few more minutes, just in case. Although it had only been a month since he and Bryce had started sharing a room, Bryce had to be suspicious of Patrick's regular disappearances.

But Patrick had bigger things to worry about. The Opera Mask Gang was back. Only one of their members had shown up at the party, but the rest had to be close behind. The criminal's powers might have been on the same spectrum as those of Artemis Wayans, one of the first supervillains Patrick had faced. Wayans, who had gone by the moniker Somna, had hypnotic powers that could influence anyone to do whatever she said. The Opera Mask gangster's seemed similar, but on a less dramatic scale.

The question was where he and his cohorts had gotten their powers. After Dr. Jeremiah Ashcroft had unleashed his monstrous nephiloids on Chicago and Washington, D.C., many people had been infected by the monsters' venoms, which turned ordinary human DNA into a superpowered gene. Ashcroft had also released a series of gas bombs carrying the same serum. As far as Patrick knew, though, none of those bombs had been released in New Echelon; but there may have been some in other Californian cities.

Stepping out of the bathroom, Patrick tiptoed toward his bed. The lights in the dorm were off, save for one lamp on the desk next to Bryce's bed. Bryce was already underneath the covers, so maybe he had fallen asleep and forgot to turn the lamp off. Patrick sat down on his own bed and pulled the covers back . . .

"Welcome back."

Patrick sighed. Bryce sat up and quirked an eyebrow.

"Thanks."

"Where have you been? We watched a whole *Lord of the Rings* movie, man. Do you know how long those are? What the heck do you have going on that keeps you so busy, you miss the whole thing?"

After checking on Asher, Patrick had waited for the police to arrive, listened as each of the partygoers gave their statement, and run through the streets looking for any sign of the thief. He had searched for hours, but there had been no sign of him—or of anyone wearing an opera mask, for that matter.

"I . . . wanted to get a head start on my youth min project." Patrick shrugged. "Just lost track of time."

"Oh, really? Where were you working on it? The library?"

"Well—"

"Because I checked there, and I didn't see you. And you weren't working on it here, either, obviously. I have a right to know the truth, man. We're roommates, and I think we're friends—"

"I think so, too."

"So, tell me the truth. Unless you can't." Bryce furrowed his brow. "You're not cheating on Lucy, are you?"

"Are you insane? Of course not! I love her."

"Then where are you going that you don't feel like you can tell me?"

"I'm . . . " Patrick sighed. "It's personal, all right? It's not that I don't trust you, it's just something that no one really knows about."

"But you ditch us randomly. When was the last time you actually sat down and hung out with the whole crew and didn't run off? Even Lucy's getting tired of it. I could tell by the way she looked when you left tonight."

A pang of regret stabbed at Patrick's heart like a shard of jagged glass. He never intended to hurt Lucy, or any of them; but he thought she at least understood why he left so many times. She knew what he was doing, after all. But if he was hurting her too, then something had to give. He had loved Lucy for years. Those feelings had come even before his powers.

He could live without Spright but not without Lucy.

"I'll try to be more consistent in spending time with you guys. I'm sorry."

"Okay." Bryce turned off the lamp and dropped back into bed. "I still wish you'd tell me the truth, but whatever."

Patrick bit his lip, considered a response, and then decided against it. He pulled the covers over himself. He didn't know Bryce well enough yet to trust him with that kind of secret. Being Spright was always going to require sacrifices. Maybe that meant he would never have the closeness with his friends that he wanted.

* * *

Cash, credit cards, watches, jewelry . . . Who would have known that raiding a college party would be so profitable? Everyone joked about college students being broke all the time; but when enough of them got together, especially spoiled fraternity and sorority kids, they had a hefty lump sum of valuables. Darius Coleman had been skeptical when he was directed to the party, but he was glad he had listened.

Most people wouldn't have been able to pull off such a heist, not to mention doing it without hurting any of their victims to scare the rest into compliance. The mass chaos ensuing from a raid on a party with so many people would have meant Darius probably getting trampled for his trouble. Luckily for Darius, his powers meant he never had to stoop to violence to force people to surrender.

He patted a wad of bills—some crisp and new, others crumpled and tattered from repeated use—into a neat stack. The cash alone totaled nearly $500. There was no telling how much he could pawn the valuables for. Of course, the cards were probably a bust. The owners would call and cancel them before Darius got any use out of them, but it had still been worth it.

The truth was this was just a practice run.

"Not bad, baby brother."

Darius looked up. Anton, his older brother—only by a few minutes, because they were two-thirds of a group of triplets—strode up to the table, clad in rumpled gray coveralls, his face and hands smeared with black grime and grease. He wiped his dark hands ineffectually on a white cloth as he examined Darius's score.

"Guess your contact was right about that college party."

"Shouldn't doubt him." Anton grinned. "Told you he'd help us get a start in this game."

"The criminal game, you mean?" Zoey, Darius and Anton's sister, appeared from the back room, clad in coveralls identical to Anton's. Her hair was dyed red and pulled back in a ponytail. "We have virtually limitless potential with these powers, and you *morons* want to use them to rob college kids."

Darius knew that Zoey—who went by Zee—had other ideas. Political ones. However Anton, being the oldest of the triplets, had the most influence. Darius went along with him because he knew from experience how Anton reacted when he was outvoted. Zee cared enough about them that she would go along with her brothers, whether she agreed or not. She would complain about it every step of the way, though. That had a tendency to make Anton angry. And with his powers, Anton had the ability to back up his rage.

"Look, we just need to get ahead of the game, Zee," Anton said. "Being a superhero doesn't exactly bring in a lot of money, now does it?"

"No, I guess not . . . "

"And how are we going to afford the super suits and other tech that heroes need to be good at saving people?" Anton shook his head. "No way. We didn't get lucky enough to have rich friends to support a life of crimefighting. We've got to make our own way in the world. I have debts to pay—to people who don't hand out past due notices. If we want to pay 'em back, this is what we've got to do."

"It's people like you that make superheroes necessary." Zee dropped down in a chair across the table from Darius. "Mom would be ashamed of us, and you know it."

"So why did you agree to help us?" Anton growled.

"Because I can stop you from getting too crazy and hurting people."

Darius released a mental burst of calming energy. It would be especially effective on his siblings. Zee's powers gave her the ability to sense others' feelings, meaning she would start to feel Darius' emotional projection more quickly. Anton's powers allowed him to draw strength from his and others' negative emotions, so the abrupt wave of calm would weaken him. They stared at each other for another moment, and then Anton grumbled and stormed away. Darius half-smiled at his sister.

"Don't give me that look," she snapped. "You went along with him. You always have."

"He needs someone to be there for him."

"Not to support his bad behavior." Zee sighed. "But I'm just as guilty of that as you are, and it's too late to go back now. At this point, we're practically public enemies one through three."

Darius set the stack of cash down on the table and picked idly at his two-inch afro. "Who are we kidding? Anton was a criminal before we got powers. It was always inevitable that we would get caught up with him. We're too close for anything else."

"I guess you're right." Zee pushed off the table and stood. "What bothers me is this contact of his. Who is he? How'd he get the information about the party? And what is he going to want in return?"

"We'll cross that bridge when we get to it. For now, we just need to keep our heads above water. Right now, that means taking whatever we need. It could be different someday. We'll see."

"As long as Anton's in charge? It won't be."

* * *

Patrick typed out his to-do list so rapidly that his phone vibrated in his hands. He had to get to work on his youth ministry project and presentation, but he also had to plan for the fall formal dance. As little time as he and Lucy had spent together lately, she would be crushed if he didn't go. And between the two responsibilities, he had to keep looking for the Opera Mask Gang.

For the past two days, he had done his best to stick with his friends as much as possible. He needed to alleviate Bryce's suspicions—and, if he was being honest, he missed their company. Spright came first, obviously, but even superheroes needed friends to help them recharge. He sat with them as they watched the next *Lord of the Rings* movie. Alexa had gained quite an appreciation for the series and was deeply invested in the second film. Later that night, they were all going to dinner together. Patrick was excited for that because Asher had agreed to meet them at the restaurant.

When was the last time he, Asher, and Lucy had hung out together? It had been too long. Even when they helped coordinate his missions as Spright, it was only over the phone. They were seldom in the same room together. Just one more reason to find a place where they could do the job in secret. Bryce's growing interest in his activities didn't help.

The door to their dorm swung open, and Bryce stepped in.

"So, you're actually coming tonight, huh? No stepping out or disappearing at random?"

"Not in the plans." Patrick finished his list. "You were right. I haven't been spending enough time with Lucy—or with the rest of you. I'm trying to do better."

"That's good. I'd still like to know your secret, though."

"Trust me, whatever you think it is, you're probably way off." Patrick went to his closet and rifled through his shirts. "But I need you to trust me. You're my friend, and I wouldn't keep secrets if it wasn't really important."

"Whatever you say, man."

Patrick pulled out a button-down navy shirt with a checkered pattern. He pulled it over his white T-shirt, buttoned it up, and picked a brown windbreaker out of the closet to go over it.

"See you tonight."

Dinner first. Prepare for the formal. Then find the Opera Mask Gang and take care of them.

* * *

In his time with the Vindicators, Carter had watched Dean Sterling work at a computer on multiple occasions. The tech genius and scion to the Sterling Enterprises empire was an aficionado on the keyboard. As his fingers flew, he made magic happen on the screens before them. It was incredible to watch. Carter assumed that no one could match Dean Sterling for technical prowess. Joanie Sellers was making him question that assumption.

If Dean was an aficionado, Joanie was a maestro. Her digits danced across the keys with almost inhuman speed, reminding Carter of Patrick Omer's superpowers. Joanie was only human, though, but she still typed with the dexterity and rapidity of a speedster. Once Silas gave her limited access to the CLOUD servers so she could hook up with the satellite, Joanie set to work with single-minded ferocity.

Whoever had broken Ty out of prison had sabotaged Stone Gate's security cameras. They had no way of knowing how the rescuers had arrived or where they had gone. But they could not hack a satellite; and according to Silas, CLOUD stored all the footage their satellites picked up on a dedicated server. The key was combing through that footage—hoping what they needed was there—and finding it.

That was where Joanie came in. She might be their only hope of finding Ty Vickers.

As Joanie worked, Carter stepped over to the window and removed his phone from a pouch on his utility belt. He knew this plan was a long shot, but there was one more thing that might tip the scales in their favor. He pulled up Dean's contact information and dialed. His friend answered on the second ring.

"You're on with Dean. How can I make your day brighter?"

Carter laughed. "Hey, man."

A dull thumping sound distorted Dean's voice somewhat. Carter figured he was probably backstage at one of his girlfriend Audrey Knight's concerts.

"Good to hear from you, Carter. Need help naming another supervillain?"

"Not quite—more like finding one you already helped me name." Carter explained the situation, from the moment of Ty's rescue—or potential capture—to their current plan. "I was wondering if we could also get access to the Sterling Enterprises satellites. Combining their footage with CLOUD's might give us a better picture of what happened at the prison and where Vickers was taken after he was freed."

Dean whistled. "That's a tall order, my friend. Tall, but doable. I'll give your hacker access to the Sterling Enterprises satellites so long as they agree not to do anything other than look at the footage. I can't have a third party moving my company's satellites. People will start asking the kind of questions that could get a CEO-slash-superhero fired."

"You're the best, Dean."

"Oh, you know. I try. I've got to go, but I'll get that information sent over. Bye."

Carter hung up the phone and walked over to Silas to share the news with him. He hoped the extra footage would be enough to put together where Ty had been taken. They were running out of options—and even worse, out of time.

CHAPTER 6

"What do you think he is going to do?" Alexa asked.

Lucy filled her lunch tray as she considered the answer to that question. With two days left until the fall formal and love in the air—she had heard of three new relationships blossoming on campus just in the past week—she had begun to wonder if Patrick had any plans for that day at all. He hadn't mentioned anything to her. Most guys had already formally invited their date weeks ago.

"I don't know. I hope he surprises me with something."

She loved Patrick. He was thoughtful and considerate, and she knew how much he loved her back. It was understandable that being Spright would take up a lot of his time. She just wished he would find a balance. He hadn't changed. He was the same next-door neighbor she'd invited to church and grown to love. But somewhere along the line, his priorities had shifted. When had it happened? It had been so gradual that she hadn't realized it until it was too late.

She had to admit that he had been doing better over the past few days. He had only left once during the movie last night, and it had been so fast that he was able to blow it off to the others as running to the restroom. Lucy appreciated his effort more than he would ever know.

Her tray now full of what EBC's cafeteria considered food, she followed Alexa to a table. They were early for lunch, so the cafeteria was relatively empty. They set their trays down on an empty table and took their seats.

"Are we still going to dinner tonight?" Alexa asked.

"Definitely." Lucy smiled. "You know, Patrick's best friend Asher will be there. As far as I know, he's single. And there's nothing saying a girl can't ask a guy to the fall formal."

Alexa crinkled her nose. "I don't need a date to the formal, Lucy. I need to focus on my studies, anyway."

"Okay, if you say so." Lucy shrugged. "Just think about it."

The chair across from Lucy skidded away from the table, and Patrick dropped into the seat. He smiled at her and reached across the table to touch her hand. Lucy smiled and turned her hand over to hold his.

Bryce sat down next to Patrick and mimed a retch. "Gross. I'm trying to eat."

Bryce's tray was filled to the brim with food. The guy seemed to eat nonstop; but since they were all going out for a big dinner that night, Lucy hoped he didn't regret the decision. Even Bryce had to have his limits. Unlike Patrick, whose superpowered metabolism meant that he had to consume multiple orders of calories more than the average human. Lucy was surprised that none of their friends had noticed Patrick scarfing down crazy amounts of food.

"Hey, Asher just called," Patrick said. "He wanted to know if it would be okay to bring a date to dinner tonight."

"A date?" Lucy side-eyed Alexa and shrugged apologetically. "I don't see why not. Is this someone new? He hasn't told me about anyone he's interested in."

"Me, either. Must be a new thing. I'll tell him she's welcome to come."

Patrick really was intending to be there tonight. Lucy squeezed his hand before letting it go to eat her lunch. Time would tell if he really had bounced back from his near-obsessive city-saving spree, or if he would fall back into the pattern. Either way, Lucy was thankful for the effort he was making in the moment.

* * *

Darius kept his hands tucked firmly inside the pockets of his black jacket as he and Zee walked after Anton into the dank alley. This was a bad idea, even for Anton. Darius was distinctly uncomfortable with his brother's criminal connections. The triplets' powers were more than sufficient to pull off their robberies, so why did Anton want to meet with an arms dealer?

Zee had put up a fight on the matter, of course. But as usual, Anton won. So here they were, all dressed in black and going to a shady rendezvous, looking every bit the cliché criminals that Anton wanted them to become. Darius glanced over his shoulder as they made their way farther into the alley—although, with Zee's powers, the precaution was redundant. She would sense anyone approaching them from behind.

"Why are we here?" Darius asked. "We don't need this."

"Maybe you don't. You can disable anyone with a thought. Zee and I can't. I'm strong, yeah, but what if I'm fighting someone who's not feeling angry or scared? Then my strength won't work. And Zee's powers aren't offensive at all. We need to be strapped, so we are ready for anything."

Zee shook her head. "I'm not carrying a weapon. It goes against everything I stand for."

"Why do you assume we'll get into a fight, anyway?" Darius asked.

"Like I said, be ready for anything. Maybe you can shut down everyone we run into. But maybe you can't, and then I'll have to fight 'em off. What if we run into a superhero? Spright's been nosing around this city for the last month. You really think he's gonna be angry or scared? I'll need an edge. And you will, too. You'll thank me later."

Zee snorted. "Doubt it."

"Guys." Darius waved a hand to quiet them. "Look."

A black car, its license plate covered by a length of black plastic that had been torn from a trash bag, sat in the alley ahead. As the Coleman siblings approached, the car's back door opened; and a man in a sharp three-piece suit stepped out. The door on the opposite side of the car opened, too; and a man dressed similarly to the Coleman siblings, armed with a submachine gun, joined the man in the suit.

"Anton Coleman," the man in the suit said. "And the siblings. My name is Walter DeMarco. Nice to meet you both."

Darius and Zee nodded. Darius wasn't sure if DeMarco knowing Anton already made him feel better or worse. It didn't make him feel less dirty about being here, though. Anton was in business with some bad people. That was his choice. If he wanted to be identified with people like this, he was free to do so. But Darius liked deniability.

"Thanks for meeting us, DeMarco." Anton shook the man's hand. "Do you have what I asked for?"

"Do you have the money?"

Anton gestured to Darius. "All here."

Darius reached into his pocket for the wrapped stack of cash that Anton had asked him to bring. It was all their earnings from the party raid, plus the extra money they'd received from the pawned jewelry. Darius couldn't believe they were going to spend it all on weapons. Anton owed a ludicrous amount of money to the Seventy-Six, a local street gang. They really should have used the cash to pay off part of those debts, not to buy guns. DeMarco looked at his friend and tilted his head toward Darius. The armed man approached. Darius extended the stack of cash.

"The stuff?" Anton asked.

"In the trunk." DeMarco gestured for the driver to pop the trunk. "I think you'll be happy with what I was able to find, especially considering the short notice on which you contacted me."

Anton's narrowed gaze was subtle, but Darius noticed it. He was sure Zee did, too. Anton wouldn't say it, but he was nervous about something. Darius took a breath and gathered his thoughts, ready to mentally strike DeMarco and his bodyguard if they tried to make a move.

DeMarco pulled open the trunk, and Anton peered down inside. Darius glanced over at Zee. Her eyes flicked over to meet his, and she nodded microscopically.

We're good.

Darius relaxed slightly. At least for the time being, DeMarco wasn't intending to double-cross them. Darius sighed and stepped up to his brother's side.

"Beautiful," Anton murmured.

In addition to an array of handguns and automatic weaponry, the centerpiece of the display of armament was a jagged, black sword with horizontal recesses running across the blade from top to bottom. Vents, maybe? The small button at thumb level on the hilt seemed to confirm Darius' assessment. What kind of weapon was it?

"A Garvin Technologies prototype," DeMarco said. "Just like you asked for."

"What does it do?" Darius asked.

Anton picked up the sword by its hilt and studied the curved blade. The corner of his mouth turned up in a smirk the way it had when he was a little boy and had come up with a mischievous new idea. He depressed the button with his thumb, and the vents along either side of the blade shone red. Anton extended the sword, pointing it at a light hanging over the alley; and a beam of red light shot from the blade and struck the light. The fixture exploded in a shower of sparks.

"A sword that shoots lasers?" Zee asked dryly. "That seems excessive."

"Hey, Spright has been hitting the criminals in this city hard," Anton said. "He's too fast to be hit with normal weapons. This gives us an edge. Literally. He can't move faster than light."

He can probably move faster than you can aim, though . . .

"I'm glad you're satisfied with your purchase." DeMarco clapped once. "If that's all, we'll be going."

"That's it?" Darius looked between DeMarco and Anton. "All that money for one weapon? I thought you said we all needed to be prepared."

"We do." Anton twirled the sword casually. "With this, I'll be able to protect you both from anything that gets in our way. No problem."

"You'll be hearing from my employer soon." DeMarco climbed back into the car. "When he calls, I recommend answering."

DeMarco's bodyguard reentered the car as well; and the vehicle pulled off, leaving the Coleman siblings standing in the alley. Darius looked at his brother in mixed disbelief and concern.

Are we working with gangsters now?

That hadn't been the plan. Anton was already in debt to one gang. The last thing the Colemans needed was to owe another one. Whatever Anton had cooking in his brain, Darius hoped it didn't get them all arrested—or worse.

* * *

Ty's throat was raw from dehydration. The two glasses of water his captors provided him per day were not sufficient for his body's needs, even if he was trapped in one place. As he swallowed, a burning pain rolled through his throat. He choked back a cough and leaned his head against the wall behind him.

His dampening cuffs were chained to that wall, but the chain was long enough to give him some range of movement. He did pushups, sit-ups, squats . . . whatever exercises he could do in place with bound hands. It had been a challenge but one that kept the threat of insanity at bay.

Now his body was growing too weak to sustain that kind of physical activity.

Maybe his captors really had brought him here to die. Maybe their goal was to torture him with a slow death. If so, providing him with food and water each morning and evening was an odd way to do it. It occurred to Ty that the food might not have even come in the mornings or evenings. There was no natural light in the basement; so for all he knew, his captors might be feeding him at random times to throw off his sense of time. Had he really been here for almost a week? It was getting harder to tell.

The metal door leading into the basement creaked open. Ty frowned. Was it time for another meal already? It had only been a few hours since his last one. He expected another two or three before the next. The only time anyone visited him was to bring him food, so what was this about?

He tucked his Bible away beneath his prison uniform and straightened, keeping his back to the wall.

Footsteps clanked against the stairway. A figure appeared in the light coming from the still-open doorway. Male, fit, a few inches taller than Ty. As the figure approached, Ty made out the features of a forty-something man with curly black hair and a matching beard contrasting against pale skin. The man stopped a few feet away from Ty—past the reach of the chain holding him to the wall—and crossed his arms.

"Hello," the man said. "My name is Ben."

Ty pursed his lips. "Hello, Ben. Are you going to finally tell me why I'm here?"

"No introduction? That's impolite." Ben tilted his head. "No matter. I already know who you are, Taro Watanabe."

"That's not my name. Hasn't been for a long time."

"Right. You go by Ty Vickers now. A bland name for a bland life—or at least, a life you wanted to be bland. But it didn't work out that way, did it, Taro?"

Ty narrowed his eyes and resisted the urge to snap at the man for continuing to use his birth name. He was not ashamed to be a Watanabe, for he loved his parents deeply; but that part of his life had been ruined by his godfather. He wanted to move forward now and start fresh. That was why he had chosen a new name.

At least, Ben did not call him Tao Liang. If he had used that name, Ty would have done everything in his power to kill the man.

"Considering you stole me from a prison cell, I think you know the answer to your question," Ty said. "Speaking of which, why did you do it? Why bring me here, especially if you were going to just lock me up like a prisoner, anyway?"

"Oh no, you're mistaken, my friend. You are not here as a prisoner. You're here for your own safety."

Ty barked out a laugh. "Is that so?"

"Yes. On my word."

"Your word means nothing to me, considering I don't know you. All I have to go on are your actions; and so far, they don't inspire confidence. Chaining me to a wall, dampening my powers, keeping me in the dark, feeding me just enough to keep me alive, not even offering a change of clothes after so long . . . " Ty shook his head. "Thanks for the intentions, but I think I was better off in prison."

"You do not understand yet, but we are protecting you." Ben backed away. "I will send someone down with a change of clothes. I cannot risk letting you bathe because that would require removing your dampening cuffs, and I can't have you leaving until I know you're safe. But at least fresh clothes might improve your mood. I'll also see about getting you an additional meal per day."

Ty glanced down at his cuffs. The green light on them was subtly shifting toward yellow. He had noticed it the day before. The battery in the dampening cuffs was wearing down. He wondered if Ben knew that the cuffs needed to be recharged. In another few days, the battery might wear down enough for Ty to use his powers. He just needed to keep Ben distracted from the light.

To do that, he decided to continue engaging the man in their verbal battle. "As nice as an extra meal would be, I'd still prefer my freedom."

"Someday. Not now." Ben turned and mounted the stairs. "You'll understand one day, I promise. For now, bear with us. We're doing the best we can."

Ty sighed and slumped back down to the floor. He did not believe Ben's words. Not even close. At least he could identify one of his captors, though. Once he got out of his cuffs, he knew who to watch out for—and, if necessary, who to kill in order to remain safe. One way or another, Ty was getting back to Emi. He didn't care what it took.

CHAPTER 7

It was not uncommon for Patrick to get the jitters. When he remained still for too long, the speed in his body built up and released itself however it could, which meant jitters. His friends who didn't know his secret merely thought he had a lot of pent-up energy. They had no idea how right they were. Patrick struggled to hide the vibrations, lest they become so rapid that his body blurred.

Because he had been trying to restrict his use of speed over the past few days, Patrick shook excessively as he prepared for the group's big dinner.

I definitely—definitely—*don't need coffee tonight.*

He struggled to still his hand so he could comb his hair. The finger-length red locks obediently fell into place, stylishly sweeping back away from his face and parting toward the left side of his head.

After two days of brainstorming ways to track down the Opera Mask Gang, Patrick had come up with an idea so simple that he did not know why he hadn't thought of it before. Back when Dr. Jeremiah Ashcroft unleashed his superhuman serum on the world, Dean Sterling had hacked into hospital records in affected cities to find patients who had been checked in with symptoms that were likely to lead to the development of superpowers. After he had compiled the list, Dean had sent it to CLOUD, a government agency devoted to observing supernatural or otherwise unknown threats such as superhumans.

If the Opera Mask Gang's powers came from nephiloids one of Ashcroft's gas bombs, they would be in that database somewhere. And luckily for Patrick, he had a friend in CLOUD. Jarrett Mercer was a soldier-turned-vigilante who had briefly joined the Vindicators. Jarrett, who went by Yeoman while fighting crime, was a high-ranking agent in CLOUD. If anyone could identify the members of the gang, it would be Jarrett.

The question was whether Jarrett would be willing to reveal that information to Patrick. Since the list had come to CLOUD via the Vindicators, it made sense that Patrick should be privy to it as well. But government agencies tended to be tight-lipped, even about things that they knew other people were aware of. Patrick hoped calling Jarrett wouldn't be a waste of his time. But he didn't have any other leads to work with. If Jarrett denied his request, all Patrick had wasted was a few minutes on a phone call.

But if the Opera Mask Gang was on CLOUD's list, why hadn't the agency intervened yet? Jarrett had told the Vindicators that CLOUD would step in if anyone on the list became a danger to the public. These criminals were clearly dangerous—although they hadn't physically harmed anyone yet—so where was CLOUD?

It was not the time to worry about that, though. He could call Jarrett the next day. At the moment, he had to finish getting ready. He didn't want to be late for dinner and cause Lucy pain or rouse Bryce's continued curiosity. At least, the latter was still in the restroom getting ready. For once, Patrick actually had an edge on him. Straightening his windbreaker and checking his reflection one last time, he stepped away from the mirror, opened the dorm room door, and stepped out into the hallway. He jogged down his stairs to the lobby and found Lucy and Alexa already sitting in plush gray-and-red chairs.

Alexa raised her eyebrows. "Wow, you are not the last one to arrive for once. Color me impressed."

Alexa had been hard on Patrick ever since beating him at dodgeball during orientation week. She thought he was slow—at least, slower than she was. If only Alexa knew how wrong she was.

"Hey, I can be fast when I want to be," he said.

He saw Lucy conceal a smile and winked at her. She looked beautiful with her blonde hair straightened so that not a single strand dared to move out of line. She wore a light blue denim top, black jeans, and an army green jacket. Her style had matured since coming to college. In the past, Patrick had been used to seeing her in shorts and graphic t-shirts. Although that was still her typical weekend wear, she had started dressing more seriously for classes and outings with their friends.

Either way, she looked gorgeous. Her kindness and relentless friendship were not the only reasons Patrick had fallen for her. As she matured, transforming bit by bit into the woman she would be for the rest of her life, Patrick only grew to love her more. He regretted that he had not done a good job of showing it lately.

"Is Asher meeting us here or at the restaurant?" Lucy asked.

He blinked, coming back from his thoughts to the present moment. "At the restaurant. He said he had to pick up his date first, so he wouldn't be able to make it here before we left."

"So, his date. Who is she?"

Patrick shrugged. "You know as much as I do. I didn't even know he was seeing anybody. But at the party the other night—"

He clamped his mouth shut. Lucy knew about the party that Asher had been to because Patrick had told her about the thief. But Alexa had no idea. As far as she knew, Patrick hadn't been to any parties recently.

Oops.

"Party?" Alexa asked. "What party?"

"Oh, a party Asher was at. He told me about it. I guess he met this girl there."

The explanation seemed to satisfy Alexa, thankfully, and it had been true. Asher had told him about the party, and he had met his date there. Patrick always preferred to keep his excuses as honest as possible. It was a good thing this hiccup had come with a simple solution. With Bryce on his tail all the time, he didn't need Alexa's curiosity added to it.

The elevator chimed behind them. Patrick turned to see Bryce exiting into the lobby. Bryce raised an eyebrow and half-smiled as he spotted Patrick. Patrick smirked and gave his friend a casual two-fingered salute.

"Wow. You actually showed up."

"On time," Patrick added. "Unlike you."

Bryce rolled his eyes. "Well, we're all here. Ready to go?"

"Let's do it. I'm starving."

* * *

Sitting in his car outside Shannon's apartment, Asher checked his phone. They should be right on time to get to the restaurant when Patrick and the others did. Asher chewed on his bottom lip and drummed his fingers against the steering wheel impatiently. If he was honest with himself, he was nervous about the dinner date. In the two days since the party, he had not talked to Shannon again, other than to ask her if she wanted to go with him and his friends to dinner. He had been elated when she said yes, but he had misgivings.

He still didn't know much about her. Given that he had fallen asleep before he could ask her anything about herself, he had no idea about her beliefs—or, really, anything other than her name and her field of study. What if faith came up over dinner and she got embarrassed and left because she hadn't realized Asher was a Christian? Or what if Patrick and Lucy judged him for going on a date with someone who was not a Christian? Or what if she was a Christian, and he was being silly?

What am I worried about?

Patrick and Lucy were two of the least judgmental people he knew. They weren't going to condemn her. And on the other hand, if Shannon did get uncomfortable because of Asher's faith, it was best to know now; so he didn't get too invested in the relationship.

Lord, just please let things go really well tonight.

He looked up as Shannon approached the car. She wore a beautiful green dress that came off her right shoulder. Her hair flowed over her shoulders in dark, curly tresses.

Wow, she's stunning.

Shannon opened the car door, slid into the passenger's seat, and smiled at Asher.

"Thanks for the invite."

"You're welcome. Thanks for coming with me." Asher put the car in drive. "All right. Here we go."

"So these friends of yours. How did you meet them?"

"Oh, I've been friends with Patrick and Lucy . . . forever, it seems like. Patrick and I were best friends from grade school, and Lucy was his next-door neighbor. He had a crush on her for the longest time.

Man, he didn't have eyes for any other girl." He chuckled. "They finally started dating last year. It was about time."

"So why did you end up going to different schools?"

"Patrick wanted to pursue ministry. Lucy wanted to be close to him; and EBC had a great journalism program, so she could pursue her degree. As for me . . . well, I guess I just didn't feel like EBC could offer me anything in the way of education."

"Ah." Shannon nodded. "Makes sense. So what future are you pursuing?"

Asher didn't have the guts to tell her that he didn't know. His career path had never been clear to him. He had come to Echelon University because it offered such a broad array of options. But thinking about it, he supposed that didn't sound so bad. He just didn't want to make her think he was indecisive, especially since she was a political science major. She, and people like her, were all about purpose. Asher didn't know what his purpose was.

"I guess . . . I guess I want to save people." Asher shrugged. "Maybe as a doctor, or maybe as something completely different—but I just knew I had to explore my options."

He glanced over at Shannon to see her reaction. She nodded understandingly but kept quiet. Had even saying that much shaken her interest in him?

Just calm down, man; you're doing fine.

He slowed the car as they approached a stoplight.

Even though he hadn't been able to admit to Shannon, the truth was Asher wanted to save people because he spent so much time watching Patrick do it. Ever since Patrick had come back to San

Francisco from Sojourn City, Asher and Lucy had been his support team. It was thrilling, but Asher wanted to be part of the action.

"Well, you've got time. You're just a freshman; you'll figure out what you want."

"And you?" Asher asked. "I realized I never asked you—are you a freshman too, or . . . "

"I'm a sophomore. But, honestly, I knew I wanted to be a poli-sci major from my first year in high school. It's just what interested me."

"Cool. Having your future together that early is . . . cool."

So far, so good.

Now, if he could just get through the rest of the night.

* * *

Patrick removed his windbreaker as the group approached the table of the upscale Italian restaurant the group had chosen. His wallet wasn't going to be thanking them at the end of the meal. Clenching his teeth behind his lips, Patrick pulled out a chair for Lucy. She smiled at him and sat down, and he scooted her chair up to the table. Taking his own seat beside her, Patrick ran his hands across the thick, navy-blue tablecloth. It was softer and made from better material than probably any outfit Patrick had ever worn.

I don't even want to look at the menu.

Bryce sat down next to Patrick. "So how's the project coming?"

"I . . . haven't made much progress." Patrick stared down at the table. The project had been his excuse for his absences several times, so he could not admit that he actually hadn't even started yet. "I don't know how to approach a subject that big."

"You came up with the idea, didn't you?"

"Yeah, but it was a last-minute thing. I kind of blurted it out without thinking—which, you know, I tend to do anyway. But with something like this, that can be kind of dangerous, as I am obviously discovering now. I—"

Lucy put her hand on top of his. Patrick realized he had been dangerously near rambling. It was another side effect of his powers, one that he was generally able to control. But when he got nervous, it tended to flare up. He chuckled sheepishly.

"Sorry."

Bryce laughed. "Man, if your brain worked as fast as your mouth, you'd have that project nailed by now."

Everyone at the table laughed. Bryce obviously hadn't meant anything by the quip; it was just his way of clearing the air between them. Due to Bryce's suspicions, their friendship had been tense lately. It would be good to move past that.

If we're going to do that, I need to operate out of somewhere other than our dorm room.

Lucy gripped his hand tighter. "Look. Asher's coming."

Patrick looked past Lucy to the front of the restaurant, where the maître d' was leading Asher and his date from the waiting room toward the table. Asher was dressed in a pair of black jeans and boots, a red Henley, and a black bomber jacket.

Asher's date was slightly taller than he was. Her face was framed with dark waves of hair that came down to meet her shoulders, one of which was left uncovered by her elegant green dress.

"Wow." Bryce's jaw was nearly on the table. "Seriously, wow."

Asher scored big time.

Patrick glanced at Lucy, wondering what her thoughts were on the new arrival. Her eyes were as wide as the others'. She glanced over at Patrick.

"Wow, do I feel underdressed," she whispered.

"Nah, you look great." Patrick turned his attention back to Asher. "Hey, man!"

"Hey, guys." Asher grinned. "Good to see you all."

"You already know Bryce. This is Alexa."

Alexa waved. "Nice to meet you."

"You, too." Asher pulled a chair away from the table. "And this is my date, Shannon."

The group greeted Shannon in chorus, who nodded and greeted each of them in turn by name, as Asher introduced them. Patrick was impressed. She carried herself with an air of authority and confidence not typical for someone their age. Patrick had no clue how someone like Asher, who was handsome but helplessly dorky, had gotten lucky enough to get her attention. But then, he was just as far out of his league with Lucy.

"Now that everyone's here, let's order." Bryce rubbed his hands together. "I'm starving."

* * *

"I've got something," Joanie said.

It had been two days since Carter and Silas first made contact with Joanie. In that time, they had been forced to wait in the hope that she would follow through with her promise to help and that she would actually find something. Those two days had been agonizing, made worse by the fact that there was little for Carter to do as the Crusader.

With Chin Liang's arrest, the Red Dogs were all but wiped out from the Brooks; and their rival gang, the Tyrants, were lying low.

But finally, Joanie had called to ask them to come back to her place. As Carter and Silas eased through the window, Joanie turned toward them and tucked a dreadlock behind her ear.

"Ty's kidnappers took him away from the prison in a beige utility van. Of course, from a satellite view, I can't get license plate numbers or any identifying markings; but if I can follow the van on the footage until it reaches a city, I can access the city's CCTV footage or traffic cams and try to get a better look."

"Access," Carter said. "You mean *hack?*"

Joanie's face flushed. "I mean . . . yeah. But you want to find him, right? Do you have any better ideas?"

Carter didn't. And truthfully, he had no room to condemn her. Dean had accessed the city's CCTV footage more than once, and it was no more legal when he did it. Part of being a vigilante was an unfortunate mass of contradictions when it came to his stance on crime. If he wanted to find Vickers, he would have to let Joanie get away with it.

He glanced at Silas, who nodded and took the lead. "We know about the van. We were able to follow it as far as the interstate, so focus your search beyond that point. As soon as you find something on the van, let us know. Especially if you find its destination. As soon as we have that, we can sweep in and rescue Ty."

"Will do." Joanie turned back to her laptop. "Let's see what I can do . . . "

CHAPTER 8

A shower of sparks rained down on the garage. Darius cringed and raised his arms instinctively to shield himself from them. Oblivious to his brother's distress, Anton trained his newly purchased sword on the far corner of the garage and fired a beam of red energy. Another explosion lit the dark building.

Darius cast a helpless glance at Zee. She shook her head in disgust and walked toward the back room. Darius followed her, ignoring Anton's rampage. If their brother wasn't careful, he was going to get the police called on them; and then they would all be in trouble. Zee went to the fridge at the back of the cramped break room and pulled out a diet soda. Darius did not know how she drank those. They were disgusting—and unhealthier even than a regular soda, in his opinion. He picked up a half-empty water bottle he had left on the table earlier and sipped from it.

"Do you think he has a plan at all?"

"Other than to sit around and wait for DeMarco's boss to call? Not likely." Zee snorted. "What a waste. All this potential . . . we could be out there, making a difference in the world. You know, since the attacks on Chicago and D.C., the government hasn't made any official statement about superhumans? Not one. It's like we don't even exist to them. The media's all over it, though. They call us 'amplified'—'amps' if they're feeling casual."

"Government support or not, superheroes are everywhere. You've got Spright patrolling everywhere between here and San Francisco, Drifter and Maestro in D.C., Rampart in Juncture City . . . "

"Exactly my point. They're practically celebrities at this point, but the government still won't acknowledge their existence—not nationally, anyway. Some of the city governments might be recognizing the heroes, but the White House? Not a peep. And there are more of us than just the famous heroes. Look at the three of us—we've hit how many locations, and we're still unknown outside New Echelon? How many more amps must be out there? But no one knows we exist." She shook her head. "I've felt marginalized all my life. Now I've got powers, and I'm *still* marginalized."

"You're really passionate about this, aren't you?"

"You know I am." Zee slammed her can down on the table. "But here we are, using our powers for personal gain. All that's going to do in the long run is make it harder for superhumans to be accepted."

"Here we go again." Darius sighed. "You know I don't like it any more than you do—"

"Sure, sure. I'm just saying."

It was too late, anyway; they were committed now—forced to pay back Anton's debt and now indebted to whatever crime boss held DeMarco's leash. At least, Anton was. But now that DeMarco had seen their faces, there was no chance Darius and Zee could get out of it. They were stuck.

"Guys?" Anton bellowed. "Where'd you go?"

Darius shook his head. For someone who fed off emotions, Anton was oblivious to everyone but himself. Most people—even Zee—probably would have left Anton to his own devices long ago, but Darius saw his brother's need for guidance and companionship. So he stayed with him. Zee stuck around because of the bond between her and Darius. At least, that was what Darius told himself. He had never asked her directly.

Anton's heavy footsteps filled the small breakroom as he stormed through the door. He set the sword down heavily on the table between Darius and Zee. Although Zee didn't flinch, Darius saw the uncertainty in her eyes. He didn't need her empathic powers to recognize it. He had known her all her life.

"We don't need that, do we, Anton?" Zee asked. "No one needs to get hurt."

"If everyone leaves us alone, no one gets hurt." Anton furrowed his brow and stared at her. "I thought you were with me on this. Are you, or aren't you?"

Zee nodded. "Yeah. Yeah, I'm in."

"Good. Because I've been thinking. Darius got a chance to show off his powers at that party the other night, but you and I haven't yet. Why don't we find a way to test what we can really do?"

Zee pursed her lips. "What do you have in mind?"

* * *

"So, you lived in Sojourn City for a year?" Alexa asked.

"Not quite a year," Patrick said. "Just a few months, really. My internship with Sterling Labs lasted the summer before my senior year of high school through the first semester. When my second semester started, I moved back to San Francisco and finished high school here."

He would have preferred to keep those details of his life quiet, but Asher had mentioned something about Sojourn City in passing; and before Patrick could stop the conversation, he was knee-deep in scrambling for an explanation as to why he had lived there. Luckily, the internship excuse had been the one Dean and Gideon had originally used on Patrick's parents, so it had been quick to come to mind.

"So did you ever see any of the superheroes?" Bryce asked. "The CEO of Sterling is supposed to be good friends with the Seraph, Gideon Turner. Did you ever bump into him?"

"I met him a few times. He seemed like a really nice guy—of course, he tended to keep to himself, since everyone knew he was a superhero. I don't think he ever meant for that secret to come out, you know? But once it did, it would've been pretty hard to put back in the box. He just kind of . . . lived with it."

"I'm jealous, man. I would love to meet one of those guys. Who'd have ever thought we would live in a world where superheroes really existed? I mean, how cool is that?"

"Very cool." Patrick scratched behind his ear. "But all this is just reminding me of my project, so . . . "

"Project?" Shannon asked. "What project?"

"Oh, you're gonna love this." Bryce grinned. "Patrick forgot to come up with an idea for a project for his youth ministry class. So, last-minute, he blurts out that he wants to study the effect living in a world with superheroes has on teens' faith."

Shannon raised her eyebrows. "That's a really good idea. I'd be interested in knowing the results of that study myself."

"You would?" Asher asked.

"Definitely. As much as having superheroes around might affect people of faith, it also has the potential to affect political leanings. For example, will the right to bear arms be as big of a hot-button topic now that superheroes are around? Will conservatives feel the need to own a gun if they know a superhero can come and save them? Or will liberals feel as strongly about gun control, knowing superheroes could potentially stop school shootings? And that's just one area where it might make a difference."

Patrick glanced between her, Asher, and Lucy. Her insight on the subject was interesting. Patrick had never considered how his existence might affect politics. Up until he came up with the project idea, he hadn't even considered the effect on faith. What would he do if he found out that he was inadvertently making people feel less of an urge to go to church because their faith was in superheroes rather than God?

No way. I'm powerful—but not all-powerful, and I can't work miracles.

"Anyway, enough about superheroes." Shannon looked back at him. "How did your internship at Sterling Labs correlate with your desire to be in ministry now?"

Patrick's throat tightened. That hadn't been a question he was expecting . . . or prepared for. Shannon was as inquisitive as Bryce, and she didn't even have any suspicions about him. This was going to be an interesting night.

* * *

Nights as a crimefighter did not offer much opportunity for dates with Raina; but crime had been slow in Sojourn City over the past few weeks, so Carter took advantage of that. As the two of them sat in a booth at Wally's Diner, enjoying burgers and fries, Carter tried to keep his mind off Ty Vickers' whereabouts. There was nothing Carter could do for him until Joanie tracked down the van, so worrying was pointless—but knowing that did not make it any easier to stop.

"You know I'm taking a sociology class this semester, right?" Raina crunched on a French fry. "Believe it or not, the professor actually brought up superheroes. He thinks their existence is going to have big ramifications for our culture."

Carter chuckled. "No doubt. I mean, two years ago, most people in the world thought that superheroes were fiction. Now they're everywhere, and the media's even got a name for them. *Amps.* Who came up with that?"

"Who knows? Some newsroom writer looking to make their mark on the world, probably. Still, it's fascinating to think about."

"And what about those of us who are vigilantes but don't have powers? Did your prof have anything to say about that?"

"Just that superhero copycats are more likely to crop up now than ever before. People are socialized to see superheroes as the highest attainable symbol of goodness, so . . . " Raina bobbed her head and grabbed another fry. Her face flushed red. "Uh, never mind. We can talk about something else now."

Carter frowned. "What?"

"Oh, nothing. Just . . . " She pursed her lips. "He said that superhero copycats were going to crop up specifically because narcissists would be seeking after the glory inherent in being a superhero and that they would probably end up doing more harm than good, both to themselves and the communities they attempt to protect."

Carter grimaced. "Ouch."

"That can't be the case for everyone, though. I bet you anything he'd change his tune if he met you or Silas."

"I hope so. Yikes."

Carter's phone rang. He scooped it from his pocket and rested it face-up on the table. The screen displayed an incoming call from Joanie. He had given her his number reluctantly, because even if she did not know his secret identity, it would be easy for someone like her to figure out who a phone number actually belonged to. He hoped she respected his privacy and did not try to dig into his personal life.

"Must be about Vickers," he said. "Mind if I take it?"

Raina gestured to the phone with her fry. "Go for it."

Carter brought the phone to his ear and spoke softly. "Yes?"

"Uh . . . is this the Crusader?" Joanie paused. "Must be. You wouldn't be so cryptic otherwise. So I have good news and bad news. The good news is, I was able to track the van's entire route. It wasn't easy, let me tell you, but I did. That brings us to the bad news, though."

"What's that?"

"As we suspected, the van is not in Sojourn City. It's not even in Michigan."

"Not even . . ." Carter furrowed his brow. "Where is it?"

"It's in New Echelon, California."

Carter blinked. "Oh. Well . . . looks like I'm taking a road trip."

CHAPTER 9

"This is not what I expected."

Zee's voice was tinny in Anton's ear, difficult to hear over the roar of the crowd. The small earpiece he had bought was cheap—not a high-quality piece of technology, by any means—but it got the job done. All that mattered was he could hear her. That was all he needed for this plan to work—provided she did her part, anyway.

"Left," Zee said.

Anton pulled his left arm up in a block as his opponent swung a right hook. The big man, dressed only in a pair of tight black and white shorts and a pair of fingerless gloves, tried to pull his hand back; but Anton reached in with his right hand, grabbing the extended wrist, and turned, throwing the muscular man over his shoulder. The crowd roared as Anton's opponent slammed into the unforgiving floor of the cage. Anton raised his right fist to deliver a blow.

"Watch his feet."

Anton stepped back as his opponent kicked back and upward in such a way that his foot would've struck the back of Anton's head. As it was, the kick passed harmlessly by Anton's face. He reached forward, grabbing the man's ankle with both hands. He sensed a surge of fear from the man, and strength surged through his body. Anton lifted and flung the man across the ring, striking the cage.

It was working. Zee's powers enabled her to predict the fighter's every move and allowed her to warn Anton before the blows could land. The more the fighter missed, the more confused and frightened he became—and the more Anton's power built. Working together like this, they were an unstoppable force. And if Darius could use his powers to amplify the fear and aggression in the fighter, Anton could feed off that, too.

He stormed toward his fallen opponent, ready to finish the job. The rules of the fighting ring—which was highly illegal, but profitable—stated that the fight continued until one of them tapped out or passed out. Anton's opponent hadn't tapped out yet; and he was still moving, his arms trembling as he struggled to push himself off the ground. He looked up and winced, no doubt blinded by the flood lights shining down on the small arena. Anton popped his knuckles and approached the fighter.

"Anton, wait. There's no need to—"

Anton's opponent, hands pressed against the ground, spun and drove the heels of his feet forward, striking Anton in the gut. He stumbled back; and his earpiece fell out, landing on the ground beside him. The fighter's gaze fell on the device, and Anton didn't need Zee to tell him what the man was thinking. His face, already red from exertion, brightened to the shade of a ripe tomato. He bared his teeth and stormed forward.

The rage the man was feeling surged through Anton's veins, pumping like adrenaline. Anton rose, bringing his fist up to connect with the man's chin. The power behind the punch flipped the fighter head over heels. He landed flat on his chest. Anton bore down on him, ready to finish the fight.

Someone grabbed his wrist, while another pair of hands fell on his left shoulder. Anton glanced behind him. A pair of thugs, hired "security" for the host, had entered the cage to break up the fight. Anton scowled and shot his elbow back, and a sharp *crack* sounded as it smashed into the skull of the man grabbing his shoulders. As he crumpled, Anton turned and used his left hand to punch out the second thug.

"Get out!" the host screamed. "Get out now!"

"Give me my money!" Anton roared.

Onlookers screamed and rushed away from the cage as Anton stormed through the gate, slamming it behind him to trap his opponent and the two guards. He cast around, looking for the owner.

I'm not leaving without my money.

This had been going so well. If only Zee hadn't had a fit of conscience and distracted Anton, that earpiece never would've fallen out; and they would be counting their winnings.

"Anton!" Darius called. "We need to go!"

"Not without my money!"

Anton saw his brother standing nearby, protectively clutching Zee's shoulders as they watched his rampage. He didn't care. They needed to toughen up and see the world for what it was. Anton continued his search.

Ah. There he is.

The fight host was rushing away from the cage in the opposite direction of the crowd, heading for an entrance to a warehouse. The cage had been set up on the docks; Anton assumed it was gang-run. The warehouse was probably a front for the gang, which meant the host probably thought he had reinforcements inside. None of them could stop Anton. The fear of the dozens of patrons increased his strength with every cry of terror.

"Come back with my money!"

He took two steps and leaped, the added strength in his legs carrying him across the fifty or so yards between himself and the host. Anton crashed to the ground next to the man, grabbed him by the collar of his leather jacket, and hoisted him off the ground one-handed.

"Now. Let's talk."

* * *

Everyone at Patrick's table laughed uproariously as Asher finished telling a story about one of Patrick's less spectacular moments as a member of the track team. He ducked his head and speared a slice of lasagna with his fork. As he brought the food to his mouth, his phone went off. Patrick downed the bite of pasta and glanced at the screen.

Carter?

Patrick tried to keep up with Carter, since they had been good friends when they were both with the Vindicators; but it was unlike Carter to call out of the blue. He was a fairly private person, one who hated to feel like he was intruding. For him to call unsolicited probably meant that something was up. Patrick rose from his seat.

"I've got to take this. It's actually a friend from Sojourn City." He glanced meaningfully at Lucy, hoping she took his meaning. "It won't be a minute."

Patrick hurried through the restaurant and pushed his way outside. He found a secluded spot on the curb and answered his phone.

"Hello?"

"Hey, man," Carter said. "Listen, I know you just moved to New Echelon, but are you up for a visitor?"

Patrick frowned. "Who?"

"Me. It's a long story; but basically, a super-criminal I captured a few months back was broken out of prison, and we just tracked his rescuers to New Echelon. Thing is, I think he might actually be in trouble. I promised his sister-in-law I'd find him, so Dean's arranged for me to get a flight out there."

"Wow."

Truthfully, it would be good to see Carter. Patrick wanted someone around who understood the struggles of superhero life. "I don't have much room in my dorm, and my roommate has been suspicious of my activity lately. But as long as we get our cover story straight and you're cool sleeping on the floor, I think we can make it work. And I'll do whatever I can to help you find your . . . *friend*?"

"It's complicated." Carter chuckled. "Sounds good, man. I'll see you tomorrow."

"Okay, then. See you tomorrow."

Patrick wove his way back through the table, careful to look nonchalant as he eased back in the chair next to Lucy. The fact that superheroes and Sojourn City had come up in conversation so recently at the table could make things awkward, considering the timing of Carter's call. Patrick just hoped no one was the wiser.

"Is your friend okay?" Bryce asked.

Patrick nodded. "Oh, he's fine. He's just planning a trip out here and wanted the chance to catch up if I have time."

"Time for a friend?" Bryce snorted, but then smiled good-naturedly. "That'll be a first."

The rest of dinner went smoothly. Patrick and his friends enjoyed one another's company; they laughed and shared stories of their past and griped about upcoming assignments . . . and Bryce never gave Patrick a sideways *when-are-you-leaving* glance. Maybe he was out of the woods.

"It was nice to meet you, Shannon," Lucy said.

"Nice to meet you all, too." Shannon waved as she and Asher walked toward his car. "Good night!"

Bryce and Alexa split off as well, leaving Patrick and Lucy alone as they walked toward his car. He reached out and took her left hand in his right, the familiar entwining of their fingers a comfortable reminder of all the good things in his life. He loved her more than she could ever know.

"That was nice," Lucy said.

"Yeah. I had a lot of fun."

"Thank you." She leaned over and kissed his cheek. "It meant a lot that you stayed for the whole meal. Other than that phone call, of course. What was that really about?"

"I'll explain on the drive home." Patrick reached for the car door. "Now let's get back and—"

His phone vibrated. He took it out of his pocket. A police alert flashed on the screen. Dean had installed the app on his phone before Patrick left Sojourn City, allowing him to pick up local emergencies. There was an altercation of some kind at the docks.

Well . . . it was almost a relaxing night.

He gave Lucy a guilty smile, but she didn't look upset.

"Go on. Give me your keys, though. I'll drive back."

Patrick nodded, removed the Spright suit from the car's trunk, and tossed Lucy the keys. Spinning in a blur too fast to see, Patrick changed from his street clothes into the Spright uniform and pulled his mask on.

"Go get 'em," Lucy said.

"Thanks. I'll be in touch."

CHAPTER 10

Darius had no idea how everything had gone south so quickly. Anton had a penchant for lashing out, though, so Darius should not have been surprised. He stood back with Zee as their brother assaulted the fight ring host, lifting him into the air and slamming him against the exterior wall of the warehouse. Zee turned to look at Darius.

"You can stop this. Hit him with your powers. Calm him down."

Darius shook his head. "If I do that, he'll kill me once he's recovered."

"If you don't, he's probably going to kill that guy!" Zee pointed at the host. "Come on, Darius, we—"

"We probably shouldn't use our real names." Darius shook his head. "And we should definitely have our masks on. Go get them from the car."

"Is this really the time for—"

"If the cops show up, and we're not wearing our masks, we're dead." Darius pushed her shoulder gently. "Go. I'll take care of our brother."

Zee furrowed her brow, studied him for a moment, and then turned and rushed for their car. Darius turned back to Anton and inched his way forward. When Anton was high on emotion, caution was the key to approaching him. If he startled Anton, he would end up flattened for his trouble. As he neared his brother, he held up his hands.

"Hey, man . . . "

We really need codenames.

Darius coughed and continued. "Why don't you put this guy down, okay? He didn't do anything."

"He owes us," Anton rumbled. "I want my money."

"I'll—I'll get it for you!" the host whimpered. "P-please! Let me go!"

"Hey!" Zee called. "Masks."

Darius looked up as Zee tossed him the golden sad-faced opera mask that he had worn when he robbed the party. Darius pulled the mask over his face. Anton, still holding the host in the air one-handed, reached out and took the angry opera mask from Zee. As he placed it on his head, he growled deep in his throat. Zee, who was already wearing the happy opera mask, put a hand on Anton's shoulder.

"Hey. Let's just let him down."

"I'd listen to the lady," a new voice said.

Darius jerked in surprise and spun around to face the speaker behind them. How had Zee not sensed them approaching? She knew better than to let herself be distracted on a job like this. Five men, all clad in black leather jackets, had assault rifles trained on the triplets. Darius shook his head.

This is a fine mess that Anton has gotten us into.

Hopefully, he could calm the gangsters before things got out of hand.

"Let me handle these guys," he said.

He stepped toward the gangsters, reaching mentally for their emotions . . .

A purple blur shot across Darius's vision, sending all five men tumbling through the air, their rifles clattering to the ground. A moment later, the blur reappeared and came to a stop, revealing a man with an athletic frame clad in black and purple from head to toe.

Darius's heart thumped in his chest. "Spright."

"Hello." The superhero waved. "Why don't you put that guy down?"

Darius looked over his shoulder at Anton. The eldest brother dropped the host and turned to face Spright. Darius suspected that even without the angry visage of the opera mask, Anton's true expression would've conveyed the same rage. Darius backed toward his brother and turned his head back to Spright.

"You know my name, but I'm afraid I'm at a disadvantage," Spright said. "I've been waiting to meet the famed Opera Mask Gang, but I still don't know your names—unless you're a different group of community theater wannabes."

Anton's fists clenched. "Shut up."

"That's not very nice. I'm not sure I want to see your show now." Spright crossed his arms. "Who are you?"

"This isn't any of your business, Lilac."

Darius shot a glance back at his brother. Antagonizing a superhero was about as crazy a move as he could imagine. Anton was no genius, but he had to be smarter than that. Darius considered sending some soothing waves in his brother's direction; but if the showdown came to a fight, Anton would need his anger to match abilities with Spright.

"Lilac?" Spright sighed. "And my dad always said that only real men could pull off purple. That's disappointing."

Zee snorted. "He's funny."

"Last chance, superhero." Anton's knuckles popped. "Step aside."

"I don't think so."

Darius extended his emotions, splayed out his hands in front of him, and projected as powerful a wave of calm and apathy as he could manage. Spright surged toward them, appearing between Darius and Zee in an instant; but he slowed and stumbled as Darius' mental projection hit him. Anton stepped in and swung a hammer-fisted punch into the hero's chest. Spright hurtled back through the air and struck a transformer. Sparks flew around the superhero.

"Let's get out of here!" Zee sprinted away. "Now!"

Darius grabbed Anton's shoulder and pulled him toward the car. Sirens wailed in the distance. The police would be there in seconds. Hopefully, between Darius' psychic attack and Anton's physical one, the superhero would be down long enough for the trio to escape.

So much for ever becoming a superhero, Zee. Looks like we're real villains now.

* * *

Spright groaned and rested against the telephone line that supported the transformer he'd struck. His limbs spasmed as the last currents of electricity channeled through them. Anyone else would have died from the power surge; but his speed powers had absorbed the electricity and turned it into energy, causing the spasms and vibrations he was currently experiencing.

He should get up and try to pursue the Opera Mask Gang, but the concept of standing seemed like too much work. He felt so tired and oddly relaxed. Why did he need to go after them, anyway?

But . . . I can't stay here.

As tired as he was, he was bound to fall asleep if he didn't move soon. At least he could muster the energy to get back to his dorm room.

"Spright?" Lucy said. "You all right?"

Oh yeah . . . I've got my earbud on.

"I'm fine. I . . . ugh . . . just took a hit. Big hit."

He pushed himself to his feet and looked around. Three police cars had pulled onto the scene. At least they could arrest the five unconscious thugs. It wouldn't be a total loss. And Spright was sure he could track down the trio . . . some other time. The one with the sad face had to have been the same guy from Asher's party. Even putting that together caused his brain to protest.

Okay, I get it. Sleep.

"I'm coming home. I'm really . . . tired. I'll see you tomorrow, okay? I'm just going to go to bed."

"Okay." Lucy sounded concerned. "Good night."

"Good night."

Spright turned away from the oceanfront. *Oh, well. Can't win them all.*

* * *

"This is all your fault!" Anton growled. "Both of you! If you hadn't interfered, I would have gotten our money from him in another minute. Now we've got nothing, and this whole thing was a waste of time!"

Darius shook his head at his brother's tirade, pulled off his mask, and ran a hand through his hair as he walked back into the garage. Subtly, he sent calming energy Anton's way, enough to be effective but not overpowering. If Anton noticed his brother's use of his powers, it would just send him into another rage.

Zee opened her mouth, but Darius held a hand up and shook his head. Any argument at this point was sure to spark a conflict. It had been a long time since Darius had seen Anton so riled up. It wouldn't end well for anyone who got in his way. His current priority was showing Anton that neither Darius or Zee were in his way.

"Spright still would have intervened. He's the one who stopped you, not us. We worked together to beat him, remember?"

Darius hated throwing the superhero under the bus. He admired Spright's actions; and in another life, he would have liked to work alongside the speedster. But crimefighting didn't pay the bills; and now that Darius had been placed at the scene of a crime, there was little chance the hero would ever consider working with him, anyway.

"That little twig." Anton hurled his mask across the shop. "Next time, I'll snap him in half."

"Next time?" Zee asked. "You're not seriously considering doing that again."

"Not a fighting ring, maybe. But we're getting better with our powers. With our teamwork tonight, we took down Spright before he could touch us. We've got potential to be a great team. Trust me. We can own this town."

"Maybe someday. For now, we need to lay low. Spright will be looking for us. We're lucky he didn't see our faces. But until some of the heat dies down, we need to stay here."

"Fine." Anton stormed away from them. "But not for too long. I've got plans—and debts to pay back, remember?"

"How can we forget?" Zee snapped.

Darius followed Zee as she strode toward the break room. It was getting late—he would just as soon go home as stay here with his siblings, but he wasn't going to leave Zee alone with Anton just yet. The tension between the two of them was likely to explode if they didn't have another party present, so he'd stay—for now. If worst came to worst, at least Darius could use his powers to stop them both in their tracks.

CHAPTER 11

As Asher drove Shannon home from the restaurant, he found himself eager for the next time they would get together. Shannon was charismatic, a brilliant speaker, always engaged and listening to those around her. It was no wonder she wanted to go into politics. She would be ridiculously good at it. And she was beautiful, too. That was a major bonus.

"Your friends are all really nice," Shannon said. "I enjoyed meeting them."

Asher smiled. "I'm glad. That means a lot to me."

He parked his car outside her apartment and looked over at her. He thought the dinner had gone fantastically—she had been engaging with them, as they had with her, and she had never seemed uncomfortable as they talked about church, faith, or God. That was a start, in his book. At least she hadn't shirked him because of it.

He decided to risk it. "I know we talked a lot about faith tonight. I realized I don't really know where you stand on the subject."

Shannon looked out the windshield. "That is a . . . long and painful conversation—one I'd rather not have right now. Can we talk about it some other time?"

"Of course." That didn't sound promising. "So are you still available for homecoming?"

"You bet." Shannon put one of her hands atop his. "Thanks again for tonight. I had a great time. I'll see you before homecoming."

She opened the car door and stepped out. Asher met her gaze as she looked back down into the car, smiled, and then shut the door and walked up the sidewalk to her home. Asher put the car in drive and pulled away.

That definitely could have gone worse.

* * *

If there was one thing Bryce knew, it was computer programming. He had always been good at it. His dad worked IT at Garvin Technologies, and Bryce had inherited his gift for it. That was why he was studying church administration. He might not have been called to be a youth pastor or a missionary, but he could do his part for the church through technology.

Adjusting the stem of his glasses with his right hand, Bryce studied the simulated church website design he'd come up with for his class project. It had been a cakewalk. Web design was at the bottom of the shelf, as far as his computer skills went. But it had been a relaxing project, and he had enjoyed it. After scanning the pages once more to ensure he hadn't missed a critical detail, he saved the project and opened his email to send it to his professor. There was nothing quite as satisfying as knowing he'd done a good job.

Computers were easy. People, though—people were not as black and white. Bryce loved people; he was a natural extrovert and had a gift for making friends. But he didn't understand people the way he did computers. They didn't have a logical flow to them. They did things that seemed against their "program." He loved it, though. It was a challenge. Bryce never shirked a challenge.

Patrick was the biggest enigma Bryce had ever met. The constant nights of disappearing for hours at a time, ignoring all his friends to do who-knows-what—that had been his code. And then, out of nowhere, he'd switched it up. For the past three days, he had refrained from running off in the middle of a hangout, and he'd made his relationships a priority. Maybe it was because of Bryce's prodding. Maybe he felt bad about leaving Lucy. Either way, the change was startling. The fact that he'd made it all the way through their dinner tonight had been incredible.

And then, he was gone again. Bryce had left the restaurant at the same time Patrick had, but he hadn't seen any sign of his roommate since then. Maybe he was just spending the rest of the evening with Lucy before he had to return to the dorm. Bryce wasn't sure of the last time the two of them had taken alone time together.

Bryce shrugged and closed his laptop. Oh, well. If Patrick wanted to open up, he would. There was no reason to push further. Bryce slid off his bed and placed his laptop inside its case. The door swung open behind him.

Ah, there he is.

"Hey, man." Bryce turned. "Where—"

It was Patrick standing in the doorway, all right. But . . . it wasn't. He was clad in a black runner's suit with purple armor plates on the chest, shoulders, forearms, knees, and shins; and he held a matching black-and-purple mask in his left hand. Only someone who had been living under a rock would have failed to recognize the outfit. And unless Patrick was suddenly able to afford ridiculous cosplayer prices, that suit was the real deal. Patrick Omer was Spright.

Bryce's jaw dropped.

"Whoa . . . um, this explains *so* much."

Bryce crossed the room in five long steps and closed the door behind Patrick, lest anyone else see his getup. Patrick looked into Bryce's eyes, and there was a numb look in his gaze that sent chills down Bryce's spine. He put a hand on Patrick's back and helped him walk over to his bed, where he slumped face-first into his pillow, not even bothering to pull the covers back. Whatever had happened to Patrick, it had done a number on him.

The pieces of the puzzle finally fell into place. Patrick's random disappearances. Patrick's penchant for fast talking and random jittering when he got nervous. Lucy must have known his secret; that was why she never seemed as concerned about him as everyone else. Bryce looked over at the door, half-expecting someone to come barging in to drag Patrick away. But it remained closed, thankfully.

"Can you turn out the lights?" Patrick asked flatly. "I need to sleep."

He was never this curt.

What's wrong with him?

Maybe some criminal had just whipped him in a fight, and it had put him in a bad mood. But there was something else off. He seemed like a totally different person. Well . . . he was, but in a different way. As Bryce crossed the room to hit the lights, he tried to process the fact that his friend and roommate was a superhero. No wonder he hadn't wanted to tell Bryce his secret.

"Don't worry, man." Bryce flicked off the lights. "Your secret's safe with me."

"Wonderful. I need sleep. Please be quiet."

Bryce climbed back into bed and scratched his eyebrow. *Maybe he'll be better in the morning.*

Bryce hoped so, anyway. There was no telling what he might accidentally reveal to the whole school if he was still like this tomorrow. But now that Bryce knew, he could help Patrick deal with whatever was wrong with him right now. That was what friends were for, and that was what Bryce was programmed for. He would be a good friend—even if Patrick didn't think he needed him yet.

* * *

Although Ty remained bound to the wall, Ben had been true to his word about the change of clothes and extra meals. Ty's guard had even provided a stick of deodorant with the clothes. Now, Ty was clad in a simple pair of dark blue jeans and a charcoal button-down shirt instead of his grimy prison uniform. His shoes had been exchanged for fresh socks and a pair of practical sneakers. He felt somewhat cleaner, at least, even if his hair still felt greasy and matted to his head and he had more facial hair than he had ever tried to grow in his life. It would be nice to get a shave. Maybe that would be Ben's next peace offering.

The light on Ty's cuffs was fully yellow now, trending toward orange. He had practiced trying to phase as his connection to his powers inched back into effect. So far, he had managed to wiggle his toes through the tips of his shoes and his fingers a few centimeters into the floor. The cuffs were still active, though, so his powers came in and out at random. He did not want to try a big phase in case they cut off mid-use, leaving him trapped or worse.

Still, just feeling his powers again was exhilarating. Being cut off from them was like having a limb severed. Now, he could feel them again, even if only at intervals. He would be able to use his powers again soon, provided Ben or the guards did not notice the fading light on the cuffs.

If Ty's estimation was correct, it was almost mealtime. He wondered if a guard would bring the meal or if Ben would do it himself this time. If Ty could build a rapport with the man, maybe he could convince him to let Ty go—or at least get Ben to lower his guard so he would not expect Ty to make an escape attempt.

God . . . Ty looked upward. *I don't know if You are real. But if You are, please get me out of here. I want to believe, but I don't know You.*

Moments later, the door swung open. The footsteps that clicked against the stairs did not match the stride of the guards, nor were they Ben's. These footsteps were softer. He frowned and looked toward the stairs as a feminine figure strode toward him. The woman, dressed in a casual T-shirt and a pair of jeans, knelt next to Ty and set a tray of food on the floor beside him. Up close, he realized she was a few years younger than he—probably in her early twenties, no older than Joanie.

"I'm sorry they're holding you here," she said. "It's not right."

Ty picked up a glass of water from the tray. "That's nice of you to say; but it comes off a bit hollow, don't you think?"

"I'd help if I could." She smiled. It looked genuine. "I tried to convince them to let you go, but they're adamant. Sorry."

Was this a trick? Some way of trying to get Ty to soften to whatever Ben wanted from him by presenting him with a friendly face? Whoever this young woman was, if that was Ben's game, it would not work on Ty.

"You'll forgive me if I don't seem convinced." Ty pressed his lips together. "I'd be more inclined to believe you if you let me out."

"I can't. I'll see if I can get them to make life a little easier for you, though. Would you like a shave? Maybe I can arrange that. How about reading materials?"

"That . . . would be a start."

"Great. I'll see what I can do." The woman rose. "It's Ty, right?"

He nodded. At least she had used his chosen name, rather than insisting on calling him by his birth name, like Ben did.

"It's nice to meet you, Ty. I'm Shannon."

With that, she turned and strode back up the stairs. Ty slumped down over his food and sighed. She seemed nice, but he doubted it meant anything. Unless someone came to help him, he was still stuck here.

CHAPTER 12

Sunlight pierced Patrick's eyelids, an unwelcome intrusion on the blissful rest that had swallowed him soon after he'd fallen into bed. Rolling over to face the wall, Patrick pulled his pillow with him and held it atop his head, the better to shield himself from the offensive rays of the morning sun.

What . . . happened?

His sleep-fogged mind searched for an answer to the question, but Patrick shut it down and pushed the thought to the back of his mind. He wasn't done sleeping yet. Once he was awake—really awake—then he could begin to solve that puzzle. But for now, a quick re-entry to peaceful sleep was all he wanted.

His left shoulder pressed down against something hard and unforgiving. Patrick scowled. What on earth could be in his bed that was so cruelly uncomfortable? He released his pillow with his right hand and reached under his shoulder to find the offending object. His fingers touched it, and he pulled—but it resisted. He tugged harder, with no success. Whatever it was seemed to be adhered to his shoulder.

Great.

He would have to open his eyes to fix this, which would surely eliminate the possibility of further sleep. Groaning audibly, Patrick lifted the pillow and opened his eyes as little as he could. The sunlight returned; and he sighed and opened his eyes the rest of the way, sitting up to get a good look at . . .

His shoulder armor. That was what he had been lying on. He looked down at himself. He had fallen asleep in the Spright suit. He was still wearing it now. And he was sitting up, in the middle of his dorm room, which he shared with . . .

Bryce.

The memories flooded back. Patrick had staggered into the room, not caring to change out of his uniform; and Bryce had been there. He had helped Patrick into bed, turned the lights off, and tried to talk to Patrick. What had he said? Patrick couldn't remember now.

What happened to me?

Slamming into the transformer was painful, but it was not the worst hit he had ever taken. Nothing had ever made him so careless.

The sad faced guy.

Just like at Asher's party, the Opera Mask gang member must have hit Patrick with his powers and made him sleepy and apathetic. The odd part was, Asher and the rest of the partiers had recovered within an hour after the thief left. They had still exhibited the symptoms of a hangover; but at least, they had their wits about them again. But Patrick still felt the weight of apathy in his mind. It was all he could do to not drop back into bed and go back to sleep. His brain urged him to do so. Why were the effects lasting so long?

Patrick forced himself out of bed, even though every step was a burden and closed the blind on the window. It wouldn't do for anyone to look in the window and see him wearing the suit. He crossed the room to his wardrobe and opened it. The bathroom door opened, the latch clicking loudly as the handle turned.

"Ah, he lives." Bryce stepped out of the restroom. "Morning, sleepyhead."

Patrick groaned. "I'm sorry. I didn't mean for you to find out . . . definitely not like this. Not my best moment."

"At least, now I get why you were so secretive. You okay?"

"Sort of? I think." Patrick rifled through his clothes. "At least, it's Saturday. Don't have to go to class. The way I'm feeling, I'm not sure I would even if I had to."

"What's wrong?"

Patrick swallowed several times, building up the willpower to continue the conversation.

"I'm not sure. I ran down to the docks last night to stop a fight. But one of the guys had superpowers—actually, more than one of them, I think. But this one guy hit me with a psychic attack or something. It just made me really relaxed, tired, and apathetic. It's still . . . affecting me, I think."

"Wow. That's crazy. Well, like you said, it's Saturday. Maybe you just need to stay in bed for the rest of the day, and it will wear off."

"I don't know." Patrick looked up at his roommate. "You're taking this surprisingly well."

Bryce shrugged. "There are way worse secrets you could've been keeping. Don't get me wrong; I'm still shook. But it's also pretty cool. My roommate and best friend is a superhero."

"Best friend? I don't think you've ever called me that before."

"What else would I call you? Anyway, don't worry. I'm not going to tell anyone your secret—not even Alexa. If you want her to know, you'll have to tell her yourself. My lips are sealed."

"Thanks, man." Patrick pulled out a long-sleeved T-shirt and a pair of joggers. "I need you to help me out. Keep me motivated today. The only way I'm going to get through this is to fight it out. I can't just veg out all day."

"You got it. Now, go get out of that costume before someone else sees you."

"Right."

Patrick could've used his speed to change in an instant, but his body instinctively protested. Even trying to walk faster than a trudge seemed like too much work.

I need to figure out why this is affecting me so strongly . . . and I need to do it before these guys strike again.

After he was dressed, he looked down at his phone. He had an unread text message from Carter with his friend's flight itinerary. With everything going on, Patrick had forgotten all about him. It looked like his flight would arrive later that afternoon. Patrick took a deep breath and turned to Bryce.

"Hey, man. We're going to have a guest. And I may need a favor . . . "

* * *

One of Lucy's favorite parts of EBC was the on-campus fitness center connected to the dorms. It was a struggle for her to get out of bed to work out in the mornings; but many times, she found a spare hour in the afternoon or evening to at least run the treadmill. But on Saturday mornings, since she got to sleep in, she liked to hit the fitness center around 11:00 and run until lunchtime.

As she ran today, she wondered if Patrick was all right. She hadn't heard from him since he told her he was coming in from the docks last night. He'd sounded . . . discombobulated. It was like he hadn't quite been all there. She hoped that he was able to sleep off whatever was affecting him. He had enough problems as it was.

She had a lot she wanted to talk to him about—his recent interest in spending time with her and their friends rather than going out as Spright, Asher's new girlfriend, the phone call that Patrick had taken from Sojourn City.

Lucy's breaths came in short and choppy pants as she increased the speed on the treadmill. Her leg muscles burned, and sweat matted her gray tank top to her back.

I wonder if Patrick ever gets this sweaty.

Probably not—at least not regularly. He would have to run farther and faster than he typically did for that kind of exertion. She could only remember seeing him tired twice. The first time had been when Alfonso Mendez, the villain known as Backfire, had nearly killed Patrick's parents. Patrick had unloaded on Backfire, dragging him across the city and beating him to within an inch of his life. That was the day Lucy had discovered Patrick's secret identity. The second time, Patrick had run from Sojourn City all the way to San Francisco to see Lucy. Both feats had been incredible; and his recovery time was unbelievable.

Across the fitness center, Lucy spotted Alexa beating on a punching bag. Alexa was still something from an enigma. She was sweet, albeit quiet and reserved. Of all their friends, Lucy knew the least about Alexa. At times, she would go for several days without seeing Alexa at all. Lucy wondered if it was an anxiety issue or if it had something to do with her family. Alexa certainly seemed dedicated to her grades. Whatever the case, Alexa didn't deserve to be alone.

The fitness center door opened; and Patrick trudged in, looking like he had just carried a two-ton boulder across the city. There were no visible bruises or wounds; but the way he carried himself, the joyless look in his eyes . . . Lucy had never seen him like that before. Patrick climbed onto the treadmill next to Lucy's and turned it on to the lowest setting.

"Hey."

"Hi." Lucy studied him. "You okay?"

"Yeah." Patrick took a deep breath. "Bryce told me I had to exercise."

"Bryce . . . *what*? Since when does Bryce tell you to do things?"

"Since I walked into our room last night still wearing black and purple." Patrick sighed. "Something's wrong with me, Luce. I literally don't care about anything."

"Bryce knows?"

"Yep. But did you hear what I said?"

"Yeah. What do you mean, you don't care?"

"I mean, I literally . . . don't . . . care." Patrick bumped the treadmill up a level, still barely rolling at a slow walk. "I can't find the energy. It's like all my will has been sapped away. It had to have been the guys from last night."

Her heart ached for him. Patrick was one of the most intense and caring people Lucy knew. Even though it frustrated her that he spent so much time as Spright, she knew it was because he had a heart for helping other people. It disturbed her to see him like this.

"That's why Bryce told me to come down here. Maybe if I keep moving, my feelings will catch up to me."

Lucy half-smiled. "I hope so."

"Bryce is going to the airport to pick up Carter, too." Patrick blinked. "Oh. I forgot to tell you. Carter Jonson is coming in from Sojourn City. Something about following a criminal that got out of jail. He's going to be rooming with me and Bryce until he finds his guy, I guess. That should be cool."

Lucy kept quiet as she processed the information. She made a mental note to talk to Bryce later. She liked the guy, and she didn't think he would spill Patrick's secret to anyone. However, as one of the three members of Team Spright—not to mention Spright's girlfriend— it was well within her rights to be concerned about someone new knowing Patrick's secret. If it went well, maybe they would have a new member of the team to help them out.

If not . . . well, Lucy would show Bryce just how protective of Patrick she really was.

* * *

He's been operating out of our dorm room for over a month. How have I never noticed?

Bryce stared at the Spright suit, which was now hanging in Patrick's wardrobe. As much of a miracle as it was that Bryce hadn't found out until now, it was also surprising that no one else on campus had, either. This school was full of some very intelligent people, both students and professors. Sure, Patrick was one of them, but he wasn't the most subtle guy around. Now that Bryce knew, everything clicked together so seamlessly that he didn't know how he hadn't figured it out before. Spright had started operating primarily in New Echelon at the same time Patrick had moved to EBC. At least Bryce could chalk it up to his lack of understanding of other human beings. Not everyone here had that problem.

Bryce's phone buzzed.

We need to talk. Meet me outside.

The text message from Lucy hung ominously on the screen. This had to be about Patrick. But Lucy was one of the sweetest human beings on the planet. If she wanted to talk to him, surely it would be a friendly chat, right?

Then again, he had been wrong before.

Bryce grabbed a gray jacket from the hook on the door and pulled it on as he walked down the hallway to the stairs. He bounded down them and stepped out into the cool September air, yelping in surprise as Lucy walked around the corner, put a hand on his chest, and shoved him back into the brick wall. The fury in her liquid blue eyes was intense and terrifying. Bryce hadn't known her face could make that expression.

"He told me. He told me that you know."

"Yeah . . . I do." Bryce held up his hands. "It's chill. I promise, I'm not going to tell. In fact, I'd like to help out, if I can. Seems like he's in kind of a bad place right now."

Lucy kept his gaze, the intensity of her glare unrelenting, for a moment longer. Then, she released his shirt and stepped back. Bryce exhaled and smoothed out the front of his shirt and jacket. Lucy gestured for him to follow her; and they walked together down the sidewalk, away from the residential building. The campus was mostly deserted since it was the weekend, so they had the place to themselves.

"How can you help?"

"I'm good with computers. Every superhero needs a computer guy, right? I know you pretty well, and I'm pretty sure that ain't you."

"No. It's not. It's not Asher either."

"Wait, Asher's in on this? Your friend from Echelon U?" Bryce huffed. "Nice. How am I the last to know?"

"Not the last. Alexa doesn't know yet. Patrick told Asher because they've been friends forever. We've only known you guys for a month. If Patrick ever felt like it was safe, or necessary, I'm sure he would've told you."

"Okay, fair. So—computer guy. I don't know how Spright gets his info on crimes, but don't you think a guy who can watch computer screens and relay information to him could be a big help? I even know how to access things that most people couldn't. Things like traffic cameras, for example."

Lucy raised an eyebrow. "How?"

"My pops is wicked smart with computers." Bryce smiled. "He taught me everything he knows. I may have fiddled around with things on my own time, though. Things Dad wouldn't have shown me on his own. I'd never use it to hurt anyone, but I had to know I could do it. I'd be glad to use that to help our boy out."

"Okay. And what does that have to do with his . . . current condition?"

"Nothing, I guess, but you'll need it eventually. And another thing— he can't keep running this gig, no pun intended, from our room. He's gonna get caught—which now means that I'd get caught, too. Besides, every superhero's gotta have a lair. I know New Echelon like the back of my hand. Let me work on finding him something."

"That would probably be a good idea. But again, the most immediate concern is his condition."

Bryce stopped walking and shrugged. "Wish I had an answer for you there, girl. But I don't know anything you don't. Maybe once his head clears up a little more, Patrick will have an idea. But for now, I'm stumped."

Lucy sighed. "All right. Good talking to you, Bryce. Thanks."

"And thank you—for not strangling me."

"Don't think I won't reconsider if you ever screw with him." Lucy pointed her first two fingers at her own eyes and then swiveled her wrists so they were pointed at Bryce's. "I mean it, Bryce."

"Cool, cool. We're cool."

"Good. You're picking up Patrick's friend from the airport?"

Bryce checked his watch. "In a few hours, yeah."

"Don't be late." Lucy swiveled and headed back toward the dorms. "See you later."

Bryce stayed where he was for a moment longer, watching her go, afraid to follow her lest he earn her wrath again.

Whoa . . . that girl's scary.

CHAPTER 13

At his core, Patrick knew that he needed to do something. While he wallowed in apathy, the trio from the docks could be planning any number of nefarious schemes. But the more he thought about it, the less he wanted to. He had lasted fifteen minutes walking on the treadmill before deciding that he had done enough for the day and dropped down into one of the chairs against the wall of the fitness center to wait for Lucy to return.

"Are you all right?"

Patrick realized he had been staring at the floor. With effort, he lifted his head to look at Alexa. She had been across the room beating on a punching bag when Patrick had entered. Now she stood right next to him. He hadn't even noticed her approaching. Alexa's arms were crossed, and her eyebrow raised skeptically; but there was concern in her eyes.

"Nothing's wrong. I'm fine."

"Yeah, right." Alexa sat down next to him. "I have only known you for a month, but I can tell something's up. You're usually energetic and smiling, no matter what. Right now, I'm not sure you could smile if you tried."

Patrick considered proving her wrong. But even lifting the corners of his mouth into a smile seemed unbearably exhausting.

"See? So what gives? I know you and Lucy didn't have a fight. I just saw you two talking on the treadmills, and you seemed fine. Big blowout with your parents? You and Bryce having roommate problems? Or are you just going through an early quarter-life crisis and don't know how to deal with it?"

"None of those things." Patrick shrugged. "Guess I'm just in a funk."

Alexa pressed her lips together and seemed to be studying him. It hadn't been his most convincing lie, but he couldn't think of anything else. And it was technically true; he was in a funk. But it was a superpower-induced funk that had inexplicably lasted entirely too long. She couldn't know that part, though.

"I've been there. When I was fourteen, I struggled with clinical depression. Before our conversion to Christianity, my parents were quite strict. I felt oppressed. There were times when I wouldn't come out of my room for days. My parents were scared. I was scared. None of us knew what to do. I got better, eventually, with medicine and therapy and by leaning into my family and friends. Most of all, our faith in Christ helped.

"It was a scary time. Even now, it's possible my depression could return. I struggle with being good enough for who my parents used to be, who they are trying not to be anymore. That's why I focus on my grades so much. But I thank God for every day I can lift my head and smile. I just want you to know that you are not going through this alone."

Patrick marveled at Alexa. That must have taken a lot of courage to admit. With effort, he placed a hand on her shoulder. "Thank you. Really. But I'm not . . . depressed. I don't think I am, anyway."

"Well, you were fine at dinner last night; and today, you are completely apathetic. I'm no psychologist, but I'd say that there is something going on in your head."

"I'm sure something is, but I'll be okay. Thank you. I appreciate the talk."

"You're welcome." Alexa stood. "If you need anything, let me know."

With that, Alexa walked toward the door. Patrick leaned his head back against the wall and closed his eyes. What was taking Lucy so long? It seemed like she'd been gone forever. Was he supposed to just stay here until she returned? What if she didn't realize he was waiting for her?

I need to do something.

One thing was certain: he had to diagnose what was wrong with him. But neither he nor any of his friends were capable of that. He knew someone who might be, though—and he had already been planning on contacting him about the Opera Mask Gang. If Jarrett Mercer didn't have a solution for what was wrong with Patrick, he might at least know someone who would.

The door to the fitness center opened again, and Lucy walked back in. Patrick stood and shuffled over to her, wrapping his arms around her shoulders in a lazy hug. Lucy patted him on the back and stepped away, grabbing his right hand with her left as she did.

"Did you talk to Bryce?" he asked.

"I did. Don't worry; I think we can trust him."

"That's good."

"So what do you want to do now?"

"A nap sounds good."

"Patrick, no."

He sighed. "It was worth a shot."

"I think you should call for help. You have that superhero group chat, right? Just send a text. Tell them what's going on and that you could use some backup."

Patrick laughed, but it came out forced. "If I do that, I'll have the entire team swarming in an instant. Not what we need right now."

It was nice to think that all his friends would respond to his troubles in an instant. He did not want to bother them, though. Carter was already on his way. All the other heroes did not need to abandon their own cities because Patrick had suddenly become emotionally disabled.

"Well, there has to be someone."

"I'm going to call Jarrett Mercer. He should have the resources to figure out who these amps are. He was a field medic, so maybe he can tell me what's wrong with me, too. But if not, I think his wife is a biologist. Maybe she can help out. And Carter will be here, too. Maybe he can help somehow."

"Now that sounds like a plan." Lucy smiled. "There's the Patrick I know."

"Thanks. But . . . it took a lot to put all that together. Do you think we could take a break? I could at least use some food. And then maybe we can call Jarrett."

"Okay. Let's go eat."

"Yay."

* * *

Darius returned to the garage in the early afternoon, grateful that he managed to get a few hours of sleep. After long periods of awkward silence last night, Zee had finally decided to go home; so Darius had also left. He had no idea if Anton had, as well, or if he'd stayed at the garage for the rest of the night.

When Darius entered the shop, Anton was actually doing auto repair work for once, lying with the upper half of his body underneath a cherry red sedan. Not wanting to bother Anton while he was being productive, Darius walked back to the break room. The coffee pot was half-full, and the smell of coffee wafted through the air. Darius took a Styrofoam cup from a shelf and poured coffee into it. He mixed in a pinch of sugar and then sat at the circular table to wait.

"No hello?"

Anton walked into the break room, wiping his hands on a white cloth. He was clad in navy blue coveralls, and grease smudged his face.

"You seemed busy."

"All done now." Anton sat down across from Darius. "I'm sorry things got out of hand last night. I'm still angry we didn't get our money from those double-timing gangsters, but we got out of there in one piece, and that's what matters."

"Water under the bridge."

Anton had a temper, but he was a reasonable person. Zee seemed to forget that at times. Darius was glad Anton saw where he'd gone wrong last night and that he had apologized for it.

"Nice work with Spright, by the way." Anton thumped Darius' shoulder. "I couldn't have clocked him if you hadn't slowed him down."

"Thanks. I'm not too happy that we had to do it; but at least, he didn't see our faces."

"Got that right." Anton smacked his hand on the table in excitement. "I told you if we worked as a team, our powers could be great! The way Zee was able to call out those hits before the guy even swung . . . and then the way you and I tag-teamed Spright. If the three of us work together, nothing can stop us."

"You're in a good mood today." Zee walked into the room. "When was the last time you were this excited?"

"The day we got our powers," Darius said.

"We've got a real chance," Anton continued without breaking stride. "We can make something of ourselves—rise up from what we were born into and become more. It's ours for the taking; no one can stop us, not even that quick-footed shrimp."

We can. That doesn't mean we should.

"DeMarco's boss should be calling me back today. One more job for him, and we should be able to clear my debts and set out on our own. No more gang ties, no more favors—we make our own fortune now."

Zee shook her head. "If we're going to do this, I have to make my displeasure about it known one more time for posterity. We're better than this, and we're playing into the superhuman stereotype by using our powers this way. But times are desperate, and we're in too deep; so if we do it, we need to decide what to call each other. We can't go around using our real names. It'll make it easier to track us down."

Darius nodded. "She's right."

"Okay . . ." Anton scratched his chin. "Any ideas?"

"As a matter of fact," Zee said, "I was thinking about it last night. For myself, I like the name Sensory. Darius, we could call you Infuser, since you infuse emotions in people. Anton, I thought Negator would be a good fit for you. You feed off negative emotions, and it's suitably intimidating."

"Negator." Anton grinned wickedly. "I like it."

"Me, too," Darius added.

"Good." Zee crossed her arms. "I just hope you morons don't make me regret this."

* * *

There were perks to having a friend who was a billionaire—like getting to ride in that billionaire's private jet when taking a trip halfway across the country. As Dean's plane angled toward New Echelon's airport, Carter leaned back in his form-fitting seat and let out a long, contented sigh. The only thing that could have made this trip better was if Raina had come with him. Unfortunately, she still had college classes to go to.

And there was another perk to being friends with a billionaire. Since Carter worked for Dean's company, Dean could give him an abrupt leave of absence; and no one could get mad at him for being gone. He would still have a job when he got home. It bordered on favoritism; but sometimes, that kind of partiality was necessary in the life of a superhero.

Silas had also elected to stay behind because he did not want both of Sojourn City's vigilantes gone in case something happened. He would protect the streets as Stonewall until Carter returned.

"We're beginning our descent into New Echelon," the captain called. "Please buckle up and stow any loose items."

Carter straightened in his seat and tightened his seatbelt as the plane descended. Although his mission here was serious, he was also excited to see Patrick. They had not met up face-to-face since Gideon and Jolie's wedding, and Carter missed his buddy. If he could spend a day or two hanging out with Patrick after Ty was safely on his way back to Stone Gate, he would try to do so.

He hoped Patrick had seen his text. He had sent his itinerary earlier that morning, but there was no response from the speedster. That was unusual.

He probably just slept in.

Carter could not imagine the kind of energy a person burned when running upward of two hundred miles per hour. His fingers wrapped around the armrests of his seat as the jet bumped against the tarmac. His grip clenched tighter, and he leaned back in his seat and tensed his shoulders. He had flown very rarely in his life, and it was not his favorite thing to do. Even flying in the Vindicators' Raptor jet was an uncomfortable prospect. But finally, the plane slowed to a halt. Carter released his death grip.

"Welcome to sunny New Echelon, sir," the captain said. "Your luggage will be waiting for you at the bottom of the ramp."

Carter exhaled shakily. "Thanks, Cap."

He unbuckled, scooped up his backpack, and hurried down the ramp. The moderate early fall air wrapped around Carter like a comfortable glove. Sojourn City was already hitting chilly temperatures. The slightly warmer climate was a nice change of pace. A flight attendant met him at the bottom of the ramp with his suitcase—which held his Crusader suit, in addition to his regular clothes and other necessities—and gave him directions through the airport. He nodded his thanks and set off to find Patrick.

As he walked, he took his phone off airplane mode and checked his messages. Still no text back from Patrick. *Am I going to be stranded at the airport?*

Carter shunted the thought aside and kept walking. Patrick would not let him down. On the other side of security, in a waiting area crowded with welcomers holding up signs, Carter scanned the crowd, looking for Patrick's signature red hair.

His gaze fell on a sign marked "Carter Jonson." But it was held by a young man about Patrick's age with skin as dark as Carter's. He boasted a high and tight afro and a pair of black-rimmed glasses. Carter frowned.

Who's this guy?

He cleared his throat and approached the stranger.

"Hi. Uh, I'm Carter Jonson."

The stranger extended his fist. "What's up?"

"Not much." Carter gave the stranger a hesitant knuckle bump. "Who are you?"

"Name's Bryce Emerson. I'm Patrick's roommate. He sent me to pick you up because he's . . . " Bryce furrowed his brow. "I'm not really sure what he is. It's a long story. I'm on the case, though. Let's get you back to EBC, and Patrick can explain himself. If he feels up to it, that is."

"Uh . . . okay. Lead on, then."

"Cool. I'm parked right this way. And can I just say what an honor it is to meet you? Patrick mentioned how you guys met. The stuff you do without powers is awesome. I'm sure you weren't expecting anyone to find out your secret identity when you came here; but don't worry, I'm going to keep my mouth shut. No one's prying your secret out of me as long as . . . "

Carter suppressed a sigh as he trailed after Bryce. This was going to be interesting.

CHAPTER 14

While Patrick prodded his cafeteria spaghetti with a fork, Lucy leaned back in her chair and watched the door. As they walked to the cafeteria, she had called Asher, hoping he might have a suggestion to snap Patrick out of his doldrums. Asher and Patrick had been best friends for longer than Lucy could remember. If anyone could cheer him up, it would be Asher—as much as that stung to admit as Patrick's girlfriend.

Finally, Asher walked into the cafeteria, his head on a swivel as he looked for his friends. He spotted Lucy, waved, and strode toward them. He sat down across from Patrick, catty-corner to Lucy, and folded his arms on the table in front of him, leaning in close so they could talk without being overheard. Not that there was much danger of that—as was typical of a Saturday afternoon, the cafeteria was all but empty.

"What happened to him?" Asher asked.

"We're not quite sure. From what I gather, the same supervillain that robbed the party you were at whammied Patrick just like he did you, only the effect didn't wear off."

"That's weird. I was fine as soon as I woke up—a little hungover, but not nearly like this." He gestured to Patrick, who was still glumly playing with his food. "He must've gotten a really good dose."

"Must have." Lucy shook her head. "We've got a few things we're working on, but I wanted to keep you updated. Speaking of which,

Bryce knows Patrick's secret now. Patrick was so affected that he went back to his room still wearing the suit."

Asher's eyes widened. "What?"

"Don't worry. I've spoken to Bryce, and he's agreed to help us out. Right now, he's at the airport picking up Carter, Patrick's . . . *friend* . . . from Sojourn City. After that, he's working on finding us a more permanent base of operations, so we don't have to run Patrick's missions out of our dorm rooms anymore."

"That's good. I can't tell you how obnoxious it was to try to talk to Patrick about this stuff while Joey was in the room. That guy's so nosy."

"Apparently, Bryce was, too." Lucy rolled her eyes. "Anyway, it doesn't matter now. We are going to call Jarrett Mercer—another of Patrick's, uh, friends. Patrick says he may be able to track down these supervillains and possibly also help with his . . . *condition.*"

"The archer guy? I thought he worked for the government now."

"He does, but he's still Patrick's friend." Lucy looked over at Patrick. "Hey, Patrick. Can you call Jarrett now?"

Patrick pulled out his phone, stared at the screen for a moment, and then handed it to Lucy. "You do it."

Lucy sighed. "See what I mean?"

"Yikes, he's got it bad." Asher reached over and snapped his fingers in front of Patrick's face. "Dude. Snap out of it. You're freaking us out."

"Sorry."

Lucy massaged her forehead.

This is going to get old really quickly.

She opened Patrick's contacts and started scrolling to find Jarrett's name . . . and stopped.

Dad.

Would Patrick's parents be able to help him? Ever since their conversion to Christianity, their relationship with him had been better than ever. And even before then, they'd loved their son like no one else. They might have an idea about how to snap him back to reality.

But Jarrett might have a simpler fix. Ignoring the idea for the moment, Lucy scrolled down, found Jarrett's name, and clicked on it. As the phone dialed, she placed it between her ear and shoulder and reached over with her right hand to gently rub Patrick's leg. He put his hand on top of hers and rewarded her with a small smile.

"That's more like it. I love you."

Patrick nodded seriously. "I love you, too."

"Hey, little speedster," Jarrett's voice said over the phone. "To what do I owe the pleasure of this call?"

"Actually, this is Patrick's girlfriend, Lucy. I'm calling because Patrick's in trouble."

The levity in Jarrett's voice vanished. "What can I do to help?"

* * *

Carter scanned the streets of New Echelon as Bryce drove them toward campus. On the whole, it looked like a clean, pleasant place to live. It was far different from Sojourn City. There were more palm trees and less skyscrapers. A few times, Carter even caught a glimpse of the beach between buildings.

During the drive, Bryce talked almost nonstop. He told Carter about himself, about how he had discovered Patrick's secret identity, and the way Patrick seemed locked in an emotional funk of some kind.

After a few minutes, Carter stopped trying to respond and just listened. It was a good thing he had come to New Echelon. In addition to rescuing Vickers, maybe he could help Patrick get back to his normal self. Patrick was usually upbeat, energetic, and encouraging. Carter couldn't imagine him acting mopey and emotionless. Bryce's mention of his computer skill piqued Carter's attention, too. Maybe he could help them track Ty within New Echelon the way Joanie had from Sojourn City.

Finally, they pulled into the Echelon Bible College parking lot. Carter stepped out of Bryce's car, leaving his suitcase and backpack inside for the time being, and followed Bryce up the sidewalk toward one of the campus's central buildings. The whole college looked warm and inviting. The environment alone was almost enough to make Carter want to enroll.

Bryce pulled open the door to the building and gestured for Carter to enter. Then he led the way to the dining hall. Carter spotted Patrick immediately and wove through the sparsely populated tables to get to him. Patrick's head lifted as the blonde girl next to him whispered in his ear. His blue eyes lit up briefly upon spotting Carter, but he was slow to rise from his chair.

Bryce was right; something's off with him.

Carter circled around the table and pulled his friend into a hug. "You okay, man?"

"Not really." Patrick sighed. "Bryce tell you?"

"The barebones, yeah." Carter gestured for Patrick to sit back down and took the seat on his free side. "Want to give me the details?"

The girl leaned over Patrick. "Hi. I'm Lucy Carmichael. This is Asher Lincoln, and you already know Bryce."

Bryce took the seat next to Asher, who extended a hand across the table for Carter to shake. Patrick slunk back in his seat and poked at his lunch with his fork. Carter furrowed his brow and stared at his friend.

"Nice to meet you all. What's going on? Patrick seemed fine when I talked to him last night."

"He *was* fine then," Lucy said. "After dinner, Patrick went out to respond to a police alert and ran into a local supervillain team called the Opera Mask Gang. At least one of them has emotional manipulation powers, but the effects are usually temporary. The guy whammied Patrick and the gang escaped, but Patrick's been in this funk ever since. He's not getting better, either."

Asher nodded. "She's right. A party I was at got attacked by the same guy just a few nights ago, and I was fine by the time I woke up. The effects shouldn't linger, unless he got a really potent dose."

Carter whistled. "Sounds like a mess."

"It is, but we'll figure it out." Lucy put a gentle hand on Patrick's shoulder. "Your friend Jarrett Mercer is on his way with his wife. Patrick thinks Jarrett will be able to help with finding the Opera Mask Gang, and his wife might be able to heal Patrick."

Carter had not seen Jarrett since Gideon's wedding, either. He didn't dislike the man, but his failure to tell the Vindicators he was working with a government agency had been a blow to Carter's trust. But then, the same thing had happened with Silas a few months before, and Carter and Silas were working together better than ever. It was time Carter gave Jarrett a fair shake as well.

"So why are you here?" Asher asked. "Patrick never told us."

Carter cleared his throat and launched into the story. "Okay. It's like this . . ."

* * *

Once Carter was settled in Bryce and Patrick's room, Bryce left them to talk about their plan and went on a mission of his own. They needed a place to operate from; and if anyone could track that down, it would be Bryce. He had told Lucy he was on it, and he intended to follow through with his word.

The requirements of a superhero's lair were obvious. It had to be somewhere secret, where no one would stumble onto it accidentally. It had to be relatively nearby so that the hero and all of his support team could have access to it whenever they needed it without having to travel great distances to get to it. It had to be large enough to hold the equipment the hero would need for his ventures: computers, gadgets, suits, weapons, and so on. In addition to all those, there was a requirement that some might consider optional. However, in Bryce's opinion, it was an absolute necessity—the lair had to be really, really cool.

Bryce's options were limited, since Echelon Bible College was in the middle of a residential area not exactly teeming with warehouses or other abandoned buildings. Eventually, though, he found the perfect solution. Before EBC was a Bible college, it had been a private high school with an extreme focus on athletics. Many of the original buildings had been torn down and replaced, but others still had the basic structure in place. One of those was the cafeteria and student lounge, originally the high school's gymnasium. When the college bought it, built its own gym, and remodeled the old gym into the cafeteria and lounge, they had basically torn the original building down from ground level upward. But there was part of the old gym that hadn't been above ground level.

One of the features of that old gym was an Olympic-sized swimming pool in the basement—a basement that was still beneath the cafeteria and student lounge but was not used by EBC. It was empty and had been for decades. The pool was drained, and the basement abandoned. The only access point was a door marked "No Entry" next to the janitor's closet. It was perfect.

Luckily, Bryce worked with IT as a student worker, so he had keys to every staff-only door in the building. That included the basement.

Carefully, making sure no one was watching, Bryce unlocked the restricted door, pushed it open, and walked inside, closing the door behind him. The stairwell was dark, so he turned on his phone flashlight and shone it down the concrete steps. Cobwebs covered the walls and floor, but that was to be expected. Bryce walked down the stairs and into the basement. The vast room was darker than his flashlight could illuminate, so he searched the walls for a breaker box. He found one on the wall to the left of the entryway and opened it and then turned on the power to the basement. Heavy-duty lights clicked on overhead.

"Whoa. This is . . . tight."

The pool itself was big enough to house everything Spright's team needed. It required some serious renovations, of course, but Bryce could handle that. He would have to come up with an excuse for being down here, so no one got suspicious. But with a little elbow grease, the pool and basement had the potential to be exactly the kind of sweet lair Spright was looking for.

"Score one for the computer geek."

CHAPTER 15

In the days since the strange occurrence at the party, Joey Paxton hadn't left his room much, except for class. He had never experienced something like that, and it scared him. What if he had still been in the pool when the masked guy had put them all to sleep? He could've drowned.

Ridiculous as it might be, Joey was afraid to leave campus for fear of running into the guy again. Joey doubted the masked man had attacked the party specifically to get at him, but it was not entirely out of the question. Joey was the heir to one of the top oil companies in the world; it was completely possible that the masked man had known that and targeted the party specifically to get at Joey. He could try to strike again.

He wondered why Asher didn't seem so spooked. In fact, the guy was thriving. He had met some cute girl at the party—a brunette from Joey's freshman year—and the two had really hit it off. Joey's relationship with Maddie, on the other hand, hadn't been going so great. She was into him, but his fear of leaving his dorm room was putting a little bit of a damper on that. She was starting to get annoyed with him, he could tell.

I need to find that guy.

Joey's dad had contacts everywhere. Maybe he knew someone who could track down the man in the opera mask and deal with him before he could strike again. Yeah. That would make Joey feel better. Even if he didn't know for sure the masked guy actually had it out for him, it couldn't hurt to deal with him, just in case. Joey picked his phone up and dialed his father's number.

"Hey, Dad? Yeah, there's a problem I might need a little help with . . . "

* * *

Whatever Darius had expected Anton's criminal contact to assign them next, it was not standing watch over a clandestine meeting between two gangs. Even more disconcerting, this meeting was taking place at the very docks where they had encountered Spright and gotten into a fight with the docks' criminal owners. He hoped the owners had a short memory or were wise enough to not provoke Anton again.

DeMarco was heading up the meeting on their side. Darius had learned that he was a high-ranking member of a gang known as the Archdukes. DeMarco's boss, the one who had assigned the siblings to this job, was the leader of the Archdukes; but so far, Darius hadn't heard his name. He wondered if Anton even knew who they were working for.

The gang they were meeting with, known as the Seventy-Six for some reason, owned the docks. The gunmen who had nearly opened fire on the triplets before Spright had intervened were probably members of the gang. So was the fight club owner Anton assaulted. They were also the gang Anton owed money to.

This meeting was a very bad idea. Darius would've just as quickly gone home and forgotten about the whole thing. Anton, on the other hand, was dead set on going through with it, so Darius came with him. Zee did, too, because her empathic powers would give them a warning if the Seventy-Six decided to play any games.

DeMarco parked his car inside one of the Seventy-Six's warehouses. It wasn't the same one they fought outside the night before, but it wasn't far. The heavy floodlights that shone on the fighting cages were visible over the roof of the warehouse. Turning his attention away from them, Darius drove the siblings' van into the warehouse after DeMarco. Anton was passive for once, sitting in the passenger's seat with his heavy sword resting across his knees. Zee was in the back of the van, along with the crates of "cargo" DeMarco had asked them to haul.

"Here we are," Darius said.

"Masks on." Anton positioned his own opera mask over his face. "Let's do this."

Darius parked the van and reached under his seat for his mask. As he pulled it on, he reminded himself that out here, he wasn't Darius. His name was Infuser. Anton and Zee were Negator and Sensory. Using their real names in front of the Seventy-Six would be a mistake.

He climbed out of the van and straightened his tanned leather trench coat. The gun that was tucked at the small of his back felt uncomfortable and weighty. He had only brought it because Anton had insisted. Darius didn't know why he needed it. Anton had the weapon he had taken to calling his "concussion sword." However, it was better just to go along with his brother's plans. Darius doubted he would have to use the gun, anyway.

DeMarco climbed out of his car and walked toward the siblings, two of his own men in tow. Across the warehouse, a shining black sedan was surrounded by six men in leather jackets.

The Seventy-Six.

Had Anton told DeMarco about last night? Darius was suddenly anxious about the gang seeing him. What if they did hold a grudge?

What if they recognized Anton as a debtor? Would they kill him for working with a rival gang?

"Unload the goods." DeMarco clapped his hands impatiently. "Come on, let's go."

Anton nodded, slung the concussion sword in a custom sheath over his back, and circled around to the back of the van. He wore a trench coat as well, but it was black to match the rest of his outfit except for his mask. He tugged the van's rear doors open. Zee, wearing a red leather jacket over a black top and blue jeans, hopped out as Anton reached in to remove one of the crates. Darius stepped up next to him and grabbed another crate.

"Hey, sis . . . " DeMarco started, but Zee jerked her head up.

"I'm not your sis. Call me Sensory."

"Oh . . . okay. Hey, *Sensory*, do you get any bad vibes off those guys over there?"

She looked across the room. "Just a lot of arrogant, macho posturing."

"I'm not sure if I'm relieved or offended." DeMarco gestured to his two men. "Let's get these crates over there and finish the deal. I don't like Seventy-Sixer territory."

Finally, something we agree on.

Darius' limbs shook in protest as he hoisted his crate and carried it toward the black sedan. Why couldn't he have gotten Anton's strength? He set the crate down in the middle of the warehouse floor with a grunt and stepped back as the members of the Seventy-Six approached—led by the fight host.

"DeMarco!" the host snapped. "What is this?"

"This is your cargo." DeMarco raised an eyebrow. "What's wrong?"

"These three. They cheated in my fights last night; and then when I refused payment, the big one tried to shake me down!"

DeMarco turned to Anton. "Is this true?"

Darius backed away from the crate and subtly brushed the edge of his trench coat away from his side as the Seventy-Sixers drew their weapons. Maybe he would have to use the gun, after all. But that was a last resort. He might still be able to use his powers to defuse the situation before it blew up. He tossed a glance at Zee, who had frozen between the van and the rest of the group.

She must have sensed it too late.

Her powers were spotty when she wasn't concentrating on them. Zee rushed to his side.

"Yeah, it's true." Anton huffed. "I didn't know you had a business deal with them."

"The Archdukes and the Seventy-Six have had an unspoken treaty for decades. If you broke it . . . "

The host crossed his arms. "I won't deal with the Archdukes as long as you have these three working for you."

"Now, wait a minute—" Anton started.

"Quiet," DeMarco said. "I'll have to consult with the boss on this one, Sloan."

The host nodded. "By all means."

DeMarco pulled out his phone and stepped away from the group. Darius sent subtle, soothing waves into the air. There probably wasn't any way to resolve this situation that ended well for all three parties; but at least, it could end nonviolently. The host—Sloan—loosened his stance, and his Seventy-Sixers lowered their weapons slightly. Now, if only DeMarco and his boss could come to a reasonable agreement . . .

"Understood." DeMarco nodded. "Yes, sir."

Sloan crossed his arms. "Well?"

DeMarco looked at Anton. "You're out. The boss can't risk war with the Seventy-Six. You can go. Your severance package is that you get to keep your life. But don't let me see you again. Any of you."

Darius sighed in relief until Anton growled, reached up, and drew the concussion sword from its sheath. DeMarco's bodyguards reached for their guns; and Anton stepped in and slashed the sword diagonally, cutting one of the bodyguards down.

"Are you insane?" DeMarco exclaimed. "Kill them!"

His remaining bodyguard and the Seventy-Sixers opened fire. Darius grabbed Zee and shoved her to the ground, reaching behind him as he fell to draw his gun. He was no fighter, but he couldn't let these gangsters kill Anton. He hit the ground, rolled, and brought the gun to bear on Sloan. He fired twice. One bullet grazed Sloan's right leg.

Anton, hyped up on his own rage and the fear and anger of the men around him, killed the other bodyguard and stormed toward DeMarco. The senior Archduke rushed behind Sloan's team of gangsters. The Seventy-Sixers opened fire, but Anton's powers increased the durability of his skin in addition to his physical strength. The bullets landed ineffectively as Anton pressed in, his weapon swinging wildly.

"Get to the van!" Darius told Zee. "Go!"

Zee nodded. "As long as you're right behind me."

"I'm coming. Just go!"

Darius stood and assumed a wide stance as Zee sprinted away from the fighting. He trained his gun on one of the Seventy-Sixers and fired. This time, his shot was more accurate; the man dropped to the ground. Anton brushed past him, hoisted Sloan off the ground, and hurled the man across the room. Sloan struck one of the metal support beams holding up the warehouse and crumpled.

They can't stop him. Maybe no one can.

"Negator!" he called. "Just leave them! Let's get out of here!"

"DeMarco's mine!" Anton shouted.

He cut through the remaining Seventy-Sixers like they were nothing and pressed in on DeMarco. The gangster, his hand shaking, fired his pistol at Anton; but none of the shots made him so much as flinch. Anton lowered his sword and grabbed DeMarco by the throat.

"Please . . . " DeMarco gasped. "Don't!"

"Let him go," Darius urged. "Let's just leave!"

"He knows who we are. That makes him a threat."

"I won't . . . tell . . . " DeMarco tugged at Anton's hand. "Please!"

"You will." Anton shook his head. "And besides, your boss already knows. You've got nothing to bargain with."

Forget codenames.

"Anton! No!"

Anton flexed—and DeMarco's neck let out a sickening pop. The gangster slumped to the ground. Darius shook his head in disbelief. What had just happened? How had it all gone downhill so quickly? He lowered his gun and examined the carnage around him.

"All right, Infuser." Anton shook his hand, loosening the fingers. "Let's go."

CHAPTER 16

Lucy loved airports. Something about the bustling energy of hundreds or thousands of people moving from terminal to terminal, checking or retrieving luggage, preparing to depart for a myriad of destinations in-country or international, had a unique feel to it that just wasn't replicated anywhere else. It was exhilarating. It was less so while trying to coax Patrick to follow her.

The fall formal is tomorrow.

Of all the times for him to be hit by a superpower that caused apathy, it would be now. Not only that, it was their first formal event as a real couple. The previous year, they had been recently reunited after Patrick returned to San Francisco; and they had still been discussing the possibility of dating. But they had not gone to their senior prom as a couple.

She knew she was being selfish because there were bigger things at stake than just her evening. If Patrick couldn't find the motivation to be Spright again, the criminals who had done this to him would get away—and not just them, but likely many other criminals that the police were too overworked to take care of, as well. New Echelon needed Spright back. But she needed Patrick back, too.

Lucy hoped Jarrett could come up with a solution to Patrick's problem, and quickly. If not, she didn't know what would snap him out of it.

"Can we sit down?" Patrick asked.

"We're almost there." Practically dragging him behind her, Lucy followed the signs to the terminal where Jarrett would be waiting. "Just . . . keep walking."

"Usually, you can't get him to stand still." Asher threw his hands up. "This is nuts."

"I'm *sorry*." Patrick pitched his voice into a whine. "You think I *want* to be like this? I . . . just . . . ugh."

He lapsed into silence, the effort of finishing the sentence apparently too much for him. Lucy sighed in relief as they came to the start of the security line. This was as far as they could go. Now they just had to wait for Jarrett to show up. Lucy nudged Patrick toward a chair. As he settled into it, Asher took the one next to him.

The three of them had elected to come to the airport while Bryce remained behind to work on finding them a lair, and Carter searched for his fugitive. At Lucy's suggestion, Patrick had loaned Carter his car. The odds of Carter finding his man tonight were slim, but he seemed determined to look anyway.

"What do we know about this Jarrett guy?" Asher asked. "Other than the fact that he used to be in the Vindicators, and he uses a crossbow to fight?"

"Well, he's a government agent," Lucy said. "He's part of an organization that specializes in finding and observing superhumans and other strange occurrences."

"Are we sure we can trust him?"

Initially, Lucy had wondered that herself. Patrick himself had been hesitant to Jarrett when that secret first came out. He had run all the way from Sojourn City to San Francisco to confide in Lucy that he wanted to trust Jarrett, but he didn't know if he could because of his lies. After a long talk, during which Lucy encouraged Patrick to return and talk to Jarrett, the two of them had made amends. Jarrett had helped the Vindicators in their final pitched battle with the villainous Doctor Ashcroft. Since then, Patrick had always spoken fondly of Jarrett.

"Patrick says we can." Lucy sat down next to Patrick. "That's good enough for me."

"All right."

"Okay, Patrick, you're the only one who knows Jarrett, so you need to tell us when he comes out, okay? We don't want to miss him because neither of us recognized him, and you just didn't feel like saying anything."

Patrick pressed his lips together and nodded glumly.

We're doomed.

"Excuse me," a voice behind them said. "I'm looking for a friend of mine. Fast mouth, messy red hair, tends to leap before he looks?"

Lucy turned. A couple stood behind them. She estimated they were in their early thirties. The man had medium-length brown hair, a wide smile, and kind hazel eyes. His wife's hair was a shade lighter than Lucy's, and her blue eyes seemed to take in the whole room at once. He was dressed casually in a pair of dark blue jeans and a forest green Henley shirt; her outfit was covered by a floor-length white dress coat. Patrick extended his right hand and pointed a finger at the man.

"There he is."

* * *

The high-tech laboratory had been designed to be reconfigured for any number of experiments, from chemical products to technological devices. At a moment's notice, pieces of the room could be shifted around, creating an environment suitable to whatever was being tested at a given time. It was the perfect location for Oscar Paxton's newest little protégé to push her limits.

Paxton had found her almost two years ago, sick to the point of death, her heart rate unnaturally high, her body covered in cold sweat. Her parents had searched for any cure to her condition, but the hospitals had been mystified. Then, one day, her problems vanished. It was like she had never been sick at all. And that was when things got interesting.

Her parents came to wake her up only to find her body vibrating so rapidly that she was a blur of motion lying in her bed. Panicking, the young girl leaped up and ran out the door—and halfway across town—in less than a minute.

When Paxton heard about her, he had immediately arranged to meet with her parents. Why had the mogul of an oil and energy company wanted to meet with them about their daughter's new . . . *condition*? Well, they had been so frantic that they never questioned it.

Paxton had offered to take her in and teach her how to control her abilities. Her parents had been grateful and even more so because Paxton had not charged them for his services. What they did not realize was that Paxton had gained something more valuable than any sum of money from his so-called act of kindness. He had gained an unstoppable enforcer.

She ran through the lab now, darting between obstacles with extreme precision, never making turns wider than necessary, her performance exceptional. All but perfect. In Paxton's eyes, true perfection was impossible for a human being, even a superpowered one. But she came quite close.

Paxton pushed a button to turn on the intercom. "Okay, stop."

She came to a halt in the middle of the laboratory. Her training suit was nothing special, just a bulky one-piece coverall made of fire-retardant material to keep her from burning up as she ran. She had never used her powers outside the lab, save for her initial experience with them. But that time of isolation was nearing an end.

"What's wrong?"

"I have an assignment for you."

Earlier that day, his son had called him. Joey said he had been robbed at a party by a man who had superhuman abilities. He was afraid that the man had targeted him specifically. Paxton was sure that Joey was wrong about that, but Joey insisted that the man be dealt with. Luckily for his son, Paxton agreed that this amplified thief needed to be handled.

"Finally." She looked up at him through the window. "What's the job?"

Paxton pressed another button. Out of the laboratory floor, a box rose. When it reached the height of her chest, it stopped; and the lid opened. Inside was her suit—her real suit, the one Paxton's people had designed for her to wear on missions.

"I'm sending you details on a target I need handled. There are rumors floating around that he and his gang may have disabled Spright. Can you handle it?"

He had a lot riding on her—the time and money he had invested in her had the potential to escalate his prestige and power beyond what money and oil could buy. But if she failed, he could face some potentially severe consequences.

"Spright's fast. I can be faster."

"I hope you're right." Paxton turned away from the lab. "It's time to show the world that he's not the only speedster out there. Don't fail me. Good luck, Friction."

* * *

"What did you do?" Zee shouted. "You're insane; you've just gotten us all killed with your stupidity! Killing members of the Archdukes and the Seventy-Six?"

"Will you shut up?" Anton said. "Let me think!"

His siblings were so ungrateful. Especially Zee. At least Darius had shot back when the Seventy-Six opened fire. Zee had just stood there, frozen. Anton had practically taken down all of them by himself. Even Darius was in a panic, talking about how Anton had doomed them all. Had they not been paying attention? DeMarco might have let them walk out of there alive, but Sloan would've come after them. And if he hadn't, DeMarco's boss would have, eventually. Anton knew too much. He owed too much money. He held too much power to be a loose end.

Anton hadn't doomed them. He had bought them time. The question was, what did they do with it? They couldn't stay at the garage. DeMarco's boss knew Anton worked there. So did the Seventy-Six, for that matter. They couldn't go to any of their homes, either; the Archdukes or the Seventy-Six would find them. But they didn't have enough money to leave New Echelon.

"We need to go back," he said. "We'll go to the garage and get all the cash I have stored away. Once we've got that, we'll find a motel. Lay low."

"How long will your cash keep us in a motel?" Darius asked.

"Not long enough."

They only had one option: get more money. Anton could work that out, but he needed time to plan. A motel room would buy them time. Zee could check in by herself using a fake I.D. and Anton and Darius could meet her in the room. That way, the motel staff couldn't tie a group of triplets to any of their rooms, even if the gangs came looking for them.

"Hey. We're going to be all right, okay?" Anton braced himself as Zee turned the van around a corner. "Just go back to the garage. I'll get the cash and be out in five minutes, tops."

"Okay." Zee sighed. "I'm trusting you, Anton. Please don't let me down."

"I won't. I'm going to take care of all of us. That's what older brothers do. Anyone who gets in the way of that can rot."

* * *

As Carter drove Patrick's compact car through the unfamiliar streets of New Echelon, he kept an eye out for utility vans. He doubted he would get lucky enough to spot the one that Ty's rescuers used to flee the prison, but there was always that possibility. It was all he knew to look for right now. Tomorrow, he and Bryce might be able to coordinate and check the local CCTV for signs of the van, but Carter did not want to wait another day. It had already been over a month. Every day he did not find Vickers was a day his so-called rescuers might decide to finish him.

He drummed his fingers against the steering wheel. Alone with his thoughts, he was forced to confront a question he had been avoiding for weeks: why was he so determined to find Ty? It had become his singular mission. But as he was reminding himself more and more frequently lately, the Crusader was in the business of putting criminals away, not helping them.

He had seen the other side of Vickers' life, though, not just the crimes he committed. Ty was no soulless mobster, no power-hungry supervillain. He was a desperate man—a father and brother-in-law—trying to support the people who relied on him, to provide for his child. Carter knew how stressful that kind of situation was. He had been providing for his mother and siblings for nearly two years.

And Carter knew what it was like to lose a father. He did not want Emi to experience the same thing, especially at her age.

So . . . I identify with Ty Vickers, a super-criminal.

Was Carter losing his edge? Or maybe this empathy was exactly what he needed to be a true hero of the people. He hoped it was the latter. It did not mean he had to go soft on those who truly wanted to hurt people, but maybe he needed to see the hurt in the eyes of the average thief and consider that their crime might be an act made in desperation. It did not make it right, and the Crusader would still stop them; but maybe the answer was not always giving out black eyes and broken bones. Some of the Brooks' criminals might be just like Vickers: down-on-their-luck people just trying to keep their heads above water. Those people didn't need a beating. They needed help.

God, give me the wisdom to differentiate between wickedness and desperation and the heart to help those who need it.

He would start with Ty. Carter truly believed that given the chance, Ty Vickers could make something great of himself. Carter had given him a Bible. He could not force him to read it or to turn his life around. But he could offer friendship and guidance.

First, he had to get Vickers home alive.

CHAPTER 17

The Mercers had reserved a suite in an upscale hotel in New Echelon. Since Patrick and all of his friends lived in dorm rooms and Bryce's only response to Lucy's querying text about a place to meet was that he was "working on it," they decided to go to the hotel room first and figure out their next move from there.

Asher let out a long whistle as they entered the suite. The wide-open living room boasted a view of the city skyline. A stairway on the left side of the room led up to the loft that held the suite's master bed. Asher had never been in a hotel room with a separate living room and bedroom.

How does someone afford a room like this?

"Wow." The intonation of Patrick's voice carried all the awe that came with watching a snail crawl. "Nice."

"He's really out of it," Jarrett muttered. "Hey, bud, why don't you lie down on the couch, okay?"

"Sounds good."

As Patrick moved over to the couch—which looked more comfortable than any bed Asher had ever slept on—Jarrett motioned for Asher and Lucy to follow him and Jan into the kitchen alcove. Asher cast his best friend a glance, ensuring that Patrick did not simply stop in the middle of the room and sink to the floor. Once he was confident that Patrick had made it safely to the couch, he turned his attention to the older superhero and joined him and the two women in the kitchen.

Jarrett crossed his arms. "Start from the beginning. I want the whole story as you know it. Every detail could be important."

Asher glanced at Lucy. If they weren't leaving anything out, they needed to start with the robbery at the party. That encounter with the solo member of the Opera Mask Gang could be a key piece of the story. He raised an eyebrow, and Lucy gestured for Asher to start. He licked his lips and took a moment to compose his thoughts, trying to remember everything he could about that night.

"A few nights ago, I was at a party. While I was there, this guy came in. He was wearing an opera mask, one of those sad-faced ones, you know? Anyway, even before he came in, there was this weird vibe about the room, like everyone was starting to relax. It hit me, too, and I started to feel sleepy—so sleepy that I just sat down on the floor, right where I was. That's when the guy in the mask came in. He started taking people's belongings, but I passed out before I could react. When I woke up, he was gone."

He continued, recounting Patrick coming to investigate and finding everyone in a hungover condition. He explained that the other partygoers agreed with his story—wherever the masked man went, the calming energy followed. He finished by relaying that the Opera Mask Gang was a known criminal organization in the area and that the robber probably belonged to the gang.

Lucy interjected, "Last night, Patrick ran into the gang at the docks. He got an alert on his phone that there was some fight going on down there, and he went to investigate. There were three people wearing those opera masks, and Patrick started to feel the same way Asher did at the party. He rushed them, but the calming feeling slowed him down before he could get to them. Then another one of the opera guys punched Patrick so hard he flew back into a transformer and got electrocuted. When he woke up, they were gone."

"What happened then?" Jarrett asked.

Lucy explained how Patrick had returned to the dorms still wearing the Spright suit and detailed what Bryce had told her about his behavior, as well as what she and Asher had observed since then.

"I'll access the CLOUD database and see if I can come up with anything on the Opera Mask Gang based on their powers," Jarrett said. "We may need concrete information to accurately pinpoint who they are, though. There are a lot of amps out there, and lots of them have similar powers."

"What about Patrick?" Lucy asked.

Jan interjected for the first time. "We'll take brain scans. It's strange that the powered attack had long-term effects on him when it didn't on anyone else, but there could be a reason for that. It could be related to his powers or even to the electrical surge he took after the initial attack. We'll try to snap him out of this as soon as we can."

"Brain scans?" Asher asked. "How long will that take?"

"I brought some portable equipment with me. Why don't you two go get some rest? Let us work on Patrick, and we'll contact you once we have more information."

As much as Asher didn't want to leave his best friend, there wasn't much he or Lucy could do to help Jarrett or Jan. It seemed like Patrick was in good hands. He rested a hand on Lucy's shoulder.

"Let's go. He'll be okay."

"Don't worry," Jarrett said. "I give you my word that Patrick will get the best care we can give. My wife's a genius. There's no one better to fix him."

Asher hoped Jarrett was right. He missed his best friend's familiar sense of humor, quick smile, and joyful demeanor. Patrick was a help for so many people, even outside of being Spright. The world needed him, and so did Asher.

* * *

As the list of known superhumans scrolled across the screen of Jarrett's laptop, he looked over his shoulder at Jan. She was hard at work next to the now-sleeping Patrick, hooking him up to a portable brain scanner. Her blonde hair was now tied back in a severe ponytail, and she had shirked her fashionable white coat in favor of a simple T-shirt and leggings. She moved around the couch with the grace and experience of a professional medical technician.

Jan was so intense when she got into her work; it never got old to watch her when she was in the zone. It was part of the reason Jarrett had fallen for her. Her passion extended to every part of her life. She was the embodiment of living life to the fullest. Knowing that he had nearly lost her to one of Ashcroft's abominations was frightening, even for someone who risked his life on an almost daily basis. Good had come from that, though. Now that she had powers, Jan was working with CLOUD, part-time as a field agent with Jarrett and part-time as a lab worker. The ability to conduct electricity was a gift with multiple uses.

Returning his attention to his laptop, Jarrett narrowed the focus of his search. It had been two years since Gideon Turner's debut as the Seraph in Sojourn City, making him the world's first publicly recognized superhero. In that time, hundreds of amps appeared across the country. Dozens of them were superheroes. Jarrett had personally worked with almost half of them, but newcomers were arriving all the time. He was sure that more would come.

That should have been a good thing. More superheroes meant less crime. Unfortunately, for every superhero that popped up, a handful of supervillains rose to counter them. Jarrett was not naïve enough to be surprised by how many amps were using their powers for selfish gain or outright evil, but he was disappointed, nonetheless. CLOUD had been busy over the past year trying to catch the most dangerous supervillains, but there were always more to fall through the cracks— such as the trio he was hunting now.

Given that all three were operating in New Echelon, it was likely that they had known one another before they got their powers. There were roughly a dozen centralized locations in the U.S. where Ashcroft's creatures or bombs had created superhumans. Odds were good that the Opera Mask Gang had been living in or visited one of those locations.

Unfortunately, CLOUD's records were incomplete. Dean Sterling had put the list together after the attacks on D.C. and Chicago, but it was comprised of those who had checked into hospitals with bite wounds—the means by which Ashcroft's nephiloids transferred superhuman DNA. The list could not account for those who had been bitten but had not checked into a hospital at all or those who had been transformed by Ashcroft's gas bombs. CLOUD had been working to update the list since its creation by monitoring those who had been initially reported and cataloging their powers when they manifested, but it was still far from complete. It was possible that Patrick's opera-masked trio were not within these files at all.

If they weren't, though, there were other ways Jarrett could help. The suit he wore as Yeoman was stuffed in a case under his bed. If necessary, he could suit up, slip out of the hotel, and beat the information out of some local criminals. *Someone* knew who these guys were.

"Any luck?" Jan called.

"Nothing yet." Jarrett put both hands to his face and rubbed his eyes. "You?"

"Just getting started. He's still fast asleep, though. I can take some scans while he's asleep; but I need to monitor his waking brain activity, so I have a baseline comparison with a normal person his age."

"He's a speedster, so his 'normal' might not be the same as anyone else's." There was a moment's pause. Jarrett smiled and swiveled in his rolling desk chair to face her. "You'd already thought of that, hadn't you?"

"Of course." Jan winked. "But I appreciate the input."

"Happy to pretend to help. Anything's more interesting than looking at names roll by on a screen."

"Good thing CLOUD didn't put you in analytics."

"You're telling me. I would've rather been imprisoned."

When CLOUD first recruited Jarrett, it had been forceful. Operating as Yeoman in Wichita, Jarrett had been apprehended by the government agency. They made him an offer: he could join up as an agent and use his skills for good, and they would allow him to continue fighting crime on the side. If he refused, they would throw him in jail for vigilantism. It really was no choice at all.

"I feel sorry for his girlfriend," Jan said. "Patrick's, I mean. Did you see how distressed she looked by his condition?"

"Dangers of being in a relationship with a superhero."

After a moment, Jan glanced back at him. "It's kind of romantic, isn't it? We're in an unfamiliar city with a few days off work in this beautiful suite, and tomorrow's our anniversary. Maybe you and I could use this as a nice, romantic getaway before CLOUD pulls us back."

She probably thought he had forgotten their anniversary. If so, she was sorely mistaken. There was not a thing in the world that mattered to Jarrett more than his wife. He might give off the air of an aloof quipster, but his love for her ran deeper into his heart than the deepest ocean trenches. He had been wrapped around Jan's finger since the day they met.

But for the sake of his reputation, he didn't let on about it. "Sounds great. Fix the kid, and we'll talk."

"Promise?"

Jarrett held out his pinky. "Promise."

* * *

Sweat sticking his shirt to his back, Bryce stood in the entryway to the basement and examined his work. He had managed to clean out the worst of the dust and cobwebs, leaving the expansive room looking cleaner than it had before, even if it was still drab and empty. He checked his phone. It was close to midnight. The project had taken him all day. He dusted off his hands and sighed.

Time to clock out for the night.

The time spent had been worth it. He already had some ideas for the eventual lair setup. With a few extension cords, cables, and surge protectors, he could set up a computer lab of sorts inside the pool. There weren't any outlets inside the pool, for obvious reasons; but with some work, he could rig something. The exterior of the basement surrounding the pool could be used as a track for Patrick to train on.

Bryce formulated a mental checklist of the things he needed to make the basement into a proper lair.

For the night, it was time to move on to other things. He had no idea what had been going on all day because Lucy hadn't tried to contact him since he dropped Carter off. Shutting the lights down via the breaker box, he walked back up the stairs, peeked out into the hallway to ensure no one was nearby, and exited the stairway, locking the door behind him. As he walked toward the exit, he passed the lounge. Alexa was inside, playing cards at a table with two other girls. Bryce waved at them and sauntered over to the table.

"Where have you been?" Alexa asked.

"Oh, uh, working on an IT project." Bryce pulled up a chair. "Big stuff."

"Well, you didn't miss much. I haven't seen Lucy or Patrick since this morning. I guess they must have taken a day off campus. Patrick did seem a little . . . *off*, though."

Boy, I hope he gets that fixed fast.

If Alexa had noticed Patrick's behavior in a brief encounter in the fitness center, then she and everyone else were sure to notice if they spent any time with him. That would lead to questions that no one wanted to answer. For now, he thought, the best thing he could do was downplay the issue.

"I'm sure they're fine. Deal me in?"

* * *

Ty drummed his fingers against the coarse concrete floor of his makeshift prison. By his best estimate, it had been close to a day and a half since the mysterious Shannon had paid him a visit. She had held true to her word and arranged for a guard to bring Ty a razor to shave with, along with a bowl of water and a can of shaving cream. The guard stood by the whole time Ty shaved and took the razor back immediately after, but the feeling of a freshly shaven face combined with a second set of clean clothes made Ty feel like a new man—at least, as close to a new man as he could feel while chained to a basement wall.

He passed the time by skimming the Bible. The stories were fascinating, and Ty's heart moved with emotion he could not understand when he read them. Nothing in this book was anything like the Eastern religions Ty's parents and godfather had ascribed to. Much of it was still beyond understanding, but one thing was obvious: Christians deeply believed that God loved them enough to sacrifice His Son. Was that really true? Ty could not say. It was a nice thing to believe, though. Comforting, even. But why would a Deity choose someone like Ty over a perfect Son?

I'm not worthy of that sacrifice.

After a while, he tucked the Bible away in the back pocket of his jeans and rose to his feet. His neck and calf muscles protested, but he ignored the cramping pain and did his best to stretch them out. The possibility of escape was unlikely but growing with every hour that Ben failed to replace the batteries in Ty's cuffs. He was determined to stay ready if the opportunity arose.

The light was bright orange. Based on the rate of decay, Ty predicted that the battery would lose enough charge for him to fully use his powers in another few days.

Ty worked through a series of stretches and muscle-strengthening exercises, letting his body fall into a familiar rhythm. He wished he had a sword or baton to practice drills with. It had been months since he was able to use a weapon. He would probably be rusty once he finally got a chance to do so again, provided he ever did. Once he escaped, that was all right with him. If he ever made it home, he would settle down with Emi. After that, he hoped he would never need to fight again. He was going to leave his life of crime behind.

A few minutes into his exercises, the basement door creaked open. Ty pushed himself back to his feet. Shannon descended into the basement and offered him an apologetic smile.

"They still won't listen to me about releasing you," she said. "I'm sorry."

"Why are they keeping me here? I don't understand."

"I don't either." Shannon shook her head and sighed. "I think they're under the impression you're important to their organization somehow. But if that's true, I don't know why they're keeping you locked up."

Ty shrugged. "Trying to break my will, maybe. If they wait until I'm out of my mind with loneliness to tell me what they want, maybe it'll make me more cooperative or . . . "

Or they're sending Shannon in as a friendly face to soften me up.

Ty narrowed his eyes at her. Why had she waited a week into his captivity to come visit him? Come to think of it, why had Ben waited so long? Ben was not a friendly face, but he was more amicable than the guards. Maybe they were trying to break him down. Ben had not come back to visit him since Shannon's first appearance, after all. Maybe they were trying a different tack.

"What's wrong?" Shannon asked.

Best to keep his cards close to his chest.

"I'm just ready to be out of here, that's all. Let me know if you hear anything else. Thanks for the shave."

With that, he moved back over to the wall and sat back down. Shannon frowned at him for a moment, and he thought she looked genuinely hurt by his abruptness. But then she nodded and walked back upstairs, leaving Ty in darkness once again. He sighed and practiced phasing his fingers through the floor.

Whatever her intentions, he could not rely on her. Ty Vickers would have to figure his own way out of the basement that had become his prison.

CHAPTER 18

The night passed with no promise of sleep for Darius. The irony of his powers was that he could use them to calm others, even put them to sleep; but he could not use them on himself. Darius sat on the sidewalk outside their cheap motel room and watched as the first glimmers of sunlight peeked over the low-rise buildings across the street. They made it through the night, which was more than he had honestly expected.

It was still only a matter of time, though. The Seventy-Six and the Archdukes held the power in New Echelon. With both gangs hunting them, Darius and his siblings were living on borrowed time. Anton said he had a plan. As much as Darius wanted to believe that, Anton's actions over the past few days had not inspired confidence.

He could've left well enough alone last night, and we would have been fine.

Had Anton just left DeMarco and Sloan alive, they would not be running for their lives.

The smart thing to do would have been to cut and run. Darius could flee the city and leave Anton to clean up his own mess. He could even bring Zee with him. But Anton was their brother. Darius couldn't leave him to die.

The sound of shoes scraping against the pavement broke the silence. Darius looked up. Anton stood behind him, his jaw locked as he stared out at the sunrise. He sat down without looking at Darius.

"It's my fault."

About time you realized it.

"Doesn't matter who's to blame; it's done. What matters is what we do now."

Anton stayed quiet for a long moment. The only sound was the sharp popping of his knuckles.

"For today, we stay inside. I've got enough money for another night or two. The gangs will be looking hardest for us today. If they can't find us, they'll dial back the search. They won't give up completely; but with the pressure off, we'll be free to move around."

"What then?"

"Then we make a big score. A bank, probably. With the earnings from that job, we can get out of here and start over somewhere . . . safer." Anton finally looked at him. "I'm sorry. I know I'm a big screw up, and I wish I could change it. But this is who I am. I don't have the same potential you and Zee do. You could make something of yourselves if I wasn't holding you back."

Darius shook his head. Anton had always been down on himself; but when it came down to it, he was more successful than they were. At least, he had his garage to make a living; Zee had gone to college but then done next to nothing with her degree and gone to work with Anton instead. Darius had worked for Anton from the start. They had been mooching off their brother's success, however modest it was, all along.

"You've kept this family together, Anton. We might fight sometimes—okay, a lot—but we're still a family. What matters is that in the end, we're all here for one another. We made the decision to back you up when you decided to use your powers for profit. We could've left, but we didn't. We're committed because we're family."

For the first time in longer than Darius could remember, Anton gave him a genuine smile. He reached out and clasped Darius' shoulder, squeezing it so tightly that Darius felt something pop. He ignored the pain and forced a smile. Anton was trying to be genuine; Darius wasn't going to kill the moment.

"Let's go inside, huh?" Anton said. "Probably isn't safe for us to be exposed like this."

"Lead the way, bro. I'm right behind you."

Every step of the way.

* * *

Lucy moaned groggily as she awoke to the sound of the shower running.

Alexa must be up early.

She rolled over to face the wall and pulled the covers around her more tightly. And she furrowed her brow. What day was it? Her eyes snapped open.

Oh, man. It's Sunday!

She had been so preoccupied with helping Patrick yesterday that she forgot to set her alarm to wake her up for church. Throwing off her covers, Lucy leaped out of bed and ran to her wardrobe. As she rifled through her clothes, she glanced at the clock on the wall. It was 9:15; she only had forty-five minutes to get to church on time.

After hastily dressing in a pair of black jeans, a white top with red floral patterns, and a light blue leather jacket, she ran to the second sink installed at the dorm's entrance and began fixing her hair.

It's also the day of the formal.

She wondered how Patrick was doing this morning. Had the Mercers been able to help him, or was he still as apathetic and drained as he had been yesterday?

Lucy finished getting ready and grabbed her phone, car keys, and purse before rushing out the door. She still had twenty minutes left; the church was only a couple miles away, so she should be fine. She would have to come up with an explanation as to why Patrick wasn't with her. The two of them had been volunteering to help Rick Walker in his youth ministry for the past several months, and it was unusual for Patrick to miss a service. At least, she could say he wasn't feeling well without lying. Patrick was very much *not* okay right now.

As she walked down to her car, she texted Patrick.

Good morning. I love you and I hope you feel better.

She stuffed her phone in her purse, climbed into her car, and peeled out of the nearly empty dorm parking lot. As she drove, she forced herself to obey the speed limit. The last thing she wanted was to be pulled over on the way to church. That would be an embarrassing story to tell Rick.

Once services were over, she would go back to the Mercers' hotel to visit Patrick. With any luck, they had finished fixing him; and the two of them could take the rest of the day off. They deserved it. Patrick and Lucy could go to the formal. They could worry about finding the Opera Mask Gang later. Even if Patrick wasn't better, Lucy wanted to do her part to help. She could be out on the streets looking for clues while Jarrett and Jan continued working on Patrick. She was a reporter for the school newspaper and had been in high school as well, so she knew what questions to ask. She knew where to start, too—the docks.

But that was for another day. She had plenty to worry about in the moment besides the Opera Mask Gang.

Lucy pulled into the parking lot of Echelon Bible Church—which, despite having the same initials as the college, was only tangentially affiliated with it—and found the nearest parking spot she could so close to service time. She rushed up the sidewalk toward the youth center built onto the side of the church.

"Lucy!" Rick called as she ran into the foyer. "Morning. I was starting to wonder if you'd make it. The band's getting on stage now. You'd better hurry if you want to join them."

"Morning, Rick." Lucy ran her hands down her clothes to straighten them. "Sorry. I slept in. Patrick won't be here today; he's not feeling well."

"Sorry to hear that."

"Yeah." Lucy walked past him into the youth center. "Me, too."

* * *

When Carter had returned to the college the night before, worn down by his fruitless search, he had been unable to get in touch with Patrick. He had been forced to text Bryce, who had let him in through the dorm's side door and offered him Patrick's bed. Jarrett and Jan had arrived earlier that day, and Patrick was staying with them until they could work out how to help him. As much as Carter wanted to help and as hesitant as he was to share a room with a relative stranger like Bryce, he needed someplace to crash.

On Sunday morning, Carter stood toward the back of the youth congregation at Echelon Bible Church. He had awakened to find Bryce dressing for church and had taken Patrick's roommate up on his offer to tag along. Carter needed some time with God after the previous day's disappointment. It was difficult to keep despair at bay. Every moment that Ty remained in the clutches of his mysterious captors was a moment they could execute him.

Bryce was Carter's best bet for tracking that van, but they had to get through the church service first. Carter shunted the thoughts aside and tried to focus on the worship. Being there was pointless if his mind was a million miles away.

Try as he might, though, he could hardly focus. He mumbled along the words to the songs the band led and sat in silence as the youth pastor spoke. Carter scrolled through his Bible app on his phone, but the words on the screen jumbled together. All Carter could think about was having to tell Emi that her daddy was never coming home, and it was because Carter had waited too late to track him to New Echelon.

God, please, please let him still be alive.

* * *

Patrick didn't remember falling asleep. As his mind swam begrudgingly back to consciousness, he searched his memory for where he was, what he was doing here, and how long he had been out. He remembered going to the airport with Lucy and Asher—being dragged there by them, more accurately—and meeting up with Jarrett and Jan. They had gone with them to their hotel and up to their suite . . .

Oh. He was at the hotel. When they entered the suite, he had gone to the couch and dropped down onto it. That was the last thing he remembered. He hoped the Mercers didn't think he was rude for bumming on their couch. But if Lucy and Asher had explained his situation to them, they would understand. Or so he hoped.

Maybe they had fixed him while he was asleep. Patrick opened his eyes, confirming he was still in the posh suite, and sat up. Instantly, a wave of drowsiness washed over him. A dozen cinderblocks seemed chained to his soul, dragging him perpetually to the murky depths of apathy. He reached up and touched his forehead. A metal band was wrapped around his skull. He probed the band with his fingers and found wires protruding from the sides. Looking down, he saw the wires snaking their way across the floor to the coffee table, where they connected to a computer-like device, which Patrick gathered was a brainwave monitor.

He put his hands on the edge of the couch, started to stand, and hesitated. He should stay connected to the monitor until one of the Mercers told him it was all right to remove the headband. He didn't want to interrupt whatever tests were running and force them to start from scratch. The problem was, he really needed to use the restroom. He tapped his foot against the floor, looked around, and considered his options.

"Hello? Anyone here?"

"Oh, you're up."

The voice came from above. Patrick craned his head around, looking upward to the balcony that overlooked the suite's main room. Jarrett leaned against the balcony railing, a coffee mug in his hand. He smirked at Patrick, backed away from the edge of the balcony, and reappeared moments later at the bottom of the stairs.

"What's up?" Jarrett asked.

"I need to use the bathroom."

"Ah." Jarrett knelt next to the monitor and set his mug down. "Well, I can pause the scan here . . . and . . . you're good to go. Bathroom's over there."

Patrick pulled the headband off, rose from the couch, and rushed toward the door Jarrett had indicated—*rushed* being a relative term for him—it was closer to a slow jog than anything, and even that required all the effort he could give. Once Patrick had relieved himself, he walked back to the couch and slumped down next to Jarrett.

The archer furrowed his brow. "You all right?"

Outside of his wife's wellbeing, Jarrett rarely showed that much genuine concern. It should have made Patrick feel good about how much he mattered to Jarrett; but the emotions to process that were suppressed, crushed down somewhere deep in the back of his mind.

"Still . . . drained." Patrick rested his head on the comfortable plush back of the couch and looked up at the ornate chandelier hanging from the ceiling above. "I've never felt like this. It's like my body can't produce any energy, and my brain doesn't want to."

Jarrett eased the headband back over Patrick's brow. "We're going to figure that out. We've gotten plenty of scans of your resting brain pattern. Now let's see how it compares with your active brainwaves."

"Where's your wife?"

"I let her sleep." Jarrett sipped his coffee. "She's a hard worker, and she didn't want to leave your side last night. I figure she's earned a late morning. Want some?"

He extended his mug to Patrick. Patrick nodded, so Jarrett rose and walked toward the kitchen alcove. Patrick studied the brainwaves displayed on the scanner's screen. He had no idea what normal brainwaves looked like or if his qualified. Would they, even if they were "normal" for him? His increased homeostasis caused by his speed powers had to increase his brain activity as well. In fact, he knew it did because he had studied entire textbooks over the period of a single class time.

His brain should have been firing off neurons like a stash of fireworks in the middle of a forest fire. But this? This didn't look like that.

Jarrett returned with another mug of coffee. "I'm glad you—well, your girlfriend—called me."

"Thanks." Patrick took the coffee. "I'm glad you came. I knew there was a chance you were busy with CLOUD stuff, and . . . " He yawned. "Well, the only other person who might be able to help me is Dean, but his specialty is in technology. I knew that even if you didn't have a solution, your wife might."

"What about Gideon? He studied biology, too, didn't he?"

Patrick blinked. "Oh. I forgot."

He was so used to thinking of Gideon Turner as the Seraph that he didn't even consider his skills in other areas. Gideon had been a surgeon before becoming a superhero. He probably would've had a few ideas. But as much of a fog as Patrick's brain was in, it was a miracle he had even thought to call Jarrett. If he hadn't already considered asking Jarrett's help before the fight, even that might never have occurred to him.

Besides, in Patrick's head, Gideon would always be a fearsome warrior. He was also a gentle caregiver, but that was hard to remember at times. Gideon was fierce, dauntless, a force of immovable heroism. Patrick supposed his mental image of Gideon came from seeing the man for the first time on a TV screen, clad in his Seraph armor and battered from a fight. On the other hand, his first experience with Jarrett was the archer bandaging up Patrick's broken leg. There was something to be said about the weight of first impressions.

"Well, I won't tell Gideon if you won't." Jarrett winked. "And anyway, it's been a while. I'm glad we have a chance to catch up."

"Same here." Patrick struggled to form a smile. "Hopefully, we get this figured out soon. I don't want to be like this much longer. It's . . . exhausting."

He sipped the coffee, hoping the caffeinated drink would spark a burst of energy to fight back against the heavy, wet blanket of mental exhaustion that rested upon him. But even the bitter explosion of black coffee across his tongue didn't stimulate a response greater than a pinched grimace. He sighed.

I don't know why I expected that to work.

He took another drink and set the mug down on the table.

He wondered how Carter was doing. He hated that his reunion with one of his closest friends was stifled by whatever was going on with his brain. Carter had his own problems, and Patrick wanted to help him out . . . but he was in no condition for that right now. Maybe Jarrett could lend a hand on that issue, too.

Patrick reached into his pocket for his phone. He had a text from Lucy.

Good morning. I love you and I hope you feel better.

Swiping his screen to open it up, he stared at the date on his lock screen with as much horror as his mind could conjure.

It was the day of the formal.

In all the confusion, Patrick had completely forgotten. Of all the days for him to be feeling completely apathetic and detached—someone had a wicked sense of humor for allowing this to happen. It wasn't God, he knew, but right now he couldn't think of anyone to blame. Himself, he supposed, for rushing into action without thinking it through.

"Any luck finding the Opera Mask Gang?"

Jarrett shook his head. "If they're in the database, their powers are unlisted. I can't find anyone that matches their description. But I have a few names that I traced to addresses in California; I'll narrow it down from there and see if I can get a match. In the meantime, I'll snoop around New Echelon's underworld for any information."

"How are you going to do that?"

Jarrett smirked. "The good old-fashioned way: striking fear into the hearts of criminals until someone talks."

CHAPTER 19

Since she was a child, Lucy had loved the thrill of the investigation. There was nothing as invigorating as digging through mysteries and lies to get to the hard truth at the bottom of a story. That was why she had chosen to study journalism. She envisioned herself as a crack reporter for some nationwide news outlet, pounding the pavement to dig up news and reveal the unbiased truth to the masses.

Dressed in black sweats, a dark gray crewneck shirt, and a black hoodie, she walked across the docks. The dark colors did not do much to camouflage her in the early afternoon sunlight, but it made her feel safer, somehow. At least, she had exchanged her heeled church shoes for a pair of more sensible black Converse. If it came to it, she could run without stumbling over her heels.

Patrick had been near a cage when he encountered the Opera Mask Gang. There had been floodlights shining down on the cage from above the warehouse. That was where Lucy would start her search. She assumed the cages could be disassembled and moved otherwise the police would have found them and shut them down a long time ago. Those floodlights were not so likely to get up and walk away.

The cool sea breeze that whipped Lucy's blonde hair up and around her face and eyes brought a welcome chill to the late summer air. She brushed her bangs aside, tugged the longer strands of hair from her face and tucked them underneath her hood, and kept her eyes on warehouse rooftops as she walked.

Her phone buzzed. She glanced at it to find a text from Patrick.

I'm so sorry about everything, and I love you very much. I'll see you soon.

She probably should have told Patrick or the Mercers where she was going, she realized. She hadn't wanted to bother them; they were busy enough trying to cure Patrick's apathy. She had at least told Asher and Bryce where she would be and instructed them that if she wasn't back by sundown, they should let Patrick's friend Carter know so he could come looking for her.

Floodlights, floodlights . . .

As Lucy passed the alley between two warehouses, flashing red and blue lights drew her attention. Two police cars were stationed at the open door of the warehouse to her left. Was this connected to her own investigation in any way?

She crept closer, kneeling at the edge of the alley and hiding behind the warehouse wall, where she could peer into the alley without being seen. The black-and-white cars were parked, and there was no sign of the officers they belonged to. She decided to risk a closer look.

Keeping low so she wouldn't be immediately spotted if the officers returned, she rushed to the open door and looked inside. The interior of the warehouse was dark, the sunlight peeking through the windows the only illumination other than the officers' dim flashlights. There were four of them, and they had gathered around a central area. One of the flashlights passed across something on the floor—a body. Lucy gasped, pulled out her phone, and used her camera to zoom in on the scene. Who had died here? Were the bodies related to the Opera Mask Gang?

After snapping a handful of pictures, Lucy backed away from the door. If the police did see her, they would send her home. She ran back out of the alley and put a few dozen yards between her and the police cars. Then, refocusing on her phone, she sent the pictures to Bryce with a text.

Bodies in a warehouse.

She checked the number emblazoned over the warehouse's main door and sent that to him, too.

Can you find out who owns this warehouse?

Sure thing, Bryce replied.

Lucy tucked her phone away and looked around. Should she continue her investigation or stop and wait until Bryce learned more? There was every chance that the murders were unrelated to the Opera Mask Gang. On the other hand, they could have everything to do with them. Either way, it wouldn't hurt to do a little more searching.

* * *

"Ow!" Bryce grimaced as a cord shocked him.

He tossed the cord to the ground and stormed away in frustration. Getting all this tech set up was harder than his first estimation, and he had to do it all while Lucy was expecting him to find out who owned a crime scene. He threw his hands up in the air. Given a few more hours, he could probably get everything hooked up; but that would mean Lucy had to wait longer to get her answers, and he still didn't want to get on that girl's bad side.

Bryce walked across the pool to where he had set his laptop bag, pulled out the computer, and sat down with his back to the pool wall.

He could research Lucy's question now and finish hooking up their permanent tech once he was done.

"Hey, man."

Bryce jumped, nearly dropping his laptop. "What on earth?"

"Sorry." Carter knelt at the rim of the pool above. "I followed you here from the dorms. Guess I should have announced myself a bit less conspicuously."

"You think?" Bryce picked up his laptop and huffed. "Man, I thought you were someone from the school staff coming to bust me for being down here. Do you know how hard it'll be to find Patrick a base of operations if this place gets exposed? There aren't that many hiding places on campus."

"I bet. Sorry. I'll be more discrete."

Bryce sighed. "It's good. What are you doing down here?"

"Looking for you." Carter eased down into the pool. "I need a favor."

"You and everyone else."

Why had he become so popular lately? It almost made Bryce wish he had never learned Patrick's secret. No one appreciated the computer nerd until they needed something researched. It was nice to feel needed, but he was getting overwhelmed. When was the last time he had even looked at homework? Not in the past few days, that was for sure.

"Sorry." Carter scratched the back of his head. "If you're busy . . . "

"No, it's cool." Bryce cleared his throat. "What've you got?"

Carter handed him a flash drive. "The whole reason I came to New Echelon. I'm tracking the van you'll see on the footage in this drive, but I have no idea where it went once it got here."

Bryce took the flash drive and plugged it into his laptop. A quick review of the .mp4 file included there showed an aerial view of the van in question. Bryce tightened his jaw as he worked. Carter remained quiet, sitting cross-legged in the middle of the empty pool's concrete floor. Bryce considered telling the vigilante that the search could end up taking a while, but he doubted Carter had anywhere else to be. He spent the next several minutes working in silence.

"Okay. Here we go." Bryce looked up from the laptop. He'd found what he needed faster than he'd expected. "I'm seeing a similar van showing up regularly at a bodega near the docks. I'll text you the address."

"Thanks, man."

"Anytime." Bryce popped the flash drive free and handed it back to Carter. "Good luck."

As Carter left, Bryce turned his attention to Lucy's dilemma. A quick search of city records showed that the warehouse in question belonged to a man named David Sloan. Bryce had never heard of Sloan, but he assumed the man was part of one of the local mobs. The docks were mob territory. He sent Lucy a text with Sloan's name and a picture of him that he found on the internet.

He looked across the room at the power cords. *Time to get back to work.* Why did he have to be so good at his job?

* * *

During the time Jarrett had known Patrick, the young man had always been a light. As the youngest member of the Vindicators, he had always been ready to brighten the mood of the others. Other members of the team were quick-witted, such as Dean and even Jarrett himself. Dean was witty and smart-mouthed, but he carried the weight of the team's technological support and the burden of running his father's company. Jarrett used his sarcasm and humor to hide the darkness he felt from his time as a soldier and the wicked things he had seen on the streets of his city. In comparison, Patrick's optimism and brightness were genuine, unsullied by darkness. It was refreshing and uplifting.

That Patrick and the one sitting with Jarrett now were two very different people. He had tried to get Patrick to smile several times; and while Patrick made an effort to respond, his countenance showed how difficult it was. Jarrett had seen similar cases of depression in some of his buddies from Special Forces, but this wasn't the same. A psychic attack—not an internal struggle—was responsible for his condition. Jarrett's ears burned at the thought of anyone taking a young, happy man like Patrick and turning him into the joyless figure on the couch. He wanted to find the opera-masked villain and beat him to a pulp.

But for now, he needed to see what the results of Jan's tests were. After she awakened, she ran a quick visual comparison between last night's scans and this morning's; but she had wanted to run some more in-depth tests before making any assumptions. Until she was finished, Jarrett was staying right here.

"This is fascinating," Jan said. "I've never seen anything like it."

"Is it because of his enhanced speed?" Jarrett asked.

"No, quite the opposite." Jan frowned. "Here. Take a look at this."

She stepped over to his side. In contrast to her fashionable white coat she had worn in the airport, today, she was wearing a pair of blue jeans and a red T-shirt. And in her husband's estimation, she was just as beautiful now as she had been then—maybe even more so, since in this getup she reminded him of the farm-bred country girls from back home. She handed him a printout of Patrick's scans from when he'd been sleeping and another from when his brain had been active.

Jarrett compared them. "There's barely any more activity on his waking scan."

"Exactly. Even a normal human would show considerably more activity while awake; and with his enhanced speed and homeostasis, his brain activity should be infinitely greater. But it's not. His brain is barely functioning as though it's awake."

"Why?" Patrick asked.

"That, I don't know." Jan furrowed her brow. "My best guess? The electrical surge you took while the attacker's psychic blast was still affecting you caused your brain to . . . well, stick. Under normal circumstances, this power would likely act like a drug, temporarily causing an emotional reaction based on whatever signal the superhuman sent. But the electricity amplified the signal. It's almost like a record that's skipping. It can't get back on track."

"How do we fix it?" Jarrett asked.

"I need to do some more research to be sure that's what's actually happening; but assuming it is, I should be able to work up a therapy for it. My biggest fear is for Patrick's powers."

Patrick leaned forward. "My powers? Why?"

"For you to use your speed properly, your brain has to be working impossibly fast. If it didn't, you wouldn't be able to process what you were seeing while moving at superspeed, let alone react to it. If you try to use your powers while your mind is still affected like this, it could lead to catastrophic results."

"And what if my mind doesn't catch back up right away, even after your therapy?"

"Then it would be dangerous for you to try to use your powers. I'm sorry; but until your mind is working at the same speed as your body, you'd do more harm than good as a superhero. I can't recommend you resume activities as Spright until I'm sure this problem is cured."

Patrick slumped against the cushioned back of the couch and groaned. Jarrett reached over and put a comforting hand on his shoulder.

"Don't worry," he said. "We'll stick around until this is fixed. If we have to, we'll find the Opera Mask Gang and deal with them ourselves. You're not going to push yourself. It's too dangerous."

"Okay. But get me back to running shape as soon as possible, okay?"

"I'll do whatever I can," Jan said. "You have my word on that."

Jarrett couldn't read Patrick's mind; but if he had been in the younger man's position, he would've probably been thinking, *And what if you can't?* Being a superhero was Patrick's life. It would devastate him if he had to give it up.

That wasn't going to happen. Jan was one of the most brilliant minds Jarrett had ever met. If anyone could fix him, she could. Jarrett had faith in that.

* * *

David Sloan.

Lucy had never heard of the man before, but the image Bryce sent her did not inspire confidence in his character. The man's appearance screamed "sleaze bag." Given the gangs' hold on the docks, that made sense. Even if Sloan was not himself a member of a gang, the likelihood of him being in their pocket was high.

After a few more minutes of searching the area, Lucy circled back to the alley where the police cars had been parked. There was another vehicle there now, also marked with police sigils. The coroner's van, Lucy assumed. She dropped into a crouch and hissed, recoiling as her knee splashed into a puddle of water. She returned her attention to the alley. The police were bringing the dead out now, but they were in body bags. No chance of identifying them, then. Too bad. Lucy backed away.

She bumped into a blue-uniformed body. Recoiling, she looked up sheepishly. Her face warmed. She had hoped to avoid this kind of confrontation. The police officer before her looked to be in his mid-twenties. His skin was a shade darker than Bryce's. A close-cropped goatee framed a knowing smile.

"Well, what do we have here?"

"Um, sorry." Lucy lowered her hood, as if that somehow made her look less suspicious. "I'm sorry. I . . . "

"Was snooping around a crime scene?"

"It's not like that. I—"

Come on, girl, think.

"I'm a reporter for my college newspaper. I was supposed to meet a source here for a story on, uh, the problem of illicit drugs in collegiate athletics. I guess he decided not to show. I heard something in the alley and thought he might have been over here, but . . . "

"And naturally, you decided to kneel around the corner and check it out first."

Busted.

"Am I in trouble?"

"No, you're not." The officer put a hand on her shoulder. "But you're going to have to get out of here, okay? This is an active crime scene, and we don't need college reporters digging into police business."

"I understand, Officer . . . "

"Gregg, ma'am."

"Officer Gregg." Lucy stepped past him. "I'll be on my way now. But I don't suppose you could tell me what happened in there, could you?"

"No, I can't. Nice try, though."

Lucy nodded and walked back to where she'd parked her car. She hoped she hadn't made Officer Gregg suspicious; the last thing she needed was the police looking into her business. It was a short leap from her to Patrick, and anyone who looked too closely into him would figure his secret out sooner or later. She wished she'd been more careful, though. Those murders had to be connected to the Opera Masks somehow.

She had done all she could. She would give everything she learned to Jarrett and then take care of Patrick. The CLOUD agent could worry about the murders.

CHAPTER 20

God, why would You let this happen?

Patrick digested Jan's diagnosis, his stomach turning at the thought that he might never be able to use his powers again. What if she was right? If his brain had been slowed past the point of being able to process his speed, he was the most useless superhero ever. He wouldn't be able to run without slamming into things—and possibly without killing himself—if his brain couldn't compensate for his speed, then it might not send the proper impulses to his body. He could break his own neck from running too fast.

He knew he was probably overreacting. Jan had not indicated that it was a permanent situation. That fear had been the first thought that occurred to him as she spoke, and it latched deep in his soul and refused to let go. It didn't help that the apathy that still smothered him kept him from countering fear with logic. It also kept him from giving voice to his fears, though, so he remained on the couch, staring at the glimmering chandelier, pondering his future.

As soon as he questioned God, he regretted it. This wasn't God's fault; and even if God had allowed it, He had done so for a purpose. God had taken Gideon's powers away once Gideon had fulfilled his purpose as the Seraph. Was he going to do the same to Patrick now? Patrick certainly didn't feel like Spright had fulfilled his purpose. He never achieved the same feats Gideon had. Patrick had never stopped a supervillain—one that wasn't part of Ashcroft's plot, anyway—and he had only partially succeeded in cleaning up New Echelon's streets. It didn't seem fair to lose his ability to use his powers now while a trio of amplified criminals terrorized his new home.

"Electricity caused this," Jan said. "I think we could use electricity to fix it—at least, in part. We don't want to do too much at once, or we could fry your brain. But if we go through a series of brief, less intense shock therapy sessions, we can at least get your brain back up to the speed of a normal human being. You won't be apathetic and exhausted anymore."

"Well . . . that would be a start," Patrick murmured.

The suite door opened. Patrick tilted his head, so he could see the door. Lucy walked in, and his spirits lifted slightly. Taking a deep breath to prepare himself for the effort, Patrick rose from the couch and walked across the room to meet her. She wrapped him in a hug and kissed his cheek.

"It's good to see you," she said. "How are things going here?"

"Slow."

"We're making progress," Jarrett countered. "Jan thinks she can use shock therapy to get Patrick's brain back to where it needs to be."

"Shock therapy?" Lucy's eyes widened. "That seems extreme."

"It was electrical shock that caused the problem." Jan kept her eyes on the monitor as she spoke. "It may be the only way to undo the damage."

Patrick walked back over to the couch with Lucy next to him, and they sat down together. She rested her forearms on her knees and leaned forward. Patrick frowned, noticing for the first time that she was dressed almost entirely in black. That was unusual for her, especially on a church day. It wasn't any of his business, but it was interesting.

"How do we do that?" Lucy asked. "I mean, what kind of equipment do we need?"

Jan half-smiled. "We won't need any equipment."

"What?"

"Why not?" Patrick asked.

"Because." Jan held up her fingers, and sparks of blue lightning danced across her fingertips. "I'll be applying the shock therapy myself."

* * *

"How many bodies?" Jarrett exclaimed.

As Jan prepared a precursory test on Patrick, Lucy had pulled Jarrett into the kitchen alcove and told him where she had been for the past few hours. Although Jarrett didn't approve of her going off without backup, he was impressed with her spunk.

"I didn't get an exact count," Lucy said. "There were several, though. And judging by how insistent Officer Gregg was that I leave, the police thought it was a big deal. I don't know if it's tied to the Opera Mask Gang, but it would be a pretty big coincidence if it's not."

"Not necessarily. If the gangs have a big presence in the docks, anything could've gone wrong." Jarrett crossed his arms. "I'll look into it. But take my advice—don't get too close to this."

"I felt like I had to do something."

That response wasn't even close to acknowledging Jarrett's request, but he supposed it was as good as he would get from the girl. She had fire—that much was evident. He hadn't even known her a full twenty-four hours, and he could already tell that. Jarrett put a hand on her shoulder and motioned for her to go back into the living room.

"Hey, babe?" Jarrett called.

"Yes?"

"I'm going to go out and see if I can dig anything up. I'll be back in a few hours."

Jan turned to face him. "Okay. Hurry back."

Jarrett smiled and nodded. He knew how badly she wanted them to have time alone that night, and he felt the same way. Their marriage had never been full of the blissful moments that most spouses longed for. From his time in Special Forces to spending his nights as a vigilante to joining CLOUD, they had either been apart or busy for as long as Jarrett could remember. He needed this as much as she did.

"Don't worry. I just need to see a man about a body."

He patted Patrick on the back as he passed him and then bounded up the steps to the loft. In the center of the loft, its headboard resting against the banister, was the suite's massive king-sized bed. Jarrett knelt, moved the fluffy, three-inch thick comforter out of the way, and pulled his suitcase out from underneath the bed. Popping it open, he removed his Yeoman suit and unfolded it.

The sleeveless uniform had been designed by Dean Sterling when Jarrett had joined the Vindicators, though Jarrett had later added sleeves because of the unpleasantness of fighting crime in freezing weather with his arms exposed. Kansas winters were nothing to joke about. Blue piping lined the shoulders, collar, waist, and legs of the brown Kevlar suit; the vambraces and boots had matching blue stripes. The case also contained his crossbow and arrows.

Jarrett walked back downstairs with the case in hand. Jarrett thought he detected a trace of a smile on Patrick's face when he saw what Jarrett was holding.

Just like old times.

Jarrett turned his gaze lastly to his wife. Jan smiled sadly, walked over, and kissed him on the cheek.

"Go take care of business. Patrick's in good hands."

"I know." Jarrett kissed her back. "I'll see you soon."

Once he was outside, he climbed into his rental car and pulled out onto the street. Where did he go from here? The bodies were no longer at the docks. They were probably in autopsy by now, but the bodies weren't the only way to get the information he needed.

He parked in an alley two blocks away from the police station, climbed up a fire escape to the rooftop, and changed into his uniform. He made his way from building to building, using a grappling hook arrow to reach his destination. When he was directly across the alley from the police station, he knelt at the edge of the adjoining roof and watched the alley. It was still mid-afternoon, so he would have to be careful; he didn't want the entire precinct alerted to his presence because someone looked up and saw a mysterious figure perched on the rooftop.

Yeoman raised his vambrace and turned on the small screen that had been installed into it. He tapped a command on the touchscreen, bringing up CLOUD's databases. He opened their files on New Echelon Police Department and selected the precinct he was watching. The officer who had ushered Lucy away had been named Gregg, she said. Yeoman scrolled through the list of officers in the department and located Gregg's name. He brought up the man's file, and his face filled the screen on Jarrett's vambrace.

Gotcha.

Sooner or later, that officer would come through here.

CLOUD probably wouldn't be happy if they knew Jarrett was using their files without a formal request. But did it matter? He was, technically, fulfilling his mandate as an agent of CLOUD. The Opera Mask Gang were unidentified dangers. They had used their powers for criminal activities, and that put them on the threat list. As much as this was a favor to Patrick, catching these guys wouldn't hurt Jarrett's standing with his bosses, either.

The precinct's back door squeaked as it swung open. Yeoman rose to attention and looked down into the alley.

That's him.

Officer William Gregg stepped out of the precinct, a cup of coffee in one hand. Yeoman attached his grappling line to the rooftop he knelt on, gave the alley a cursory scan to ensure Gregg was alone, and rappelled down to the officer's side. As his feet touched the gravel, Gregg jumped in shock and reached for his sidearm. Yeoman held out his hands.

"Easy! Easy; I'm not here to hurt you!"

"Who are you?" Gregg asked. "Some new vigilante?"

"Some new— I was one of the Vindicators, Officer Gregg."

"You were?" Gregg frowned and took his hand away from his gun. "I don't remember you. And how do you know my name?"

"I'm flattered." No one ever remembered the archer without powers. "Look, I'm here helping Spright with a little issue he's having. I know your name because I have resources, but these resources haven't helped me find my targets. I think you have information that could help me."

"I-I'll do the best I can."

"Thank you." He angled his thumb toward the roof. "Meet me up there."

Flipping the switch on his grappling arrow, Yeoman reeled himself back up to the rooftop. He disconnected the line, slipped the arrow back into his quiver, and replaced the crossbow on his back. Gregg joined him a few moments later, his breathing heavy from the exertion of climbing the fire escape. Yeoman crossed his arms over his chest and waited for the officer to regain his breath.

"How . . . can I . . . help?"

"I'm looking for three individuals who wear opera masks. I believe they may be related to the bodies that were discovered at the docks this morning."

"How did you know about— Oh, right. *Resources.*"

"I was told the dock belongs to a man named David Sloan. What can you tell me about him?"

"I can tell you he's one of the bodies we discovered. Those resources couldn't tell you that much, huh?"

"Sloan was killed at the warehouse?"

"That's right. Broken back. From the look of the scene, he was thrown across the room and slammed into a support beam. Killed him on impact."

"Thrown across the room?"

"That's the best way I know to describe it." Gregg shrugged. "No bruising to indicate he was hit by a car or anything; whatever delivered the force that threw him into the beam, it didn't leave a bruise. That's why I say he was thrown."

"An amp."

"Sounds reasonable enough; they've been cropping up more often. Hey, do you have powers, or is your thing just the crossbow?"

"No powers. But don't knock the crossbow until you've tried it."

Gregg raised his hands, palms outward. "Hey, hey. No judgment. I got mad respect for a regular guy who runs around with superheroes. Anyway, the rest of the bodies were killed by somewhat more conventional methods—gunshots and slash wounds. From the length of the cuts, we think the bladed weapon was a sword, not a knife or hatchet."

A sword? So not only did the Opera Mask Gang have superpowers, they also had a flair for the theatrical. Yeoman supposed he should've guessed that, based on their choice of disguise. What purpose did a sword serve, especially if at least one of the others was armed with a gun? And why had Sloan been killed by brute force, while the others had been taken down with weapons?

"So you said these guys wear opera masks?" Gregg asked. "We've heard of the Opera Mask Gang, but we had no reason to connect them to these murders. You really think it was them?"

"Possibly." Yeoman worked his jaw. "Sloan had gang connections?"

The cop laughed. "Oh, yeah. He was one of the top lieutenants in the Seventy-Six. But one of the other victims, a guy named DeMarco, was a lieutenant in the Archdukes. We thought it was a gang meeting gone south at first, but the CODs didn't match that."

"The Opera Mask Gang could be connected to the other street gangs, then. Thanks for your help."

"You're welcome." Gregg stepped forward. "Anything else?"

"That'll be all. But I may be in touch."

Yeoman turned, drew and loaded his crossbow, and fired the grappling arrow. He swung away from the precinct and back toward his car.

If the Opera Mask Gang just slaughtered lieutenants from two other gangs, then all this just got a whole lot more complicated.

They weren't just looking at a few rogue superhumans anymore; they were also racing against a gang manhunt.

* * *

"Hello, Mr. Watanabe." Ben knelt next to Ty. "I trust you are comfortable?"

Ty edged away from the other man and sneered at him.

Comfortable?

Even in new clothes and with a fresh shave, Ty was chained to a wall. No amount of food, water, or hygiene was going to make him feel comfortable as long as he was trapped down here. There was no sarcasm in Ben's tone, though. The question was, in some odd way, genuine.

"What do you want from me?" Ty asked. "Whatever it is, just tell me. You've had me here for over a week now. If you wanted me dead, I would already be dead. If you wanted information, you would have tortured me by now. So what is it? Why am I so valuable to you that you are willing to keep me chained up in a basement for so long?"

"You cannot begin to fathom your true value, Mr. Watanabe."

"Vickers," Ty growled. "You know my name is Ty Vickers now."

"That is not your name. It is the name of a man who felt the need to hide. You should not be hiding, Mr. Watanabe. You are a warrior, a champion. Your destiny is far greater than living in an unassuming house in a bad part of town, barely scraping by as you strive to provide for the child you desperately cling to as the last memory of your wife."

That was all Ty could handle. The mention of his daughter sent him into a frenzy, and he seized the moment. Phasing free of his cuffs, he lunged forward, launching a knife-handed strike at Ben's throat. Ben backed off with startling speed, standing just outside the reach of Ty's chains; but Ty was free of the chains. He jabbed his fingertips into Ben's throat, choking the man. Ben recoiled, clutching at his throat. Ty stood over the man with his fists clenched. He could press his attack . . . or he could run.

Ben lashed out and grabbed Ty's ankle. Ty tugged away and phased free.

At least, he tried to. His leg remained solid, clutched in Ben's grasp. Still struggling for air, Ben thrust his other hand forward. Too late, Ty realized Ben was holding a taser. Electricity coursed along Ty's body, wracking his limbs with painful convulsions. He cried out and fell to the ground. Ben pulled himself to his feet.

"Seems I struck a nerve. I'm sorry." The man massaged his throat. His voice sounded hoarse from the strike, but his breaths came in more evenly. "Good thing you're not a killer. You could've easily crushed my windpipe."

"How . . . " Ty clenched his teeth as his body trembled. "My . . . powers . . . ?"

"Did you think you were the only amp in the room?" Ben clicked his tongue. "Pity. I've had the ability to mute the powers of other superhumans for some time now. It's why I wasn't worried that the battery in your cuff was dying. I figured you would try something like this sooner or later. I was just hoping I could convince you of my goodwill before it came to blows."

"My daughter . . . " Ty swallowed a lump growing in his throat. "If I never see her again, I'll hold you responsible, Ben. You'll pay."

Ben held out his hands, palms outward. "One day, I fully intend to see you reunited with your daughter. However, that depends on how willing you are to cooperate."

Of course, Ben wanted something. They always did. There were very few people Ty had met in his life who were genuinely unselfish.

Rachel, Joanie, Carter, Silas—he hoped his parents were on that list, but he remembered too little about them to truly know. They were members of the Sicaran order. Could they truly have been good people if they were assassins?

He tried to access his powers. They felt distant, though, with his concentration scrambled by the taser shock. For the moment, he was immobile.

"What do you want from me?" Ty demanded.

Ben pocketed his taser and turned toward the top of the stairs. At his gesture, two thugs clambered down the steps.

"For now, a new place to hold you. In the long term? Something much greater. You have a destiny, Mr. Watanabe, and it is time you fulfilled it." Ben locked gazes with Ty, and there was a righteous fire burning in his eyes. "With your help, we can finally bring about the destruction of the Sicarans."

CHAPTER 21

Jan's superpowers didn't come as a surprise to Patrick. He had been there the day a nephiloid bit her. He and Jarrett, along with Dean Sterling and Audrey Knight, had been fighting Doctor Ashcroft's forces in Washington, D.C. Jarrett's wife had been there, and Jarrett had asked Patrick to find her and get her to safety. When Patrick had arrived at her location, she had already been bitten, infected by the superpowered serum contained in the creatures' fangs. He had run her to the hospital himself before rejoining the fight.

What surprised him was that she had the power to manipulate electricity. Jarrett had been quiet about what her powers actually were. He had joked multiple times that she had developed the ability to shoot lasers from her toes, but Patrick knew there was no way he had been serious. What were the chances that she had the powers that he needed to repair the damage to his brain?

Of course, even if she had different powers, it would have been simple enough to procure the equipment needed to perform artificial shock therapy, but the fact that she did have these powers only reinforced to Patrick that Dean and Gideon's theory that God gave each person their powers with a specific purpose in mind was true. God had known that Patrick would go through this crisis, and he had given Jan electrokinesis so that she would be able to help Patrick through it.

He lay across the couch, his head propped up against the armrest, while Jan studied his brain scans again. It would be a delicate operation. Too much electricity, and she could fry his brain. Too little, and she might not jumpstart it back to its normal condition. Patrick would have been terrified of most strangers shooting lightning into his brain. But Jarrett trusted Jan, so Patrick did, too. That didn't keep him from being nervous, though.

Even that nervousness was just a glimmer of emotion, smothered beneath the weight of the superhuman apathy. Patrick was ready to return to his normal self.

"Okay," Jan said. "I'm going to put you under now. Once I do, I'll begin shock therapy. I'm going to start slowly and try to get your brainwaves back to normal human patterns. After that, we'll wake you up and see how you're feeling before we try anything else."

"Sounds good." Patrick reached for Lucy's hands. "Just tell me I'll be able to take Lucy to the formal tonight."

"With any luck, you will." Jan smiled. "Are you ready?"

"As I'll ever be, I guess."

Jan administered a sedative. "Count backward from ten."

"Ten . . . nine . . ."

Patrick frowned.

He wasn't in the hotel room anymore. He stood in the middle of a racetrack—a NASCAR-sized one, but it was empty. There were no cars on the tracks, no fans in the stands. How was this happening? Although not unheard of, it wasn't common for people to dream while under anesthesia. What made it stranger was that it was a lucid dream. Maybe it had something to do with his speedster's physiology.

"I hope I don't feel her shocking me."

He walked toward the starting line, the black-and-white checkered pattern standing out amidst the otherwise gray scenery. Lining himself up in the center of the track, Patrick dropped into a runner's crouch. If he couldn't use his powers in the real world, maybe he could use them in his dream. Patrick adjusted the placement of his right foot behind him and pressed down with his left foot, ready to push off with it.

"And . . . go!"

He pushed off and started running—at an incredibly average pace. Before getting his powers, Patrick had been on the track team in high school; so he remembered what a normal run felt like. This . . . felt exactly like that. He scrunched his face in concentration and pumped his arms, struggling to move faster; but his body would not cooperate. He moved his legs faster and faster, but Usain Bolt could've lapped him without breaking a sweat. This was no speedster's run. It was barely an impressive normal person's run.

Patrick stopped a hundred yards from the starting line and looked back. This was a dream—impossible things were supposed to be possible within a dream. If he couldn't even run like Spright in his dream, would he be able to in reality?

This was no dream, he realized. It was a nightmare.

"Why is this happening?" he shouted. "Why?"

"Patrick."

Patrick turned and jumped back. The voice had come from a man who'd suddenly appeared behind him. The man wore khaki pants, a green shirt, and a cargo vest. His bald head shone under the lights of the racetrack, and his face boasted a full, gray beard. The man smiled kindly—one of the most genuine smiles Patrick had ever seen and as familiar as his own. It was not the man's sudden appearance that had startled Patrick. It was who he was.

"Grandpa?"

"Hello, Patrick." Joshua Omer beamed even more widely. "I'm glad you remember me."

Patrick's grandfather had disappeared from his life years before, excommunicated from his family because of his Christian beliefs. At the time, Patrick and his parents had been devout Orthodox Jews; so when Joshua had converted from Judaism to Christianity, it had been a slap in the face. But Joshua was one of the reasons Patrick himself had eventually converted, which had led to Patrick's parents being saved, as well.

But Patrick had never seen Joshua again. He had later learned that Gideon had met Joshua in Venezuela, when they had both been kidnapped by guerrillas. Like Gideon, Joshua had developed the power to project light after being experimented on by Ashcroft; but Gideon said that Joshua had most likely never known about his powers. But as Gideon had escaped from the guerrillas, Joshua had sacrificed his life to save Gideon, staying behind to fight the captain of the guerrillas while Gideon ran.

"I . . . haven't even dreamed of you in so long," Patrick said.

"I know. Time goes on, and our hearts heal. It doesn't mean we forget; it just means we can move forward."

"I miss you."

Joshua nodded. "That's normal, too."

"Why . . . why are you here?"

"Why are you angry, Patrick? You ask God why, and you are angry at Him; but you have no reason to be."

"My . . . my powers. I don't know if I can use them again."

"Well, that's the thing, isn't it? You don't know. Why be angry about something you're not even sure will happen yet?"

He had a point. Patrick raised his eyebrows in surprise and took a step back. It was true; Patrick didn't know that he would be without his powers *forever. It was just a fear. Even if he couldn't use them initially, there was every chance that he'd regain the use of them in time.*

"I just got scared. God took Gideon's powers away, and I guess I didn't want Him to take mine, too."

"Everything is in God's plan. If He will take your powers, then He will; and He has a reason for it. Being angry about it won't stop Him. It will only hinder you from moving forward."

"You're right." Patrick sighed. "I'm sorry."

"Don't tell me." There was that smile again. "I'm just a dream, remember?"

"Right." Tears welled in Patrick's eyes, and he wiped them away as they began to roll down his cheeks. "I miss you, Grandpa. I wish I could've told you about the day I got saved or when I got powers."

"I miss you, too." Joshua turned and began to walk away. "But what are you waiting for? Run."

* * *

Jan's breaths were ragged and choppy as she struggled to contain the outpour of electricity from her fingers. She had become adept at firing electrical bolts; the effort came from trying to ensure that the voltage was not too powerful. Rendering Patrick brain-dead altogether was the last thing she wanted to do. As slivers of silvery-blue energy coursed from her hands and into Patrick's head, she glanced over at the brainwave monitor. She was nearly done; the patterns were nearing normal human functions.

Focus. That was the key. If her mind wandered or if she began to feel anxious, she would lose control. As long as she maintained her focus, she would be fine. Sweat beaded her forehead. Jan inhaled again, shakier than she would have liked.

"Can you . . . wipe my forehead?"

"Of course." Lucy knelt next to her with a paper towel and dabbed at the sweat. "How are you doing?"

"Almost . . . done."

"Is he all right?"

"Yes." Jan looked at the monitor again. "Just a few . . . more . . . seconds."

Patrick's brainwaves rose and fell . . . and matched the standard. Jan sighed in relief, cut off the electricity, and lowered her hands. She slumped down onto the floor, resting her head against the couch. Lucy rushed off and returned a moment later with a glass of water. Jan took the glass and downed half of it.

"Thank you."

"You're welcome." Lucy sat next to her. "So where do we go from here? You said that even with normal human brainwave patterns, Patrick can't use his powers, right?"

"It would be dangerous. He wouldn't be able to process what he was seeing, nor would his body compensate for the abnormal speed. Trying to use his powers at all would be . . . well, it would be suicidal."

"But you can get his brainwaves back up to speedster levels, right? This is temporary."

Jan hesitated. With time, she could use her powers to increase the output of Patrick's brain. The problem was, unlike with human brainwaves, she didn't have a pattern of reference to compare to. She could easily go too far and cause serious harm.

"It is temporary, right?" Lucy pressed.

"I hope so. But it's going to be very dangerous to fix him completely. Ideally, I would like to have a readout of a speedster's brain while they're using their powers. I don't suppose you happen to have one?"

"No, we never studied Patrick's brain."

"That's what I was afraid of." Jan forced a smile. "Don't worry. We'll do the best we can. We'll put all the resources we have toward making sure that Patrick can use his powers again soon."

"I hope so. They mean the world to him."

"He'll be okay. Besides, he's got you."

"Thank you," Lucy smiled.

"That was good work at the docks today, by the way. You've got quite the investigative talent in you."

"I've always liked unraveling mysteries."

"A useful talent for a member of a superhero's team. But don't let it go to waste—there's a lot of good you can do with a gift like that. You have it for a reason; you should use it."

"I will."

Jan pushed herself to her feet. "Patrick should be awake soon. I'm going to go wash up, if you want to stay with him."

"Of course. And thank you again for helping him. I know in his current state he may not have seemed grateful, but he really is. And so am I."

"I'm happy to help." Jan walked toward the restroom. "I just hope it's enough."

CHAPTER 22

The Seventy-Six owned several blocks' worth of real estate surrounding the docks, and they maintained control of their property with ruthless efficiency. The Archdukes, who were longtime rivals with the Seventy-Six now working their way toward a partnership, stuck to upscale parts of town, as their name suggested. It would be difficult to approach the Archdukes in daylight, but the Seventy-Six did not present the same problem.

Yeoman trained his crossbow scope on the five-story building across the street. The ground floor was a bodega, which was no doubt a front for the Seventy-Six. Yeoman spotted six obvious gangsters patrolling the streets outside; and the third-floor window was open, revealing several more inside.

There's bound to be someone in leadership here.

If he could find someone in charge, they might be able to tell him who the Opera Mask Gang were. The trio had obviously had some dealings with the Seventy-Six before, since they had been at the docks twice. But shooting the place up was unlikely to get him any answers. If he wanted to talk to them, he'd have to simply do that—go down there and talk to them. That might be difficult to do dressed in his super suit, though. He had a change of clothes in his car. He could go down, change, and walk to the bodega within a few minutes.

Click.

"Don't move."

Yeoman raised his head from the scope of his crossbow. A man stood next to him, pointing a gun at Yeoman's neck.

Well, that was sloppy of me.

He should have known better than to be caught unawares; he had been in Special Forces. And yet, he had let a two-bit gangster sneak up on him. If the man had been so inclined, he could've killed Yeoman; and the archer never would've known the gangster was there.

"Put the crossbow down."

"No." A new voice came from behind the gangster. "You put the gun down."

Yeoman smirked as Carter Jonson, dressed as the Crusader, locked his forearm around the gangster's throat. Growling, the gangster tossed his gun down.

"Hey, Crusader." Jarrett inclined his head toward Carter. "Thanks for the save."

"My pleasure."

"Who are you?" the gangster demanded.

"We'll ask the questions," Carter said. "I'm assuming you're with the Seventy-Six?"

The man clamped his jaw shut. Carter rolled his eyes, shoved the man to his knees, and detonated an adhesive bead against his wrists. Blue-green gel bound the man's hands in place behind his back. Jarrett grabbed the gangster by his shoulders and tilted him backward, so they were looking each other eye to eye.

"I'm Yeoman. I'm a vigilante, but I'm not from around here. I'm just in town helping a friend. You know, it's kind of insulting that none of you know who I am. Doesn't anyone watch the news? I was with the Vindicators, so I don't know why—"

Carter cleared his throat. "Yeoman."

"Right. Anyway, I have a few questions I needed to ask your bosses. I was just scoping out the area to make sure it was safe to come closer."

Why was Carter here, though? Jarrett eyed the other vigilante. If they were not careful, they could end up working at cross purposes. If Carter would let Jarrett take the lead, maybe they could both get what they wanted. Carter locked gazes with Jarrett for a moment, then stepped back and gestured toward the gangster.

"What kind of questions?" the criminal asked.

"About David Sloan. And how he died."

The man was silent for a moment. Had Jarrett gone too far? The mention of Sloan's death could make the gangster clam up. If it did, Yeoman would have to go down and enter the bodega the hard way.

"Why are you asking about that?" the gangster demanded.

"I have reason to believe the people I'm searching for are the same people who killed Sloan. Seeing as he's one of your bosses, I figured the Seventy-Six would be itching for payback however they could get it." Jarrett removed a capsule from his belt. "If you agree to help me, I'll let you go. You can go tell your bosses why I'm here; and if they let me in to talk with them, we can work out an arrangement."

The gangster huffed. "Fine. But you're going to have to change—the bosses won't want to be seen talking to no vigilante."

"Fair enough. I'll go change and be back in ten minutes."

"We'll be expecting you. But take my advice: the bosses smell anything up, and you'll be dead, just like that. No second chances. So I'd really consider whether you want to do this before you come in."

"Understood."

Yeoman popped the capsule and drizzled the solvent it contained across the gangster's bonds. The gel dissolved instantly. The man scooped up his gun, backed away, and walked toward the door leading back into the building. As he left, Carter crossed his arms and stepped closer to Jarrett.

"What was that about?"

Jarrett removed his goggles. "Playing the long game. I'm not interested in some street gangs. They can lead me to the amps who messed with Patrick's head. That's all I care about."

"Well, it's not all I care about. These gangsters could be holding a man I've tracked all the way from Sojourn City. I'm not leaving here until that man is rescued, so forget your deal—I'm going in there suited up, and I'll beat every man in there black and blue until I find the guy I'm looking for."

"Just . . . let me go in first," Jarrett said. "I'll keep an eye out for your guy or anyplace in the bodega that looks like it could be hiding a captive. If I see something, I'll let you know once I'm out. If not, you can go in there and beat them up to your heart's content."

Carter clenched his jaw. Jarrett tensed. Would he take the offer? There was no reason they could not work together. Carter was Patrick's friend, after all. He had to want what was best for Patrick. At the moment, that meant finding the Opera Mask Gang. Finally, Carter nodded and uncrossed his arms.

"Fine. For Patrick. But if you need backup, you call. I'll be inside in seconds."

"You got it."

They stood in silence for several moments. Jarrett looked Carter up and down. His suit was different from the last time Jarrett had seen him. The simple silver cross on his breastplate had been replaced by a larger, electric blue cross that glowed softly. His domino mask was gone. In its place, the Crusader wore a helmet-like cowl with an opaque blue visor. He carried a shield on his left arm and had a sword slung across his back in place of his typical staff.

"New getup?" Jarrett asked.

"Dean gave me an upgrade, so I could deal with a supervillain." Carter crossed his arms. "It's a bit flashier than I'm used to, but it's growing on me."

Jarrett nodded. "And the sword?"

"The groove is electrified. Unless I'm using the edge, it's still a nonlethal weapon. But I do still keep my staff on-hand for engaging big groups." He tapped the small of his back, where a pair of short truncheons rested in a horizontal sheath. "The more weapons, the better."

"Nice."

"Thanks. I see you added sleeves." Carter looked down at the street below. "Oh, hey. Our guy's back."

The man they had accosted stood in the street, waving up at them. Presumably, that meant his boss was amicable to a visit. Jarrett patted Carter on the shoulder and stepped past him toward the fire escape.

"Wish me luck, kid."

Jarrett descended it into the alley, followed it back to his car, and quickly changed from his suit into a blue polo shirt, black jeans, and a pair of casual boots. He put his crossbow and suit in the trunk and studied his pistol.

Keeping it was a calculated decision—if he did bring it, the Seventy-Six might see it as a threat and end the conversation before it began. But if he didn't bring it, they might see it as an insult. What kind of fighter would come to them unarmed? That might end the discussion just as quickly. Finally, Jarrett tucked the pistol into his waistband at the small of his back and walked out of the alley. If worst came to worst, Carter was there to back him up.

Out of his Yeoman suit, he doubted they would take him too seriously. Yes, he was strong and well-muscled; he always kept his body in peak fighting condition. But his features were . . . *soft*. It was unfortunate, but the fact was that Jarrett had a babyface. He looked too nice, and there was no cure for that. Maybe the gun would show them he meant business.

As he approached the bodega, two patrolling Seventy-Sixers looked up at him and stopped in their tracks, but they did not train their guns on him or acknowledge him in any other way. The man on the roof must've told them to expect him. Jarrett didn't acknowledge them, either. He continued walking toward the bodega at a casual stroll. He wasn't nervous because he knew he could take either of them out in a second, and he wasn't offended because he knew that ignoring him was typical gang tactics.

The gangster who'd accosted him on the rooftop was waiting at the bodega door. He pushed it open as Jarrett approached, the top of the metal frame catching a bell inside the store as it swung inward. Jarrett spared him a brief nod and walked past him. He spotted several more Seventy-Sixers inside, mixed with civilians who either didn't know or didn't care that the store was run by the gang. The man from the roof pointed to a door in the back corner. Jarrett wove his way through the aisles to the door, where yet another gangster was waiting for him. The burly man inclined his head to the door and pushed it open, stepping inside as he did. Jarrett went in after him.

The bodega's stockroom looked like any other in millions of stores across the world. This one, however, boasted racks of assault rifles in addition to shelves full of stock. A man in a tailored dress suit looked up from a game of cards as Jarrett entered.

"So, you're the guy who's snooping around my territory." The man stood. "I hear you're asking about David's death."

"That's right." Jarrett approached the man cautiously. "His killers might be involved in a case I'm working on."

"A case?" The man barked out a laugh. "You're no cop, pal. My man told me who you are—a vigilante—but given how you arm yourself, probably not a superpowered one. Just a man. I assume you're still armed?"

Jarrett nodded. "Pistol at the small of my back."

"Smart man. I won't ask you to disarm; I'll trust your honor to not shoot me while we're talking business. If you try, Raymond over there will do you in."

The burly man who had opened the door for Jarrett made a rumbling sound deep in his throat. Jarrett forced a smile at him. He scanned the stockroom as he returned his gaze to the lead man. There was a large metal door set in the back corner of the room, bolted shut from this side. Jarrett narrowed his eyes.

Good place to keep a prisoner.

His gaze swept past the door in an instant and returned to the leader.

"So," the man said, "the killers. I know one of 'em. The big guy owes us money. Don't know about his friends, other than that they used to work for DeMarco from the Archdukes. But they did him in, too, so I guess that business has come to an end. Fine with me—just means that killing 'em won't sour business with the 'Dukes."

"They must've had a reason for killing your man David, not to mention DeMarco."

"Well, it's possible David was . . . overeager. He runs the fighting ring down at the docks, see? Two nights ago, those bozos in the opera masks show up; and the big one jumps in the ring. He's winning pretty good, too, but then his earbud falls out. Cheater. David tries to get 'em to leave, but the big guy jumps all over David and demands his winnings. Before he can do anything he surely would've regretted, that little runner—Spright, is it?—scares off the masks. Thing is, they weren't wearing the masks when they first came on the scene, so David got a good look at their faces. That's how I know the big one owes us. Maybe that's what went down last night. David saw their faces; their cover was blown; so they decided to just kill everyone and split."

"Why wouldn't DeMarco side with the masks?"

"Would've been bad for business." The man shrugged. "The Seventy-Six and the 'Dukes are on unstable ground. Anything that smelled of deception could've ruined everything. It was better for DeMarco to betray the masks than to stand up for 'em and risk war with us. Even though it got him killed, DeMarco did the right thing."

"I'm sure." Jarrett frowned. "You said that when they showed up to the fight ring, they weren't wearing masks. Do you have footage from that night? Security cameras, anything?"

"It's possible. But why should I part with it? I need that footage, so I can find these fools myself and put 'em in the ground."

Jarrett scoffed. "You won't be able to kill them. They have superpowers. It's how they managed to kill your people and DeMarco's. If you send your soldiers after them, there will be a bloodbath. Let me go; I know how to handle people like them. I'll ensure they go to jail and get a fair trial."

"Fair trial? Ha! I want to watch them bleed."

"You must've already studied the footage by now; you know what they look like. Why do you still need it? Just give it to me."

"Hmm . . . no. You see, the thing is, I need to be sure that I'm the one who catches David's killers. Because David was my cousin."

The man raised his hand, which now held a gleaming silver pistol. Jarrett lashed out with his left hand, turning the gun aside, while with his right hand he drew his own weapon and fired at Raymond, the hulking gangster at the door. Jarrett's bullet blasted through Raymond's knee, dropping the big man to the floor. Immediately, he swiveled back to the man in front of him—Sloan's cousin. The boss fired his gun; but since his gun hand was still in Jarrett's grip, the bullet harmlessly struck the concrete floor. Jarrett jabbed his right hand forward, striking the man across the brow with the butt of his gun.

The door to the bodega crashed open, and two gangsters rushed in. Jarrett threw himself behind a shelf as they opened fire. He stuck his hand between the shelves and returned fire, hitting one in the shoulder and the other just above the waist. He crossed the room, kicked the man with the wounded shoulder in the face, and locked the door. As he passed Raymond, who was struggling to get to his feet, he grabbed the big man's head and shoved it face-first into the floor. He tucked his gun away and knelt next to the boss.

"Now that you've got that out of your system, let's talk. Where is the footage?"

CHAPTER 23

Frigid air seeped into Ty's bones. He clenched his jaw to keep his teeth from chattering and pressed his arms close to his chest, preserving what warmth he had. While Ty was incapacitated from Ben's taser attack, the two burly guards had thrown a bag over his head, hauled him upstairs, and tossed him in a meat locker.

At least I know I'm probably in a restaurant.

And for the first time in ages, his hands were free.

Unfortunately, he quickly learned the limitations of his powers. After his head cleared and his strength returned, Ty attempted to phase out of the meat locker. Something about the cold did not agree with him, though. When he attempted to push through the door, it felt like a normal person trying to walk straight through a chain-link fence. The frigid molecules bit into Ty's essence like daggers. He quickly phased back out and huddled in the corner of the meat locker. Since that attempt, he had been afraid to try again.

So he could not phase through frozen objects. That was good to know. He wondered how Ben had discovered that or if the mysterious captor was just taking a chance. Either way, Ty was once again trapped.

A heavy *clunk* signaled the meat locker door unlocking. Ty straightened and clenched his fists. Not long ago, he had heard the distinct sound of gunshots.

Ty knew little about Ben, but he was obviously involved in some criminal dealings. The clamor from outside could have been the result of a disagreement between conspirators, or a shootout with the police, or any number of things. However, something deep within Ty feared that it was something more. He had to be ready for anything.

It was a strange coincidence that a fight broke out right after Ben mentioned the Sicarans. Now that Ty knew the order of assassins was part of the picture, he had to consider the possibility that they were hunting him. Had they finally arrived to finish him off? If so, he was determined to go down fighting. That would not be easy to do while his body was stiffened from the cold, but Ty would not just lie down and die.

He still did not know why Ben had chosen him. Shortly after throwing Ty into the meat locker, Ben had explained he was an enemy of the Sicarans and that he thought Ty could play an important role in taking them down. Certainly, Ty was not opposed to fighting the group of assassins that had sent a killer after him and murdered one of his friends, but he did not know if he wanted to be a soldier in Ben's war, either. After all, Ty's father had been a Sicaran. What if Ty was wrong about them? What if they were the good guys, and Ben was on the wrong side? Ty's stepfather, Chin Liang, had betrayed the Sicarans in favor of an ancient cabal called Charybdis, and Liang was an awful person. Did Ben also work for Charybdis? If so, could Ty trust him?

Either way, if the Sicarans had arrived to kill Ty, he would fight back no matter whether or not they were on the so-called good side. His life was more important to him than an idealistic war between two ancient groups of criminals.

The meat locker door opened. Hands in the pockets of his tailored trousers, Ben stepped inside. Ty sighed and let his shoulders relax. He still did not trust the man; but at least, he knew Ben was not here to kill him.

"We need to move," Ben said.

Ty frowned. "What's going on?"

"I trust you heard the commotion earlier. I was not here at the time, but a vigilante attacked several of my men. I fear this location has been compromised. We must move you elsewhere."

A *vigilante?* A spark of hope lit in him, bringing a lightness to his heart he had not felt in months. Perhaps God had heard Ty's pleas, after all. There were many vigilantes and superheroes in the world; but somehow, Ty clung to hope that it was Carter Jonson. If the Crusader was there to save him, he could go home and return to prison, where he could serve out the rest of his sentence in peace and eventually earn his freedom to a life with Emi. He did not have to get caught up in a centuries-old war. Unless it was a different vigilante. Or the Crusader did not believe he had been kidnapped.

If Carter thought Ty had gone along with the escape willingly and was here to bring him back by force, Ty might never see the outside of prison walls again.

Will he listen to me if I try to explain?

The Crusader knew how much Ty cared for Emi. Surely, he would understand.

Ben gestured for Ty to follow him. "You'll excuse me if I keep my dampening field up. I can't trust you not to use your powers just yet."

He released the chain from the wall, though, and then he ushered Ty toward a pair of guards standing just outside the locker. Ty scanned his surroundings. He had been incoherent due to the taser when they brought him up from the basement, and he had been blindfolded to boot. For the first time, he got a better look at his prison. It was a gray stockroom lined with racks of guns. A door to his right bore a window that looked out into a small storefront.

Not a restaurant, but I was close enough.

"Out the back." Ben drew a gun from inside his blazer. "A van is waiting."

Ty spotted bloodstains on the concrete floor. If the Crusader had been in the stockroom, he was not here anymore; and there were no bodies to be seen. Had Ben's guards killed him? Ty's spirits sank back down.

God, if You're out there, please let Carter be all right.

Ty sincerely hoped the blood did not belong to the vigilante. Or that if the blood was from his would-be rescuer, that it was some random local vigilante, not the young man who had taken a chance that Ty could be redeemed.

One of Ben's guards pulled open a door that exited into an alley. Fresh sea air hit Ty like a wave. The afternoon warmth chased away the lingering chill from the meat locker. He took deep breaths, enjoying air that was not stale and recycled. Distantly, he realized that he was a long way from Sojourn City. The warmer climate and ocean breeze indicated one of the coasts. It was no wonder that no one had found him yet. Would Carter or the police even think to look outside of Michigan?

Ben yanked open the rear doors of a beige van and gestured for the guards to put Ty in.

"You have to understand; we need you," Ben said. "We don't want you to be a prisoner, but we cannot risk anything happening to you until you've come around to our side of things."

"I'd be more inclined to trust you if you treated me like an ally, not a prisoner." Ty shook off one of the guards and stepped toward the van.

"I'm not happy about this, but I'll hear you out. It's not like I have much of a choice. But stop treating me like a flight risk, or I'll act like one."

"Understood." Ben nodded. "I'll explain everything once we're—"

Thump. A red-clad figure landed atop the van in a crouch. Ty looked up at him and gaped. It was the Crusader! Carter's familiar dark features glared down at the group from behind his mask. Ben snapped out an order, and Ty's guards swiveled their guns toward the Crusader. Ty dropped prone as they opened fire.

The Crusader burst into motion, leaping off the van as the guards opened fire. His staff lashed out left, then right, knocking the guns from their hands. With his free hand, the Crusader drew his sword and tossed it.

"Heads up, Ty!"

Ty snagged the weapon from the air. Energy instantly flooded his palms. It was invigorating to be holding a sword again after so long.

The Crusader pressed in, striking one in the abdomen. The other guard lunged forward to take the Crusader in a bear hug from behind. Ty lashed out from the ground, snaking his leg in front of the man's ankles. The guard cried out and stumbled forward. The Crusader turned and rammed the end of his staff into the man's solar plexus, sending an electrical charge through the guard's body. Ty rolled over and pressed the blade of the Crusader's sword against the first guard's neck.

Ben backed away from Ty and Carter, training a pistol on the vigilante. Ty sized Ben up. He was surprisingly in control for someone in his position. His hand was level and steady, his eyes locked on his target, his shoulders straight.

He's not afraid.

Ty pushed himself to his feet and stood behind Carter. The vigilante twirled his staff and stared Ben down.

"Who are you?" the Crusader demanded. "Why did you take him?"

"We need him." Ben's eyes shifted to focus on Ty. "You know the Sicarans have to be stopped. Come with us. Help us. Together, we can take them down. They're an order of assassins, Mr. Watanabe. They will stop at nothing to reshape the world in their image. Do you really think they'll let you stay alive after you killed one of their own? Sooner or later, they will come for you. You're a threat to them. Get ahead of the game. Help me take them down before they take you out."

Carter shook his head. "He's not going anywhere, except back to prison."

Ben scoffed, but his eyes remained locked on Ty's. "And is that what you want? I can offer you freedom—a life. All he's offering is a cell."

"Freedom? You've kept me locked in a basement for almost two weeks!" Ty raised his borrowed sword, its tip pointed at Ben's throat. "If that's your idea of freedom, I think I'll take captivity that I know I'll get out of eventually. I want my daughter back, Ben. I want a regular life with her. If I help you in your war with the Sicarans, I'll never get that life. I'll spend the rest of it fighting for a cause I don't even know if I believe in yet."

"Your life will never be normal. They will hunt you. They will hurt you by any means necessary. That includes your daughter."

Ty's chest seized at the thought of Emi being hurt by the Sicarans. *I can't let that happen.*

But he could protect her better when he had her with him. Couldn't he?

Ben knelt and put his gun on the ground. "Go with your vigilante friend. I can see you're not ready for this conversation. When the truth strikes you, I'll be waiting. We need you, Mr. Watanabe, and you need us. It's time to reject this false life you've built for yourself and become the man you were always meant to be."

Ty glanced at Carter. "Leave him. Let's get out of here."

"Sounds good to me." Carter broke his staff into two short truncheons and sheathed them. He spared one last glare at Ben. "You come after us, and I'll take you down hard."

Then Carter turned and strode past the van. Ty hurried after him, and the two of them stepped out of the shaded alley and into the sunlight on a dockside street. Ty closed his eyes and basked in the warmth of the sun. How long had it been since he had felt it directly? Too long. He let out a long sigh and found himself smiling. When he finally opened his eyes, Carter was standing with his hand held out.

Ty frowned. "What?"

"I'll take my sword now."

He had almost forgotten he was holding it. Ty sized up Carter. He couldn't see the young man's eyes behind his blue visor, but he could almost sense what Carter was thinking. Ty had his powers back, and he was armed. It would be easy to take out the Crusader and run. He had no reason to do that.

He handed the sword back to Carter. "Thanks for the rescue."

"You're welcome. I knew you didn't run away." Carter grinned and patted Ty's shoulder. "I'm glad I was right. Let's get you back to Sojourn City."

"Right. How did you find me, anyway?"

"It wasn't easy, but we had a lot of help. Starting with your sister-in-law, actually. Joanie used satellite footage to track the van in that alley from the prison all the way here to New Echelon."

New Echelon?

"That's near San Francisco, right? We're in California?"

"Yeah. Whoever the guys were that sprung you, they wanted you as far from Sojourn City as possible." Carter gestured for Ty to follow him and led him toward an alley across the street. "Was that guy back there serious? He really wanted you to help them take down the Sicarans?"

"I think so. I have no idea who they were, though. The only thing I can think of is that they belong to Charybdis, the rival organization of the Sicarans my godfather worked for." Ty shuddered. "I don't want any more to do with them than I do with the Sicarans."

"Good for you."

Carter brought Ty to a compact car. The vigilante quickly changed from his red uniform into casual street clothes, stuffed the costume into the back seat, and gestured for Ty to climb in the car. Ty slid into the passenger's seat and buckled up. Carter started the car and pulled out of the alley.

"Hey, Carter?"

Carter glanced at him. "Yeah?"

"You were an answer to prayers. You have no idea."

Carter smiled. "Glad I could help."

CHAPTER 24

Lucy sat on the edge of the coffee table and watched as Patrick roused from his sleep. She'd been sitting here for almost half an hour, but she didn't care. She was determined to be at his side when he woke up. Jan had not returned since finishing her shock therapy session, and Lucy did not blame her. If she had been in the older woman's position, she would have wanted to shower and change into fresh clothes after that kind of exertion. The precision it must have taken required a kind of discipline Lucy didn't have.

Patrick's eyes rolled beneath his eyelids, and he groaned softly. He was still wearing the same clothes he'd been in yesterday, Lucy realized. He probably needed a shower, too. With any luck, he would be back to himself once he awoke. A glance at her watch confirmed that they had plenty of time for him to return to his room for a shower and still be able to make it to dinner.

"Mm," Patrick muttered. "I'm . . . all right?"

"Easy there. You'll still be coming down from the anesthesia."

"I'm fine." He sat up. "Oof . . . maybe not fine. Dizzy."

"You probably need to get some food in you. When was the last time you ate?"

"Um . . . I can't remember." Patrick laughed softly. "Yesterday in the dining hall? Man, I was a wreck, wasn't I?"

"A little bit."

Lucy rose and walked to the kitchen alcove. A bowl of fruit sat on the counter; she took an apple from the bowl, poured another glass of water, and returned to Patrick. He took them and bit into the apple, chasing it down with a sip of water. He smacked his lips, nodded, and leaned back.

"I feel better. Normal. Where's Jan?"

"She went to clean up. She worked hard to get you this far. It was like watching a miracle."

"We definitely made the right call asking them to come here. Hey, thank you for all your help yesterday. I'm sure I was a pill to deal with, but I don't remember you complaining once. It means a lot."

"What are girlfriends for?" Lucy winked. "Once Jan comes out and checks you, we can probably get going. If you're up to it, that is."

"Up to it . . . " Patrick smacked his forehead. "The formal. I'm so sorry I forgot."

"It's okay. We've still got plenty of time. We don't have to dress up all fancy. I just want to spend time with the old Patrick, the one who won't fall asleep while I'm talking to him."

Patrick chuckled. "I'll do my best. The way that anesthesia hit me, no promises. But I think I can manage."

The front door opened. Jarrett walked in, dressed in plainclothes rather than his super suit. He was clutching his right arm, and a gash on his forehead crossed from the corner of his right eyebrow up to the edge of his hairline. He closed the door behind him and leaned against the wall.

"Are you all right?" Lucy exclaimed.

"I'm fine." Jarrett grimaced. "Just had a little . . . *disagreement* with a gang boss. It was going fine until I tried to leave. There were a few more guys between me and my car than I had planned on, but I made it out. Hey, Patrick. Good to see you up."

"Thanks." Patrick rose unsteadily from the couch. "Why were you out fighting gangs?"

"Trying to determine the identity of the Opera Mask Gang." Jarrett crossed the room, sat on the couch, and rolled up his shirtsleeve. "I'm lucky they only hit me twice. I should be able to stitch these up easily."

That could've been me.

If Lucy hadn't stopped investigating the docks, she might've been the one to run into the gangsters. Maybe it was for the best that Officer Gregg had forced her to leave. Jarrett, at least, knew how to handle himself in such situations. But she felt a pang of guilt that he had been hurt because of an investigation she'd started.

"Did you find anything?" she asked.

"I got a recording of the night Patrick fought them at the docks." Jarrett pulled a flash drive from his pocket. "I'll comb through the footage later tonight. But how are you feeling, Patrick? Any better?"

"Jan did a great job. I'm feeling like myself again."

"That's good. Well, you might want to stay here for a little bit longer so she can test you again; but after that, I don't see a reason why the two of you shouldn't go enjoy your evening. The masks, wherever they are, can wait until tomorrow. Besides, tonight's our anniversary, and I think we'd like to get some alone time. It's not often we're set up in a hotel like this one."

Patrick nodded. "Thank you, Jarrett. For everything."

It was good to see him back to his gracious, happy self. Lucy just hoped he stayed that way once he learned that it wouldn't be safe for him to use his powers yet.

* * *

The garage belonging to Anton Coleman was dark. Friction—rookie speedster and trainee under Oscar Paxton—watched from across the street. Obviously, no one was home. The exterior lights should have come on half an hour ago as the sun dropped below the horizon. No interior lights shone through the windows, either. The Colemans had obviously chosen to abandon the shop in their escape. But that didn't mean that they hadn't left any clues behind. It couldn't hurt to check inside, just in case.

Friction did not know how Paxton had learned the identity of the opera-masked thief who had attacked his son at a party. Paxton said that the thief's name was Darius Coleman and that he and his siblings spent much of their time here. Last night, however, the siblings had gotten involved in gang violence. Paxton said they would likely have left the garage already. It appeared he had been right. But if there was a clue inside and Friction didn't investigate, Paxton would never let her hear the end of it. It would take less than a few minutes for her to search, anyway.

Darting across the street, Friction approached the front door and tested the knob. Locked, of course, but that was no problem for her. Vibrating her hand, Friction touched the doorknob. The brass knob rattled, fell off the door, and clattered to the concrete porch.

Friction pushed the door open and stepped into the garage, probing the wall for a light switch as she did. She found one and flipped it on. The garage was dusty and cluttered, as if it had been abandoned far longer than a single day. Anton Coleman was not a clean person. Friction scanned the room. Where might she find a clue to the Colemans' whereabouts?

Time to put my powers to use.

Friction sped around the garage, searching for anything—a home address, a printout of a plane or train ticket . . . anything. She came up empty. Stopping back at the front door where she'd started, Friction growled deep in her throat. Paxton had finally given her an assignment. She had been begging for real experience for weeks. He took a chance on her, and she had run into a dead end after her first lead. How would he ever trust her to really be a superhero?

She touched her earbud communicator. "The garage is clean. There is no sign of them."

"Understood," Paxton replied. "And nothing that hints at their current location?"

"No, sir." Friction stepped outside and looked around. There had to be something. Anything. She couldn't bear the thought of disappointing him. Finally, her eyes fell on a solution. "There is a single security camera installed outside the garage. If I can find the footage from the past twenty-four hours, perhaps it will show me something."

"Good work. Get to it and let me know what you find."

Friction disconnected the line and rushed back inside. A computer was set up against the right wall in the back, near the door to the break room. She zipped over to it and grabbed the mouse. Whoever had used the computer last must've been in a hurry because that contact alone brought the screen to life.

Their mistake, my gain.

Friction pulled up the computer's link to the camera and rewound the footage. As she passed that morning, she saw several cars pull up to the garage and armed men exit—gangsters out for revenge, most likely. They, too, must've found nothing because they left as quickly as they arrived.

A few moments later, the footage reached the previous night. Friction stopped it and then played it forward as a dark van pulled up to the garage. Zee Coleman was in the driver's seat; she pulled the van into the garage and out of view of the camera. Friction sped the footage forward. The van pulled out of the garage again and turned left, driving out of range. Friction sighed. That hadn't been much to go on. But at least now, she knew what kind of vehicle they were driving and a general direction.

Friction tapped her earbud. "Mr. Paxton."

"Anything to report?"

"I have a make and model of the Colemans' vehicle and a general direction they headed, but that doesn't tell me anything." She pursed her lips. "They could have driven out of town, for all we know."

"No, they stayed here."

"How do you know?"

"If the Colemans planned on leaving New Echelon, they'd need money to do it. Given that they were working for a gang, they clearly didn't have the kind of money they'd need for that. I imagine they will stay local until they have acquired the kind of money necessary to build a life outside of New Echelon."

"How will they do that with the gangs hunting them?"

"Only one way that I can think of: robbery." Paxton was silent for a moment. "Take the rest of the night off. The Colemans will make their move soon. And when they do, it won't be subtle, not as long as Anton Coleman is pulling the strings."

Friction thought to ask him how he could be so confident, but she didn't want to anger him. He had just told her she could have the night off. It would be foolish to question that offer.

"So I should wait until they make their move and then catch them in the act?"

"Precisely. And then, when you stop them, the news will have a new darling superhero to adore. Make me proud."

"I will." Friction broke the communication. "I hope."

* * *

The movies made superhero life look glamorous. Live life by day, fight crime by night, and listen to friends—who were always witty and attractive—banter over comms all the while. The part of crimefighting that the movies never showed was how said witty and attractive friends had to do menial labor to ensure that the superhero's lair was upkept. No wonder Batman kept a butler around. No one else would have willingly cleaned the Batcave.

I am nobody's butler. Bryce sulked.

It had taken most of the day, but he had finally gotten the pool transformed into something resembling a superhero's lair. The wiring had been redone so the old Mac computer he had set up was working, and he had jacked directly into the cafeteria's internet line. There were a few other tables set up around the interior perimeter of the pool; Bryce figured they could use them as a space for Patrick's suit and whatever other tech he had. And he had bought a few cans of spray paint and used them to outline a crude racetrack around the exterior of the pool. It was far from Batcave quality, but it was something.

Now if he got out of here, he might just be able to catch a good time tonight. He didn't have a date, unfortunately; but Alexa was equally dateless, so the two of them were going together. She insisted it was not a date, but Bryce didn't care what she called it. He was hanging out with a pretty girl on the night of the formal. That was a win in his book.

Dusting his hands off on a now-dirty rag, Bryce climbed out of the pool and headed for the stairs. He hit the power on his way out, mounted the stairs, and ascended back to the student lounge. He had to be careful coming out of here. Maybe he could install a camera, one so small no one would notice it, so he could see the hallway outside the basement door before he exited. That would help him avoid any questions he couldn't answer—not to mention the rest of the team, once they started using the lair. But for now, he'd have to take his chances.

Cracking the door open, Bryce peered out. So far, so good. He creeped out, edging the door shut behind him, and took out the key to lock it . . .

"What are *you* doing?"

"Whoa!" Bryce jumped and spun around. "What—who—?"

Alexa stood behind him, hands on her hips and a confused expression on her face. She wore a sleeveless silver dress and had her hair down in wavy tresses. Bryce flicked his gaze up from her outfit to her eyes. She raised an eyebrow.

"What are you doing?" he asked.

She pointed past him. "The ladies' room is that way. And I asked you first."

"Um . . . " Bryce scrambled for an answer. "Still doing some important work for IT."

"In the basement?"

"Uh . . . yeah." Bryce locked the door. "That's right."

"You are a terrible liar, Bryce." Alexa rolled her eyes. "Don't tell me if you don't want to, but at least hurry up and get changed. The formal is in half an hour, and you are filthy."

"I know. I was on my way to do that right now."

Bryce circled around her, maintaining eye contact as he backed away. He chuckled nervously, made it to the corner where the hallway intersected with another, and darted away.

That was way too close.

He just hoped she didn't get as invasive with him as he had with Patrick. If Alexa found out because of Bryce's mistake, Lucy was going to kill him. And he really didn't want to die.

CHAPTER 25

Patrick adjusted the cuff of his button-up gray shirt and nodded in satisfaction. It was nice to feel something so simple as pride in his appearance again. After feeling nothing but dreary exhaustion and apathy for a whole day, it was a welcome change. Lucy had been so patient with him through it. He was ready to take her out and show her how much that meant to him.

He combed his hair, pulled on a black leather jacket, and laced up his boots. They still had time to make it to the formal. He wondered what kind of food the school was serving. Anything that wasn't fast food would do. Regardless, he was just glad they were able to go. The formal meant a lot to Lucy.

As Patrick finished putting his outfit together, the door opened. He looked up as Bryce stepped into the room. He was covered in dust and looked exhausted. Patrick's heart leaped into his throat. In all the chaos, he had forgotten one little detail: Bryce knew his secret now.

"Hey!" Bryce said. "Feel any better?"

"Lots." Patrick stood and walked over to his roommate. "Thanks for being discreet with my identity. I know it had to come as a shock, and I'm sorry that I never told you before. It was for your safety as much as mine."

Bryce slapped Patrick's hand in a high-five. "Don't even mention it. I've got something pretty cool to show you tomorrow. I know you've got somewhere to be tonight, and so do I."

"Sounds good. Where's Carter, by the way?"

"He came back a few hours ago with some Asian guy. He said they needed a place to lay low until tomorrow, so I took them to . . . well, to the place I'm going to surprise you with."

"So, he found his man, huh?" Patrick pressed his lips together. "That's good, I guess."

He was happy that Carter's mission was accomplished; but truthfully, he wished his friend could stay in New Echelon a bit longer. It was unfair that the few minutes Patrick and Carter had gotten together were sullied by Patrick's deflated mental state. Even a few minutes to talk and catch up would have been welcome.

Moments later, Patrick ducked out the door and walked down to the lobby and out into the cool evening air. Lucy was standing next to her car, now dressed in a denim skirt that stopped just above her knees, a pink top, and a brown jacket and matching boots. Patrick smiled as he walked up to her and gave her a hug.

"You look amazing."

"So do you." Lucy gestured to the dining hall across campus, where the formal was set up. "Come on. I'm starving."

"Me, too."

Patrick hooked his arm, and Lucy grinned and hooked her hand through it. Together, they strode toward the dining hall; and hopefully, their first quiet night together in far too long.

* * *

Asher's leg bounced against the floorboard of his car as he waited for Shannon. He did not know why he was so nervous. It was just homecoming. They would sit in a stand and watch a football game.

Still, he wanted it to go well more than anything he had ever wanted. She was sweet, smart, and gorgeous. The fact that she was interested in a guy like him and that she had made the first move was almost too good to be true.

Seeing how she'd dressed just to go to a group hangout, Asher expected something equally dazzling tonight. Because of that, he had also dressed to impress—as well as he was able, anyway. He was sporting a checkered blue-and-gray button-down shirt with a solid blue tie, a pair of black jeans, and black dress shoes. He didn't want to look like he was trying too hard, but he wanted to match her style and not look like he was way out of his league—which, obviously, he was, but everyone else didn't need to know that.

Shannon stepped out onto the sidewalk.

Oh, who am I kidding? Everyone knows she's a million miles out of my league. In fact, I'm so far out of my league, we're not even playing the same sport.

Although she was not dressed formally, Shannon was still dazzling in an outfit that looked far too nice for a football game. She wore a pair of black skinny jeans, a flowing button-down blouse with a floral pattern, and a tan leather jacket. Her dark hair was curled in long waves that bobbed as she walked. Asher struggled to keep his jaw from dropping as Shannon climbed into the car.

"Hi. Are you ready to go?"

He swallowed. "Uh . . . yeah. You look . . . wow."

"Thanks." Shannon beamed. "You look pretty good yourself."

"Thank you."

Asher pulled away from her apartment and found himself scrambling for anything to say. It wasn't just her looks that had him mute; it was his urgent need for this date to go well.

Why did I put this much pressure on myself?

What if he couldn't think of anything to say all night? What if he did, but everything he talked about bored her?

"Did you do anything interesting yesterday?" Shannon asked.

"Not really. I had to go pick up some friends at the airport with Lucy and Patrick; but other than that, I really just caught up on some homework and watched TV. You know, a basic college Saturday."

Shannon laughed. "I know."

"What about you?"

"Well, my father had a business dinner with some important family friends, so he asked me to come. It was boring; they just talked about finances and politics all night." She rolled her eyes. "But I stayed and listened because when you're the oldest child . . . "

"You've got to play the good daughter card. Right." He chuckled. "I'll do my best to be more interesting than whatever stuffed suits your dad works with."

"That shouldn't be hard." Shannon winked. "At least, you'll be easier to look at."

Asher's face flushed, and he kept his eyes on the road and hoped she didn't see.

So far, so good.

* * *

Although Jan didn't know it, Jarrett had taken their anniversary into consideration when he had packed for the trip to New Echelon. While she got ready in the bathroom, he opened his suitcase and took out a tailored white dress shirt, a red tie, and black slacks and dress shoes. He wished he hadn't gotten a gash on his forehead, but there was nothing to be done about that. He had cleaned it, and it wasn't deep enough to need stitches; so they would just have to pretend it wasn't there.

He tightened the tie around his neck, folded down his collar, and walked downstairs to wait for Jan. He had chosen this hotel intentionally—it had a five-star restaurant on the top floor that overlooked the city skyline. It was the perfect place for a romantic date, something the two of them needed in a bad way. He just hoped the Opera Mask Gang wasn't going to make a move tonight. If they were, they would see a side of Jarrett that he rarely let loose.

"Are you ready?" Jan called.

"Ready? For what?"

Jan stepped out of the bathroom. She was clad in a blue dress that fell to her ankles, its edges and curves sparkling in the gentle lamplight of the living room. As she moved, the colors seemed to bend around her like an electrical current. How Jan had managed to find a dress that perfectly represented her powers, Jarrett didn't know; but it was really working for her. After so many years together, his wife's beauty never ceased to stun him.

"Look at you," she said. "You clean up nice."

"Me?" Jarrett scoffed. "Look at you."

"Yeah, but . . . " Jan stepped in front of him and traced his jaw with her finger. "I'm looking at that cute farm boy who won my heart all those years ago, desperately trying to look like you belonged in the city."

Jarrett laughed. "I have always been more comfortable in the country."

"But you tried for me." Jan adjusted his tie, reached up and ran her hands through his lightly tousled hair. "And if I do say so, I think city life has treated you well."

Jarrett kissed her deeply. "Thank you. Shall we go?"

He held out the crook of his left arm, and she hooked her right arm through it.

"It would be my honor."

CHAPTER 26

"And then Mr. Paxton says, 'Oh-ho, not everyone can have a stake in the oil business, but really, Benjamin, choice beef?'" Shannon lowered her voice as deeply it would go, mocking one of the businessmen who had met with her father. "I wanted to hurl. Like seriously, just because we didn't have prime steak, it's like we offended his billionaire sensibilities or something."

Asher laughed over the shouting fans around them.

"I can't believe you know Joey Paxton's dad. What are the odds? I mean, the guy's my roommate, and his dad and your dad are business partners . . . It's crazy!"

"Small world, right?" Shannon sipped a large soda. "So Dad told him if he didn't like the cook's choice of meat, then maybe he should go cook his own. That took him down a peg."

What did I get myself into?

The more Asher talked to Shannon, the more he liked her; but he hadn't realized she came from such a wealthy family. To be rubbing elbows with Oscar Paxton like that—it was more than a little intimidating. What if Shannon's father didn't think Asher was good enough for her?

It didn't help that as she was talking about one of her father's associates mocking his choice of steak, they were eating hot dogs and popcorn. Why had she picked Asher out of the crowd, anyway? What had attracted her to him?

"Shannon . . . why me? There were dozens of guys at that party; and out of all of them, you came up to talk to me."

She smiled, her eyes practically glowing, and took his hand. "Because I know a genuine soul when I see one. All my life, I've been surrounded by either sycophantic boys who only want to date me so they can get in good with my father or guys just looking for a meaningless fling with a rich girl. I didn't want that. Never have."

"That's . . . very mature. And very down-to-earth for . . . "

"For a rich girl?"

Asher gaped. "I'm so sorry. I didn't—"

"It's okay. You're right. Honestly, I grew up around the rich and powerful; and for the most part, your assessment is accurate. It's why I want to go into politics. I can show people I know what I'm talking about, and I'm more than just a spoiled heiress."

Asher looked back up at her. The passion behind her eyes conveyed the truth of her words. She was amazing.

He smiled. "Wow, you sound like Joey."

"Oh, heaven forbid."

"Well, it's true. That's the whole reason Joey came to Echelon U. He wants to make a real life for himself."

"He thinks he does." Shannon sighed. "Joey is attracted to the idea of life outside of his family's bubble of protection. But when it comes down to it, he'll always have that cushion; and he'll always rely on it."

Asher frowned. "That seems kind of harsh."

"I'm sorry, I didn't mean to be rude. I know he's your friend, and I would never speak harshly of him. He and I had some good talks, back when we were young and forced to attend our fathers' meetings. I'm just afraid for him; I don't want him to fail."

Asher understood her concern. He often wondered how far Joey would make it. He had to help the rich young man with his homework so often that he feared if he weren't around, Joey would have no idea what to do. But Joey had determination. He just needed a push to take control of his own life and not rely solely on the help of others.

"Don't worry about it. I get it."

"While I'm apologizing . . . I didn't mean to be rude the other night when you asked me about my faith. It just wasn't a topic I was ready to broach; and like I said, it comes with some difficult baggage. But I like you, and I think you deserve an answer. I can see how important faith is to your life."

"Hey, I don't want to make you uncomfortable . . . "

"No, it's all right." She sat forward and looked him straight in the eyes. "The truth is, I was raised Catholic. My family was devout, going to Mass every week and confessionals as often as necessary. I didn't know anything else. But . . . all that changed one day when our priest . . . "

Shannon's eyes flitted away. Although the crowd continued to roar around them, it was almost like no one else was there. He felt like he and Shannon were the only two people in the world. Asher suspected he knew where this was going, and his heart broke for her. No one should be taken advantage of by someone they trusted, let alone a little girl.

"He took advantage of me." Shannon returned her gaze to Asher's. "As you can imagine, my family distanced themselves from church. After that . . . after that, religion didn't appeal to me much anymore. How could someone who claims to be a man of God do something as cruel as he did to me? I was ten. I barely even knew what was happening, but he didn't care."

"Shannon, I'm so sorry . . . "

"So, that's why I said that faith was a difficult subject for me. I find it hard to trust anyone in a position of religious authority. How can I, after that?"

"Shannon, I understand." Asher reached out and took her hand. "I see stories like that in the news all the time. Religious leaders—priests, pastors, whatever they call themselves—they're only human. A lot of times, because they're leaders, we act like they don't have to be accountable. It makes it easy for them to abuse their power."

"If people like that are the cream of the crop when it comes to faith . . . " She laughed and shook her head. "How could I ever give religion another chance?"

"I won't even begin to excuse that kind of evil. The way he hurt you is wrong, and it's inexcusable whether he had accountability or not." Asher forced himself to maintain eye contact with her as he spoke. "I understand your reservations. All I can say is, there's so much more to the faith I hold than wicked men pretending to be good. It can be life-changing . . . but I'd never try to force it on you. Take your time. If you ever want to talk about it, I'll be here."

Shannon sat back and looked down at her lap. "Thank you. That's a lot to think about."

"Hey, are you okay? I'm sorry, I hope I didn't overstep—"

"No, no, you didn't. I'm fine." Shannon wiped her eyes. "Let's just talk about something else for now. I promise I'll consider everything you said."

"I'm glad."

Hopefully, I didn't just kill my chances with her.

But if he had, at least he'd given her a push in the right direction.

* * *

"Jan and Jarrett seem so cool," Lucy said. "I mean, can you imagine? They're both heroes. Jarrett doesn't have powers, but he fights crime and works for the government; and Jan can manipulate electricity. And they seem so perfectly in sync."

Patrick nodded as he took a bite of a tortilla chip covered in salsa. "It's really cool to see. Of course, I worked with Jarrett in the Vindicators, but I only met Jan briefly."

"Maybe that will be us one day."

"Something like that." Patrick smiled. "Of course, it'll be a little different—Jan's the one with powers who doesn't really do much physical action, while Jarrett is powerless but fights all the crime. Of course, I'll be fighting the crime with my powers, but I could never do it without your help."

"Right. But, I mean, me not having powers doesn't mean I have to stay behind all the time. I'm not saying I'd actually fight with you, but . . . "

"But what?"

Lucy knew she and Patrick would inevitably have to talk about her outing at the docks. She hoped he didn't get upset and overprotective. After all, she'd never been in any danger. The police had been there all along, and she'd never come close to any criminals. She'd just done some investigative work.

"But I can help in the field in other ways." Lucy shrugged. "For example, the reason Jarrett even knew who to look for today was because of some legwork I did after church. I poked around the docks, found some clues, and sent the information to Jarrett."

"Really?" Patrick considered, and then nodded. "Nice work."

"Wait . . . for real?"

She'd been expecting a blowup, followed by some speech about how he "couldn't do his job right as long as he was worried about her potentially putting herself in danger out there," and how foolish it had been for her to do that. After all, even Jarrett had given her a gentle dressing down. Was he really okay with this?

"I have superspeed. Even if you get in trouble, I can be there in seconds."

I hope he's not fooling himself.

Patrick was assuming that he would get his powers back. Lucy hoped he would; and she believed if anyone could do it, it was Jan. But he was taking for granted that it would ever happen. She hoped he wasn't ignoring the fear that he might not regain his superspeed. That could be just as harmful as clinging to that fear and exploding about it to everyone. She didn't need to bring that up tonight, though.

"I guess you're right. I'm glad you understand."

"I do. I guess I'm just curious about why, though. I mean, you've never mentioned wanting to go out and do field work before. What brought this on?"

"It's . . . been a long time coming, I think. Sitting in my room and doing nothing but talking to you while you're out there darting around and saving the day is tough. And I don't think it was until today that I realized that what I wanted wasn't for you to stop being Spright; it was for me to be able to help you more."

Patrick smiled at that. "Well, I'm more than happy to accept your help."

* * *

"When was the last time we did this?" Jarrett asked. "I mean, had dinner together in a scenario that wasn't a quick dine-and-dash or a few stolen moments in the cafeteria at CLOUD base? I really can't remember."

"Neither can I." Jan stared out the window at the city skyline. "It's been too long."

She was thrilled that Jarrett had put so much effort into the date. It showed that he had thought it out in advance, even before she had mentioned it in the hotel room the night they arrived. As much as this had been a trip to help Patrick, she now realized that he also wanted a getaway for the two of them. The fact that he had bothered to pack a dress shirt and tie was proof of that.

It was a nice change of pace. Jarrett was a dedicated man, very focused on his job. He didn't neglect her; but he took his work very seriously, both as a CLOUD agent and a vigilante. And if Jan was honest, she was equally intense when it came to her own work. And now that she had powers, she was still learning how to fit in at CLOUD, both as a scientist and a part-time field agent. They were both busy, and no one would blame them for skimping on their alone time. And for a while, that was how it had been.

But Jan knew where that road led. She had seen it in her brother and his wife, both just as dedicated to their work as Jan and Jarrett. Nothing nearly as interesting, of course—Jan's brother was a CPA and his wife a teacher. But they had been so busy with their respective jobs that they had lost time for each other. It had broken Jan's heart when they filed for divorce. That would never happen to her and Jarrett. She had determined as much in that moment. But that didn't mean that things didn't occasionally get stretched between them. They just had to learn to love each other despite those things.

"It's a beautiful city," Jan said. "You'd never know looking at it from here that its streets are so overrun with crime."

"You think this is beautiful, you should see Sojourn City sometime. I wasn't there for long, but the view from the Vindicators' tower?" Jarrett whistled. "It was astounding."

Jan laughed. "Astounding? When have you ever used that word before?"

"Well, right now, for one. What? You think just because I'm a muscle-bound farm boy, I don't know any big words?"

"Okay, that's not what I said." Jan stifled her continued laughter, so she wouldn't disturb the other guests in the five-star restaurant. "It's just a new word for you, that's all."

"Okay." Jarrett smirked. "Whatever you say."

They lapsed into silence as they ate their meal—a mouth-watering collection of lobster, shrimp, vegetables, and foods that Jan could only dream of finding back in Kansas. Every bite caused an explosion of flavor in her mouth, and she ate slowly to savor each one.

"Do you think superpowers are genetic?" Jarrett asked.

"What do you mean?"

"I mean, will someone with powers pass those powers down to their kids?"

Jan considered. "I think the chances of that are very high, yes. The superpowers given by Ashcroft's serum are the result of a mutation to the recipient's DNA, effectively changing them from human to—what did the Vindicators call it? A Nephilim? That DNA would be passed on to the child. So statistically, it would be likely for the child to develop powers."

"Interesting. So even though Ashcroft's serum only affected a few hundred people, within a few generations, the world could have thousands of superhumans."

"That's the future we're looking at." Jan tilted her head. "What made you think about that?"

"Oh. I was just thinking about children."

Jan smiled sadly. She and Jarrett had never had time for kids. They had tried before he left for the army with no success. After he returned, the timing was never right. They were still young and could still theoretically have children; but as busy as they both were, she still didn't know if the timing was right.

"Do you want kids?"

"I don't know . . . " Jarrett drummed his fingers on the table. "Maybe. I know why it might not be the best idea right now, but . . . "

"I know. Me, too." Jan would've loved a houseful of kids, but she didn't want to neglect them, either. "Maybe in a few years, once all the chaos surrounding the new superhumans has died down some; we could take some time away from CLOUD and start a family. But with how much is going on right now, we just couldn't risk it."

"Yeah." Jarrett picked up his glass of water. "I know. Sorry, I didn't mean to . . . bring down the mood."

"You didn't, love."

She reached across the table and ran a finger across the back of his hand. "Tell you what. Let's finish up here and go back to the room."

"All right." Jarrett raised a finger, gesturing for their waiter. "Check, please."

CHAPTER 27

As Ty awoke, he found his head resting on a pillow—rough and lumpy, but far better than the floor he had been on since Ben's people "rescued" him. His body was splayed out on an air mattress, and a soft blanket covered him from abdomen to toe. He rolled over and sat up, running a hand through his sleep-tousled hair. It was dark, almost pitch-black, just as it had been in the basement of Ben's hideout. At least, he was free and comfortable—for a few more hours, at least. Then, it was back to his cell.

He did not love the idea of going back to prison, but it was the only way he could ever have a free life with Emi someday. And Carter had risked a lot to leave Sojourn City and come halfway across the country looking for Ty. Ty was willing to pay back that generosity.

Ben's words about the Sicarans gnawed at the back of Ty's mind, though. Regardless of his intentions, Ben was probably right. The Sicarans did have a reason to hunt Ty, and they did not seem like the kind of people who would be squeamish about hurting innocents. If they had a chance to target Emi because of Ty, they would do it. Could Ty really stop that by helping Ben fight the Sicarans?

For a moment, Ty was tempted to phase out and find his way back to Ben. Emi's safety was most important to him—even more important than actually being with her. Maybe hunting Sicarans meant Ty could never be with her again; but if he knew she was safe, it might be worth it.

On the other hand, if Ben was with Charybdis, Ty was unsure that his side was any better. He still did not know what hand Charybdis had played in his parents' deaths, but Liang had worked for Charybdis. With Mac Tíre's dying words still ringing in his ears, Ty knew that Liang had betrayed the Watanabes. Did that mean Charybdis was actually behind his parents' deaths, not the Sicarans? It certainly seemed that way to Ty. But the Sicarans were enemies, too. Ty could not trust either side.

And even if he did trust Charybdis, going back to Ben would mean betraying Carter. Why did Ty care so much about the young vigilante? Carter was the one who had convinced Ty to turn himself in. But he was also the one who had found a home for Emi, offered Ty a Bible, reached out to Joanie for help, came to Ty's rescue . . . for some reason, Carter cared about him. Could Ty really betray that kind of loyalty by running back to Ben?

No. Ty shook the thought away. He had made his choice. He was staying—staying with Carter, of course. Not in another musty basement. The basement he now occupied looked like it had been recently cleaned, though, and decorated like a hideout of some sort to boot. Carter had given Ty minimal information about the location, other than that it was a safe place that Ben and his cohorts would never find.

Footsteps shuffled on the upper ring around the alcove Ty was in. He frowned at the shape of the room. An empty swimming pool, perhaps? It was an odd layout. Carter mounted a set of wide steps leading down into the pool.

"Morning," Carter said. "Our ride's here, so we're set to leave whenever you're ready."

He tossed Ty a bundle. Ty snatched it out of the air and unwrapped it. It contained a fresh set of clothes, a stick of deodorant, a comb, and a bottle of water.

"If you want, you can get an actual shower," Carter continued. "We're on a college campus, so I can arrange to sneak you into my friend's dorm room. I bet you haven't had a nice warm shower in a while."

Ty chuckled. "I haven't. And it's been even longer since I had one where I didn't have to watch my back the whole time."

"Well, let's get you up there. Then we'll see about going home."

"Right." Ty pressed his lips together and nodded. "Home."

* * *

Beep! Beep! Beep!

The screeching wail of Patrick's alarm filled the bedroom like a panicked bird trapped in a cage with a pack of predators. Patrick's eyes snapped open; and he shot up in bed, scrambling for the device.

Shut up!

He found the phone and jammed his thumb down hard on the screen, and the room was blessedly silent.

That's the thing about smartphones. You can't really turn them off angrily.

He'd never had a flip phone—they were before his time—but the thought of clapping the thing shut was much more satisfying than an angry tap on the screen. Grunting, he hauled himself out of bed, glancing at the time on the screen as he did.

Oh, shoot.

He had five minutes before class started. He sped across the room only to slam face-first into the door. Groaning, he stumbled back and collapsed to the floor in a heap.

Right. Jan had said not to use his powers yet. His mind couldn't keep up with his body.

"You all right, man?" Hands fell on his shoulders and helped him stand. "That looked rough."

"Yeah, I'm . . . " Patrick blinked as he recognized his helper. "Carter!"

Carter grinned. "Hey, man."

They laughed and pulled each other into a back-slapping hug. A wave of relief rolled through Patrick knowing that Carter had not left yet. He might have to soon; but at least, they had a few minutes. A few minutes . . .

Oh man. My class!

Patrick walked to his wardrobe and got ready as fast as humanly possible. He realized the shower was running, and he wondered if Bryce was also running late or if Carter's missing person was using Patrick's shower. Either way, he did not have time to find out. He hurriedly pulled on a shirt and glanced at Carter.

"Hate to say hey and run, but I'm late for class."

"No biggie. I get it. Looks like you're doing better emotionally, though."

"I am." Patrick hopped up and down as he pulled his pants on. "And I heard you found your guy."

"I did. He's showering now. We'll probably head back to Sojourn City in a few hours; but if you have time around noon, maybe we could grab lunch before we go."

Patrick raised an eyebrow.

"Lunch. With a super-criminal."

"He's cool." Carter chuckled. "I'll explain everything then."

The walk across campus was surprisingly lonely. Everyone else was already in class or still sleeping because they had a later class.

Patrick trudged across the lawn and tugged open the door to the Masterson building.

Time to power through the stairs.

Patrick made his way through the building to the stairwell, climbed them with effort, and ducked into his classroom. Rick met his gaze as he entered and stopped lecturing.

"Ah, Patrick. Feeling better?"

"Hmm?"

"Lucy said you were sick yesterday; that's why you weren't at church."

"Oh. Yeah. I'm . . . getting better." He forced a smile. "Don't worry, I'm not contagious or anything."

The class chuckled. Patrick dropped into the chair and pulled out a notebook and pen. But as Rick lectured, he found his mind wandering from the class and to what was, in his mind, a much more urgent situation. He couldn't keep this up. He needed his powers back. He'd go back to the Mercers' hotel tonight and have Jan finish the therapy.

What if it didn't work, though? What if he was stuck without his powers forever? His thoughts went back to the dream of his grandfather—being scared or angry wouldn't change his situation. There was no reason to worry about it until he knew for sure. But how? How could he keep from worrying when something so monumental in his life could be changing forever?

" . . . and in practicality, the effectiveness of a youth ministry can be measured . . . "

And what about the Opera Mask Gang? Who was going to stop them if Patrick didn't get his powers back? Sure, Jarrett had some skills, but could he handle three superhumans on his own? Even if Jan helped him—and Patrick was unsure how much combat experience she had, if any—they would still be outnumbered three to two. Patrick had never had to worry about numbers; his speed gave him the advantage even when he faced poor odds.

Maybe he had nothing to worry about. The Opera Mask Gang hadn't shown up in the news the day before, so maybe they were lying low until everything blew over. Patrick knew they would pop back up eventually—if not in New Echelon then somewhere else—and someone would take them down, but he would prefer to do it himself. He had never faced an amplified opponent without at least one of the Vindicators at his side. He wanted to prove that Spright had the same mettle they did.

The thoughts continued to haunt him until Rick finished his lecture. Patrick looked down at his notebook. He had only written two lines of notes, and even they were vague. He had no idea what his teacher had said; his thoughts had been consumed with his powers. Patrick slammed his book shut, stuffed it in his backpack, and zipped it up as the other students rose and filed out of the classroom.

"Hey, Patrick," Rick said. "Is everything all right? You seemed distant today. Well, more distant than usual. Normally, I can tell your attention is here, even when it looks like you're a million miles away. Today, it was like your body was in the classroom, but you were . . . anywhere but here."

"Sorry, sir." Patrick searched for an excuse. "It's this superhero stuff."

"Well, don't get too stressed about it, all right? It's just an assignment."

Patrick stepped out into the hallway and exhaled. That was too close. He walked away from Rick's classroom and pulled his phone from his pocket. He had a text from Bryce.

Meet me in the lounge after class.

He pushed the doors open, stepped outside, and jogged across campus toward the lounge, zipping his jacket up to the collar as he did. Fall was on the way. Patrick appreciated a break from the heat, but he had never been a fan of the cold. At least, New Echelon's cold was nowhere near Sojourn City's cold; while he stayed with the Vindicators, he had feared hypothermia every time he stepped outside.

Patrick walked into the student center and looked around. The cafeteria was to his left, the student lounge down the hall and to the right. Patrick followed the latter course and found Bryce waiting outside the lounge. As Patrick approached, his roommate scanned the hallway before gesturing for Patrick to follow him and walking farther down the hall. Patrick had never gone this way before, but he thought it led to the janitor's closet.

"Where are we going?"

"Shh." Bryce held a finger to his lips. "This needs to be on the DL."

Patrick raised an eyebrow and looked off into the distance, shrugging at no one in particular, confused by his friend's sudden secrecy. This had to be about Spright, he assumed; but he didn't know where Bryce could be taking him that would be relevant. His confusion grew as Bryce stopped at a door next to the janitor's closet, which was marked "No Entry," and took out a key ring.

"Where did you get all those keys?"

"I work in IT, remember? I have to get into lots of places where students aren't allowed." He began unlocking the door. "Such as the student center basement."

Bryce opened the door and made a grand sweeping gesture with his left arm, motioning for Patrick to enter. Patrick stepped forward and looked down the dark stairwell before him, the concrete steps looking like they had been poured long before the rest of the school had existed—possibly before the rest of New Echelon had existed. Patrick looked around to make sure no one was watching and then descended into the darkness of the basement. Bryce shone his phone light in after Patrick and then shut the door behind them.

Patrick's feet met the basement landing. He shuffled around to ensure he wasn't still on a step, so he wouldn't fall and crack his head open on his next step. Bryce's light lowered as he reached the bottom of the steps, too, illuminating the floor and proving that Patrick was, as he'd suspected, at the bottom. Bryce stepped past him, opened a breaker box, and flipped a switch. As the lights in the basement came to light, Patrick looked around . . . and whistled.

"Dude. This is awesome."

The basement, apparently, had been an underground swimming pool. The area around the pool had been spray-painted with concentric lines that resembled a runner's track. The interior of the pool itself had been filled with a tool chest nearly as tall as Patrick, as well as several tables, one of which housed a computer. It was sparse, but it had potential.

"I didn't know how much gear you had, so I brought the extra tables so we could store bigger stuff. That tool chest there is for your smaller stuff—assuming you have any. I don't know, I'm just working with what little I know about superheroes. And I painted out this track so you could just . . . run."

"I love it." Patrick grinned. "At least I won't have to operate out of our room—or my car—anymore. You don't think we'll get caught down here, do you?"

"Nah. Even maintenance workers don't come down here. And I'm working on installing a spy cam outside the door, so we can check that the hallway's clear before we exit. Should help us avoid getting found out. I know there's still a lot of work to do before it's a real superhero's lair, but I thought I could get you started, at least."

"It's definitely a start." Patrick turned and pulled Bryce into a backslapping hug. "Thank you, man. This means a lot. We need to get Lucy and Asher down here ASAP—they're going to want to see this."

"Sweet. Team Spright's first lair meeting!"

"Don't . . . don't do that." Patrick shook his head. "Don't use the word 'meeting.' It makes it sound boring."

"Sorry. Uh . . . first lair strategy session?"

"We'll work on it." Patrick chuckled. "Come on, let's go find Lucy and show her what you've been working on."

Anything, he thought, to keep his mind off the possibility that his powers would remain dormant.

CHAPTER 28

"It's time," Anton said. "Remember the plan."

Darius' leg bobbed against the floorboard of the van as they circled the bank, looking for a discreet place to park. Anton had concocted a plan for robbing the bank, and he spent the past day drilling it into his siblings. They both knew their roles; but judging by Zee's creased brow, she was as uncertain as Darius.

Anton's plan hinged on Darius going in first and lulling the place into a sense of rest, as he had at the college party. Once everyone inside was either asleep or compliant, Anton would come in and speak to one of the tellers, ordering them to empty the registers into his bag. Zee would keep watch by the door, using her powers to keep a lookout for anyone who might try to hit a silent alarm or call the cops. If it all went smoothly, they should be in and out in less than ten minutes.

The problem that Darius had come across was that if he entered without his mask, the security cameras would get a good look at him; and once everyone came out of their emotional fuzz, they could give the footage to the cops. On the other hand, if he went in wearing his mask, it would alert the employees; and he might not be able to calm them down before they called for help. He would have to get the timing just right to pull this off.

Anton pulled the van into an alley half a block away from the bank. Darius looked down at the golden mask in his hands, its sullen expression appropriate for his own mood. There was a lot of risk to this plan; but if they didn't do it, the odds were good that the Archdukes or the Seventy-Six would find them sooner than later—and then they'd be dead, anyway. This was their best option for getting out of New Echelon in one piece.

How did it come to this?

When Darius had awakened in the hospital and discovered his powers, he never would have guessed that he would use them to help his brother rob a bank because it was their only hope for survival.

"You've got this." Anton put his hand on Darius's shoulder. "Just keep your head down; don't engage. Everything will be fine. We're going to get out of here and start up a new life in a place where the gangs will never find us. We'll set ourselves up for a good life."

Darius licked his lips, nodded, and tucked the mask under his gray fleece jacket. He would pull his hood up, keep his head down until the bank's occupants were disabled to make sure the cameras didn't catch his face, and then pull the mask on. There was still a risk that a bystander could catch a glimpse of his face, but this was a bank robbery. Nothing about it was risk-free.

Anton's grip tightened. "Two minutes. Then Zee and I are right behind you."

"And remember," Zee added, "No names from here on out. We wouldn't want to get caught because someone overheard us calling each other."

Darius—*Infuser*, he reminded himself—stilled his bouncing leg and opened the door. *Don't think twice.*

He hopped out of the van, slammed the door behind him, and pulled his hood up as he exited the alley. Infuser kept his head low, only raising it enough to see across the street to the bank. His right hand, tucked in his jacket pocket, brushed the gun that he'd tucked there—the same one he'd fired at the Seventy-Six just nights ago. It was for emergencies only—or so he told himself. Its presence both comforted and terrified him. Looking both ways, Infuser crossed the street and bounded up the steps to the bank's front door. Ducking inside the building, he moved to a corner and stared at the floor.

The bank was full. There were at least two dozen patrons, not to mention nearly a dozen employees. It was a lot of people to influence at once, but he'd done it at the college party; he could do it again. Reaching out psychically, Infuser touched each mind and began to pour out relaxing vibes. He imagined soft piano music, the sound of a babbling brook, gentle rainfall on a rooftop as he drifted to sleep. The imagined sounds slowed his heart rate and calmed him, and he poured those same feelings out to each person in the bank.

Someone dropped into one of the comfortable chairs in the waiting area. Another yawned. Darius reached into his jacket and wrapped his fingers around the edge of his mask. A few more seconds, and he should be able to pull it on without alerting anyone; they'd be too calm to react.

One, two, three.

He removed the mask, placed it over his face, and adjusted his hood to ensure it still covered his telltale red hair. Scanning the bank, he confirmed that everyone inside had succumbed to the emotional repression.

The door swung open behind him. He turned to face it as Anton and Zee—Negator and Sensory—entered. Sensory stayed by the door, while Negator stormed across the bank toward the nearest teller. He had his concussion sword strapped to his back. Infuser hoped he didn't lose his temper and use the weapon. Even Infuser's powers wouldn't calm the kind of panic that would create. Infuser extended the reach of his power, subtly touching his brother's mind, just enough to keep him placid.

"Your drawer," Negator said. "Open it."

He hoisted a duffel bag and dropped it on the counter. The teller on the other side looked at the bag, and her eyes widened slightly; but that was the only reaction she could manage under the weight of Infuser's power. As she complied with Negator's instructions, Infuser glanced over his shoulder at Sensory. Her gaze was fixed on the steps outside. So far, they were in the clear.

"Next!" Negator shouted. "Open the drawer."

"Someone's coming," Sensory called.

"Infuser! Mute 'em."

Infuser strode toward the door, ready to expand his powers to calm whomever was about to enter the bank. As he did, Sensory swiveled around and gestured toward the tellers.

"They're getting nervous."

"The money!" Negator shouted. "Now!"

"Negator, calm down. You're riling them up."

"Don't tell me what to do! *Open that drawer!*"

Infuser grimaced in concentration and poured out more calming vibes; but his own center was wavering, nervousness building as the situation spiraled out of control. He pressed harder on Negator's emotions, trying to force down his anger, pushing aside all subtlety and hammering at his brother.

"What are you doing?" Negator roared. "Not me!"

The door swung open, and someone gasped. Infuser spun around. The woman who had just entered the bank held her hands to her mouth, stifling a scream. Sensory stepped toward her and grabbed her forearm, pulling her inside the bank. Infuser turned his head back and forth from her to Negator, who was still shouting at the teller. It was too much; the flurry of emotions was too difficult to dampen.

"We need to go!"

"No! Not until we have what we need." Negator drew his sword. "Now give me the money and do it faster!"

The woman who'd just entered screamed at the sight of the weapon. The concentration Infuser had already been struggling to maintain broke. He dropped to his knees, the exertion of energy overwhelming him. Several more screams joined that of the newcomer. Someone was at his side now—his sister.

"Are you okay?"

He nodded. "We need to go."

He heard Negator growl incoherently.

Oh no.

The sudden ripples of fear coursing through the room would feed Negator's power, especially now that Infuser wasn't dampening his emotions. Pushing himself to his feet, Infuser staggered toward his brother.

"Negator, you need to calm down."

"I'll calm down when I have all the money!"

"He's giving you the money! Look!"

The teller had, indeed, been shoveling stacks of cash into the duffel bag, but Negator's outburst had caused him to recoil. He sat in his chair, trembling, his eyes fixed on the massive sword in the hands of the maniac robbing his bank.

"P-please. Don't hurt us."

"Shut. Up!"

Negator slammed his sword into the ground, and a shockwave rolled through the bank. Infuser cried out as his feet left the ground, carried by the force of the blast the sword delivered. And then everything devolved into chaos.

CHAPTER 29

"Wow," Lucy said. "This is . . . *wow.*"

When Bryce said he would work on finding a hideout for Team Spright, Lucy had never expected the results to come so quickly, let alone this extravagantly. The fact that he had found an ideal place actually on campus, which wouldn't be discovered accidentally by any other student and was big enough to suit their needs, was almost too good to be true.

"Okay, Bryce, I'm glad I didn't have Jarrett kill you."

Bryce chuckled nervously and scratched the back of his head. "Thanks. Wait . . . who's Jarrett?"

"I am."

Bryce yelped and spun around. Lucy smirked. Jarrett and Jan descended the stairway into the basement and looked around. Jarrett was carrying a briefcase with him. He raised an eyebrow and looked at Bryce, who was fiddling nervously with his glasses.

"Who's this?"

"My name's Bryce Emerson." He extended his hand. "Nice to meet you."

"Okay . . . " Jarrett shook Bryce's hand. "Honestly, this isn't a bad setup. Could use a little bit of work, but for a bunch of college students? Not bad at all."

"One college student." Bryce grinned sheepishly. "I set this all up myself."

"No one likes a braggart, Bryce." Jarrett descended into the pool. "But good job."

Jan and Patrick followed Jarrett down; and Lucy went after them, patting Bryce on the shoulder as she passed him. The guy was just trying to help. She'd been hard on him at first, but it was obvious that they could trust him.

Footsteps clunked on the stairs. "Hello?"

Lucy recognized Asher's voice. "Come on down!"

Lucy poked her head over the edge of the pool as Asher entered the basement. He looked around and whistled. Lucy gestured for him to join the rest of them in the pool and then walked over to Patrick's side. Everyone was here now. Carter had entered the basement at the same time Lucy arrived with his . . . friend? Prisoner?

"We can finish my therapy here, right?" Patrick asked.

Jarrett and Jan exchanged glances. This was the part Lucy had been dreading—the moment Patrick realized that they couldn't continue therapy yet.

"Patrick," Jan said, "we need more time. I don't know what your brain patterns should look like as a speedster. If I go in half-cocked, I could kill you or cause irreversible damage to your brain. I'm not saying we won't continue the therapy, but we do need to wait until I have a better handle on what I'm doing."

Lucy took Patrick's hand. He would need comfort. If he started to get belligerent, she could give him a quick squeeze to bring him back.

Patrick took a deep breath. "How long?"

"Realistically, I can't give you an estimate." Jan shook her head. "If we had another speedster to compare brain scans with, we could move faster; but we don't. I'm sorry."

Before Patrick could respond, Jarrett spoke up. "Until then, we've got some things to help you get by."

He set his briefcase on one of the tables Bryce had placed in the pool. Jarrett popped the case open and turned it to face Patrick. Inside was a plethora of technology. Lucy could guess the use of some of the items, but she had never seen anything like some of the others.

"What's this?" Patrick asked.

"Tech. If Carter and I can fight crime without powers, you can, too—at least for a little while."

Lucy watched Patrick as he studied the gear in the briefcase. His brow was furrowed, and his posture was tense. He was deeply upset, and she understood why. For two years, his powers had probably been the biggest part of him. Running at supersonic speed had been, for him, just another bodily function. Not using it would be tremendously difficult.

"I'm not trained like you and Carter. You have Special Forces and CLOUD training, and Carter learned martial arts from Gideon. I don't have any of that."

"I'll teach you. And I know it's only temporary, but you should still know how to handle yourself without powers."

Carter nodded. "We can do this together, man. I didn't realize how bad you had it. I'm sorry for not asking sooner. Tell you what—I'll get Ty back to Sojourn City; and then I'll come back here, and we'll get you trained up right."

"Okay." Patrick pulled his hand gently from Lucy's and reached toward the case. "What do we have?"

"You're familiar with Sterling Enterprises' adhesive beads?" Jarrett held up a marble-sized sphere. "These are new and improved, courtesy of CLOUD. Sterling's beads could hold anyone of normal strength and ability; but these have been upgraded so the adhesive gel is unbreakable, even by someone with super strength. It has a breaking point of up to two tons."

Lucy whistled. For someone to break out of that adhesive, they'd have to be impossibly strong. She knew Patrick had faced super-strong villains before, but that kind of strength was all but unheard of.

"Jealous," Carter muttered. "I need some of those."

Jarrett smirked before continuing. "And then, of course, we've got your run-of-the-mill listening devices, GPS trackers—all that good stuff. And these will be especially important for the bad guys we're chasing—neural dampeners. They'll block out the Opera Mask Gang's psychic attacks. But the real cream of the crop? These babies."

He held up a pair of black bars, approximately three inches long, each of which had four holes through the sides. They looked like the brass knuckles Lucy had seen criminals use. But they were not metal, and the ends of them were not sharpened or ridged. Instead, each knuckle had a small, grooved circle in place of a spike.

"Shock rings," Jarrett said.

He placed one of the devices over his left hand and squeezed that hand into a fist. The four circles lit up blue, crackling with energy. He turned and punched an empty table, and volts of electricity rippled across its surface.

Carter's jaw was agape. "Silas has been holding out on me. I need to get a set of those!"

"Nice," Patrick said. "That could be useful even when I get my powers back."

Jarrett nodded. "But for now, they'll give you the edge you need to survive."

Patrick's phone—and then Jarrett's—sounded an alarm.

The police alert system.

There was a crime in progress somewhere in New Echelon. Lucy felt her heart drop. With this gear in front of him, there was no reason for Patrick to sit this one out. He couldn't use his powers, but there was no way he would wait here while Jarrett went out there alone.

"Looks like it's time to give this stuff a test run." Jarrett handed Patrick the shock ring. "Suit up. This city needs to see that Spright isn't out of the game."

* * *

Riding shotgun in a car on the way to a crime scene was a new and uncomfortable feeling for Patrick, to say the least. He was usually the first one on the scene, a streak of purple dashing in to save the day and stop the bad guys. Even when he was with the Vindicators, he had been the first responder in many situations.

He wondered how he must've looked to anyone outside the car—he was already wearing his black-and-purple suit, mask and all, but he was just sitting in the passenger's seat, waiting for their arrival at the bank before he could do anything. It had to have been surreal for anyone who noticed.

Surreal . . . and awkward, if I happen to look up and make eye contact.

"Been a while since I foiled a bank robbery," Carter said from the back seat. "Funny. I first got on Ty's trail because he robbed a bank."

Patrick glanced over his shoulder. "Speaking of Ty, are you sure it's safe to leave him in the lair with my friends?"

"Don't worry. He'll behave. He's got too much to lose if he doesn't."

Jarrett turned the car onto a side road. "Carter and I will take the lead on this one. I don't have time for a full tutorial, but I can tell you that you should still be able to use your powers to enhance the speed of your punches—not too much, or you'll risk breaking your arm, but enough to give you the added *oomph* you'll need."

"I think I can do that." Patrick slid the shock rings over his fingers. "Any idea what else we should be expecting?"

"No clue. Lucy said the Opera Mask Gang killed some gangsters using at least one gun and sword, though, so keep your eyes out for that." Jarrett swung the car around another corner. "Like I said, let Carter and I take the lead. I trust you, but I don't want you getting hurt. Use the openings you see; work with me on this, and we'll get these guys."

Four police cruisers sat parked on the street ahead. Jarrett pulled to the side of the road, parked the car, and jumped out, unslinging his crossbow as he slammed the door shut. Patrick stepped out onto the sidewalk and followed Yeoman. Wiggling his fingers to adjust them to the feel of the shock rings, Spright looked up at the bank in front of them and then at the officers stationed behind their cars. The Crusader patted Spright on the shoulder as he stepped past, his staff already in hand.

"What's the situation?" Yeoman asked.

An officer looked up. "Hey! It's you. The, uh, archer guy."

"It's Yeoman." He sighed. "Good to see you again, Officer Gregg."

"You, too." The police officer looked over Yeoman's shoulder. "Hey! It's Spright! It's been a few days since you've been on the streets."

Spright nodded. "Had a little . . . hiccup . . . but I'm back."

"That's good. And you've got the Crusader, too, huh?"

Yeoman scowled. "Oh, come on."

Gregg shrugged. "Anyway, three wackos in opera masks went into the bank and started demanding money. One of 'em waves a sword around, and it causes a massive explosion that sends everyone into a panic. One of the tellers hit a silent alarm, but we didn't really need it at that point, considering the explosion alerted everyone outside the bank."

"They're still inside?" the Crusader asked.

"Yep. Good thing, too; whatever modifications that sword has, it's more than we're equipped to handle. I'm glad you guys showed up, because if we had to go at them alone, this would've gotten ugly."

"We'll take care of it." Yeoman looked up at the bank's façade. "But we can't just go in the front door. They'll start killing hostages, or, at best, start a shootout. Then they'll get caught in the crossfire. Either way, a lot of people would die if we did that."

"Any side doors?" Spright asked.

"There's an employee-only entrance on the west side," Gregg said, "but that presents the same problem. You go in through there, and you'll come out behind the teller windows. They'll still see you coming."

If only I had my powers.

Spright could've darted in the front door and taken out all three Opera Masks before they knew he was there, or he could've rescued the hostages in a blink and left the Opera Mask Gang without leverage.

"We're looking pretty short on options," Yeoman said. "What about a rooftop entrance? We could cut in and drop down on them, take them by surprise."

Patrick stroked his chin. "Still runs the risk of crossfire casualties."

"The only realistic way to take these guys out without hurting the hostages is a sniper." Gregg gestured to a rooftop across the street.

"We've got one at the ready, but we were hoping to pursue less lethal options. It's never a good day to fill out the reports that come with shooting three people."

Carter ran a hand over his head. "There must be some way to get them out of there."

"Why can't you run in and do it, Spright?" Gregg asked. "Aren't you fast enough?"

Spright grimaced beneath his mask, thankful that the officer couldn't see the expression. "Yeah. About that—"

A gust of wind blew past them, trailing a red streak that appeared out of nowhere. Spright stumbled back, knocked off-balance by the force of the blast, and landed on one knee. Gregg and the other officers raised their weapons and trained them on the bank, while Yeoman looked back at Spright.

"What was that?" Spright asked.

Yeoman stared. "I think that was another speedster."

* * *

Paxton was right. The Coleman triplets had not waited long to make their move. Friction had been going about her daily business when Paxton alerted her to the in-progress robbery being perpetrated by three suspects in opera masks. In a flash, Friction changed into her super suit and sped across town to the scene of the crime.

As she ascended the stairs toward the bank, she noticed a trio of costumed men standing with a police officer. One of them she didn't recognize; he wore a brown-and-blue costume and carried a crossbow. The second, a red-clad black man, looked familiar. The third, though, was as distinct to the New Echelon and San Francisco area as the Seraph was to Sojourn City.

Spright.

A rush of excitement surged through Friction's body. She might actually get to work side-by-side with Spright—the first speedster superhero and her idol. Ever since she started training, she had looked up to Spright. And here he was. After what Paxton said about the Masks "taking him out," she was worried she might never get the opportunity.

She didn't have time to think about it, though. She had to focus on the task at hand. If Spright joined in, even better; but either way, she would go in and take down the Coleman siblings. She wondered how Paxton wanted her to deal with them once she incapacitated them. Would she turn them over to the police? She had to assume that was what he would want. Still, she had to get clear instructions from him once the job was done. For now, she needed to take them down before anyone got hurt.

The world moved in slow motion around her as she reached the top of the steps leading up to the bank. The front doors and windows had been completely blown out, leaving a trail of glass shards that crunched underfoot as Friction approached the bank. Then she was through the door. Hostages were lined around the room, and the biggest of the Coleman siblings—Anton, she had no doubt—stood in the middle of the room, a large high-tech sword gripped in his right hand. The other two stood in the back corner, heads pressed together as though they were talking in secret. Darius clumsily held a gun while Zee was unarmed.

Friction darted across the room, snatched the gun from Darius's hand, and returned to the middle of the room, taking the gun apart as the world returned to normal speed. The fragments of the gun clattered to the floor, and Friction spread her hands. Darius stumbled to the floor, tugged forward by the force of Friction's pull. Anton turned to face her and growled, the sound coming from beneath the angry visage of his opera mask.

"Who are you?"

"The name's Friction. I'm here to make sure you don't hurt anyone ever again."

"Enough with the theatrics," Paxton said in her earbud. "Take them down—quickly!"

"Friction, huh?" The voice came from behind her. "I kinda like it."

She turned. Spright and the other two vigilantes stood in the broken door frames. The archer had his crossbow trained on Anton; and the red-clad man was crouched with his staff at the ready, while Spright stood casually, sparks popping around his knuckles.

Has he always been able to do that?

Then she processed what Spright had said and beamed.

"Thank you!"

"You want names?" Anton rumbled. "Mine's Negator. And I'm about to take all three of you down!"

He raised his sword and drove the blade toward the floor. Friction sped up; and once again, everything else slowed down. She ran toward Anton as his sword came ever closer to the gray-tiled floor of the bank. She reached him in half a second, grabbed his wrist, and turned it aside. Before he could react, she slammed her fist into his jaw and darted behind him to kick the back of his knee. That knee sagged to the floor, and Anton crouched there. His sword fell—and as the tip struck the floor, another concussion blast detonated.

Friction grunted as the full force of the blast struck her. Her feet left the ground; and she flew back and slammed into a cubicle, knocking its wall over onto the desk it surrounded. Her ribs screamed in protest, and she rolled off the fallen cubicle and into a crouch. Anton, clutching his wrist, reached unsteadily for the sword.

"Don't do it!" The archer stepped forward, an arrow at the ready. "Not another inch."

"Infuser!" Anton shouted. "Ramp up the fear."

Ignoring the pain in her ribs, Friction pushed herself up to her feet as Darius stepped forward.

What is he planning?

Friction planted her foot, ready to push off into a run . . . and she gasped and clutched at her head as paralyzing panic gripped her body and tore through her mind.

Oh, that's what he meant.

CHAPTER 30

"Infuser! Ramp up the fear!"

What does that mean? Spright spared a glance at the new speedster, Friction, who was staggering to her feet. She wore a silver costume with burgundy gloves, boots, belt, and domino mask. *Where did she come from?*

Time for that later. Spright turned his attention back to Negator. He couldn't let the big guy use his sword again. Its devastating blast had torn the cubicles around the bank apart and knocked all the hostages flat. Whatever that weapon was, it was no ordinary sword. But as Spright moved forward, the hostages, along with Friction, screamed and clutched at their heads. That explained the command about fear.

Yeoman's crossbow didn't waver. "I'll take Negator. You guys get the other two!"

Spright nodded and rushed toward the back corner of the bank, past Friction's trembling form, where Infuser and the female Opera Mask stood. Infuser did not react as Spright approached; he must've been too busy maintaining the psychic assault. Good. All Spright had to do was punch him out, and this would be as good as over. He raised his fist, the shock rings crackling, swung it forward . . . and a hand caught him by the wrist and tugged him away from Infuser, throwing him back into a support beam. Spright grunted. The female Opera Mask stepped toward him, clutching a bank security guard's nightstick in her left hand.

"You're not running," she noted. "Your powers on the fritz?"

"Don't need my powers to teach you a lesson." Spright dropped into a fighting stance. "Who are you?"

"They call me Sensory. Let me show you why."

Before Spright could lunge, the Crusader stepped in and swung his staff at Sensory. The woman stepped deftly aside, slapping the back of the Crusader's weapon with her nightstick as it passed. Spright stepped back to let the Crusader handle her. He turned to Infuser. But as he charged, Sensory stepped in front of him again. Spright swung; and again, she dodged the blow. She grabbed his arm, ducked under it, and struck him on the elbow. Before he could react, she struck again beneath the ribs. Finally, she hurled him over her shoulder. Spright landed hard on his back and groaned.

She's anticipating my moves.

She must've been sensing his emotions, if not his thoughts, so she knew exactly what he was about to do. Gideon had been capable of doing much the same when he still had his powers. Patrick grimaced and pushed himself to his feet. He winced at the pain that shot through his abdomen.

"You should still be able to use your powers to enhance the speed of your punches," Jarrett had said. *"Not too much, or you'll risk breaking your arm, but enough to give you the added oomph you'll need."*

Even if she could anticipate his blows, Sensory was only human. Her reaction time couldn't beat Spright's enhanced punches.

Just be careful. Tearing my own arm out of my socket won't do anybody any good.

Sensory was engaged with the Crusader again. They traded a flurry of powerful strikes from their respective weapons. The Crusader was doing a good job of keeping just ahead of her strikes. Training with the Seraph had paid off. Spright charged in and rammed his left fist at her elbow, driving it with the added force of his speed. The shock rings connected with her limb, sending blue sparks running up and down her arm. Sensory hissed and staggered back, her hand going limp and the nightstick clattering to the floor. The Crusader took advantage of the opening and jabbed at her. She barely stepped out of the way of the blow. Spright pulled back his foot for a kick . . .

And another blast ripped through the bank.

Spright stumbled forward and landed flat on his chest. He looked around. Sensory and Infuser had been grounded, too, but the Crusader was staggering to his feet. Good. Turning, Spright ran back toward Yeoman and Negator. It was time to end this.

* * *

As Spright and the Crusader ran toward the two Opera Masks at the back of the bank, Yeoman squared off with Negator. The burly man had retrieved his fallen sword—a piece of technology that was foreign to Yeoman. Once this was over, he would need to determine how Negator had obtained the weapon and ensure that no other criminals could get a hold of something like it.

"Who are you?" Negator asked. "Arrow Guy?"

Yeoman smirked. "Did it take you all this time to come up with that?"

He fired an arrow. Negator heaved his sword up to block it, but he was too slow. The shaft buried itself in the brute's right shoulder. Yeoman flicked the auto-reload switch near the trigger. It was a feature of the weapon CLOUD had come up with. Without it, using a crossbow would've been impractical and suicidal.

Negator straightened, ripped the arrow from his shoulder, and snapped the carbon-fiber shaft in half with his bare hand. Yeoman took a step back. Negator squared his shoulders and took his sword in a two-handed grip.

He's getting stronger.

Yeoman looked around at the whimpering hostages. Was it possible that Negator fed on their fear?

"Hey, Happy. How about you put the sword down and—"

A beam of red light shot from the blade of the sword and struck Yeoman in the chest. He was hurtled into the metal doorframe. Pain shot up and down his back at the impact; and he slumped to the ground, dropping his crossbow next to him.

Oh . . . the sword shoots lasers, too.

He reached up and touched his chest. The blast of energy had seared his armor-weave vest, leaving a black scorch mark behind; but it hadn't punched through.

Thank you, Dean.

Yeoman pushed himself to his feet and tucked into a clumsy roll as Negator swung the huge sword down at him. He came up behind Negator and drove his elbow back into the brute's kneecap. The joint didn't bend. Negator spun and raised his weapon for another blow. Yeoman rolled aside and grabbed an adhesive bead from his belt. Time to see if these things could hold as much as the CLOUD techies boasted. He squeezed the bead to activate it and drew his hand back to throw.

Negator's blade, still descending on Yeoman's previous position, struck the floor. Another concussive blast erupted from the weapon, knocking Yeoman off his feet again. His adhesive bead slipped from his hand and detonated harmlessly against the counter. Yeoman grunted as he landed in a wrecked cubicle next to Friction, who was still clutching her head and moaning in fear.

"Yeah," Yeoman muttered. "Same."

He started to push himself up. Negator was running out the door; and the other two Opera Masks were close behind him, the female leaning against Infuser. Yeoman drew his gun and took aim, but they were already out the door. He staggered in that direction and leaned against the doorframe.

Another blast erupted outside. This one was far enough away that it only knocked Yeoman back a step. He grimaced, shook his head, and looked outside. Two of the police cars had been knocked aside, and the officers lay flat on their backs. There was no sign of the Opera Mask Gang. Yeoman sighed, holstered his gun, and knelt to retrieve his crossbow.

"Spright? Crusader? You okay?"

"I'm good!" Patrick called.

"Me, too." Carter rubbed his head. "That chick was good."

Jarrett walked back into the bank. The hostages were up and about now, looking dazed and confused. They had to be reeling from the double whammy of emotions Infuser had hit them with. Patrick crossed the bank to stand next to Jarrett and looked over at Friction, who was still leaning against the pillar. Who was she? Yeoman hadn't heard reports of any new speedsters. Her suit didn't look homemade—either she had been around for longer than they knew, or she had funding from someone.

"Who are you?" Spright asked her. "Where'd you come from?"

The girl backed away. "I have to go."

"What? N-no, don't go—"

Friction vanished in a streak of red flashing past Yeoman and Spright and out the door. Spright rushed to the entrance and looked out at the street, but Yeoman knew she was already long gone. In pursuit of the Opera Mask Gang? Maybe. Or returning to wherever she considered her base to recoup from the loss.

Patrick stepped outside. "We have to find her."

"Don't worry, kid. I don't think she's a threat."

"No, no, you don't understand. If we can convince her to come back with us, then Jan could scan her brain. She could see what my brain needs to look like when I use my powers." He stepped up to Jarrett and grabbed his shoulders. "She could fix me."

⚭ ⚭ ⚭

"What was that?" Paxton's voice demanded through her earbud comms.

"I—I'm sorry, sir," Friction panted. "I don't know."

Friction had run from the bank at top speed, putting as much distance between her and the scene of the crime as she could. Finally, she came to a stop behind a warehouse that smelled of fish and seawater. She leaned against the building and clutched her stomach, hoping she didn't vomit right there.

Whatever she had expected when facing the Coleman siblings, the abrupt surge of terror she had experienced had not been part of it. She had been unable to move, her body paralyzed by horrors she couldn't comprehend. And as abruptly as it came, the terror was gone again, leaving Friction in a state of confused numbness. Her stomach rolled as she tried to straighten.

"Darius' powers. They're stronger than I expected."

"You have to stop them," Paxton said. "They can't have gotten everything they wanted from that botched job, so they'll try again; and you have to get them this time. If you don't, they will disappear from New Echelon."

"I'll . . . I'll stop them." Friction pushed off the wall and staggered away from the smelly warehouse. "Do you think I should talk to Spright? Maybe we could work together. After all, I am outnumbered."

"No. You have to do this alone. And next time, don't hesitate. You were moving too quickly for the Colemans to see you. You could have taken them all out as soon as you went in."

"Taken them out, sir?"

"Killed them, Friction. What did you think I was sending you to do?"

Friction stopped in her tracks, her boots scuffing against the soggy planks of the docks. *Kill them?*

She hadn't expected this to go that far. Heroes didn't kill. She had watched the Seraph and Spright and the other Vindicators on the news; they never killed the criminals they fought. They disabled them and turned them over to the police.

"I—I can't."

"You can, and you will." Paxton's voice was eerily calm. "This is the real world, Friction. Spright and his cohorts live in a fantasy. The people they imprison will return someday because they didn't have the guts to end them."

"Sir, I'm not a killer."

"Well, then you'd better learn how to be one quickly. You will kill the Colemans. That's an order."

Friction stared down at her crimson boots and then looked up and out at the ocean. The docks and the water alike were covered by a light fog. Appropriate, considering how clouded her mind felt right now. Could she really follow through with what Paxton was asking her to do? But what other choice did she have? She had no one else. Paxton had trained her and made her suit and molded her into the hero she was becoming.

"Yes, sir."

As she turned and sped away from the docks, the fog parted like a curtain in her wake. Friction wished she could leave her doubts behind as easily.

CHAPTER 31

Patrick pulled his mask off as he, Carter, and Jarrett descended into the lair. His hair followed his mask, splaying wildly around his forehead and dangling down into his eyes. It had only been a week since his last haircut. Maybe it grew faster because of his powers. He ran his hands through it, pulling the strands back away from his eyes, and walked down into the pool, where Asher, Lucy, Bryce, and Jan were busy at work. Ty sat in the far corner, his elbows resting on his knees.

"There's another speedster," Patrick said.

Lucy looked up from the computer. "We know. We saw her on the news."

"Who was she?" Asher asked.

"No idea." Patrick set his mask down on a table and began removing his suit's outer plates. "She called herself Friction, but she sped off before I had time to talk to her. She seems like a rookie; she made some pretty basic mistakes out there."

"She made the same mistake you made the first time you went against them." Jarrett took off his goggles. "She rushed in without assessing the situation, and it got her into trouble. The only difference is, she didn't slam into a transformer, so she'll recover."

Patrick raised his eyebrows. Jarrett was usually snippy but in a good-natured way. That, though, sounded like an out-and-out put-down. He blushed and looked away from the older hero. As much as he wanted to respond, he knew Jarrett was right; and he was only stating the facts. Carter put a hand on Patrick's shoulder and gave him a subtle shake of the head. Patrick smiled at his friend's quiet encouragement.

"What about the Opera Mask Gang?" Lucy asked. "What happened?"

"The strong one—Negator—has some kind of high-tech sword." Patrick waved his arms in an expansive sweep. "It shoots out these shockwaves whenever he hits the ground with it. He used it to knock us back, and they used that time to escape."

"The sword shoots lasers, too." Jarrett gestured to his burnt suit. "Learned that the hard way. We need to find out who manufactures weapons like that; if they start selling to common criminals, there would be chaos."

"The other two called themselves Infuser and Sensory. Infuser was the one who robbed your party, Asher. And apparently, he can project more than just apathy and calm. He made the hostages panic. It was like everyone in that bank was experiencing their worst phobias."

Jarrett nodded. "And that fear made Negator stronger."

"What about Sensory?" Jan asked.

Patrick turned to her. "Sensory was the female of the trio. She was predicting every move we made before we did it. I think her powers are similar to Gideon's empathic abilities."

"Yeah, it was like fighting someone who was thinking a step ahead," Carter said. "I knew how to counter her a little bit, since I've trained with Gideon; but she was more advanced than he ever was, I think."

But this doesn't matter right now.

Patrick knew they needed to stop the Opera Mask Gang; but as far as he was concerned, that would be easier to do once he had his speed back. Their priority should be finding Friction, convincing her to come back to the lair with them, and letting Jan take her brain scans so that she could continue her shock therapy on Patrick and return him to normal. The Opera Mask Gang could wait.

"Well." Jarrett thumped Patrick's upper back. "You did good for your first time in the field without powers. I'm sure next time will be even better. We'll keep training and—"

"I don't need training. I need to find Friction."

"Patrick—"

"No, listen to me." He slammed his hand down on the metal table. "This is Team Spright, isn't it? That means I call the shots. You want to keep looking for the Opera Mask Gang, fine. But my priority is getting my powers back. I need them. Which means I need Friction. You do what you want, Jarrett, but my team—"he waved at Lucy, Asher, and Bryce—"my team is going to find her."

Jarrett squared his jaw, and there was a fire in his dark eyes. Patrick didn't care. Jarrett was his friend, but that didn't mean they had to agree on everything. How was he supposed to catch the Opera Mask Gang while he was depowered? Today had proven that he couldn't be a superhero without his speed. No matter how well Jarrett claimed he had done, it didn't matter because the bad guys got away. Carter studied Patrick with wide, assessing eyes but said nothing.

"You know, Patrick, you've changed. Do what you want." Jarrett grabbed his laptop and moved over to another table. "I'll catch these guys before they hurt anyone else."

Patrick glared at him for a moment, threw his hands up in the air, and turned back to his friends. Lucy's arms were crossed, her brow furrowed in concern, Bryce's eyes were wide and full of shock; and Asher's hands were in his pockets, his gaze fixed intently on his shoes. Jan brushed past Patrick and walked to her husband's side without a word.

"Well?" Patrick raised his palms. "Do we have anything on Friction?"

Bryce scratched the back of his neck. "I'll . . . see if I can find anything."

Patrick chopped his head in a short nod. His friends understood. They had to. He might have seemed harsh and unreasonable to Jarrett, but how could he be a hero without his powers?

Carter pursed his lips. "Don't lose sight of why you do this. Jarrett and I operate without powers. Being amplified doesn't make you a hero."

He strode away without waiting for Patrick's response, dropping onto the floor next to Ty. Lucy still looked upset. After seeing Patrick under Infuser's power and their conversation at the formal the other night, she understood his priorities, right?

"Something wrong?" he asked.

She turned away. "You didn't used to be this obsessive. Carter's right. If you think your powers are what makes you a hero, you've got a lot of learning to do."

* * *

"One bag," Anton shouted. "We only got *one* bag of cash. This isn't enough for us to get a fresh start anywhere!"

They were running out of time. The Archdukes and the Seventy-Six had to be closing in on them, especially after the robbery. If they'd been on a clock before, it would be running down into seconds now. Anton kept an eye on the shabby hotel room's curtained window, peering through a narrow slit. He expected to see armed gangsters or cops approaching at any moment.

"We still got several hundred dollars." Darius placed bills in a stack as he counted. "It'll buy us a few nights in a motel, and who says that we have to stay here in New Echelon? Let's just start driving, get as far as we can, and set up somewhere else. Then we can plan a new job."

Anton quirked an eyebrow. "Are you actually suggesting another robbery?"

"I don't like it. But it's too late now. Spright and those other heroes, the cops, the gangs—they're all after us. Our only choice is to get all the money we can and start fresh."

"Zee?"

"Yeah." She huffed. "Yeah, I'm in. I still say all this was avoidable in the first place, but we are where we are. We work with what we've got. Right now, Anton, you're our best chance of survival."

He would never tell them, but that meant the world to him. Anton had always tried to look out for his siblings but had always worried they would be better off without him. Maybe they would have in any other situation. He knew he was practically useless—muscle, and nothing more, good to fix a car or break a few heads, but otherwise nonessential. But finally, he could prove his worth.

"Okay. But we can't go anywhere yet. It's too risky, especially now that the van has been near the scene of the bank robbery. We need to pull another local job."

"Isn't that just as risky?" Darius asked.

"Potentially, yes. But if we run now and the cops connect the van to us, then we could get pulled over in the middle of nowhere, and then what would we do?" Anton shook his head. "We need new wheels. And if we hit the right place, we could deal with all our problems at once."

"We're robbing a car dealership?" Zee asked.

"No." Anton smirked. "We're going to hit the gangs where they live. We're going to take their money, steal one of their vehicles, and put so much hurt on them that they'll be too scared to ever come after us again."

* * *

Asher didn't know EBC's campus very well, but he knew where people in general liked to go when they wanted to mope—somewhere up high, where they could look down over everything around them. He didn't know if it was because it gave them perspective or because the view was calming. But unless it was someone terrified of heights, they were probably going to get to the highest point they could find when they were facing a crisis and needed to think.

Patrick was no exception. Although he had confessed to Asher and Lucy that he no longer enjoyed heights after he was nearly dropped to his death by Jeremiah Ashcroft, he didn't have a phobia; so it seemed likely to Asher that he would find a good vantage point. He climbed the stairs out of the team's newly minted lair and looked around for someone to help him.

A tan-skinned girl in the lounge looked familiar. She sat at a light brown circular table in the student lounge, her cheek resting against the palm of her left hand while she flipped pages in a textbook with her right. She might not have seen where Patrick had gone, but she might know what Asher was looking for. He pushed his way through the glass door into the student lounge. The room was an inviting, air-conditioned space with blue-and-gray checkered carpet and medium gray walls, which made Asher want to drop into one of the oversized beanbag chairs in the corner and take a nap. Unfortunately, he had other business to tend to. He stepped up to her table.

"Excuse me. Hi. It's Alexa, right? Do you remember me?"

She looked up, pushing a lock of dark hair behind her ear. "You're Asher—Patrick and Lucy's friend, right?"

"Yeah. Did you see Patrick come through here recently? I'm looking for him."

"No, I didn't."

"Do you happen to know the highest accessible place on campus? Somewhere quiet and up high that someone might go to think?"

"The rooftop garden, maybe. It was built to be an outdoor dining area for students during warmer months." Alexa paused for a moment. "Is everything okay?"

Asher looked around the lounge. There were a handful of other students inside; a pair of guys in jerseys playing ping-pong, a guy and a girl sitting at another round table and chatting over their coffees, and a mixed group playing video games on the TV in the corner. They were all occupied, at least.

"I'm not sure. Patrick's been going through some stuff lately, and I think it's hitting him hard. I need to talk to him."

"I noticed he has been a bit off. Let me know if there is anything I can do to help."

"For now, just tell me how I can get to that rooftop garden you were talking about."

Moments later, Asher exited onto a rooftop covered in foliage, interspersed with tables and chairs. Patrick stood on the far side of the roof, near the edge, looking out over the campus and the distant city business district.

Asher strode toward his best friend, not bothering to hide the sound of his footsteps. He wasn't trying to sneak up on Patrick. He just wanted to talk. But as he approached, Patrick made no acknowledgment of his presence. Asher stopped when he was side by side with Patrick and tucked his hands in his jacket pockets. He looked out over the city in silence, waiting for Patrick to speak.

"I was a jerk," Patrick finally said.

"No, you . . . " Asher sighed. "Yeah."

"This is all wrong, man. What happened to me? Here I am, blessed with this amazing gift from God; and as soon as it looks like it might get taken away, I throw a tantrum. Gideon didn't do that when he lost his powers. I don't know why I couldn't have the same composure. I'd like to say that it's because I know I still have more to offer, but . . . "

"But really, you just like your powers and don't want to give them up."

"Yeah." Patrick sniffled. "I had a dream about it and everything. I saw my grandpa. He told me God would do what God wanted to do, basically, and that it would always work out for the best. And here I am, still trying to hold on."

Asher half-smiled. "Kind of reminds me of the premise of your project. Forget how superheroes affect teens in their relationship to church; it's affecting you and your relationship with God."

Patrick turned to look at him, his expression almost comically dumbfounded. Asher put a hand on his shoulder, squeezed, and looked back at the city. For years, Patrick had been the best of his friends, the most mature for his age, and the quickest to come up with a biblical solution to any problem. Now, he was facing his own crisis. Asher would repay him.

"Maybe that's why we're here," Asher said. "Lucy and I don't do much to help you in the field, but we can keep you accountable for not getting addicted to your speed."

"Addicted? Is that what you think this is?"

"A little bit. I mean, think about how often you went out to fight crime before that night at the docks. Think about how long you stayed out on the streets every night. You sacrificed a lot to do that: time with your friends, good grades because of missed homework assignments, dates with Lucy. And, yes, you could say that those are the sacrifices a hero makes, but there's a fine line between hero and adrenaline junkie."

Patrick grimaced and clutched his chest. "Ouch."

"I'm not trying to rake you over the coals or anything, man. I just want to give you some perspective. You sure could use some."

"Thanks. I'll think about it." Patrick gestured to a chair. "Sit down. Let's talk. How are things with Shannon?"

"Oh, pretty good. Things got kind of heavy the other night, though." Asher dropped into one of the chairs. "She told me she was abused by a priest when she was a kid. It turned her off from religion. I told her that I understood and that if she ever changed her mind and wanted to talk about faith, she could talk to me."

"How'd she take it?"

"Surprisingly well. I don't know if I won her over, but I think it was a start. I'll keep chipping away and try to get her to come to church with me."

Patrick grinned. "You're not missionary dating, are you?"

Asher looked down at the table. "I don't think so. I just want what's best for her."

"Good for you." Patrick stood. "I should probably apologize to Lucy. She was pretty mad—no reason to let that fester. And thank you. I needed to hear what you said."

Asher rose and hugged Patrick. "Anything for my best friend."

* * *

Although there was not much for Ty to do in Spright's lair, he did not mind being left alone. It was enough to be in the presence of others, watching them as they went about their business. The tense argument between Spright and his friends had been awkward to watch, but Ty kept out of it and waited for Carter's next move.

The bank robbery had provided Ty with time to read his Bible. Appropriately, some of the passages he found today spoke of the joys of being released from captivity. Ty did not think those verses were talking about physical captivity, but he was still trying to wrap his mind around concepts like sin and forgiveness. Oh, the world was full of sin. That was easy to see in the neighborhoods Ty lived in and frequented. He was even ready to admit to the sin in his own life. He had done things that were undeniably wrong. Stealing, killing . . . he was no saint.

What was hard to understand was that God was ready and willing to forgive someone like him. Someone like Carter, sure. The young hero was noble and selfless. But Ty had lived most of his adult life selfishly. Could God really forgive that? The fear of rejection made Ty recoil. He had put the Bible away before the vigilantes returned from the bank.

When Carter finally sat down next to him, Ty could tell the younger man was conflicted. He understood that conflict too well. Despite his continuing desire to return home, Ty was also drawn by Ben's warning that the Sicarans would continue to pursue him. The idea of slipping away during the bank robbery to find Ben had occurred to Ty at least half a dozen times. Only the thought of never seeing Emi again kept him from running.

"You want to stay, don't you?" Ty asked.

Carter bobbed his head. "Patrick needs all the help he can get. But the longer we keep you away from Sojourn City, the more severe your punishment will be. I don't want years added onto your sentence because of me."

"With your support, a good lawyer, and an honest explanation of my captivity, I think we can convince the courts I don't deserve extra time." Ty pressed his lips together. "I would prefer to return with you; but if you want to send me on ahead to turn myself in while you stay here to help . . . "

"No. I'll be there with you. No one should have to face that alone."

"Thank you. I don't deserve your kindness."

"I know." Carter smiled and put a hand on Ty's shoulder. "I don't care. I believe in you, and I want to give you a chance to do better."

Ty's stomach somersaulted. Was that how God felt about Ty? Pieces of the puzzle started to click together in his mind. Maybe God would accept him, after all.

"We'll stay," Ty said. "You're right. They need your help—our help. If I have to face consequences for it when we return to Sojourn City, so be it. You want me to do better? This is how I start."

"All right, then." Carter rose to his feet. "Let's catch some bad guys."

CHAPTER 32

The walk of shame returning to the lair so soon after his tantrum-fueled exit lasted longer than Patrick would have liked. He trudged down the stairs and circled around toward the ladder that descended into the pool. Bryce looked up as he approached; and Lucy had to have heard him, too, but she made no move to acknowledge his presence. Fair enough; he had earned that. Jarrett and Jan kept busy on their side of the lair. Carter, for his part, at least shifted away from the corner of the pool.

Turning to clamber down the ladder, Patrick wished he had asked Asher to come back with him before leaving. He could have used the emotional support. He walked over to the table where Bryce and Lucy were poring over feeds from traffic cameras. How Bryce had access to those, Patrick didn't know; and it was probably better that way.

"I'm sorry," Patrick said. "I was a jerk."

"A little bit." Lucy kept her gaze on the computer. "But you came to your senses pretty fast, so maybe you're not a total jerk."

"It's chill, man," Bryce said.

Lucy finally looked up, smiling a little bit. "Yeah. It's chill."

"No, it's not." Patrick pulled up a chair. "I got distracted, so focused on my powers that I forgot about all the things that really matter. I didn't even see it until now, but it's been going on for months. I thought taking a few nights off to hang out with you guys would make up for it, but it's more than that. It was my attitude about everything that really stunk."

Bryce shrugged. "Hey, I've never had powers, but I'd bet it's pretty easy to get that way."

Easy or not, it didn't make it right. Asher's observation had been close to home. Patrick had become consumed with his powers to the point that he relied on them more than he did on God. Maybe that was why God had allowed this to happen. He needed to get Patrick's attention. Patrick just wished he had seen it sooner.

"I'm going to try to do better. But I need you to keep me accountable—all of you, but you especially, Luce. You're the closest person to me in the world. You'll see sooner than most if my powers start consuming me again. If they do . . . "

"I'll call you on it." Lucy moved over to him, knelt behind his chair, and wrapped her arms around his neck and shoulders. "You're a good man, Patrick Omer. But even good men need a wakeup call sometimes."

He wondered if he could use this experience for his project. If he, a superhero himself, was guilty of relying more on his powers than God, how many teens in churches would start to think they could count on superheroes for things they'd normally pray about? A superhuman who could heal illnesses could quickly take the place of prayers for a sick family member; a few heroes like Patrick and his friends could give such a sense of safety that prayers for protection could fall by the wayside.

"Superheroes should be tools of God. We should never replace Him."

Lucy playfully shoulder-bumped him. "Sounds like you've got the thesis for your project."

"Not just that. A new philosophy for my life." Patrick stood. "Now, I have a few other apologies I need to make."

"Good luck."

By the time Patrick rose, Carter was standing next to him. Patrick opened his mouth to speak, and Carter chuckled and slugged Patrick gently across the shoulder.

"You don't even have to say it, man." Carter shrugged. "I know what it's like to get so intensely focused on something, you lose sight of everything else. Being a superhero isn't easy. We're good."

Patrick grinned, hugged Carter, and then glanced across the pool to where Jarrett and Jan were working. He still had one more apology to make. Jarrett was intently focused on the laptop in front of him, while Jan was making notes on a tablet. Patrick crossed the room and cleared his throat as he approached.

"Jarrett? Can I talk to you for a minute?"

The older man looked up from his laptop. "Sure."

"I'm sorry. You were right. No matter how much I want my powers back, it's more important to find the Opera Mask Gang and stop them from hurting anyone else. With that big sword Negator has, they could do a lot of damage."

"Anton."

"Huh?"

"His name's Anton." Jarrett smirked. "And I forgive you. Everyone gets a muddy head sometimes. You cleared it faster than others."

"Didn't do it myself. It's good to have wise friends."

"It certainly helps."

"So, you figured out who the Opera Mask Gang are?"

"I did." Jarrett waved a hand at the laptop. "I used the security footage from the docks—they had their masks off when they first arrived. Ran facial recognition and found out that they are triplets: Anton, Darius, and Zoey Coleman. Anton's the big one with the sword. You can work out the other two easily enough."

"Any idea how they got their powers?"

Jarrett leaned in closer to the computer. "We don't have a record of any of them presenting bite-related injuries, but they have relatives living in Phoenix. It's possible they were there when one of Ashcroft's gas bombs went off. That explains why they're not in the CLOUD amp database."

"Do they have criminal records?"

"Anton has a few minors: drug possession, a handful of B&E's . . . but his siblings are clean. Zoey is a known political activist, but she's never taken it beyond peaceful protesting. Career-wise, Darius is about as interesting as cardboard."

"What makes three relatively innocent people go supervillain?"

"Had to have been Anton's influence. But whatever the case, he's shown that he's willing to commit violent crimes now; and his siblings are going along with it. They need to be stopped."

"Agreed." Patrick looked at Jan. "I take it you're still not ready to continue?"

She pursed her lips and shrugged. "Not until I have a better idea of what a speedster's brain activity should look like. I'm sorry."

"It's okay. In that case, I'm going to need something from you, Jarrett. If we're going to stop the Coleman siblings before they cause any more trouble, I need to be able to handle myself without my powers. Gideon helped me hone my speed; you can help me with my skills."

"It would be an honor." Jarrett put his palms on the table and pushed himself up. "We'll start first thing in the morning."

"Oh, but . . . I have class . . . "

"Before class. You want to do this? You're starting bright and early."

Oh, joy.

* * *

Sleep still fogging his brain, Patrick threw his hands up in a sloppy attempt to block a strike from Jarrett's foam *escrima* stick. The older man slapped Patrick's guard aside almost effortlessly and stepped in, reaching around Patrick's neck to grab him in a chokehold. Patrick shoved his elbow into Jarrett's ribcage before the lock was completed, and he slipped out of the hold. As he stepped past Jarrett, his ankle hooked Jarrett's leg, sending Patrick sprawling face-first onto the foam mat.

"Wake up!" Jarrett slapped Patrick's leg with his baton. "Crime isn't going to wait for you to be alert. When you're a speedster, you have the luxury of being able to respond to any situation in seconds. You won't have the same luxury without your powers. You'll have to be ready to go at any moment."

Patrick rolled into a crouch, coming up with his left knee pressed down into the blue padding and his right foot planted, ready to spring. Jarrett had brought the mat—along with the *escrima* sticks and a stand-up punching bag—with him that morning. Patrick was relieved that there would be a surface softer than the unforgiving concrete for him to fall on.

But padding or no, Jarrett wasn't taking it easy on him. It shouldn't have been possible for a foam baton to leave a stinging injury, but

Jarrett delivered so much force with his blows that Patrick was already sore. Sweat soaked the back of his blue workout T-shirt.

"Sorry. Just . . . haven't had my morning coffee."

"Didn't think a speedster needed coffee."

Jarrett lunged. Patrick pushed off with his right foot, tucking into a somersault and coming up behind Jarrett. He turned and, picking up a foam baton of his own, struck Jarrett behind the knee. Jarrett turned and brought his baton down. Patrick's baton came up to block. The black foam weapons met, forming a cross as they locked.

"Plant your feet!" Carter called from the sidelines. "Use momentum and leverage to your advantage."

Patrick had been thrilled when Carter told him that he was going to stay in New Echelon to help out until Patrick got his speed back. Carter apparently trusted Ty Vickers enough that he did not believe the convict would try to escape. Patrick wondered what the thief's story was. The rapport between him and Carter was odd, considering Carter had put him in prison. That was a conversation for another time, though.

Jarrett swung his baton in a tight circle. "He's right. For someone of your size and build, leverage will be key. You'd never be able to overpower Anton Coleman physically. You have to outsmart him—use his own mass against him. Wear him out."

"What about Darius and Zoey?"

"Neither of them is as physically formidable as Anton. As long as you're wearing your neural inhibitor, Anton is your biggest threat—but Zoey could be your downfall."

"Her predictive powers?"

"Exactly."

Patrick pulled his baton back, rolled to the side, and pushed himself to his feet, keeping his weapon between him and Jarrett. It would be just like the government agent to attack in the middle of their conversation.

"You only managed to hit her at the bank because you used your speed, and you've got to remember that. Don't be afraid to augment your strikes with it. Your powers aren't gone; you just can't use them to their fullest extent yet."

"Have you learned anything about Friction?"

"Nothing. There are no speedsters in the CLOUD database. That doesn't mean anything, though. Many of the reported bite victims haven't manifested their powers yet. It's possible that she has, but we haven't correlated her with someone on the list."

"She could have gotten her powers the same way I did—one of Ashcroft's bogus flu vaccinations. Or even one of his gas bombs."

"And she's only showing up now?"

Patrick shrugged. "We need to know more about her."

"Agreed. But first . . . "

"The Coleman siblings. Don't worry; they'll be my focus." Patrick pointed the tip of his baton at Jarrett. "Go again?"

"Let's do it."

* * *

Oscar Paxton drummed his fingers against his desk as his son droned on about the struggles he was having in school. Joey could've had everything—down to the very chair that Paxton now sat in—but he had refused out of some misguided desire to pave his own way in life. It was all very noble, and Paxton would have supported it . . . if Joey had any idea what he actually wanted to do. This was nothing more than a flight of fantasy, an idealized concept of trailblazing when he didn't realize the kind of work it would take to accomplish it.

But Joey was Paxton's only son. That meant that whatever Joey did, Paxton had to act like he supported it. Otherwise, he lost any hope that Joey might one day return to the fold. So, he listened.

"And who knows where Asher's been the last couple days," Joey muttered. "He's usually around all the time, and he's glad to help me with whatever problems I'm having. But ever since he met Shannon at the party . . . "

Paxton furrowed his brow. "Shannon?"

"Yeah, Shannon Weeks. You know, Benjamin Weeks' daughter?"

Benjamin Weeks. The man was a sometimes-partner, sometimes-rival of Paxton's, and he was familiar with Shannon. Weeks had brought his daughter with him to many cocktail parties at Paxton's home. The man was arrogant, though. His daughter . . . perhaps the same. What were the odds that she would find herself dating Joey's roommate?

"Well, I'm sure Asher is just infatuated. In a few days, they'll settle into a new normal; and he'll return to being there for you." Paxton leaned forward. "Are you doing all right, son?"

The question was vague but subtly pointed. He was not referring to grades, nor to Joey's mental state, nor even his relationship with his friends—he was referring to the boy's fear that the masked men would come after him again—an irrational fear, as Paxton had already known, and as the bank robbery had proven. If they had truly been after Joey, they would have just come for him, not attacked a bank.

"I'm okay. It's been a few days, and that masked guy hasn't come back. I was probably being paranoid. You can call off whoever you put on his scent."

"Of course."

Never.

Friction had to prove herself by taking down the Colemans. Paxton had too much riding on her to let her give up now. If things had gone differently with the Colemans, they might have been suitable replacements for the girl; but that ship had sailed. And besides, he had put too much effort and money into Friction to cast her aside now.

And if she didn't work out, he had a backup plan in place. He checked his watch. In fact, the first test of that backup plan should be ready within the next half hour. If he hurried, he could make it in time. Paxton put on his best fatherly smile and nodded to Joey.

"Hang in there, son. I've got a meeting I need to get to. You know the way out, yeah? I'll see you later."

"Sure, Dad." Joey rose. "Good luck with your . . . meeting."

As the boy crossed the office, Paxton reached into his desk for his car keys. The cherry wood desk cost more than Joey's tuition, and the car that these keys went to even more. Paxton did not believe in hoarding his wealth. He used it. After all, people would always need energy, oil or gasoline, or otherwise. And Paxton had his fingers dipped into every aspect of the energy business. Running out of money was unlikely—which was good because this project he had running on the side had cost a cool billion. That wasn't even counting the money he had already poured into getting Friction the training and care she needed—not to mention the super suit she wore.

Oh, well. Nothing lasted forever, even money. Best to use it in the way that benefited him most while he was still alive. He had all the money he could ever need. More of it would not give him satisfaction. Only completing his mission would do that. Training Friction gave him satisfaction that he had not felt for years. And if that was a sign of what Paxton was meant to do for the rest of his life, he would pursue it relentlessly.

* * *

As Ty watched Carter train with Patrick and Jarrett, his own muscles twitched with longing for action. Ty had never been one for idleness. His father and godfather had trained him in hand-to-hand combat, swordplay, and many other forms of combat before he was old enough to drive. After that, he had set his sights on becoming a police officer, only for those aspirations to fall apart when Ty's godfather was connected to organized crime. That was when Ty became a criminal. All his life, he had been active. The last few months had been torture. It was time for him to do something again.

Something like fighting the Sicarans.

Ty scowled and pushed the thought aside. How often would he have this same argument with himself? He had made his decision the moment he followed Carter instead of staying with Ben. He did not even have a moral or philosophical reason to want to fight the Sicarans. If he did, it would only be to protect himself and Emi. But even if he did slip away and find Ben, Carter would only hunt him down again. This time, Carter would bring him back by force. Ty would have to fight him, and Ty respected the younger man too much to do that.

But the Sicarans . . . Ty needed to know more about them. Why had his father served them? Why had his godfather betrayed them? Were they as sinister as Ben said, or was there something the mysterious man was omitting? They were assassins; surely, they had to be evil. But Ty's chest tightened with the thought that his father could ever serve an evil organization or that his cruel godfather could have done the right thing by betraying them—by betraying Ty's father.

And Ty wanted to know what Kane McCrory, the assassin sent to kill Ty's godfather, meant by his hints that Ty had some greater destiny.

I have to know the truth.

If he went back to prison, he might never get his answers. But if he did not, he might never get Emi back.

He leaned his head back against the pool's concrete wall and stared up at the ceiling. Neither answer was easy. Which one was right? He was running out of time to decide.

CHAPTER 33

DeMarco—the Archduke captain Anton killed at the docks—had
a brother, Dexter, who owned an upscale Italian restaurant in New
Echelon. The restaurant, which was simply named "DeMarco's," was also
a front for the Archdukes. They used the back rooms of the restaurant to
host leadership meetings, card games . . . everything. It was the perfect
location to catch the leaders unaware and deal with them.

Anton checked the charge on his concussion sword. It was running
low, and he had no idea how to charge it. DeMarco would have known,
but he was dead now. Maybe while Anton was inside the restaurant,
he could get the brother or one of the other Archdukes to explain it to
him in exchange for their life. If not . . . well, the sword could still be
a powerful weapon in Anton's hands, even without its energy charge.

"Are you sure this is the right place?" Zee asked.

"I'm positive," Anton said. "Look, I know you guys have only been
involved in this for a few months, but I was in for a lot longer than that.
I know these things. You've got to trust me; if the Archduke leadership
is anywhere, it's here."

"Okay. You'd better be right because I'm not going to prison for tearing
up a restaurant full of innocents. Gangsters, fine. But not innocents."

"Try not to use that concussion blast in here," Darius said. "As small
of an area as it is, it's bound to kill someone."

"Isn't that the idea?" Anton asked.

"It's uncontrollable. A blast like that could kill bystanders—or one of us—as easily as the Archdukes."

"Fine." Anton nodded. "But that means this'll get bloody."

Darius blanched. He didn't have the stomach for this. Neither of them did. Anton should have left them at the hotel and done this job alone, like he had initially wanted to. He was honored by their support, but they did not need to get their hands bloodied for him. That was why he was around—to do the things they couldn't. That they shouldn't.

"We'll cover the exits." Zee twirled her baton. "Just make this quick."

"One of you get us a vehicle. The Archdukes usually park around back, and they hang their keys on hooks just inside the back door. It's some kind of solidarity thing."

"I'll get the car. Darius can watch the front, and you can go in and get the money from the Archdukes. You know, there's a police station like two miles from here."

"I know. That's why we make sure no one calls them." Anton picked up his mask. "Now, let's get moving."

He popped his door and dropped out onto the street, realizing it was likely to be the last time he exited this van. It had been with him for nearly a decade. It was almost an injustice to discard it so unceremoniously, but keeping it would only endanger them.

"Infuser, front door."

Infuser, now wearing his mask beneath a gray hoodie, rushed to the front door, while Negator and Sensory circled the building. There would be at least one guard at the rear entrance, Negator was sure; but Sensory would detect him before they got close. Negator slipped his mask on.

"Sensory, anything?"

"One, on alert."

"Take care of him."

Sensory pressed herself against the wall, peered around the corner, and then lunged out, extending her collapsible baton. The sounds of a struggle met Negator's ears as he cleared the wall. Sensory knelt next to the guard, who lay flat on his face, and picked up his gun. Negator stepped past her, put his hand on the door the man had been guarding, and pushed.

The door flew inward, cracking off its hinges and smashing into the far wall. Negator stormed inside—his sword held at high guard—and scanned the back room. Five men gathered around a table intended for six. Negator assumed that the DeMarco brother he had killed was the absentee. The men were half-standing, two of them reaching for concealed weapons. At the other end of the room, two more guards stood next to the door leading into the restaurant. They raised weapons as Negator cleared the door.

"Kill him!" one of the bosses shouted.

Sensory fired. One of the guards dropped before his finger touched the trigger. As the second guard fired, Negator leapt across the room, his concussion sword descending toward the man. He managed a single shot, but it bounced harmlessly off Negator's skin. The fear and rage swirling about the room fed his strength and durability. Negator slashed out with his sword, killing the gangster instantly.

"Stop!" Sensory shouted. "Don't touch those weapons."

Negator turned. The two bosses who had been reaching for their guns were frozen, staring at the weapon Sensory had trained on them.

Atta girl, sis.

Negator lowered his sword and stormed back to the table.

"*You* . . . you're the one who killed my brother," one of the men spat.

Negator studied the speaker. He had the same warm skin tone and jet-black, gel-slicked hair as DeMarco, the same arrogant curve to his eyebrows that indicated he was looking down on everyone around him, the same tailored three-piece suit. But he was not the man Negator had come to see. He was not the leader of the Archdukes. Negator scanned each of them in turn and stopped at the man who sat at the head of the table.

He was in his late forties, sandy blond hair beginning to creep away from his forehead but still prominent enough that most would not consider it receding. Although he was dressed as immaculately as the others at the table, the weathering on his face indicated a man who did not fall prey to the amenities he was afforded. He used them but did not let them use him. He was smart and strong.

The man looked unafraid as Negator made eye contact. "What do you want?"

"All the money you can give me, a free ride out of town, and the promise that your men will not pursue me or my siblings anymore. Give me those three things, I'll spare your life, Mr. Paxton."

* * *

Patrick's phone buzzed in his pocket—a unique buzz that he had set for Dean's police alert system. Emergency. He looked around. This *would* happen while he was in the middle of apologetics class.

Leaving his backpack and notes behind so it would appear he was returning—the other students and his professor would hopefully assume he was going for a bathroom break—he ducked out the door, pulled out his phone, and opened the alert app as he walked down the hall toward the exit. He eyed a hallway security camera. Before the

Opera Mask Gang's antics, most of his crime fighting had been done at night. Of late, he had been sneaking out during the day too often. Someone was going to notice when he stopped returning to classes.

That was a problem for another time, though. Saving lives came first. DeMarco's, the Italian restaurant he and his friends had visited just a few nights before, was under attack. Patrick dialed Jarrett and put the phone to his ear.

"You got the alert, too?" Jarrett asked.

"I'm on my way to the lair now."

"No time. I already grabbed your suit. You can change in the car."

Patrick hung up and pushed through the door leading to the streetside sidewalk. Jarrett's rented car skidded to a stop next to him. Carter was in the back seat, geared up and ready to go. Patrick tugged the front door open and dropped into the passenger's seat.

"It's the Colemans, right?"

Jarrett nodded. "Sounds like it."

Patrick unbuttoned his shirt and began pulling on the Spright suit in its place. He missed the ability to change clothes in a fraction of a second. He worked his way into the suit and pulled his gloves and mask on.

"Friction could be there," he noted.

"Could be, but we'll talk to her after the Colemans are dealt with. Anton is the dangerous one, remember—let me deal with him if possible."

Lord, help us get these guys here.

"Understood. Any idea why they're attacking a restaurant?"

"Best I can tell, DeMarco's may be a gang cover. They could be out for vengeance."

"This could be bloodier than the bank, then."

Jarrett set his jaw. "Which means the Colemans are even less likely to come quietly."

"That's what I was afraid of." Patrick activated his shock rings. "But one way or the other, they're coming."

"Glad we're in agreement."

The car skidded to a stop across the street from DeMarco's. Jarrett slid his goggles down over his eyes and climbed out of the car as Carter clambered out of the back seat. Patrick followed suit, his vision turning purple as the lenses came down. Jarrett pointed at a dark van parked half a block down.

"That's the Colemans' van."

"Want to take care of that?"

Yeoman pulled his crossbow, unfolded it, and trained it on the van, not even slowing his stride. An arrow struck its driver's side front tire, instantly deflating it. He gestured toward the restaurant's front door and broke away from Spright, heading for the back. Spright understood. They could flank the Colemans and catch them by surprise. He approached the front door, losing sight of Yeoman as he circled the building. The Crusader stuck with Spright, and Patrick could not help but feel a twinge of relief that he would not have to fight alone.

Spright's heart pounded as he reached for the door.

I can do this.

He and Carter had nearly beaten Infuser and Sensory the last time they confronted them; if not for that last concussion blast from Negator's sword, they would have had them. The key would be taking that sword away from him—or at least keeping him from striking the ground with it.

"I'm in position," Yeoman said over the comms. "Go."

Spright tugged the door open and rushed inside and barely ducked in time as a fist shot toward his head. He shunted his body to the left. The Crusader stepped into the gap, striking the attacker with the face of his shield. Spright brought his right hand up to strike under the arm of his assailant. Sparks crackled around Spright's shock rings, sending the attacker reeling back away from him. Spright stepped back and dropped into a ready stance. The Crusader drew his staff and flanked the attacker. Their opponent was a male of average build wearing a gray hoodie, black jeans, and a sad-faced opera mask.

Spright waved. "Hey, Darius."

Infuser froze. So, Jarrett's analysis had been accurate. Darius Coleman was Infuser. He was also the least likely of his siblings to be violent. He was alone in the restaurant lobby, which put Anton and Zoey in the back room. That would make things difficult for Yeoman. Spright scanned the restaurant to be sure it was empty of civilians. It was. Darius must've ushered them all out.

Across the restaurant, sounds of battle emanated from a side door. Spright nodded to the door, and the Crusader stepped in that direction.

"You sure?" Carter asked.

Patrick gave him a thumbs up. "Go. I've got this."

* * *

Yeoman bent over and half-ran, half-crept toward the back door of DeMarco's, scanning the windows as he approached. They were fogged—no doubt to keep prying eyes out of whatever business the mob had going. A body lay next to the back door. Yeoman knelt next to him and placed his finger on the man's neck. There was a pulse. This hadn't been Negator's takedown, then; he would have just killed the guy.

The back door hung wide open, and voices spilled out—one voice shouting over the rest. That would be Negator. Yeoman stood, pressed his back to the wall next to the door, and peered inside. Negator and Sensory stood with their backs to him, facing a table surrounded by five men in suits. Two more men lay on the ground next to a door across the room—which no doubt led into the restaurant proper. There was no sign of Infuser. He must have been at the front of the store. Spright and the Crusader were more than capable of handling him, though.

Yeoman tightened his grip on his crossbow. Right now, his biggest threat was Sensory. If she detected even a trace of his intent, his cover would be blown. Luckily, her focus was on the gangsters around the table; but if Yeoman was too obvious, he could still alert her.

Calm thoughts.

An early morning in his backyard, the cool air of a Kansas morning clearing the sleep fog from his brain as he centered his crossbow on a target and squeezed the trigger. Jan coming out to bring him a cup of coffee. Pulling her close, kissing her forehead.

Yeoman raised his crossbow and trained it on Sensory. The shock arrow he had loaded would scramble her nervous system, rendering her paralyzed and dazed for half an hour. Finger on the trigger, he centered his crossbow on her back . . . and fired. She turned at the last second, but the arrow still struck just behind her shoulder blade. Sensory cried out as her body seized. She slumped to the floor.

Negator turned. *"Zee!"*

"Fire!" one of the gangsters said.

The Archdukes raised their guns and opened fire, but the bullets bounced from Negator's skin harmlessly. The door on the other side of the room swung open, and the Crusader rushed in. His staff lashed out, knocking the guns from the hands of two Archdukes. Yeoman raised his bow and shot the closest gangster. Negator hit another, sending him crashing through the door the Crusader had just entered from. The Crusader grappled with Negator while Yeoman stepped into the back room. The gangsters turned to face him.

"Why did you shoot our man?" one of them exclaimed.

"No need to escalate things." Yeoman shrugged. "Besides, you're criminals, too. Did you really think I was on your side? Now stay here and let me handle him, understand?"

The lead man glared at Yeoman. Likely weighing his options, deciding whether he and his companions could take Yeoman and Negator. Finally, he nodded and gestured for his two remaining companions to back away. Yeoman nodded to the Crusader, shouldered his crossbow, and moved into the front of the restaurant, ready to engage Negator.

* * *

"Please, leave us alone," Infuser said. "We just want to get out of this city, so they won't bother us anymore."

Patrick furrowed his brow beneath his mask. "They?"

"The gangs." Infuser pointed behind him. "We made a mistake working with them. We want to leave New Echelon and start over somewhere they can't follow us. We never wanted this."

"But Anton had other plans. Why did you follow him, Darius?"

"He . . . he's my big brother. He's always taken care of us." Infuser leaned against a table, rubbing the spot on his ribs where Spright had punched him. "But he also needs us to take care of him. We all need each other. And he never would've listened to us."

"So instead of just leaving him, you became criminals."

Infuser didn't respond, but his head wavered slightly as though he were looking around for an answer. He was lost, Spright realized. He didn't want to be involved in this, but he had no choice while Negator was calling the shots. What if Sensory left first? If Infuser's sister was out of the equation, would he follow suit? Or if Spright could convince Infuser to surrender, would Sensory agree to do the same?

Gunshots sounded from the restaurant's back room. Infuser straightened, his hand falling to the small of his back. Spright stepped forward, holding out a hand in what he hoped was a calming gesture. Infuser flinched but didn't draw his gun. He stared back at the door across the restaurant. The gunshots were joined by the sound of bodies and furniture crashing together. Yeoman and the Crusader had engaged, then. Spright needed to get back there and help them—but he couldn't do that until he dealt with Infuser.

I don't need my powers for this. Talk him down.

"Come on, Darius. You know if you run, you'll be looking over your shoulder forever. Surrender now. Make this easier on yourself. You may go to prison; but you can make a case that you were coerced by Anton, and your sentence may be reduced. Once you get out, you can be free of all this . . . maybe use your powers for good. You have potential. Don't let Anton drag you down with him."

"I—"

The door crashed open, and a suited gangster stumbled out and crashed into a table. Negator stepped out after the man, his shoulders heaving as he inhaled heavily. His sword was still clutched in his right hand, the vents on either side of the blade shimmering with red light.

With a roar, the enraged berserker leaped in to attack.

CHAPTER 34

Friction shot upright as her alarm buzzed. She must have dozed off. When she awoke, she couldn't remember where she was at first. She looked down at her phone.

Paxton.

The alarm was a unique signal he had set up to notify her if he was in danger. Heart pounding, she darted out the door, changing into her super suit in a microsecond. She sped across town toward Paxton's location. He was at a restaurant—DeMarco's. She recognized the place; it was one of the better Italian restaurants she had eaten at.

She crossed town to the restaurant in a minute and a half. Coming to a stop on the street outside, Friction surveyed the restaurant. From here, she didn't see any signs of trouble. However, only two vehicles were parked across the street, and the parking lot was empty. One of the vehicles was a black van that she recognized as the Colemans,' and an arrow had pierced the front tire. One of the vigilantes with Spright had used a crossbow; the other heroes must have arrived already.

Friction froze outside the restaurant. If the Colemans were in there, she had to kill them. She couldn't imagine taking a life, even the life of a criminal; but it would be even harder to do with other superheroes here. Spright wasn't a killer. He would never let her land a killing blow on any of the Colemans. She just had to be faster. Based on the encounter at the bank, she suspected Spright's powers were on the fritz. She could use that. Reaching up, she activated the neural inhibitor that Paxton had given her. It should protect her from Infuser.

Friction took a deep breath, sped her body up until the world around her was nearly still, and sprinted inside DeMarco's. The state of the restaurant was chaos, perfectly preserved as a frozen moment in time in Friction's perspective. Spright was leaping aside in a frantic dodge. Negator was halfway across the room, his sword raised as he charged in Spright's direction. A man in a business suit lay atop a collapsed table between the hero and the villain. In a doorway on the other side of the restaurant, Spright's friend stood with his crossbow at his shoulder, trained on Negator's back, while the Crusader hurled himself onto Negator's back, wrapping his staff around the brutish villain's neck.

Friction's heart pounded in her chest.

I can't do this.

Taking down bad guys was one thing, but killing them? All life was precious. How could Paxton ask her to take it away?

She had to do something *now*. Time hadn't stopped; she was just moving so fast that they seemed to be standing still. But if she just kept standing here, her momentum would die down. It was time to move. Negator was in position to kill someone, so he had to be taken down first.

Friction ran toward him, leaped, and planted both feet on his chest. She kicked off into a backflip and grabbed the Crusader, pulling him free as Negator flew back and slammed into the rear wall. Friction landed in a crouch. The vigilante stumbled to the ground next to her as the world returned to normal speed.

"What . . ." The vigilante looked around, confused. "Friction?"

An arrow shot over Friction's head, lodging in the wall. It had, no doubt, been aimed at Negator. Spright slammed into Infuser, taking him down to the floor. The man lying on the table grimaced and rolled onto the floor. The archer lowered his crossbow and looked at Friction. Her gaze locked with his, and she looked past him into the back room. Paxton stood next to a table with two other men. His gaze hardened, and he nodded to her.

It was time to prove herself to him . . . or fail his test.

Negator pushed himself to his feet. His sword had fallen, but she doubted that made him any less of a threat. Friction looked from him to Paxton and back again. She knew what he expected of her. The archer swiveled to face Negator and fired an arrow. The metal shaft struck Negator's shoulder and bounced off, clattering to the floor. The Crusader charged and leaped into a spinning kick, driving Negator back a step.

Dropping his crossbow, the archer drew a pistol and fired. The bullet hit Negator in the knee. Friction saw it tear through his jeans. Still, the brute was unfazed. He advanced on the archer. Spright crossed the room toward him—running at normal human speed, Friction noted—and jumped onto Negator's back. The archer fired again.

"Friction!" Spright yelled. "A little help?"

Friction rushed in, spurred on by hearing the hero call her name. She dropped into a slide and hit Negator's knee with a speed-enhanced punch. The joint popped, and Negator screamed and sagged to the floor. Friction slugged him across the jaw.

"Infuser!" Negator said. "I need rage!"

Negator jerked his arms backward, hurling Spright aside, and brought his arm in a backhanded strike against Friction's sternum. Her feet left the ground, and she gasped as her back struck the doorframe. Negator rose and yanked the archer's pistol from his hand, crushing it in his fist. The archer snapped out a kick, but Negator caught his leg and threw him across the restaurant. The Crusader rammed his staff into Negator's chest, but the metal rod spun aside. Negator punched the vigilante. The Crusader caught the blow on his shield, but his knees buckled beneath the weight of Negator's fist. He crumpled to the floor. Negator turned back toward Spright.

The criminal froze in place as a mass of blue-green goo spread across his feet. Friction recoiled in surprise and disgust. What was that stuff? Negator surged forward but went nowhere. Whatever the goo was, it was impossibly strong.

Spright stood and clenched his fists. Sparks crackled across his knuckles. He drove his fist into Negator's jaw and then landed another punch on his chest. Despite lightning bursts that exploded from Spright's knuckles with each punch, Negator seemed unmoved. He grabbed Spright's wrist. Friction sped toward him, striking him in the back. Negator reeled forward into Spright's fist.

The oldest of the Coleman triplets finally collapsed as electricity coursed over his skull. He hit the floor, his legs sinking into the strange adhesive. Friction looked down at him and then up at Spright.

Then her comms went live.

"Finish him!" Paxton shouted.

Friction stared down at Negator's still form. He was unconscious and held in place by Spright's mysterious goo. The police could take him into custody. Why did Negator have to die? She looked across the room at Infuser. He was leaning against a booth, his gaze fixed on Negator. What would Darius do if he saw Friction murder his brother?

What kind of person would he become? She was not convinced that Darius or Zoey were monsters like Anton.

"Coward," Paxton growled.

He stormed into the restaurant and nudged Friction aside. Negator flinched—ever so slightly, probably just rousing from his unconscious state—and Paxton drew a gun and fired.

"No!" Friction shouted.

Too late. Negator could be bulletproof when charged with negative emotion, but he was weakened by the sustained assault of the superheroes and only just returning to consciousness. A circle of crimson blossomed on the back of Negator's shirt. Friction shook her head in horror and looked up at Darius. He had slumped to the floor, his hands covering the downward-turned mouth of his opera mask. Spright stepped forward and jerked the gun away from Paxton.

"Why did you do that?" the hero demanded.

"He was getting up. He was still dangerous. You don't know if that substance would've held him. I couldn't take the chance he would get free. He's already hurt too many people!"

"That wasn't your call to make."

"Yes." Paxton turned away. "It was."

Before Paxton could take another step, Spright's arm shot out to punch Paxton across the jaw. The man crashed to the floor, unconscious. Friction dropped her gaze to her shoes. What Paxton had just done and what he had expected her to do—how could she continue working for him in good conscience? This was the man who had taken her in and trained her. He helped her control her speed. She had never seen this ruthlessness in him before. Was this a single, overzealous moment, or was there more to it?

Friction looked up to see where Darius was. There was no sign of Anton's brother. He must have fled while they were focused on Paxton. She glanced over her shoulder. There was no sign of Zoey in the back room. Had she witnessed her brother's death, as well?

"Looks like I'm done here." Friction walked toward the front door.

Spright grabbed her arm. "No. Wait."

Friction stopped and looked back. The archer had risen now and was limping over to the Crusader's side to help him up. They made no move to come after her, though. For now, it was just her and Spright. The other speedster released his grip on her arm.

"I need your help," he said. "Darius—or Infuser, whatever you want to call him—did something to me, and it affected my powers. I can't use my speed. With your help, I might be able to get it back. Will you help me?"

Friction's eyes widened. She had imagined him welcoming her to the hero's life or thanking her for helping them. Maybe even offering to team up someday. But she never could have imagined someone like him needing her.

She shook her head. "I-I'm not sure. I'm just an amateur. There's nothing I can do; I barely know anything about my powers."

"You don't have to. All you have to do is let one of my friends take a brain scan. We can compare how your brain works when you use your speed, and she can adjust my brain to match it. I'll be able to use my powers again. But if you don't do this, it could be a long time before I'm able to. Maybe never."

Spright . . . never able to use his powers again? Friction couldn't imagine what that must be like. Ever since she received her powers, she had grown so used to them that not having them would be like losing one of her senses. She had the power to help him. That meant she had the responsibility to do it, right? And yet she suspected Paxton would be more than happy to see Spright off the streets, if only so his protégé could take the superhero's place. Paxton wanted her to be a star. Friction didn't particularly care, though—not after watching him murder Anton in cold blood.

"Okay." She bobbed her head. "Yes. I'll help."

"Really?" The relief in his voice was palpable. "Thank you."

Spright stepped toward her, looked around, and reached up to grab the corner of his mask. Friction mirrored his quick glance around, ensuring no one was around to see the hero's secret identity. The other men had cleared out. Only the vigilantes remained. She sped across the room, shut the door to the back room just in case, and returned. Spright pulled off his mask, revealing boyish features, red hair, and kind blue eyes. That face belonged to one of her closest friends.

Friction gaped. "Patrick?"

He furrowed his brow. "Do we know each other?"

Friction reached up, removed her mask, and flipped her hair aside. She allowed the speed vibration around her face, which she usually used for added disguise, to fade away. Patrick's eyes widened, and his jaw went slack.

"Alexa?"

She pursed her lips. "Good thing I don't have any more classes on my schedule today. We've got a lot to talk about."

CHAPTER 35

Of all the twists and turns that came with being a superhero, Patrick never expected to experience a reverse identity reveal: finding out that one of his friends was secretly a superhero and had been keeping it from him all this time. He had been the one to reveal his identity but never the opposite. It was kind of a gut punch.

But strangely, it made sense. He did not know much about Alexa, despite her proximity to his friend group. Maybe this was why she was not always present with the others and had always been reluctant to open up to them. Patrick always thought it was because of some awkwardness about her recent conversion to Christianity and her former Muslim faith or something. He never could have imagined this.

He would process that later. For now, they needed to discuss their next move regarding both his powers and the Coleman siblings. With Anton dead, he was afraid Zoey and Darius might have tipped over the edge. Then there was the mob boss who murdered Anton. Patrick suspected he would be a problem.

Patrick pulled open the door to the lair and gestured for Alexa to enter, allowing Jarrett and Carter to lead her down. Jarrett had been limping since the fight with Anton; his leg had likely been sprained when Anton had grabbed it and thrown him. It was a miracle it wasn't broken. Patrick followed them in, closed the door behind them, and descended into the lair. He had texted Lucy to meet him down there; she needed to know about Alexa.

Alexa frowned. "Has this been down here all along?"

"The pool has, but our lair here is new." Patrick stepped past her and out into the lair. "Bryce set it up over the weekend."

"That . . . makes so much sense."

Patrick realized that just as he was putting the pieces together around her identity, she must've been doing the same with his. All the little clues that made no sense to someone without context fit perfectly once she had the whole picture. He guided her down toward the pool and descended the ladder. Lucy was already in the pool, along with Jan. And, as ever, Ty secluded himself in one of the corners.

Lucy walked toward Patrick as he reached the floor. "Hey, I got your text. What's going on—Alexa?"

"Hey, Lucy." Alexa climbed down into the pool. "I guess I've got some explaining to do. Tell me I wasn't the last one to know about this little operation."

Patrick lowered his head. "Sorry . . . you were. If it helps, Lucy and Bryce both found out by accident, and I told Asher because he's my best friend. Not that I'm the only one with secrets. Turns out, Alexa is Friction."

"Surprise." Alexa hoisted the backpack that held her suit. "I had no idea you guys were a super-team too. We could've been working together a long time ago."

Lucy blinked. "Wow. That's . . . wow."

"Sorry I never told you." Alexa blanched. "We may be roommates, but I have still only known you for a few months."

Lucy shrugged, then smiled. "I suppose fair's fair. No hard feelings."

Patrick gestured to Jan. "The good news is, we can use Alexa's brain scans to get my powers back. And don't worry, I made sure the Colemans were taken care of before I asked her. Which brings us to the bad news: Anton died, and Darius and Zoey escaped."

"He died?" Jan gasped. "What happened?"

"A gangster happened." Jarrett slammed his quiver down. "We had Anton contained, and then this guy came up and shot Anton in the back. In the confusion, Darius and Zoey escaped. Now they're probably going to be bent on getting revenge for their brother."

"Who was this gangster?" Lucy asked.

Patrick shook his head. "Not sure. We may have to do some digging."

"No need," Jarrett said. "I recognized him. Oscar Paxton, one of the world's leading names in oil and clean energy. He's got a monopoly on the energy business. But he's also the leader of the Archdukes."

Alexa was blinking rapidly. Patrick wondered why. Maybe it was just the flurry of information being a lot to take in. He wasn't sure. She would get used to it quickly enough, if that was the case.

"Why would Paxton kill Anton?" Patrick asked.

"Maybe because Anton killed some of his lieutenants? Or made business tense with the Seventy-Six?" Jarrett shrugged. "I can't be sure. What I do know is Paxton's not going to stop at Anton. He'll want Darius and Zoey dead, too."

"But we knocked him out. The police have him in custody, right?"

"Sure, but between his wealth and his underworld connections, Paxton will get out quickly. After all, he was the victim of the Colemans' attack. He can make a valid self-defense plea that no one will refute—which means we need to find Darius and Zoey quickly. Otherwise, we'll have them and Paxton shooting up the town, gunning for each other."

"Lovely. Looks like I'll need my speed back now more than ever."

"I'll get right on it." Jan extended a hand. "Alexa? If you come this way, I can get you hooked up to a brain monitor."

Alexa nodded. "I'll be glad to help however I can."

Good.

The way things were progressing, they would need as many people as they could get out there, or the streets of New Echelon were going to get very messy.

* * *

Paxton had killed him.

It hadn't been self-defense. It was murder, plain and simple. And Darius had to watch, unable to do anything as his brother was shot before his eyes.

At least for Darius, watching it happen had been over quickly. After he had found Zee and dragged her out of the restaurant, she hadn't stopped screaming for nearly an hour. She had roused from unconsciousness just before that gangster had shot Anton, and she had sensed her own brother's death—felt it as keenly as if it had been her own. Now, she was curled up on the dusty hotel bed, staring at the wall and crying silently. She had always been the strongest of the three emotionally. But this . . . no one should have to go through what she was experiencing.

Darius sat down next to her. "You okay, Zee?"

"No." Zee sniffled. "No, I'm not. Anton was a bully, and he didn't know when to quit while he was ahead; but he didn't deserve to die for it. He was our brother. He was just trying to take care of us."

"I know." Darius wrapped his arm around her shoulders. "I know."

"That murdering scum has to pay."

"He will. Spright knocked him out. The police have him in custody now, I'm sure."

"You don't get it. Do you know who that man was? Oscar Paxton is a millionaire. He'll never see the inside of a jail cell."

Darius stood and crossed the room, scratching the back of his head. They were now enemies with a millionaire who also led a powerful gang. Paxton had killed Anton, so there was no reason to assume he would let Darius and Zee go—not since they had killed DeMarco and especially not now that they had launched a second attack against him. Darius and Zee would be at the top of the hit list.

"We've got to go."

"Get real, Darius. How can we do that? We've barely got any money, a stolen car . . . where are we going to go?"

She was right. When they fled the restaurant, they had found an arrow stuck in one of the van's tires. With no other option, they had hurried back to steal one of the Archdukes' cars. But even if they got out of town, the small bag of cash from the bank robbery would only last them a few weeks, tops. Not nearly enough time to put down roots and start making the kind of money they needed to survive.

"What do you propose?"

"We need to stop the people trying to kill us." Zee stood, and the rage burning in her dark eyes was frightening. "We need to kill Oscar Paxton and the rest of the Archdukes' leadership. While we're at it, let's take out the Seventy-Six for good measure. I doubt they'll forgive Anton's debt just because he's . . . " She swallowed. "Once they're all dead, we'll be safe. It's what Anton would've wanted."

"But not what you would've wanted. This isn't you talking, Zee."

"Feeling your brother's death changes your outlook on life." Zee picked up her opera mask and stared down at it. "Those superheroes aren't going to help us. If they were worth anything, they would've taken down the Archdukes a long time ago."

Darius thought back to his conversation with Spright. The hero seemed genuine; he really had wanted to help them, not just beat them up and throw them in jail. Before Anton came crashing through that door, Spright had been willing to talk. He might have listened to Darius. He might have helped. He wanted Darius to turn himself in and get clean. He seemed to have genuinely wanted to put Darius on a better path. That path wouldn't have included murdering Oscar Paxton.

"I don't know, Zee . . . " Darius stopped walking next to the window and peered out. "We can do the right thing. If we turn ourselves in and testify against Paxton, maybe we could put him away, regardless of his wealth."

"That's not how the world works, and you know it. Paxton is so strapped up with lawyers that anything we say will get twisted against us. Who would believe us over him, anyway? The legal route won't cut it. Our government is too corrupt."

If anyone would know, it was Zee. Her political activism wasn't just idealistic. She did her research. Darius balled his hands into fists and pounded one against the wall. How had it come to this?

"Do we have enough money for a few more nights in this motel?" Zee asked.

Darius picked up the bag of cash Anton had left underneath one of the beds and counted their coffers. There was enough. Zee must have sensed the affirmative, because she nodded.

"Good." Zee crossed to Darius's side, locked the door, and pulled the curtains. "We'll lie low for a few days, wait for all this to blow over. Ditch the car. The Archdukes will be looking for it. And while we wait, we can put together a plan."

"Whatever you say, sis." Darius sighed. "Whatever you say."

CHAPTER 36

Asher had never seen Joey frantic; but following him into the police station, weaving between officers, visitors, and a few perps being ushered in, Asher was hard-pressed to keep up with his roommate. They had been at lunch when Joey got the call that his dad had been arrested. In support of his friend, Asher agreed to go with him to the police station. Joey wasn't really in the mental state to drive, anyway.

Joey stopped at the front desk and rapped his fingers impatiently against the surface. Asher stepped back to a makeshift waiting area where a few dingy plastic chairs were set against a wall. He pulled out his phone and dialed Patrick. Spright was far from being involved in every arrest in New Echelon, especially in his current condition; but there was still a chance he might know something.

Patrick answered on the second ring. "Hello?"

"Hey, I'm at the police station with Joey. Apparently, his dad was arrested today. Do you know anything about that?"

Patrick sucked in a breath between his teeth. "Is his dad Oscar Paxton?"

That didn't sound promising. "Yeah. What happened?"

"He shot Anton Coleman in cold blood. The Colemans attacked DeMarco's. I don't know if you're aware of this, Asher, but your roommate's dad is the leader of the Archdukes gang."

"Wait . . . *what?*" Asher laughed. "That's ridiculous. He's, like, the world's top energy manufacturer."

"And a gangster on the side. I watched him shoot Anton. The only other people in that restaurant were Archduke leaders. He's a criminal, man."

"Oh man." Asher ran his hand through his hair. "Do you think Joey knows? How could he not?"

"I don't know. I'm glad you called me—at least you've got a heads-up. And while I've got you, there is some good news. I made contact with Friction, and she agreed to help me get my powers back."

"That's great! How'd you convince her?"

"Didn't take much convincing. Friction is Alexa."

Asher blinked. He needed to hang up before Patrick dropped any more bombshells on him. He seemed full of them today. Asher glanced at the desk where Joey was speaking with an officer. Joey gestured for him to come over.

"I've got to go," Asher said. "I'll stop by later."

Asher hung up and weaved his way toward the desk. The officer Joey was speaking with pointed to a hallway across the bustling lobby. Joey nodded and walked toward the hall. Asher fell in behind him. How did he bring up Paxton's gang affiliation? If Joey didn't know, this was not a good time for him to find out. If he did know, he hadn't told Asher for a reason. Either way, he would wonder how Asher had gotten that information. Talking about it would only put Patrick's identity at risk.

Another officer met them in the hallway and led them to the temporary holding cells. As they stepped through the door to the cell block, Asher wondered if Shannon's father associated with Paxton through his legitimate business. What if it was it through the gangs, and she was connected to criminals, too?

"Dad?" Joey rushed to the cell bars. "What happened?"

Paxton, who was sitting on a stone bench in a crowded cell, looked up at his son's voice. The other criminals in the cell were giving Paxton plenty of space.

They know who he is.

However good he was at concealing his identity from the public, that anonymity clearly did not extend to the underworld. Paxton rose and crossed to the barred cell door, the other suspects clearing a path for him.

"Thank you for coming so quickly, son. This is a terrible mistake—I was the victim, and Spright took me down instead of the attackers."

Joey shook his head. "That doesn't sound like him."

"I don't know what happened. All I know is, two of those thugs got away while he was busy punching me out. Did you bring the bail money I asked for?"

Joey reached into his pocket. "Yeah, Dad. I got it."

"Good. Get me out of here, so we can get justice on those who really deserve it."

Asher shuddered. Whatever Paxton had planned, Asher suspected it had nothing to do with helping the police find the Colemans.

* * *

"So." Patrick studied the group before him. "How do we start?"

Alexa stood off to the side as Patrick, Jan, and Jarrett gathered around a table full of lab equipment and spoke. Bryce had left the lair half an hour ago. He had an early afternoon class to get to. That left Alexa waiting on the sidelines, which she had never liked. It was why she had so much trouble keeping friends until now. She had always been training with Paxton, but she couldn't tell anyone that.

Patrick, Lucy, and the others were different, though. They had never questioned where she was when she hadn't been able to make a hangout because of training; and when she had been with them, they made her feel important. She was just as much a part of the group as the rest of them. And despite that, she couldn't find it in herself to be angry that they never told her Patrick was Spright. After all, she had kept an equally big secret from them.

"What's it like?" Lucy asked. "Being a speedster, I mean. I've asked Patrick before, but I wondered if the sensation might be different for you."

Alexa glanced over at her. Like Alexa, she was only waiting as Patrick and the others figured out their game plan. It was nice to have someone to talk to. She had never had that with Paxton.

"It's . . . peaceful. Like the whole world stops, and everything makes sense. You have so much time to think, and to process, and to plan; and there's no noise or movement to distract you."

"Sounds great."

"Yeah, it is. Especially in the middle of a test."

The girls laughed. It felt so good to be open and real with someone. Paxton was so distant, and his lab workers had been instructed to keep conversation with her to a minimum. She wasn't there to make friends, Paxton said. She was there to become a superhero. Friends were a distraction. Maybe Paxton was wrong about that. Patrick kept his friends close, after all; and he was still a superhero.

A superhero who lost his powers, whispered a small voice at the back of her mind. She pushed the thought away. That could have happened to anybody. It was simply a misfortune that had nothing to do with his friends. And besides, without them, he wouldn't be able to get his powers back at all.

"We've got something," Jan said. "The ideal way to get a precise brain scan match for Patrick's speed is to analyze your brainwaves while you're in motion. I'm going to modify the equipment I have to work with a portable brain scanner you can wear while running."

Alexa nodded. "Whatever you need."

"This is going to take some time," Jarrett said. "No reason for all of you to hang around down here. Go get some lunch. We'll call you when we've got something."

* * *

Oscar Paxton was not a worrier by nature. If something became a problem, he dealt with it. He did not concern himself with what might be or how things might go badly. He reacted to events as they came. His son, on the other hand, was a chronic worrier. Paxton wished he could beat that out of Joey.

"Why are we at the office, Dad?" Joey frowned. "We should go home. You've been through a lot today. What if those masked people come after you again?"

"We're no more in danger here than we are at home. Relax, Joey."

Paxton had some things he needed to get from the office before he went home. Now that the Colemans had made themselves an enemy, Paxton had no choice but to prepare extreme measures in response. Ideally, he would have liked to recruit them. Alongside Friction, they would have made a powerful team. Unfortunately, their tangled web of connections with the Seventy-Six made them too dangerous to use. Paxton had expected them to run, not to retaliate with force. Anton had surprised him. He would not be taken by surprise again.

He strode out of the elevator and down the carpeted hallway toward the double doors leading into his office. Joey trailed behind him, his aimless, meandering gait raising Paxton's ire when he glanced back.

This boy should have been a warrior.

Paxton had failed his son; he saw that now. He wished he could go back and do it all over.

Paxton reached for the doorknob and realized the door was already slightly ajar. He frowned and glanced over his shoulder at Joey. The cops had taken Paxton's gun; he was unarmed now. Someone of his skills was never defenseless, but Joey might get in the way. He turned and put a hand on his son's shoulder.

"Wait here. I'll be right back."

Joey frowned but stepped back and leaned against the wall. Paxton eased into his office and closed the door behind him.

"What have you done?" a voice demanded from the shadows.

Paxton turned in time to see a black-clad figure step out from the deepest corner of the office. A sword was sheathed across the figure's back. Reaching up, the intruder removed his mask, revealing dark brown skin crisscrossed with scars. Paxton relaxed. At least, the intruder was an ally.

"Keskin." Paxton inclined his head. "It is good to see you."

Keskin—the Sicaran assassin Roland Demirci—sneered. "Niceties will get you nowhere, Adranis. I asked you a question. What have you done?"

Paxton shrugged. "I protected myself. Anton Coleman was going to kill me. I had no choice but to strike first. Isn't that our code?"

He moved toward his desk as he spoke and dropped into the comfortable rolling chair on the other side and removed a bottle of whiskey from the bottom drawer of his desk. He needed a drink now, something to take the edge off. Keskin strode closer but made no move to sit in either of the plush armchairs on the other side of the desk. The assassin stood with his arms crossed, a deep frown etched on his face.

"Coleman and his siblings would have been useful to us," Keskin said. "You were tasked with recruiting superhumans for the Sicarans. The Colemans already worked with your man DeMarco. They would have been easy recruits. Why did you push them away?"

"Our peace with the Seventy-Six was hard-won." Paxton poured himself a glass and took a sip of the strong drink. "I could not risk it. Besides, I already have a superhuman for you."

"Yes, the speedster." Keskin looked around. "I don't see her here."

"We've had some . . . disagreements regarding her training. She'll come around."

"She'd better. And for the record, Adranis, I would not worry so much about your peace with the Seventy-Six. It will not last." Keskin removed a knife from the sheath on his belt and twirled it between his fingers. "Their leader is from Charybdis. Once he learns of your association with the Sicarans, your alliance will fall apart."

Paxton scowled. Charybdis? He slammed his glass down on the desk. All this time, Benjamin Weeks had been a member of that ancient cabal, the sworn enemies of the Sicarans. Paxton had sacrificed the Colemans to keep peace with Charybdis?

"Keep that card close to your vest for now," Keskin said. "It's possible that your alliance could be a useful tool someday. If we get close to Weeks, we can sabotage Charybdis from within."

Paxton nodded. "Understood."

"Deal with the Colemans. Find us superhumans, Adranis. Don't fail again." Keskin slammed his knife on the desktop. "Otherwise, next time I visit, I won't leave the door ajar. You will not see me until it's too late."

CHAPTER 37

The testing center for Garvin Technologies rested on ten acres of open land between New Echelon and San Francisco. The building was a three-story state-of-the-art slab of metal and concrete, a monument to progress. As Paxton, dressed down in a pair of khakis and a gray polo, strode up the sidewalk to the front door, he examined the face of the building with its massive infinity symbol, a *G* resting in the center of one loop and a *T* in the other. Garvin had been struggling to keep up with Sterling Enterprises for the past few years but was climbing in the ranks since their development of energy weapons, such as the concussion sword Paxton gave to Anton Coleman via DeMarco. Unfortunate that Coleman had used the weapon against him. Garvin Technologies had another weapon in the works, one Paxton had been collaborating on. With any luck, it would help him with his little amp problem.

It was clear that he had pushed Friction too hard, too quickly. She was too young and naïve to do what needed to be done. She did not understand that a real hero wasn't an idealistic child who couldn't kill. Sometimes, death was a necessity. Even the police understood that. If they could use lethal force, why did she think herself above them? She was just following the example of costumed do-gooders like Spright, but that was not heroism. It was cowardice. Once she was with the Sicarans, she would learn. That naïveté would be stripped away. As an assassin-trained speedster, Alexa might well be the deadliest person on the planet.

But for now, Paxton would take matters into his own hands. He had not risen to the top of the Archdukes by keeping his hands clean. He had done more than his share of killing, both as a Sicaran and as a criminal enforcer. When Joey was born, the Sicarans had allowed Paxton to return to the United States to raise the boy, provided he used his skills and resources to further their cause. He had not forgotten. He had not lost his skill. He just needed a new set of tools.

Paxton pulled open the glass door to the testing facility's lobby and stepped inside. Everything about the lobby screamed progress—the stark white, almost shining furniture, the abundance of transparent walls and fixtures, the plants in gleaming ovular growth jars that provided them nutrients automatically. It was almost too much. Garvin seemed to be trying too hard to beat Sterling.

"Mr. Paxton!" a lab assistant called. "Dr. Marsden is waiting for you in Lab H."

Paxton followed the assistant down the hall, concocting an air of aloofness about himself. Few knew about his dealings with Garvin Technologies. In fact, Mark Garvin himself remained unaware. Garvin and Paxton had been in negotiation for months; Garvin needed energy, and he wanted Paxton to provide it. But while Paxton had been working aboveboard with the CEO and owner of the company, he had been working in secret with Dr. Eliot Marsden on this little side project. The fewer people who noted Paxton's presence, the better. Mark would not take kindly to Paxton's involvement.

The door to Lab H slid aside, and the assistant gestured for Paxton to enter. He nodded his thanks to her and strode inside as the door whooshed shut behind him. The lab was ten degrees cooler than the hallway or the lobby had been, colder even than it had been outside. Ignoring the temperature, which raised instant goosebumps on his arms, Paxton examined the contents of the lab. By all accounts, Marsden was a tidy scientist. Everything was in its place on a pair of white workbenches attached to the far wall. Most of the lab was wide open and empty of clutter. One standout caught Paxton's attention: a pile of haphazardly stacked files against the right wall, its contents spilling over onto the floor around it.

Standing at a computer station on the left wall, Marsden looked up, spotted Paxton, and jumped. Paxton shook his head and strode over to the man, taking advantage of his imposing height and muscle mass to keep the scientist off guard. Marsden was a useful tool, but Paxton couldn't have him thinking that he could do this on his own. He needed Paxton. Otherwise, he was a liability.

"Mr. Paxton," Marsden said. "Right on time."

"As always, Dr. Marsden." Paxton shook Marsden's hand firmly. "Tell me, Doctor. What have you accomplished since our last meeting?"

"The prototype is nearly complete, sir. I should have a functional model within the day."

"Excellent. Let me see."

Marsden bobbed his head and typed in a command on the computer. A circular hatch opened in the lab floor, and from the hatch rose the instrument of Paxton's judgment. A suit of sleek, high-tech armor, the metallic figure gleamed silver under the fluorescent lights. The helmet was featureless—an intentional choice, giving the impression of an emotionless hunter. The wearer would be able to see through the helmet via a micro-camera embedded in the machine's forehead that fed directly to the helmet's head-up display.

Every inch of the armor had been designed to Paxton's specifications. Concussion gauntlets, reverse-engineered and modified from the models manufactured by Sterling Enterprises, gave the suit the strength of someone like Anton Coleman. The suit was form-fitting and narrow to increase its aerodynamics. Powerful thrusters in the legs, combined with an interior inertial compensator, would allow the wearer to run with speeds rivaling those of Spright and Friction. Those same thrusters could even provide a short burst of flight. The right gauntlet hid a miniature version of the concussion sword. The suit was made of indestructible aionium, a metal "borrowed" from Sterling Enterprises.

"The HUD and onboard computer are reactive." Marsden tapped the helmet. "A neural link will enhance your own reflexes. In addition to providing superspeed, it will give you the ability to react to a speedster's moves, thinking almost as fast as they do."

Paxton stepped up to the suit, examining his reflection in the faceplate. *Who says we need amplified fighters, Keskin?*

With suits like this, the Sicarans could compete with any amp. Paxton would prove it with this prototype; and then, perhaps, Keskin and the Elite would be so pleased, they would realize recruiting superhumans was unnecessary.

"And no one has any idea about this? It can't be traced back to me?"

"The only one who knows is Kate." Marsden gestured at the door, no doubt referring to the secretary who escorted Paxton in. "She's loyal to me, and she knows I'll protect her. She won't tell anyone."

"Good." Paxton looked the suit up and down. "Have you heard about Archduke Franz Ferdinand's hunting habits, Marsden?"

The scientist raised an eyebrow. "No, sir."

"Archduke Ferdinand was considered an . . . excessive hunter." Paxton half-smiled. "He killed three hundred thousand creatures. An unnecessary amount, by anyone's estimation, but he continued anyway. He did so because he could and because he loved the game."

"I see."

"This suit, Marsden, will make me the greatest hunter the world has ever seen. A hunter feared because he doesn't hunt out of necessity or fear. No. I hunt because I love the thrill of the sport—I'm not living for the trophies I will gain from my targets, but from the game of it all. The challenge."

"I'm afraid I don't understand, sir." Marsden looked from Paxton to the suit and back. "This . . . this prototype is going to production for Garvin Technologies, isn't it?"

"Oh, you may use the blueprints to create one for such a purpose, yes. But not this one. This suit is *mine,* Marsden. Why do you think I've been funding it all along? Out of charity? I wanted this suit for me."

Marsden's gulp was audible. "Sir . . . and what will you be hunting?"

Paxton removed the suit's right gauntlet and slid it over his hand. "Superhumans."

* * *

"They just let him go?" Patrick asked.

"What choice did they have?" Asher replied. "Joey brought the bail money. And even if this goes to trial—and given Paxton's power and wealth, I doubt it will—you know as well as I do that he can claim self-defense. Who's going to argue it? Is Spright going to show up in court to dispute his statement? Or maybe Anton's siblings, the super-criminals, will do it."

"There's got to be some dirt we can find on Paxton," Lucy said.

The three original members of Team Spright were meeting in the student lounge. Alexa and Bryce were both in class, and Asher's classes at Echelon U had been canceled for the day. It was the first time the three of them had been alone to strategize in . . . Patrick didn't remember how long. He didn't count the time when he had been under the influence of Infuser's psychic attack; he might as well not have been there at all.

Asher looked at her. "What kind of dirt?"

"Something tying him to the Archdukes. They're practically public enemy number one to New Echelon PD. If they knew Paxton was the leader of the Archdukes, they'd have him behind bars before he could even say, 'I want my lawyer.' Especially if we can prove he's used any of his company's funds to help the gang."

Patrick patted her hand. "Good point. Any ideas on how to do that?"

Lucy shook her head. "Unfortunately, no."

"What about Joey?"

"No way," Asher said. "He doesn't know about his dad's gang involvement. Trust me. He was completely dumbfounded when he found out his father had been arrested; and when I watched them interact when Joey sprung him, I could tell that he genuinely had no idea what his dad could've done."

All the stories Asher had told about Joey's reluctance to study aside, Patrick didn't think the guy was actually an idiot. There had to be some clue he'd noticed that hinted at his father's allegiance to the Archdukes.

"There is one thing," Asher continued. "I didn't want to bring it up, but . . . maybe it'll get us the win, so I'm willing to risk it."

"What is it?" Lucy asked.

"Shannon. She mentioned that her father and Paxton know each other. They've worked together, and she's even been to Paxton's house before. I didn't want to think about it, but what if their business association is gang-related?"

Patrick grimaced. Asher clearly liked Shannon a lot. Asking her if her father was involved in gang activity was practically relationship suicide. But what if it was the only way?

"We can't ask you to do that, buddy. We'll find proof somehow. I mean, we've got Jarrett Mercer on our team. He's a government agent. If anyone can find out the truth about Paxton, it'll be him."

"Thank you." Asher sighed in relief. "Just wanted to put it out there."

Lucy smiled. "And we appreciate it. Don't worry. I'm sure Shannon has nothing to do with the gangs, even if her father does."

"Yeah, I mean, she's going to school for politics." Asher laughed nervously. "She's above all that. Right?"

"Don't sweat it, buddy." Patrick bumped his friend's shoulder. "I'm going to go take a walk. See you guys later."

Patrick stretched and rose from his chair. They still didn't have a plan to catch Paxton, but he knew someone who might be able to give him some advice. Leaving the student lounge behind, Patrick pulled out his phone and called the man who taught him everything he knew about being a superhero.

"Hello?" Gideon Turner answered.

"Hey, Gideon. Do you have a few minutes to talk?"

"Sure thing. Is everything okay?"

"It's . . . I just really need someone to talk to—someone who understands what I'm dealing with."

Patrick took a breath. The sound of Gideon's voice reassured him, fortifying the waning determination in his heart. Gideon had poured his heart into making sure Patrick was ready for whatever he faced. Patrick couldn't have asked for anyone better. He wished Gideon were here now. He'd know exactly what to do. He'd faced far worse than Paxton. He would've dealt with him easily.

"Have you seen anything on the news? There's a new speedster in town. Calls herself Friction."

"I saw. Dean makes sure that all the Vindicators get regular updates about that sort of thing. She's a problem?"

"No, actually. She's helping me out . . . you know, maybe I should start from the beginning. If you're not sitting down, you might want to. This might take a while."

Patrick walked down the hallway toward the stairs that accessed the rooftop garden. As he did, he explained his situation to Gideon from the moment Asher had called him about the theft at the party until Paxton had murdered Anton. Through it all, Gideon never interrupted. Patrick found a chair on the rooftop, pulled it over to the edge so he could look out at the city as he talked, and finished the story.

Gideon blew out a breath. "It sounds like you've been through the wringer."

"I have. Jarrett and Carter have been a big help; and, of course, so have Lucy and Asher and everyone else, but I've never dealt with anything like this before—not without you or Dean or one of the others. I know you probably would've dealt with the Colemans and Paxton the first time you fought them, but I—"

"Don't compare yourself to me. You said it yourself—this is your first supervillain encounter without support from an experienced superpowered hero. Not to mention that you've never gone against organized crime before. My first outing as a vigilante was against organized crime, and I nearly died . . . at least three times."

"Yeah, that's true, I just . . . I hate that I can't do this on my own. I had to call Jarrett for help, and now you . . . "

"Trust me, Patrick, I never did this on my own—not successfully, anyway. If I hadn't had Dean's support my first year as the Seraph, Luca Serban would be running Sojourn City now. He wasn't my only help, either. Jolie, Carter, Carter's dad . . . they all played an important part in my defeating Serban. It wasn't a solo effort."

"I hadn't thought of it that way before. Thanks, Gideon."

Patrick stared out at his campus, watching as handfuls of students walked from one building to another. They were energetic, full of life, probably completely unaware of what was going on in their city, certainly unaware of the personal crisis Patrick was experiencing. Was being a superhero always this isolated?

"Rely on your team. They'll get you through this."

How could I have missed that?

Unintentionally, Patrick had always thought of Lucy, Asher, and now Bryce as an auxiliary part of what he did. They were there for support, but they didn't influence what happened on the streets. That was on Patrick, and Patrick alone. But if what Gideon was saying was true, they were more important than that. He needed them as much as—or more than—he needed his powers.

"While I have you, do you have any tips on taking on a gangster like Paxton?"

"Hit him where it hurts—his wallet," Gideon said. "Draw him into making a mistake. The more you hurt him, the angrier he gets and the more likely he is to slip up. Once you have viable evidence you can give to the police, even Paxton's wealth won't save him."

"What about his son—Asher's friend, Joey? Asher says he's clueless about his dad's gang activity. Finding out the truth will wreck him."

"It's unfortunate, but Dean had to find out about his own father's criminal activity the same way. Telling him was one of the hardest things I had to do; but once he realized the truth, he came around."

"Thanks, Gideon. Just talking all this out, it means a lot."

"You're welcome. Tell Jarrett I said hello—and Carter to hurry back. And if there's ever a threat that requires the Vindicators to get back together, tell Friction she is more than welcome to join us."

"I'll tell them. Bye, Gideon."

Patrick hung up and stared down at his phone. Gideon had given him a lot to think about. There were a lot of changes to make in his life. God had given him his friends for a reason, he realized. Treating them like secondary members of Team Spright had been a mistake. If they were going to stop Paxton and the Colemans, it wasn't going to be his efforts alone that got it done. It would be all of them. Together.

"Calling the boss man?"

Patrick turned. Carter stood in the rooftop doorway, leaning against the frame and smirking. Patrick chuckled and tucked his phone away. Carter stepped up onto the rooftop and took one of the metal patio chairs. Patrick sat down across from him.

"I don't blame you," Carter continued. "Gideon knows his stuff. I couldn't have taken Vickers down without Gideon's support."

"He does. Do you think he misses the superhero life?"

"I know he does." Carter smiled. "He's content, though. Probably more content than I'd be in the same situation."

Patrick frowned. "And way more content than I've been."

"That's not what I meant."

"I know." Patrick leaned back in his chair and looked up at the sky. "I appreciate that you stuck around. I feel like I haven't been a very good friend since you've been here; we missed out on the lunch we had planned, and I've barely spoken to you."

"You're busy. I know how it is."

"Yeah, but you've made a big sacrifice by sticking around to help me. I hope you know I don't take that lightly."

"It's cool, man. Promise."

Patrick looked back to Carter. "We've got time now. Come on, let's go grab a bite. We'll catch up; you can tell me what's going on in Sojourn City and exactly who Ty Vickers is; and then we can figure out how the two of us and our friends can stop the Colemans and put Paxton out of business for good. Spright and the Crusader—together again."

Carter grinned. "Sounds like a plan."

CHAPTER 38

Jarrett was beginning to think that his estimate that working up a portable brain scanner would "take a while" had been an understatement. Jan had been working around the clock to rig something that would be able to transmit a speedster's brain scans to her terminal. Jarrett was doing his best to help; but although he had experience as a field medic, his expertise did not lie in this area.

The work provided them a lot of alone time together, though. With Patrick and the others juggling their classes with their hero work, the lair was often empty for hours at a time. The only occupant was Carter's friend—or prisoner—Ty, who kept to himself. Jarrett didn't care. The opportunity to sit in privacy with his wife and simply talk to her was a rare privilege.

Jan peered up at him.

"Okay. Hold this together while I finish the wiring."

Jarrett reached down and pressed the two halves of the wireless headset together as Jan used a thin pair of clamps to guide the wiring together with one hand, while with the other she fused them together with thin streams of blue electricity. Jarrett studied his wife, smiling at the intense gaze she had locked on the device.

"You look really cute with your nose scrunched like that."

A trace of a smile flickered across Jan's face. "Don't distract me."

"Sorry." He looked up at the ceiling and whistled innocently. "I was just thinking we need to revisit our conversation about kids. After all, you've been doing such a good job with these teenagers that it would be a shame to deprive an infant of the same care . . . "

"Jarrett . . . "

"Sorry."

Jan's fingers flickered with sparks for another moment, and then the crackling blue light vanished. She put the clamps down on the table and took the headset from Jarrett, turning it over in her hands to examine every angle.

"Good?" he asked.

"I think we've got it. We'll see if it can keep up with speedster brainwaves once Alexa gets down here; but for now, we can give it a test run to make sure it works at all. Do you mind?"

"It would be my pleasure."

Jan slipped the scanner over Jarrett's head. It was heavier than he expected—not enough to weigh him down but heavier than a baseball cap. He straightened as Jan walked over to her computer.

"Let's just hope this doesn't explode."

Jarrett gaped silently, his eyes widening as he struggled to think of a reasonable response to her taciturn statement. He glimpsed a subtle smirk on Ty's face, but the convict turned away and said nothing.

Jan reached for the switch. "Turning it on . . . now."

"Wait, wait, no—"

Jarrett cringed and stiffened as the headset hummed to life.

I swear, if I blow up . . .

But nothing happened.

Jarrett relaxed, though he could still feel his own eyes bugging out of his head as he stared at his wife. Whether she was joking about it blowing up or not was impossible to tell. Jarrett was a master of deadpan humor, but his wife was almost as talented in the art.

"It's working," Jan said. "And don't worry. It wouldn't have exploded, per se. Probably just caught fire. You would've lost some hair, but it wouldn't have been anything you couldn't recover from."

Jarrett shook his head. "Speak for yourself. My hair's my best feature."

Smirking, Jan walked over to him as he removed the headset. She reached up and ran a hand through his thick hair.

"True. But if it burned off, I bet it would give you a reason to grow a beard—another of your better features."

Jarrett chuckled. "Thanks. I'm not sure I could pull off the bald and bearded look."

"I bet you could." Jan took the headset. "Well, with everything working, we should be good to go once Alexa gets down here. We can run the tests, compare her brain scans with Patrick's, and then I can get him back in running shape. And then, I guess, our work here will be done."

"Yeah, I guess so."

But with the situation surrounding the Colemans and Paxton unresolved, Jarrett wasn't sure if he could leave in good conscience. He had already been gone from CLOUD for nearly a week, but he thought he should be able to stay until this situation was resolved. If he didn't and Patrick or one of his friends got hurt, he didn't know how he would live with himself.

* * *

Stealing a car was not as difficult as Darius imagined, especially with the power to influence emotions. Using his powers to subdue a cocky teenager with a car that wasn't nearly showy enough to live up to the boy's pride, Darius took his keys without incident and drove away with the teen convinced that he had given up the car of his own volition.

Maybe I can even return it . . . someday.

They wouldn't have long before the boy came to his senses and reported the car stolen; but by then, it wouldn't be an issue. Driving the car back to Anton's shop, he replaced the boy's license plate with one of the many hanging on Anton's wall, put a few dents in the vehicle so it would less match the description the boy provided to the police, and even pained a sloppy pair of white racing stripes down the middle of the black hood.

Satisfied with his work, Darius returned to the motel, where Zee waited outside their room. Two small suitcases sitting on the sidewalk beside her. The dilapidated building and its dusty room had been more a home over the past week than Darius' own house, he realized. It would feel strange to leave it behind. But they had remained in one place too long. Sooner or later, the manager would get suspicious. Darius climbed out of the car and picked up both of the dinged-up black suitcases.

Zee studied the car. "Good find. Any trouble?"

"None." Darius tossed the suitcases in the back seat. "And the car's just boring enough that it won't stand out no matter where we park it."

"Even with the racing stripes?"

"It was that or give the whole thing a new paint job, and I didn't have time for that." Darius returned to his seat behind the wheel. "We'll just have to trust the blandness of the car itself will outweigh the paint job."

"It had better." Zee climbed into the passenger's seat. "If it doesn't, we're toast. Paxton won't hesitate to kill us, too."

She was right, but Paxton was also less likely to attack them on the street outside of his legitimate business. He still had a front to put on. He could call security and have them escorted away, yes, but he would never stoop to murder while he was on the premises of his energy company. That was their sweet spot.

The plan, currently, was to wait for Paxton to leave work and follow him home. They would ambush him as he arrived at his house, Darius using his powers to lull Paxton into a sense of security and Zee sneaking up on him and taking him down. They hadn't decided yet who would be the one to actually kill him—both of them simultaneously wanted to be the one to get revenge for Anton and did not want the guilt of murder on their conscience.

It didn't help that neither of them had been able to grieve properly. Anton's body had been taken by the police, and Darius and Zee couldn't retrieve it without being implicated in his crimes. The cops knew Anton worked with two accomplices, and his siblings would be at the top of the list of suspects. Without his body, they hadn't been able to perform even a private funeral or ceremony. It was a wound that was slowly scabbing rather than healing.

"Where do we go from here, Zee?" Darius asked. "We kill Paxton. Then what? How do we find the rest of the Archdukes? How do we get them and the Seventy-Six off our tails? It's never going to end."

"One step at a time. Revenge first."

Darius clenched his jaw, nodded, and kept his eyes on the road. Zee had changed since she sensed Anton's death. This was not the sister he knew. When she finally came to her senses, Darius hoped she hadn't fallen so far that she didn't recognize herself anymore.

* * *

The streak of red circled the lair so rapidly that it nearly formed into a solid circle, fencing in those inside the pool from the outside world. Patrick leaned against the cool metal of the table he had set his gear on. With one hand, he reached up and scratched the back of his head as Alexa's blurred figure continued to run.

Lord, please let this work.

Jan appeared confident that the brainwave scanner was functional. As long as Alexa's brain put off the same kind of energy Patrick's did when he ran, this test should gather all the data Jan would need to begin reprogramming Patrick's brain.

He had to get it back before someone else got hurt. If he had been able to use his speed at DeMarco's, he could have saved Anton's life and brought all three Coleman siblings in unharmed. But now, one of them was dead; and the other two were likely being hunted by a millionaire gangster—and were just as likely hunting that gangster in return.

Jarrett nudged him. "She's really moving. Have you ever run this fast?"

"A few times. When I ran from Sojourn City to San Francisco, for sure. Maybe when we fought Ashcroft at his lab, too."

He glanced down at a speedometer resting on the table. Alexa was nearing 250 miles per hour. It was an impressive speed. Even Patrick was awed that she could reach it. Whoever had trained Alexa had pushed her far harder than someone her age deserved to be pushed.

I need to know more about her past.

Alexa had to have gotten her suit, at least, from someone. It was professionally crafted, not some homemade spandex body glove.

"She's slowing down." Jarrett motioned to the speedometer. "195."

Building endurance had been one of the hardest parts of learning how to use his powers. Well, that and stopping. It was understandable that Alexa would have similar problems. She had been running at this rate for five-and-a-half minutes; if he was doing his math correctly, she had run over twenty miles in that time.

"Just a few more minutes, and I should have what I need," Jan said. "Then, we can take a break, and I can get her resting brain levels."

"Why didn't we do that before?" Patrick asked.

"It's better to do it after she's used her powers. I want to get as accurate a feel for speedster physiology as I can."

Patrick glanced at the speedometer again—170. She was decelerating. He turned his attention away from the test and to his laptop. A document pulled up bore the title "Heroes and Their Effects on Christian Teens." He hadn't had much time to work on it. The past few days, he, Carter, and Jarrett had followed Gideon's advice—hitting Paxton's wallet. They had taken out four Archduke safehouses and left them for the police to find. Any money in the safehouses had been confiscated.

He had managed to type out a page and a half of content that he had formed from his own thoughts as well as a few interviews he had done during the Wednesday night youth group at Echelon Bible Church. The results were surprising—from the batch of nearly thirty students he polled, almost four out of five of them believed superheroes were irrelevant to Christianity. That was a good thing, he supposed, but not if taken too far to the extreme.

He was sure that some ultra-conservative pastors somewhere in the country were pounding their pulpits and screaming about how superhumans were from the devil. Even the superheroes would see their powers as demonic, to be feared. Ultimately, their words would be harmless, but they would spread their message enough that their faithful followers would believe them.

On the other hand, those four-fifths also didn't see a negative aspect to superheroes. Their faith just did not come into play in their opinions about them. Patrick knew that Rick didn't hold anything against superheroes, and neither did EBC's pastor.

Another segment of students believed that superhumans' powers could be gifts from God, depending on how they were used, but that superhumans themselves were only people. Although they could physically save people, God was ultimately still in control of spiritual and eternal salvation. Those students fell in line with Patrick's own beliefs. He knew God had given him these powers for a reason, but he wasn't fooling himself into thinking that having those powers in any way replaced God's sovereignty.

It was the final group that concerned Patrick. They believed that not only were superheroes gifted by God but that they were also an active part of His plan for saving humanity. That, in Patrick's opinion, could be a dangerous slope. It put *entirely* too much faith in all-too-human superheroes.

"What's that?" Jarrett asked.

"Research project for youth ministry." Patrick chewed on his lip as he typed. "Crazy that superheroes are now a valid topic for that kind of thing, huh?"

Alexa skidded into the pool and stopped dead center. Patrick saved his paper and turned away from the laptop. Jan walked up to Alexa and removed the headset while Jarrett handed her a water bottle. Alexa squeezed the bottle, downing a quarter of its contents at once.

"That was a good run," Patrick said. "Your consistency is impressive."

"Thanks. I was pushed . . . pretty hard."

Patrick raised an eyebrow but didn't pursue the statement. If she wanted to talk about her training, she would. Otherwise, he'd wait to ask. She didn't continue, though, so he walked to Jan's side as she studied the data on her computer. Patrick's brainwaves occupied the left side of the screen, while Alexa's filled the right. Hers spiked wildly, far higher and lower than Patrick's did; but there was a consistency to it. It wasn't random or chaotic.

"I can work with this," Jan said. "Give me a couple hours to study it and run simulations. Then, we can continue with your shock therapy."

Finally.

* * *

Carter sat with Ty in the corner of the pool, watching as Alexa ran and the others worked on the brain scanner. Bryce had dragged some metal folding chairs down from a supply closet; so at least, they did not have to sit on the concrete floor anymore. The lair was still a work in progress, but Carter was glad Patrick had somewhere to work from.

Carter glanced up at Alexa's speeding form. "You could use your powers for good, too, you know."

Ty blinked. "I think that would be hard to do from prison."

"You won't be in prison forever." Carter smiled. "We'll make sure you don't get extra time for being kidnapped. And on good behavior, you should be free to go in a couple years."

"I hope you're right." Ty pressed his lips into a thin line and stared at his shoes. "I'm not sure the hero's life is for me, though. I would like to settle down with Emi, find a boring job, and be a dad."

"I respect that. Nothing says you can't do both, though."

Carter studied Ty. He had grown fond of the other man, despite himself. Ty might have been a criminal, but he was more complex than most of the enemies Carter fought. He was kind, friendly, loving, moral . . . he was a good man. Carter could see himself becoming friends with Ty. Who would have ever predicted that?

"I've noticed you reading that Bible I gave you," Carter said. "Any thoughts?"

Ty chuckled. "Lots. I'm still . . . processing, though. If I have any questions, I'll be sure to ask you."

"No pressure."

"Thanks." Ty exhaled through his nose. "You know, Ben told me he wanted me to help him fight the Sicarans. He said they would come after Emi to hurt me. As much as I want to be with her again, I have been tempted to return to Ben and help him. But the thought that I would live the rest of my life on the run . . . no. Carter, I need you to promise me something. If the Sicarans do come after Emi, you have to protect her."

"With my life. I promise."

"Thank you." Ty's shoulders sagged, and he slumped back in his seat. "You have no idea how much that means to me."

CHAPTER 39

Darius knew very little about guns. The one he carried was a blocky, black handgun with a built-in safety rather than a manual switch. Anton had given him the gun. That night at the docks when everything first spiraled into chaos seemed so long ago now. He stared down at the weapon and struggled to bear the overwhelming weight of grief that threatened to crush him. He grieved not only for Anton but also for how far his own life had fallen in a few weeks.

I should've taken a stand.

Darius had never been able to stand up to Anton, and that was what had gotten them into this situation. Zee would have taken Darius' side if he had told Anton no from the start. On his own, Anton still might have tried to use his powers to commit crimes; but things might not have gone as spectacularly wrong as they had with Darius and Zee involved. Now Anton was dead. And it was, at least partially, Darius' fault.

The same went for Zee's disturbing shift in behavior. She had withdrawn so far into herself since Anton's death and became so vengeful that Darius feared she was on the verge of a psychotic break. She wasn't allowing herself to grieve properly. The more that grief built up, the more likely it was to explode into a violent external episode. If she was never involved with their criminal activities, she wouldn't be in this state at all.

Darius glanced up at her as she stared at Paxton Energy headquarters. Her gaze was intense, focused. Tears welled, filling her eyes to the brim; but she did not allow them to fall. Darius realized he had the power to help her. He could project any emotion he wanted to; he could help her grieve. Reaching out, he tested her mind. Zee swiveled to face him, her hand dropping to the gun in her lap.

"Don't. Don't do that."

Of course, her empathic powers picked up his intentions even before he was able to project anything. And in her state, she wouldn't want to feel comfort or grief. She wanted her anger to fester. Once again, Darius was powerless to help.

"We shouldn't be here, Zee. This is all wrong."

"You're right. It is." Her eyes didn't flinch from his. "But this is where we are; it's too late to turn back now. We've dug ourselves in this deep. It's impossible to climb out."

Darius sighed and turned his attention back to the tall, charcoal-colored building. Staying here with her only supported her bad behavior the way he had with Anton, but she would stay with or without him; she was too far gone. If he left, she would find and kill Paxton on her own. Staying with her was the only way to ensure she remained safe. He couldn't lose her, too.

"It's almost over, Darius. Almost over."

* * *

Patrick glanced up as Lucy walked into the lair. He looked over his shoulder at Jan, who was almost ready to begin shock therapy. Before she did, he wanted to address the team. He had been meaning to do it ever since his conversation with Gideon, but the time had slipped away from him. There was no time like the present, and everyone was here for once—Lucy, Asher, Bryce, Alexa, Carter, Jarrett, Jan, even Ty. He might not get another chance like this.

"Hey, everyone?" Patrick cleared his throat. "Listen, I've got something I'd like to say while we're all here. Things are about to get crazy; and with my powers hopefully coming back after today, some of you may not be here much longer. So I need to say this now."

Everyone looked up from what they were doing, some moving in closer to him. Jan stayed at her table but leaned back from her computer and focused on Patrick.

"Here goes." Patrick inhaled deeply. "I'm sorry. For the past few months, I've been acting like I'm the only member of the team with anything important to contribute. Because I had powers, I thought I could do everything on my own and that you guys were just moral support. I realize now that I need you for so much more than that. I couldn't do this without any of you. If Jan and Jarrett hadn't come, I might still be in an apathetic funk. Lucy, you got us the information that led Jarrett to the Colemans' identity. Asher, you knocked me out of my bad attitude when I was salty about losing my powers. Bryce, you gave us this sweet lair. Alexa, without you, I might never get my powers back. Carter . . . you're awesome, dude. Enough said.

"Being Spright is a dream come true for me. I love being a superhero. Running around, stopping bad guys, and saving lives. But I never should've made that my main focus in life. There are things that are so much more important. I didn't honor God with the powers He gave me. But I'm going to try to change that. He comes first; all of you come second; my powers come way, way after that. You all mean the world to me; and if I could still be Spright and save the world all by myself, I wouldn't want to—because none of you would be there. I'm sorry for being a jerk. I love you all, and I am so thankful for your help."

The room was quiet for a moment. Then Lucy stepped forward and pulled Patrick into a hug. Asher joined her, crushing him from the side. Thankfully, the others chose not to join in, or else Patrick may have been suffocated. But they did come by and pat him on the back. He smiled and finally stepped back.

"You're the team leader, Spright," Lucy said. "Where do we go from here?"

"Glad you asked." Patrick grinned. "We're going to catch some supervillains."

* * *

The lobby of San Francisco's Sterling Enterprises building was nearly three stories tall. Its front walls were floor-to-ceiling glass. The security guard at the marble desk monitored the security feed on the screen in front of him as Lucy pushed her way through the glass doors. She walked with as much confidence as she could muster to stand across from him. She put a hand on the desk and waited for him to acknowledge her.

The first step of Patrick's plan was simple—follow a money trail. Jarrett suggested they start with the high-tech sword that Anton Coleman had used. Given his former allegiance with the Archdukes, it seemed likely that Paxton—or, at least, one of his lackeys—had procured it and given it to Anton. If they could trace where that weapon had come from, they might find some incriminating evidence on Paxton.

Patrick had contacted Dean Sterling, CEO of Sterling Enterprises; and Dean had confirmed that the sword had not been made by their company but that someone in research and development might be able to place it. Equipped with a video of Anton using the weapon, Lucy set out to Sterling Enterprises while Jan began Patrick's shock therapy.

"Can I help you?" the guard finally asked.

"I'm here to see Mr. Holcomb."

"Do you have an appointment scheduled?"

"I was directed to speak with him by Dean Sterling. He told me Mr. Holcomb would be expecting me."

The guard raised an eyebrow.

"I'll have to verify this before I send you through." He picked up his desk phone. "Mr. Holcomb, there's a young lady here to see you. Says she was sent by Mr. Sterling . . . yes, sir. I understand." The guard cleared his throat. "Go on ahead, Miss. Fourth floor."

Lucy circled the desk and walked toward the elevator bank on the back wall. She stepped into the first one that opened and rode it to the fourth floor. She stepped out into a cacophony of technology and hurried scientists. One man stepped over to her, his middle-aged features friendly and calming.

"Hello, young lady. You must be the student Mr. Sterling mentioned."

"That's right. You're Mr. Holcomb?"

"I am." Holcomb gestured for her to follow him into a cubicle. "He said you had some questions about a piece of technology."

"That's right."

The cramped cubicle contained Holcomb's desk, which was cluttered with papers and knickknacks, as well as three chairs. Lucy took one of the two chairs in front of the desk while Holcomb circled the desk to sit.

"So, how can I help?"

"Here." Lucy handed him her phone, which had the video already displayed on it. "I'm interested in the sword that the man in the video is using. I've never seen anything like it. Do you know who developed it?"

Holcomb studied the video. "Fascinating. We have similar technology in development for military use but nothing this advanced or sophisticated. The only other company I can imagine came up with this weapon is Garvin Technologies. I've heard rumblings that they have something new in the pipeline. This must be it. Perhaps this man, whoever he is, simply got his hands on a prototype."

"Garvin Technologies." Lucy nodded. "Yes, I'm sure that's what must've happened."

"Anything else I can help you with?"

"No, I think that answers my questions."

Holcomb returned Lucy's phone, nodded politely, and guided her back to the elevator. As it descended to the lobby, Lucy dialed Bryce. He could check up on Garvin Technologies. Maybe this lead would get them closer to the answers they needed.

* * *

There was a part of Asher that was terrified to take Shannon to a fast-food restaurant, even for a lunch date. He knew the kind of money she came from and the kind of food she was used to. Unfortunately, he was short on time and taking her to an upscale restaurant wasn't a speedy endeavor. Patrick needed answers, so he had asked Asher to talk to Shannon about her father's business meetings with Paxton. Asher would not accuse her of anything. He doubted Mr. Weeks was a gangster; but even if he was, that didn't mean Shannon knew it.

He smiled ruefully. "Sorry it's so cheap. College student budget, you know?"

Shannon laughed. "Asher, I don't care where you take me. I'm just glad to spend time with you."

Asher blushed as he parked the car and walked up to the restaurant door, holding it open for Shannon as she went in.

She just wants to spend time with me, and I'm about to give her the third degree.

They ordered their food and sat down. She was dressed more casually than he was used to seeing her. Her hair was tied back in a casual ponytail, and she wore a long-sleeved blue shirt and black jeans. It put him at ease; if she had been decked out like normal, he would've been even more nervous than he already was.

After a few minutes of small talk, Asher mustered up the courage to broach the subject.

"Listen, I wanted to ask you something. You may have seen on the news that Joey's dad was arrested the other day. I went with Joey to bail him out, but Joey seemed so surprised that his dad was there. You mentioned that your dad and his dad met sometimes. Do you know anything about what might've happened?"

Shannon scoffed. "Is this a date or an interview?"

"Uh, date, of course." He laughed nervously. "I was just wondering . . . I mean, he is my roommate, after all. I was just worried about him."

"I didn't mean to snap." Shannon sighed. "The truth is, I know more than I probably should. As a kid, I was always more interested in listening to the adults than I was in playing with the other children. So yes, I heard things; and I know things."

Asher furrowed his brow. "What kind of things?"

"Asher, I can't . . . I'm just not sure we're close enough yet that I can trust you with this."

"What if I said that someone could get hurt? I told you. What I really want is to help people. If Joey's father really deserves to be in prison, then he needs to go there before he hurts anyone else—maybe even Joey himself."

Shannon stared down at her half-eaten burger, both hands gripping the edge of the table. Asher opened his mouth to continue but drew back. He had already pressured her, and he felt guilty enough about that. He didn't want to use her; she was his friend, not some source. It was her choice whether to talk about it or not.

"Okay." Shannon tossed her hair back and locked eyes with him. "You want the truth? Here it is. My father and Paxton have been in business together for a long time because Paxton is the head of the Archdukes gang and my father is the leader of the Seventy-Six. There have been off and on wars between the two gangs for years, but Dad and Paxton have always tried to keep things peaceful."

Asher gaped. It was worse than he feared. The thought that Mr. Weeks could have been involved in criminal activity had occurred to him, but that he was a gang leader?

"That's why I want to go into politics," she continued. "I have to get away from the family business. I want to be the kind of politician that cracks down hard on crime. My dad should pay for all the terrible things he's done. Are you happy now? I've spilled all my family secrets."

"Shannon, I'm . . . so sorry." Asher leaned forward and put his hand on hers. "Thank you for confiding in me. But now, I need to ask you something else."

Her brow crinkled. "What else could you possibly want?"

"I have a . . . feeling . . . that Paxton will be arrested soon. Do you think, if his case goes to court, that you could testify against him? As a direct witness to a criminal conspiracy, your testimony would carry a lot of weight—especially with what you said about your own father. It may be our best chance of getting him locked up."

Shannon shook her head, pulling away from him and staring at him in confusion.

Oops.

He'd taken it too far, too fast. He should have just left it at that and changed the subject. If that scared her off, they were in trouble.

"What is going on, Asher? Are you working undercover for the cops or something? This really has been more of an interview than a date—or maybe a more accurate word would be 'interrogation.' I thought you liked me. Has all this really just been about Mr. Paxton?"

"No, I . . . " Asher sighed. "I do like you. Really. I'm just . . . I'm working on something important relating to Paxton. I can't go into details, but—"

"You can't go into details? After everything I just confessed to you? Wow. Asher, can you take me home, please? I'm not hungry anymore." Shannon stood. "Or do I have to walk?"

"No." Asher stood and picked up their tray of half-eaten food. "No, I'll drive you home."

* * *

"Got word from Lucy and Asher," Bryce called. "The sword was most likely manufactured by Garvin Technologies, and Shannon confirmed that her father, Benjamin Weeks, is illegally involved with Paxton. He's the leader of the Seventy-Six."

Patrick whistled. "Asher knows how to pick 'em."

Jarrett checked his gear while the two younger men talked, and Jan prepared a place for Patrick to lie down while she worked her magic. Alexa leaned against one of the pool's walls, arms crossed and staring at the floor. Something about her posture showed she was uncomfortable. Jarrett studied her out of the corner of his eye. She was hiding something. He should know; he was a special agent. Hiding things was his specialty.

Jarrett wasn't sure if he trusted her yet. Sure, she was Patrick's friend, but that made the situation even more convenient. What were the odds that she would befriend him, not knowing he was Spright and just so happened to be a speedster herself? Where had her suit come from, and who had trained her? The girl was a mystery; and Jarrett didn't like mysteries, especially in his inner circle.

That made him a hypocrite, he realized. He had kept his position as a CLOUD agent secret from the Vindicators when he first joined the team of superheroes, and it had taken time to rebuild their trust after they had learned the truth. He had been in Alexa's place, so maybe he should give her the benefit of the doubt. But that didn't mean he would take his eyes off her.

Across the room, Ty rose from his chair and approached. "Did you say Shannon? And Benjamin?"

Bryce nodded. "That's right. Why?"

Ty clenched his fists. "The man who kidnapped me said his name was Ben. And a girl named Shannon came to take care of me a couple times while I was imprisoned. She did not seem to approve of Ben holding me prisoner."

"That tracks with what Asher said about Shannon," Bryce said. "She's definitely not a fan of her father's activities."

Carter pressed his lips together as he geared up. "But why would a street gangster have a vendetta against an ancient shadow organization like the Sicarans? There has to be more to Ben Weeks than Shannon is telling us—maybe more than she even knows."

Jarrett slipped his quiver over his shoulders. "Whatever he's hiding can wait. Right now, we need to make our move. I've dealt with the Seventy-Six before. I'll go back into their territory and see if they can provide me with information about Paxton. And if they won't, I'll just take it."

"I'm coming with you," Ty said. "I need to know the truth."

"No way." Jarrett shook his head. "I don't know you; and no offense, I don't trust you."

If he could not even trust Alexa, how was he supposed to trust a convicted criminal? Ty seemed genuine, but what if it was a ruse? Just because Carter was chummy with the thief didn't mean Jarrett had to be.

"I'll come, too," Carter said. "I'll keep an eye on Ty. Besides, the Seventy-Six know you now. They'll probably stack up their defenses in case you come back."

Jarrett clenched his jaw. Finally, he sighed. "All right. The three of us will hit the Seventy-Six. Bryce, keep working on the Garvin Technologies angle. See if you can dig anything up on that front."

"What about me?" Alexa asked.

"Stay here with Patrick and Jan." Jarrett checked his crossbow before clipping it to the outside of the quiver. "They may need a speedster's eye on their side of things. We'll be back. Make sure comms are on and keep me updated on all fronts."

"Good luck." Jan blew him a kiss.

"Thanks." Jarrett headed for the stairs with Carter and Ty in tow. "But I'm not the one who'll need it."

CHAPTER 40

Friction had not checked in for days. When she had run off with Spright, Paxton had believed she would return before long; but he had not heard a word from her since. Now he was starting to get worried—not for her safety but, rather, that she had chosen to cut her ties with him and work with the other superhero instead. That would be *problematic*. Keskin would be unhappy with another failure, to say the least.

Paxton resisted the urge to rise from his desk and pace his office. It was demeaning to pace. It indicated that he was actually worried about something; and while he was, he would never debase himself by showing it externally. Even alone, he could not present weakness. He could never be too sure when someone was watching. That was part of the life of a Sicaran. He remained in his comfortable leather chair, the only sign of his anxiety an occasional finger drumming on his desk.

I need her back.

He had too much riding on Friction. If the situation with the Colemans had worked out, they would have been a suitable replacement for her. However, with Anton dead, the strongest of the three was out of the picture; and the other two were unlikely to listen to anything he had to say, considering Paxton had killed their brother. He had to get Friction back.

That was why he had his new suit of armor. If they would not fall in line, he would hunt them down instead. And perhaps Keskin would see that the Sicarans did not need amplified soldiers, after all. They only needed technology and the training to use it.

The desk phone rang. Paxton frowned. Rarely did a call come all the way to his office; he was CEO, so many calls were taken care of by one of his executives before they ever got to him. He leaned forward and clicked the speakerphone button. It would, he assumed, be his secretary connecting him to a caller.

A rich baritone voice emanated from the speaker. "Adranis."

Paxton straightened.

Keskin.

"Hello, my friend."

"We are on our way. Have the superhuman prepared for us when we arrive."

"Wait, I—"

The line went dead. Paxton's blood ran cold. He had run out of time. He either had to convince Friction to come back to him or else find her or the Colemans and bring them in bound and ready to be shipped off. If the Sicarans arrived and Paxton had nothing to give them, he was as good as dead.

He rose, unbuttoned his suit jacket, and crossed to the hidden panel in the far wall of his office. It had been installed months before, when Marsden first began development of the suit. Until now, it had sat empty. Paxton placed his hand against the palm reader camouflaged in the wall. The hidden panel slid aside, revealing the armored suit.

It was time to hunt.

* * *

Bryce pored over Garvin Technologies' financial records. They had not been easy to come across. In his high school years, though, Bryce had been a troublemaker—a troublemaker with a computer. He knew how to access all kinds of back doors. It had to be illegal; but he wasn't stealing anything, and he wouldn't leak the files to the public. More importantly, he was doing it for a good cause.

So far, he had found one potential point of interest. Every three months, Garvin Technologies received an anonymous donation for seven-and-a-half thousand dollars. The memo gave no purpose for the donations, and they did not show up in the company's main accounts. Where did they go?

Bryce pushed up his glasses. A private project, maybe? It was unlikely to be the sword they were looking for, though. As high tech as it was, seventy-five hundred dollars a month for one sword was insane. This had to be something much bigger.

He looked past the computer to the other side of the pool. Lying on a cot that had been covertly brought down, Patrick was unconscious as Jan held her hands near his head, currents of electricity pouring between them. Bryce shuddered at the idea of so much foreign electrical energy coursing through his brain. He was glad that wasn't him.

Bryce returned his attention to the laptop. All of Garvin's employed scientists had at least three recorded projects at any given time. One man stood out: Dr. Curt Marsden. He only had a single project on record. The project was called . . .

Excalibur.

"Sounds like a sword to me," he murmured aloud.

And if Marsden only got one project to everyone else's three, perhaps he was also working on whatever secret project Paxton had going on. Lucy might want to head over to Garvin Technologies for a talk with Marsden.

* * *

It had been hours, and there was no sign that Paxton would leave his workplace anytime soon. The longer the Colemans' stolen car sat across the street, the more likely a guard would come over and ask them to leave. If that happened, Darius feared that Zee would just shoot the guard. She was unstable and growing worse.

"Let's just go," Darius said. "We can come back tomorrow. Maybe . . . maybe Paxton's not in today. He could have an appointment, or maybe a family thing. Sitting here won't do us any good."

"Family thing." Zee frowned. "You're right; let's go."

"Huh?"

"I've been thinking about this all wrong. I just wanted to kill Paxton, but that wouldn't teach him anything. We need to hurt him the same way he hurt us. He took Anton from us. Let's take someone from him."

Darius' eyes widened. "Zee, no! What's happening to you? My sister would've never thought to hurt an innocent just to get at their loved ones. That's . . . evil."

"Anton wanted us to be supervillains, didn't he?" Zee raised her gun, pointing it at Darius. "Drive. It shouldn't be too hard to find out who Paxton's immediate relatives are. We find that information, find the family, and show Paxton that he can't take people's lives just because he has money and power. We'll show him that we have power, too, and that we'll hold people like him accountable for the way they trample on the weak."

Darius put the car in drive. His own sister, pointing a gun at him. *How could she?*

He pulled away from Paxton Energy, realizing as he did that he would, very soon, be forced to choose whether to go along with Zee's newfound dark side or stop her from doing something she would regret one day. He wasn't sure which one would hurt her more.

* * *

The precision and focus that Jan Mercer poured into her powers was fascinating. As she worked on Patrick, Alexa never saw her attention flicker, even for a moment. She never showed a hint of exhaustion, though she had been at this nonstop for over an hour. Alexa aspired to have that kind of control over her own powers. Sure, she had endurance, but that was about it—there had to be possibilities beyond simply running fast for a long time. She sensed the untapped potential of her powers; she just didn't know how to unlock it.

Alexa wondered how Bryce's search was progressing. She still hadn't decided how she felt about hunting Paxton. She was angry with him for murdering Anton Coleman, but he had trained her and taken care of her when she had been unable to control her powers. He helped her become Friction. She couldn't just turn on him, could she?

That was why she hadn't told them yet that he was the one who had trained her. Plus, Alexa was afraid that they would not trust her anymore. Would they believe her when she said she hadn't realized the kind of man Paxton was? Or would they dismiss her, seeing her as too dangerous to continue working with?

These are your friends. They're good, godly people. You don't have to worry about them abandoning you . . . right?

"Hey, Alexa," Bryce walked over and sat down next to her. "You ever use your powers to, you know, speed over to a teacher's desk and sneak a peek at an answer sheet on a test?"

She chuckled, shaking her head. "No, Bryce. I use my powers responsibly . . . for the most part."

"For the most part?"

"Yeah." She combed a lock of hair behind her ear. "Once or twice, I've sped out of the dorms after curfew when I've had a craving; but I always come back in a few minutes. Not like I'm actually sneaking out, right?"

"Eh . . . debatable. You are out past curfew, a few minutes or not." Bryce wagged his finger. "You should be ashamed of yourself, young lady."

She rolled her eyes. "I . . . "

Something—she wasn't sure what it was—maybe a shift in the ambient noise of the basement, maybe something subtler—set off her enhanced senses. The world crawled into slow motion around Alexa as her body reacted instinctively to a potential threat. Bryce slowed until he was practically frozen in time. Jan was equally still, but energy continued to crackle from her hands to Patrick's head.

Right. Speed of light—still faster than I am.

She looked up. The lair's ceiling—which, she realized, was the student lounge's floor—was crumbling. Hints of red energy shone through the cracks. Alexa darted across the room, grabbing Bryce and bringing him out of the pool and under the stairs, where he would be safe from falling debris. She sped back into the pool, changing from her plain clothes to her super suit in an instant. She could not move Patrick or Jan because disrupting the flow of her electricity now could damage his brain, but she had to protect them somehow.

Friction stopped next to the cot. Her body continued to vibrate at a far higher frequency than the rest of the room, keeping her in motion so that she would have time to react to whatever happened next. She slowed just enough for the rubble to begin its descent. There had to be some way to shield Patrick and Jan from the debris.

Shield them.

That was it. She could literally shield them from it. If she moved rapidly enough, she could change the direction of the wind—create a wind shear—that would knock the debris aside, forming a safety bubble around them. The rest of the pool would be filled with rubble, but it was the only way to keep them safe that she could think of.

She broke into a tight sprint and circled around Jan and Patrick. The debris fell faster now, and Friction sped up until she created a blur of red around them. The debris falling toward them dropped away, crashing to the floor. Several chunks crushed Bryce's computer and the equipment table next to it.

Good thing I moved him.

Friction skidded to a stop next to the table as the debris stopped falling. Jan looked up from her work as the catastrophe registered, but she did not react beyond that. On the other hand, Bryce's voice yelped from the stairwell. She hoped that was more surprise than injury.

Several chairs and tables had fallen through the hole, but they were crushed nearly beyond recognition. She looked up at the ceiling. What had happened? Was anyone up there hurt? The hole continued up through the lounge to the roof, and the sun shone through. Then a shadowy figure dropped through the hole, moving in a silvery blur. A blade protruded from the figure's right wrist, red energy pulsing around the weapon.

"Friction," the intruder growled as he landed on the bottom of the pool. "It's time to come home."

She frowned. The figure rose from its crouch in the center of the pool and stepped between debris as it approached. The armor's faceplate was featureless. Friction had never seen anything like it. And yet, it had called her by name . . . and wanted her to come home. She bent her knees and raised her hands in some semblance of a fighter's stance.

"Who—*what*—are you?"

The faceplate lifted, revealing Oscar Paxton's visage. Friction's eyes widened. Her ears burned in embarrassment and rage. This was not how her friends should have found out the truth. Worse, Paxton had risked hurting so many people just to get to her. How dare he?

"Get out," she said. "I want nothing to do with you. You're a monster—a *murderer*—and I won't be like you."

"Won't you?" Paxton laughed. "I trained you. I made you what you are. Without me, you would be nothing. Leave me now, and what do you have? These friends? They don't have what it takes. They play pretend hero, but nothing they do is effective. Three times, Spright engaged the Colemans; and he accomplished nothing. I did. I killed Anton Coleman."

"He didn't have to die."

"This debate is pointless." Paxton lowered his faceplate again. "You're coming with me, Friction. Your services are needed."

"Never."

"Very well." Paxton mimicked Friction's fighting stance. "Then I'll take you by force."

Friction darted forward and came in low, vibrating her hand to enhance the force of her punch. She drove her fist up toward Paxton's solar plexus. He turned and shoved her hand aside.

How?

Friction recovered from the block and snapped a kick out. Paxton blocked it with his left forearm.

How is he this fast?

Paxton raised his sword and swept it at her. Friction rolled underneath the blow. He was astonishingly fast. Somehow, his armor must have analyzed her moves and told him where and when to block, while also providing the speed to keep up with her. She had never fought another speedster before. Could she do this?

Just remember—it's all the armor's doing.

She could work around that. Friction aimed her fist at Paxton's faceplate and immediately broke off the punch, dropped low, and snapped a kick at his knee. The blow landed, and Paxton's armor creaked in protest.

I did it . . .

Something hard and heavy slammed into the top of Friction's head. She crumpled to the ground and scrambled away from Paxton. It was a good thing he wasn't aiming to kill; if he had hit her with the sword, her head would've split in half.

"Stand down, Friction. This little exercise is pointless."

He stepped forward; and a stream of electricity shot across the room, striking his chest. Paxton reeled back, sparks crackling along the armor. He growled and raised his sword arm to block the blast. Friction glanced over her shoulder. Jan stood between Alexa and Patrick, both hands extended and long arcs of blue lightning crackling from her fingers. The older woman clenched her jaw in concentration and shoved her hands forward, redoubling the force of her attack.

Now was Friction's chance. She rose and sped forward, leading with her shoulder. She slammed into Paxton, knocking him back two steps.

She circled around behind him and drove her vibrating fist between his shoulder blades. Paxton dropped to one knee, still trying to ward off Jan's attack.

"Enough!" Paxton roared.

He slammed his sword into the floor. A shockwave erupted. Friction grunted as it caught her, blowing her backward. She slammed into the pool wall and grimaced. Slumping to her knees, she looked up as Paxton stood. Jan was down, too, and Patrick's cot had been knocked over. He lay on the floor, unmoving.

"I forged you into the weapon you are, girl! And you would turn against me?"

He stormed toward her—and slammed face-first into the ground. Behind him stood Spright, now clad in his black-and-purple suit when seconds before he had been in plain clothes. Stepping toward Paxton, Spright vibrated his fists, which also crackled with the electricity of the shock rings he wore.

"Oscar Paxton," Spright said. "It's time you and I had a talk."

CHAPTER 41

Yeoman crashed feet-first through the bodega window, raising his crossbow as he landed. He fired an arrow into the shoulder of a Seventy-Sixer who raised an Uzi. The Crusader leaped through right behind him and took out another gangster before he could swivel an automatic rifle to train it on Yeoman.

This attack was risky. A daylight raid on a public store could put Yeoman and the Crusader on the public's naughty list. They would have to be very careful to only target the people they were sure were gangsters and usher out those who were not. They did not have time for niceties. Every moment that passed, the bubbling cauldron of conflict between Paxton and the Colemans grew hotter, ready to blow. If they ended this now, the Seventy-Six would have information Jarrett and his team could use against Paxton.

As he passed the injured form of the man he shot, Yeoman kicked the gangster's Uzi aside and dropped his elbow into the man's face. He continued walking through the store, crossbow pressed against his shoulder and ready to fire at a moment's notice.

A gangster jumped out from an aisle and opened fire with a handgun. Yeoman ducked back and fired another arrow. It struck the gangster's knee; so Yeoman fired again, knocking the gun from the man's hand. He pushed onward.

His throat closed as an arm wrapped around his neck. Yeoman grabbed the wrist of that arm with his free hand, but his accoster had an iron grip. Suddenly, a dull *thunk* sounded from behind, and the grip on Yeoman's neck loosened. He turned to find Ty standing over the unconscious form of a gangster. The thief was disguised with a ski mask and armed with the Crusader's sword. Yeoman nodded his thanks.

Someone shouted, and a pair of gangsters—a man and a woman, both armed with knives—rushed Yeoman and Ty. Yeoman raised his crossbow to block the woman's knife while swiveling his body to allow Ty access to the male attacker. The man's blade swept harmlessly through Ty's body as the former criminal used his powers. Yeoman jabbed his left hand forward, and the woman pulled back to block his blow. Yeoman disengaged from her and fired a blind shot from his crossbow.

The woman cried out and staggered forward, but she kept coming and swept her knife at him. Yeoman blocked it with the end of his crossbow, ducked under an attack from the man, and fired another crossbow bolt into the man's knee. Ty finished off the man with an elbow strike to the jaw. The woman attacked again. Yeoman turned aside, the blade nicking the sleeve of his suit, and struck the woman under the armpit. He followed that up with a blow to her knife hand and took her to the floor with a kick to the solar plexus. Yeoman turned his kick into a spin and brought his fist cannoning down into the woman's jaw. She dropped and didn't get up.

Yeoman scanned the bodega. An elderly woman cowered in one of the aisles, holding a bag of potato chips in front of her as if it would shield her from view. Yeoman sighed and took a cautious step toward her.

"I'm not here to hurt you. These are bad people. Please leave, so you aren't in any danger."

The woman screamed and scrambled for the door, taking the chips with her.

"Hey." Yeoman frowned. "That was petty theft."

Ty shook his head and walked down the aisle into the open front area of the store. Yeoman strode after him. The Crusader was just finishing off a pair of gunmen. He brought his electrified staff forward, shocking the last one standing into unconsciousness.

"You all right?" Carter asked.

Jarrett nodded. "Your buddy had my back."

"Let's finish this." Ty stepped forward and flourished his sword. "I'm ready to go home."

Jarrett led them to the back room where he had met Sloan on his previous visit. Five armed men stood in the stockroom, Sloan in front. Behind them was a man Yeoman had not seen before. He carried himself with authority. Brown, curly hair framed his head; and though he was unarmed, Jarrett could tell he was dangerous.

"Ah, you're back." The man's gaze was locked on Ty. "That is you, isn't it, Mr. Watanabe? I saw you using your powers on the security feed."

"That's Ben," Ty growled. "He's mine."

"Mr. Weeks, before you open fire and things get messy," Yeoman said, "maybe you should listen to why I'm here."

Sloan narrowed his eyes, the big pistol in his hand not wavering a centimeter. He looked back at the gang leader, who furrowed his brow as if in thought. Finally, Benjamin Weeks nodded and gestured for his men to lower their weapons. Yeoman eased his crossbow down to his side. Weeks stepped past the gangsters.

"Although I appreciate you bringing Taro Watanabe back to me, Vigilante, this is the second time you've broken in here and made a mess. There will not be a third. Why are you here?"

"I want to talk to you about Oscar Paxton—and what you can do to help me put him behind bars."

Weeks laughed. "Is that all? My friends, while I have no intention of helping you, I can assure you Oscar Paxton will not be a problem for much longer. I have him right where I want him."

Yeoman shook his head. "Paxton's dangerous—volatile. You know as well as I do that he's too ambitious to keep his treaty with you forever. Eventually, he'll want something he can't have; and when he does, he'll turn on you without a second thought. Get out now. Take him down."

"You don't understand. Unfortunately, the Seventy-Six are at a disadvantage right now. If a gang war broke out, there would be chaos—and I would be on the losing side. My daughter lives in this city, and I will not let her be hurt. But once Paxton is lulled into a sense of security, I can end things in one fell swoop. You see, Vigilante, I have it all planned out."

"Paxton could use your daughter as leverage. When he does break your deal—and he will—he could kidnap your daughter. As long as he's a free man, she'll never be safe."

"No?" Weeks drew his gun. "Maybe you're right. But there's more at stake here than you know. Paxton is an enemy older than time. I won't lose my chance at bringing him down."

Older than time? Yeoman frowned at the turn of phrase. What did Weeks mean? Judging by Ty's sharp intake of breath, he had a guess. Jarrett would have to ask him about that later. For now, though, this had to end.

Yeoman sighed. "Sorry you feel that way."

The gun tucked at the small of his back was in his right hand in an instant, while with his left, he reached out and twisted Weeks' gun hand until he dropped the weapon. The Crusader and Ty burst into motion, making short work of Weeks' guards. Yeoman pulled the gang leader in close and jammed the barrel of the gun against his head, keeping Weeks between him and the other gangsters.

"Stand down!" Yeoman snapped. "I tried to do this nicely—same as last time I came here. You know, your customer service is terrible."

"You think you're walking out of here?" Weeks sounded calm, unbothered. His gaze was still on Ty. "I've got a dozen more men on the streets outside and nearly a hundred more spread through the docks. Even if you get out of the bodega, you won't make it far. Shoot me if you want; at the end of the day, all three of you will be in the ground, just like me. Think about it, Mr. Watanabe. You know what you have to do."

Yeoman clenched his jaw. "Don't talk to him. Talk to me."

Unfortunately, Weeks had called his bluff. Yeoman could either kill him, at which point the Seventy-Six would mow him down; or he could let him go, showing that he had no teeth, in which case he would still probably wind up dead. Neither option was ideal. But they were not his only choices.

Turning his gun away from Weeks' head, Yeoman instead shot out the kneecaps of the two remaining Seventy-Sixers and turned his gun on Sloan. The man trembled. Yeoman could almost see the flashbacks of his last visit tumbling through the gangster's head. Sloan, unlike Weeks, feared Yeoman.

"I knew you couldn't do it." Weeks sneered. "You're no killer."

"I've killed before. But not when I don't have to." Yeoman pressed the gun back to Weeks' head. "Now, Sloan. You have financial records of deals your boss has made with Paxton?"

Trembling, the smaller man nodded.

"Sloan, you coward, don't do it," Weeks said. "Don't you do it! I'll kill you!"

"H-he's right," Sloan said. "You say you've killed before, Vigilante, but I haven't seen it. But I know the boss will kill me. I-I can't help you."

"Fine." Yeoman fired, clipping Sloan's leg. "I'll find them myself."

As the gangster screamed and clutched his leg, Yeoman bashed the butt of his gun into the side of Weeks' head. Weeks slumped to the floor, unconscious. Yeoman grabbed Sloan's head and drove it into his raised knee. Sloan's cries ended as he crashed to the floor, out cold. Yeoman walked past him as Ty hurried to Weeks' side.

"Come on, Crusader." Yeoman patted Carter on the shoulder. "Let's give your friend some time with Mr. Weeks and see if we can find these records."

* * *

Patrick had never felt more alive. His body coursed with speed, humming like a racecar engine as he stood over the armored figure who had attacked the lair. Patrick didn't know how this had happened. His last memory was of lying on the cot as Jan gave him a dose of anesthesia to put him under while she began her shock therapy. He had dreamed again while he was under—at the racetrack once again, he came face to face with his grandfather. Joshua Omer had smiled and put a hand on Patrick's shoulder.

"You're ready, my boy."

"Ready?"

"You proved yourself." Joshua looked him dead in the eyes. "You showed that you are more than your powers, that you can be a hero without them,

that God comes before them, and that you care more about your teammates than about being Spright."

"This was . . . a test?"

"No." Joshua beamed. "But things not intended as tests can still prove us."

Patrick tilted his head, confused at the wordplay. Even in life, his grandfather had been cryptic like that.

"What happens next?"

"Now . . . you run."

At that moment, Patrick's eyes had snapped open to the sight of debris filling their lair and an armored figure battling Jan and Alexa. No sooner had he awakened than his body began to vibrate, the world slowing around him as he sped up. The armored figure spoke to Alexa, and Patrick recognized his voice. Paxton. Patrick's suit had been crushed by one of the chunks of rubble. But it was predominantly cloth, and the portions that were metal were made of aionium; no mere rubble would damage that metal. Patrick put his suit on and crossed the pool to knock Paxton to the ground.

Spright stared down at him. "Oscar Paxton. It's time you and I had a talk."

"So you know who I am." Paxton pushed himself to his feet and pointed at Friction. "Did she *tell you*?"

Spright frowned. What did Alexa know about Paxton? He turned to Alexa. A look of guilt washed over her face. What did Paxton mean? Patrick's mind whirled, and the pieces clicked together. Alexa's training, the quality of her uniform . . . Paxton had trained her. Why had she kept it from them? But it did not matter. Alexa had chosen her side. Spright wouldn't hold her past against her.

"She didn't have to," Spright said. "But I'd bet there's plenty she could tell us. For now, let's just start with what's right in front of us. What are you doing here?"

"I need a superhuman. I'm going to take one."

Paxton shot forward, propelled by rocket thrusters on the back of his armor. His metal-gloved hand wrapped around Spright's throat, and he lifted him into the air and through the hole in the ceiling. Spright struggled against Paxton's grip as he rose into the sky.

"And it's not Paxton. Call me Adranis."

"Did you say Adonis? You're not handsome enough for that." Spright kicked Paxton's chest and repeated the blow, again and again, speeding the kick up each time. "Let. Me. Go!"

His foot struck the seam between the chest and stomach regions of Paxton's armor. The older man grunted; his grip loosened; and Spright drove his fist into the armored chin. Paxton reeled back and released his grip completely. Spright tumbled toward the ground and landed—harder than he would've liked—in the middle of the street. Moaning, he pushed himself up and scanned the sky for Paxton.

Their flight had taken them over the campus to one of its bordering streets. Paxton was hovering overhead, wobbling slightly as he struggled to recover from Spright's blow. Spright darted out of the street as a car honked its horn at him. He shook his head.

Can't they see that I'm busy superheroing?

Adranis descended toward Spright with his right arm pulled back. The blade on that arm glowed with red energy.

Oh, great.

Adranis had a weapon like Negator's. Spright dashed out of the way as a blast struck the sidewalk where he had been standing. He leapt onto the back of a parked car, used it to propel himself into the air, and caught Adranis by his ankle. Paxton cried out and crashed into the lawn in front of the Masterson building. Spright bounced along the yard, grunting with each impact. Finally, he rolled to a stop.

Ow . . .

It was a blessing that his superspeed granted enhanced healing; otherwise, he would be feeling these bruises for weeks. Gingerly, he touched his shoulder—and quickly pulled his hand back as the injury protested. Spright stood, his body screaming in pain. He ignored it and turned to the patch of torn lawn and kicked up dirt where Paxton had landed.

"You're going to regret that, boy. I—" He broke off mid-threat.

"What, can't think of a witty follow-up?"

"Joey."

"That makes no sense. I'm not even dressed like a kangaroo."

Adranis turned and sprinted away from the college at super speed. Spright frowned and watched him go.

Joey?

Whatever was happening was serious enough that Paxton was prioritizing his son over finishing off Spright. If Joey was in trouble . . . was Asher with him?

"Spright!"

He turned. Friction and Jan rushed up to him. Jan had pulled a ski mask down over her face to conceal her features, and her hands crackled with electricity. When the women saw that Paxton was gone, they loosened their stances; and Jan's powers dissipated.

"Hey, it worked," Friction said. "Your powers are back!"

"They are." Spright nodded at them. "Thank you. Both of you."

"Where did he go?" Jan asked.

"He said 'Joey' and flew off. I think his son might be in danger."

"What kind of danger?" Friction asked.

"I don't know. Unless . . . "

The Colemans.

Would they really be vengeful enough to hurt Paxton's son to get back at him for killing Anton? Darius hadn't seemed the type, but Spright didn't know Zoey well enough to say whether she would or not. Either way, as quiet as they had been over the last few days, they had to have been planning something.

"We need to follow him. Jan, get in contact with Yeoman. Tell him where we've gone and that we may need backup."

"Will do." Jan nodded. "And I'll help Bryce contain the situation here. With the lair out in the open right now, we don't need anyone discovering your secret. Go take care of him and the Colemans; I've got this."

"Thank you. I owe you way more than one." Spright looked at Friction. "You up for this?"

"Absolutely."

"Then let's get moving."

CHAPTER 42

Lucy kept her left hand pressed to her ear as she walked through the courtyard toward the opulent Garvin Technologies building. Bryce had called to keep her updated on the attack on their lair. Patrick had gotten his powers back and, in Bryce's words, was *teaching a lesson to some Iron Man looking dude.* Bryce was lying low inside the damaged student center while Jan and Alexa went to help Patrick.

They were in so much trouble. There was no way the school wouldn't discover the lair down there. Once they did, it wouldn't take a genius to figure out who had been operating out of it. There had to be something they could do. But if Bryce started moving stuff out of the basement now, someone was bound to notice.

"Should I head back?" she asked.

"Nah. You can't do any good here. Getting to the bottom of this Paxton situation is going to be a lot more helpful. Just keep doing what you're doing, and I'll keep you posted."

"Will do." Lucy stepped into the building. "I'll keep comms on."

She lowered her hand from her ear and took in the sights of the lobby. A guard at a desk to her right studied her, half-rising from his seat. She should probably start with him. Putting on as confident a front as she could, Lucy strode toward his desk.

Don't think about how you might be going to meet up with a scientist who's working with a mobster-turned-supervillain.

The suit that Paxton had used to attack the lair had to be the secret project he had been working on with this Marsden guy. If that was the case, Marsden could be just as deadly as Paxton. She was glad she had thought to bring along a few adhesive beads when she left the lair. If Marsden turned dangerous, she could throw a bead at him and run.

"Can I help you?" the guard asked.

"Yes. I'm looking for Doctor Marsden. I'm running an article about famous local scientists for my school newspaper; and since Marsden was born and raised in these parts, I was hoping for an interview. My name's Lucy Carmichael."

It was, of course, a lie, but it was the only thing she could think of on the fly. She had done as much research on Marsden as she could when she arrived at the labs. She didn't have a lot of information, considering she had done it on her phone sitting in her car in the parking lot. But maybe it would buy her some time.

"I'll contact his assistant. Please take a seat."

Lucy thanked him and moved over to the waiting area, dropping into a white-padded ergonomic chair. Everything in here was white, giving the lobby a futuristic vibe that made it seem like they were trying too hard. Sterling Enterprises didn't go nearly this far out of their way to look like they were progressive.

Eventually, a lab assistant with bleached-blonde hair walked up to her, a big smile fixed on her face.

She's trying really hard to look friendly.

Lucy just smiled back and shook the woman's hand. The lab assistant gestured for Lucy to follow her down a hallway.

As Lucy fell in behind the assistant, she hid her surprise that Marsden had accepted her request so quickly and readily. Most people would have been too busy to take that kind of last-minute interview, no matter what line of work they were in. But then, if Marsden really did have fewer projects because his time was focused on Paxton's suit—and Paxton now had that suit—Marsden might not have much work to do at all right now.

The hallways were just as garishly white as the lobby had been. Lucy stuck behind the assistant, who rambled on about Marsden's achievements as they walked, and paid attention to every turn they made, every doorway they went through. If she had to cut and run, she wanted to know how to get out of here. Marsden could easily turn security on her; and if she got lost in this building, they would find her in no time. It wouldn't be easy to explain to the police why she was here.

The assistant stopped at a lab door, entered a passcode, and opened it. Lucy nodded her thanks and entered the lab. It too was all white, but the walls and floor were segmented into perfect squares that, to Lucy, looked like they could slide aside to reconfigure the lab for whatever purpose Dr. Marsden needed at a given moment. His workspace was tidy—everything stacked neatly on his worktables. One stack of files stood out, sitting on the floor rather than the table, haphazardly organized and nearly falling apart. Lucy made a note to remember those files. If they were apart from everything else, they might be important to Marsden.

The doctor himself stood in the middle of the room with his hands clasped in front of him, a smile on his face that Lucy could tell wasn't genuine any more than his assistant's was. She looked over her shoulder. The young assistant had not entered the lab, and the door had closed behind her. Could the woman lock the door from outside? If so, Lucy might be in trouble. But she suspected that the interior of the lab had a safety feature to keep a scientist from getting locked inside with an experiment gone wrong.

"Hello, Miss Carmichael. My assistant tells me that you wish to conduct an interview with me for your school newspaper?"

"That's right." Lucy looked for a seat but realized the lab did not hold any chairs.

No concern for the comfort of his guests, I see.

"I'm writing about local scientists. Since you were born here in New Echelon, I thought who better to feature in my article?"

"Of course. I'm honored. What would you like to know? Perhaps about my own time in college and moving forward into my career here at Garvin Technologies?"

"Actually, I'd like to come at it from a different angle. I'd really like to focus on what projects you're working on right now."

Marsden's smile faltered—just a little bit but enough that she knew she was on the right track. Whatever Marsden was working on, he didn't want to talk about it. That, combined with the evidence they had from Garvin Technologies' files, made it almost certain that Marsden was working with Paxton. The trick would be getting him to admit it. Lucy opened her phone's audio recording app, tapped the start button, and held it up.

"Whenever you're ready," she said.

"You must understand, Miss Carmichael. My projects are confidential. If I talked about them to a young reporter and that information was published in a college newspaper, rival scientists could see it and steal my ideas. Until my projects are completed and patented, they are strictly confidential."

"But they're not your projects, are they, Doctor? They're Garvin Technologies'."

"Even more confidential, then. My job would be in danger if one of Garvin's rivals, such as Sterling Enterprises, scooped our ideas."

"I see. I guess that makes sense."

"But like I said, if you want to hear about my life and journey to becoming a scientist, I would be more than happy to share. Otherwise . . ." Marsden gestured to the door. "I'm afraid we have nothing to talk about."

Lucy clenched her jaw. That hadn't gone anywhere although she hadn't really expected it to. It would've been too easy for Marsden to just confess his secret project funded by Paxton to a college journalist. But she just couldn't leave yet.

"Aw, come on, Luce." Bryce's voice spoke softly from the Bluetooth earpiece she wore. "Just roast him."

She smirked. "Dr. Marsden, are you or are you not working illegally with Oscar Paxton to create technologies that have not been approved by your employers?"

Marsden gaped. "Excuse me?"

"Answer the question, Doctor. Are you working with Oscar Paxton, and did you design both the concussion sword that he sold to Anton Coleman and the suit of armor that Paxton is now wearing in a fight with Spright?"

"He's . . . what?"

"Haven't you seen the news? Your funder is using your tech to become a supervillain."

"Turn off that recorder right now."

"I don't think so." Lucy stepped forward. "You still haven't answered my question. Did you or did you not design the weapons that he has been using to perpetuate crimes in this city?"

Marsden stepped back as Lucy approached, reached into his lab coat, and withdrew a pistol. Lucy froze as he pointed the gun at her. His fake smile, long vanished, was replaced with a scowl.

"You know entirely too much for your own good, young lady."

"Everything okay, Lucy?" Bryce asked.

"What are you going to do, Doctor?" Lucy stood her ground. "If you shoot me, everyone here at Garvin Technologies will know what you did. And you won't get away because if I'm right, then Paxton has used you. He won't help you now."

"Shoot you?" Bryce exclaimed.

"This lab is soundproof," Marsden said. "I can shoot you, and no one will ever know. It will take some doing to hide your body, but it's not impossible."

"I don't think you're a killer, Doctor. You make weapons, not use them."

She lowered her phone hand toward her pocket, as though she was going to put it away. That same pocket, however, held the adhesive beads she'd borrowed. If she could get her hand on one of them, she could use it on Marsden. The problem was, even doing that wouldn't make the gun go away. Even with his feet glued to the floor, Marsden could still shoot her.

Maybe a good throw could coat the adhesive around his hands and chest.

But even that was a risk. He could shoot as soon as he saw her pull back her hand to throw.

"Don't move."

Lucy swiped out of the recording app. She had one other option. Patrick had installed an emergency alert app on her phone that would send a distress signal to him as soon as she pressed a button. But he was occupied with Paxton. Would he get to her in time?

She didn't know what other choice she had. Subtly, she tapped the alarm button. Then, dropping her phone, she held her hands up.

Marsden stepped forward. "Now, let's figure out what to do with you."

* * *

Joey had been right all along. The guy in the opera mask had been after him. His fears had gradually diminished as days passed without the guy coming anywhere near him again; and he had started to think that he had just been another unfortunate victim of the party attack, that he had never been the intended target.

He had been wrong.

As he left his dorm room that morning, the man in the opera mask appeared, a gun pointed right at Joey's chest. He grabbed Joey's sleeve and shoved him down the hallway. As he did, panic and fear set in, and Joey nearly dropped to the floor in the fetal position. But the man urged him on, finally shoving him into the middle of Echelon University's football field. A woman wearing another opera mask was waiting for them.

"Wh-what do you want?" Joey stammered.

"This isn't about you," the man said.

"Shut up, Infuser." The woman pointed her gun at Joey. "This *is* about you, kid. Your dad ruined our lives. Now we're getting even."

Joey shook his head. "Please . . . please . . . you c-can't do this. Whatever my dad did, I'm sure he didn't mean to. This all has to be a mistake!"

"Didn't mean to?" The woman laughed. "He knew exactly what he was doing."

Joey looked around. Surely someone, anyone, would see his predicament and call for help. Sweat beaded on his forehead and neck. The man—Infuser—wasn't paying attention to Joey. His gaze was sweeping across the perimeter of the football field. Maybe he was watching for anyone to show up, too. Why was this place so vacant? Now that he thought about it, he hadn't seen anyone in the hallway, either. What had Infuser done?

"Is this about money?" Joey asked. "I've got a stash back in my room. Or—or I could go to the bank and withdraw everything in my trust fund. It's yours. Just please, don't hurt me."

"It's not about money, either. This is revenge. Pure and simple."

"Let's get this over with," Infuser said. "Call him."

The woman used her free hand—the one not pointing a gun at Joey's head—and brought an old flip phone to her ear.

"Oscar Paxton? You know who this is. You know what you did. And now we're going to make you pay. We have your son. You can't stop us—but if you want to try, we're at the Echelon University football field. You have ten minutes. If you're not here, we'll shoot your son."

She slammed the phone shut and tucked it away. Joey looked up at the eerily joyful expression on her opera mask. What could his father possibly have done to elicit this kind of reaction in these two? Joey didn't care much; he just didn't want to die. He had never really believed in God, but now he prayed to anyone who would listen.

Please, please help me! I don't want to die!

* * *

As Jarrett and Carter searched the bodega's back room—including the basement Ty had been held in—Ty hoisted Ben to his feet and shoved him against the far wall. The other gangsters were bound with adhesive gel from Carter's beads, and the door to the front of the bodega was barricaded. No one would get inside to interrupt Ty's interrogation.

Ben's eyes flickered open. "Ah. Alone at last."

"My friends are going to prove you're a criminal. But while they do that, I want to have a long talk with you."

"I imagine you do." Ben smirked. "I don't suppose you've come to accept my offer."

Ty jerked his ski mask off. He drove the blade of Carter's sword against the concrete wall next to Ben's head and glared at the man. If Ben was afraid, he did not show it.

"You're with Charybdis, aren't you?"

Ben nodded. "I am."

Ty fought to keep from showing the twinge of surprise he felt. Although he had suspected that Ben belonged to the organization, he had never expected the man to admit it so readily. Perhaps Ben thought that honesty would win Ty over. If that was the case, he was sorely mistaken. Ty took a step back but kept Ben boxed against the wall.

"And Oscar Paxton is with the Sicarans?"

Ben's head bobbed in another nod. "He is."

"Did you take me from prison because of my godfather?" Ty asked.

"I knew Chin Liang for many years," Ben said. "He saw great value in you, and he spoke often of your potential to serve Charybdis. His opinion of you changed as you grew older, but mine did not. I have watched you, Taro Watanabe. I know your skills. I know your power. If any man can bring down the Sicarans, it is you."

"My father was a Sicaran," Ty growled. "Why would I fight his organization for one that my godfather betrayed him for?"

"Because as honorable as your father was, he was on the wrong side. I think you know that. The Sicarans have manipulated the world for centuries. Their machinations bring death and destruction on an unspeakable scale."

"Like Charybdis is any better."

"Sometimes, death is necessary to our cause, yes . . . but our goal is only to shape the world into the utopia we know it can be. The Sicarans? Their only goal is to destroy us. They have no greater aspirations. Their hatred for Charybdis has blinded them to the good we can do for all."

Ty shook his head. "The Sicaran I fought in Sojourn City—Kane McCrory. He talked like I have some kind of destiny. Do you know what he's talking about?"

Ben's gaze flickered away for the first time.

He knows.

Whether he would admit it or not, Ben knew exactly what McCrory was referring to all those months ago. Anger welled in Ty's chest. Someone was going to tell him what was going on! He tightened his grip on the knife and pressed it to Ben's throat.

"You don't want to do that." Ben swallowed. "The last thing you want is for both Charybdis and the Sicarans to target your daughter."

Ty narrowed his eyes. "Leave her alone. I know you have a daughter, too—would you really harm mine?"

"Me? Never. I can make no promises for my allies."

"I see." Ty snorted. "So Charybdis really is no better than the Sicarans. You know, your daughter knows exactly what you're up to, and she hates it. She wanted me to go free. Sounds like even your own blood isn't a fan of Charybdis. If I were you, Ben, I'd worry less about me and more about what your friends in Charybdis might think if that tidbit got out."

With that, Ty lashed out, striking the pommel of the sword against Ben's skull. The man slumped to the floor again. Ty stood over him, staring at his still form, and sighed. He would get no answers here. There was still one man he could ask, though. Maybe Oscar Paxton knew what Kane McCrory and Ben Weeks wanted with Ty.

Carter hurried back into the stockroom. "We've got what we need, but we just got a call. Patrick needs us at Echelon University."

Ty backed away from Ben's body. "All right. I'm done here. Let's go."

* * *

Spright weaved through New Echelon traffic, keeping his eye on Paxton's distant form as the armored Adranis ran toward his son. That suit made him almost as fast as Spright. If the situation was not so dire, Patrick might have been impressed.

It had to be the Colemans endangering Joey. They had lost their brother, and now they were going to take the son of the man who murdered him. It made sense—to a supervillain, anyway. It was disappointing, though. Based on his all too brief interaction with Darius, Spright didn't believe that Darius was villain material. He seemed like a genuinely good person.

But unfortunately, everyone had a tipping point. For Darius, that must have been losing Anton.

Spright glanced over his shoulder. Friction was right behind him, a red streak matching his purple. Turning his head back around, Spright took a moment to enjoy the thrill of running—the wind against his masked face, the impossible rush of his arms and legs moving at hundreds of miles an hour, the brief brush of his feet against the concrete. It was ecstasy. He let out a whoop of pure joy, enjoying the simple reality of his powers despite the severity of the situation.

"Spright, I got a hold of Asher," Bryce said in Spright's comms. "He said he can't find Joey anywhere. But as he was walking around campus, he started to feel intense fear when he got close to the football field."

"That's got to be Darius. Thanks, Bryce."

"What's the plan?" Friction asked.

"We've got to save Joey first. But we also have to stop both Paxton and the Colemans from killing each other. I can take Paxton; can you deal with Darius and Zee?"

"No problem."

Even if Paxton hadn't been the bigger threat, Spright still would have chosen to deal with him. Knowing that Friction had been trained by Paxton, Spright couldn't risk the gangster talking to her and convincing her to stand down. She was still new to this game, still impressionable. Even though she had already fought him off once, she might change her mind if Paxton convinced her that what he was doing was right. After all, he could always use the excuse that he was trying to save his son.

And even if Friction didn't listen to Paxton, she could be too invested in fighting him. She could take it too far the other way—going far harder on him than necessary to stop him. If that happened, Spright would have a lot of fires to put out on his own.

"We're getting close. Get ready. I'll sweep in and grab Joey; you take care of the Colemans."

"Understood. And Spright? Thanks for giving me this chance."

The football field appeared ahead. Spright leaped, clearing the fence surrounding the field. Adranis had launched himself into the air, propelled by the repulsion units on his back, and now descended toward the field with his sword extended. Spright sped forward and grabbed Joey, carrying him up to the top of the bleachers surrounding the field. He spun back around in time to see the red line of Friction's blur intersect with both Colemans, sending them tumbling through the air. Friction came to a stop next to Spright.

Paxton landed half a dozen yards from the Colemans, his weapon glowing. Darius and Zee pushed themselves off the ground, looking around in confusion.

"Is that . . . ?" Joey asked.

"That's your father." Spright turned back to the field. "And we have to stop him."

"What—"

Spright rushed down into the field, activating his shock rings as he ran, and slammed his right fist into Paxton's head as the armored man raised his sword to attack the Colemans. The blow did nothing more than jerk Adranis' head to the side, but it stopped his attack. Friction skidded to a halt between the Colemans and put her hands on her hips.

"Stand down. No one needs to get hurt."

"Pathetic," Adranis growled. "All of you."

Spright dropped into a fighting stance, and a shrill alarm filled his earpiece. Patrick's stomach churned. That alarm meant someone from his team was in trouble.

"Bryce, what's going on?"

"It's Lucy," Bryce said. "She's being held at gunpoint at Garvin Technologies."

Spright swiveled his head around to look at Friction. He didn't want to leave her here alone, but Lucy needed help. He wasn't going to leave her in danger. With any luck, Yeoman, the Crusader, and Ty would be here shortly to back Friction up.

"I've got this," Friction said. "Go."

"Thank you."

Spright blasted away from the field, rushing toward Garvin Technologies as fast as his legs could propel him.

CHAPTER 43

"Get out of the way, girl," Paxton said. "They tried to kill my son. Now, I'm going to take care of them, like you should've done from the start. If you get in my way, I'll kill you, too."

The silence on the football field was heavy. Friction stood in the middle of a triangle formed by Paxton, Darius, and Zoey. The latter two each had a gun trained on Paxton—as if a mere handgun would damage his armor. Paxton's shoulders were squared, his hands clenched into fists, the sword on the back of his right arm glowing a fiery red. Joey was up in the stands, watching from a safe distance.

The Colemans were out of their depth. Friction had each of them in her peripheral vision. If they moved, she would know it. But regardless of what they did, this was the end of the road for them. Friction had a neural dampener on, and Paxton was smart enough that he probably had one installed in his helmet. That made Darius' powers useless; and while Zoey could predict any move Friction or Paxton made, she wasn't fast enough to stop either one of them at the speed they moved.

Paxton was the real threat. Although he was not as fast as Friction, he was not far behind. His armor was tough; and that sword was deadly, even for a speedster. All he had to do was avoid her strikes long enough to get in one good hit, and Friction would be dead.

"I'll give you one more chance." Paxton's voice was surprisingly calm, considering his son had been in mortal danger seconds before.

"Surrender to me now, and you will not be hurt. I have use for people like you—all of you."

"You murdered Anton," Zoey spat out. "Why should we believe you?"

"Very well." Paxton sighed. "Friction?"

Friction scowled and shook her head. "You're a criminal, just like they are. You said you were training me to be a hero. Why would I ever go along with you now that I know the truth?"

"Such a disappointment. Let's get this over with, then."

Paxton lunged at lightning speed. Friction turned to her left and sped forward, shoving Darius to the ground. As he fell, she ran over to Zoey and pushed her aside, too. She returned to her previous spot as Paxton descended.

His blade crashed toward her. Friction weaved around its blade and smashed her vibrating fist into the joint at Paxton's elbow. The joint buckled, and the blade turned inward. Paxton, destabilized by the blow, crashed to the ground. Friction leaped on his back and ran her hand through one of the thrusters of his jetpack. It sparked and crackled.

Good luck flying now.

She backed away and crossed her arms as Paxton pushed himself up. The treads of his armored boots left heavy indentations in the lawn. He retracted his faceplate and scowled at her.

"I could've made you a champion. You would have been renowned across the world for your bravery, but you just couldn't listen."

"I'm not like you." Alexa shook her head. "You're a murderer. A monster."

"You have no idea what I am." Paxton took a thudding step forward. "But because you betrayed me, I'm going to make sure you do—you, and everyone you call a friend. I'm going to string them all up for you to see. I'll start with these two." He gestured to Darius and Zoey.

"The petty thieves you thought deserved your protection. Then I'll kill Spright. Then that archer. The other vigilante, too. And when I'm done with them, I'll find all the little friends you call a team and kill them in front of you. But I won't stop there. I'll track down your parents and kill them; and once everyone you love is dead at your feet and you realize that you were wrong to betray me, then I'll kill you."

Friction screamed. "No!"

She sped forward. Time seemed to freeze around her as she closed on Paxton so quickly that he couldn't possibly have seen it coming. Her fist cannoned into his exposed face, and then she turned and drove her hand down onto his armored gauntlet. The force and speed of the blow shattered it at the seams, cracking it apart and sending his blade tumbling toward the ground. She leaped, planted both feet in his chest, and pushed off, driving him to the ground. Backflipping to land on her feet, Friction pressed in.

Paxton must have tried to react, though it was too slow to even register to her, because his left fist was up. She ignored it and punched his head again, cracking the helmet and sending the retracted faceplate flying off and across the field. She turned and kicked him again; and this time, a hairline fracture formed on the chest plate.

Friction breathed heavily as she continued to exert herself, pummeling Paxton before he could react. With each blow, her knuckles swelled. Blood stained her gloves, their already-maroon color patched with almost black splotches where his aionium armor tore open her skin. She ignored it. Another punch blackened his eye, and another drew a stream of blood from his nose and the corner of his mouth.

With a final kick, Friction knocked Paxton onto his back and slowed down. Her shoulders heaved. Her breaths were choppy as she struggled to fill lungs that expanded too quickly. Friction tried to calm herself. Paxton lay flat on the ground in front of her, his armor cracked and shattered in half a dozen places, his face one big bruise. He looked up at her, wheezing and coughing, and shook his head.

"See?" Paxton laughed, but the sound grated on her ears. "You are just like me."

* * *

With every passing second, Lucy's fear that Marsden would pull the trigger grew—not because he wanted to kill her but because his hands shook so violently in his anxiety that she worried his finger would spasm. He clearly had not been trained in firearm usage because he kept his finger firmly on the trigger. Lucy had fired a gun under the supervision of her aunt who was a police officer, so even she knew proper trigger discipline.

Keep your finger outside the trigger guard until you're ready to fire, her aunt always said.

Patrick should be here any second now. Lucy had pressed the alarm button almost two minutes ago. He had to be closing in. But what if he wasn't available? If Paxton had him pinned down or he was busy saving innocents, he might not reach her in time. Lucy let her fingers fall toward her pocket again, ready to risk using the adhesive bead if it looked like he wasn't going to show up.

Trust him. He'll be here.

"You . . . you should've left well enough alone." Marsden was babbling now, panicked. "You shouldn't have come."

"You're not going to kill me, Doctor. But you are going to go to jail. You had to know the risks when you started working for a gangster."

"Gangster?"

The gun shook in Marsden's unsteady grip. "I've got to think now. I've—"

A purple blur filled the lab, and Marsden's gun clattered to the floor. Lucy drew out one of her adhesive beads and threw it. The bead exploded at Marsden's feet, coating his legs in blue-green gel. He reeled back and fell to the floor—an awkward position, considering his legs were still upright from the knees down. Spright stopped between Lucy and Marsden.

"Heard you needed a hand," Patrick said.

"Thanks for the assistance." Lucy kissed his masked cheek. "Your timing was perfect."

"Aw, shucks. Nice throw, by the way." He looked down at Marsden. "You should've just confessed, man."

"Hey, guys?" Bryce's voice said. "You may want to get back to the field—*pronto*."

"On my way." Spright looked at Lucy. "You'll be okay here?"

She nodded. "I'll call the cops and have them pick up Marsden. Go."

* * *

Darius' head spun from the shock of being knocked flat by a speedster twice within the span of no more than a minute. His opera mask had been cracked on one of the hits. The broken corner of the plastic bit into his cheek. Darius pulled his mask free and dropped it to the ground. He didn't need it anymore—they were as good as done. Police sirens wailed in the distance. Zee was out cold from one of the speedster's punches. He would never be able to drag her away in time, even if he was in peak condition.

And from the look of things, Friction would not be distracted with Paxton for much longer, anyway. The gangster was lying limply in the middle of the field, surrounded by shards of his armor. Where had he gotten that suit, anyway? The sword on the arm was like the one Anton had used.

Darius staggered to his feet and limped to his sister's side while Friction spoke with Paxton. Maybe this was their revenge. Letting the gangster get defeated and captured by the superhero was justice, wasn't it? Neither Paxton nor his son had to die for that. Darius was relieved. The boy did not deserve to die. He didn't need to pay for his father's crimes.

"Zee. Wake up, Zee!"

She groaned.

"What happened . . ."

"It's over." He looped his arm around her back. "We've got to go."

"Not so fast," Friction called. "I'm not done with you two. You may be victims of his cruelty; but you still committed crimes, and you tried to kill his son."

Darius slumped to the ground next to Zee. There was no point in running; Friction was more than fast enough to stop them. Surrendering now was their best option. He picked up the gun Zee had dropped and tossed it away, where his sister wouldn't be tempted to use it. That would only get her hurt.

Friction stepped around Paxton and toward Darius and Zee. Darius stood and lowered his head, indicating surrender. He reached out to his sister's mind and poured calm thoughts in. She needed to come willingly, too. Friction knelt to help Zee stand. Behind her, Paxton turned and began to rise, a compartment in his left gauntlet opening. Friction was distracted with Zee. Only Darius saw what was coming.

"Look out!" Darius cried.

Friction turned as a hidden gun unfolded from Paxton's gauntlet. An arrow soared past Darius' cheek, so close that he could hear it, and embedded itself in one of the fractures on Paxton's chest plate. The gangster gaped, stared down at the shaft protruding from his abdomen, and slumped to the ground.

"No!"

Two voices shouted the word in unison. One belonged to Joey. Darius looked up to the stands as the young man rushed down to the field. Zee laughed darkly, and Darius turned and stared at his sister in revulsion. Friction's jaw was slack with horror, but Zee was just sneering. Darius completed his turn, searching for the other voice, and saw the archer—the same vigilante who had fought them at the bank and the restaurant—standing in the end zone, his crossbow still shouldered. Next to him stood the red-clad vigilante and an Asian man. Judging by the look of despair on the Asian man's face, he was the one who had cried out. As the archer lowered his weapon, the Asian man hurried across the field.

Darius extended his wrists as the red-clad vigilante approached and slapped a pair of handcuffs on him. The vigilante gave Friction another pair, which she put on Zee. The police sirens wailed louder. Spright appeared again, examined the scene, and dropped into a crouch next to Paxton.

"He finally got what he deserved," Zee murmured.

Darius shook his head. "What happened to you?"

"Doesn't matter." Zee jerked her head toward a pair of approaching cops. "Looks like we're not going to be seeing much of each other for a while, anyway."

* * *

"Don't you die, Paxton!" Ty growled. "I need answers. Don't die!"

The young man kneeling next to him—Paxton's son, Ty assumed—looked up with tears streaming down his face and confusion evident in his eyes. Ty ignored him and focused his attention on Paxton. If they had just been a few minutes earlier or if Jarrett could have taken his shot non-lethally . . . but it was too late.

Paxton was gone.

"Why did they kill him?" the boy whispered. "He was trying to save me. Why?"

Despite his frustration, Ty's heart went out to Paxton's son. They shared one thing in common: a father belonging to the Sicarans, beloved by their sons, killed before their time.

A hand fell on Ty's back. "He's gone. I'm sorry."

Ty looked up at the Crusader. "He was my last chance at answers. The Sicarans, what they think my destiny is, Charybdis . . . I'll never know the truth now."

"Maybe that's for the best." Carter took Ty's hand and helped him rise. "You don't need this mess in your life. You need to go home, serve your time, and be a good dad to Emi. That is way more important than any destiny these wackos think you have."

A lump formed in Ty's throat. He struggled to swallow it. "You have to remember your promise. Protect her while I'm in prison. If they come for her . . . "

"You know I will."

"I'll hold you to that." Ty lowered his head. "All right. Let's go. I'm done here."

CHAPTER 44

The adrenaline high that came during a mission was more intense for a speedster—which meant that the comedown from that surge of emotion was worse, too. As Patrick and his friends gathered in the airport the next day, he struggled to stay focused on what was in front of him. He felt almost as tired as he had while under Darius' power, although he knew that this slump would end soon on its own.

Paxton was dead on the scene when Patrick arrived back at the field. He didn't blame Jarrett for killing him. It had been his only option at the distance he was at, since most of Paxton's armor was impenetrable aionium. Alexa had been too distracted with Zoey to realize the threat Paxton still presented, and she would have died had Jarrett not acted. It was not the first time the archer had killed a villain to save a friend's life. He had done it for Patrick, too, killing Alfonso Mendez in Washington, D.C.

Joey was distraught, though. Asher's roommate believed his father had arrived at the football field to save him from the Colemans. He still had no idea about Oscar Paxton's criminal activity or why Spright and Friction had battled his father.

Alexa had been as subdued as Patrick since the encounter. Patrick could tell she felt guilty about how violently she had beaten Paxton. He would have to talk to her about it. At least, she hadn't killed him. He was confident that with time, she would recover and even become a better hero because of it. Lucy, on the other hand, remained surprisingly strong, despite Marsden nearly killing her. Her tough spirit made Patrick proud to call her the woman he loved. If not for her work, they wouldn't have as much evidence against Paxton as they now did.

The real damage was to their lair. Thanks to Jan's quick thinking, she and Bryce managed to get rid of any evidence that Team Spright operated from the basement. She had used her powers to cause a small electrical fire that burned any equipment they could not move from the basement beyond recognition. It looked like it had just been the result of Paxton's attack. None of EBC's students had been hurt, and they would be able to rebuild the student center before the spring semester started. But that left Team Spright without a lair for the foreseeable future. Maybe Bryce could work some more of his magic.

That was a problem for another day, though. For the moment, they had to say goodbye. Jarrett and Jan had booked a flight for that morning, and Carter did not want to wait any longer to get Ty back to prison. Dean's private jet was already waiting for them at the airport. The group stood just outside the security line and exchanged handshakes and back-slapping hugs.

"Sorry we can't stay longer," Jarrett said. "CLOUD has an urgent assignment for us."

"You've done more than your share," Patrick said. "I'm glad you both came, and I can't begin to thank you for everything you did."

"It was our pleasure." Jan held out her hand. "It was very nice to get to know all of you."

"You, too." Patrick smiled and shook her hand. "Take care of yourself—and your husband. We may need you again someday."

"Anytime."

Jan and Jarrett waved to the others as they entered the TSA security line. Patrick smiled and waved one last time before turning to Carter and Ty. Carter offered him a wide grin and pulled him into another hug. Patrick gripped his friend for dear life. He wished he and Carter had been able to spend more time catching up before he had to go.

"Don't worry, man." Carter stepped out of the embrace. "I'll be back soon. I've got to get Ty back to Stone Gate, but there's some unfinished business here that needs taking care of. There was more to the feud between Paxton and Weeks than you know, and I need to get to the bottom of it. I'll fill you in when I get back."

Patrick nodded. "Guess I'll see you soon, then."

"Without a doubt." Carter waved goodbye to Lucy and Bryce. "You two take good care of this bozo. He needs it."

Lucy stepped in and grabbed Patrick's hand. "We will."

Patrick glanced at Ty. "I don't know you well, but I hope you know you're making the right decision. I'm very impressed by your dedication."

"Thank you." Ty inclined his head. "Perhaps we'll meet again someday."

Then Carter and Ty were off, hurrying toward the private tarmac where the private jet awaited them. Patrick let out a long sigh, and then he and Lucy turned to head for the exit with Bryce trailing behind.

"Your friends are nice," Lucy said. "I hope we get to see them again under better circumstances."

"We will." Patrick pulled her hand up and kissed her knuckles. "Come on. We've still got a lot to take care of."

* * *

Spright stood in the shadows of the alley behind the police precinct as Officer Gregg exited through the back door. As soon as the door shut,

Spright sped over to the policeman's side. Gregg jumped and reached for his sidearm. He stopped when he saw who had startled him.

"You guys have got to stop doing that." Gregg sighed. "Where's your archer friend?"

"Had to leave town. But he wanted me to give this to you."

He extended a folder that had been stuffed with the paper files taken from Marsden's lab, along with a flash drive containing the video of the Colemans fighting the Archdukes and the Seventy-Six at the docks, the records of dealings between Paxton and the Seventy-Six, and the digital copies of Paxton's deal with Marsden.

Gregg tilted his head. "What's this?"

"Everything you'll need to put Darius and Zoey Coleman away, as well as Dr. Marsden from Garvin Technologies. They were all part of a larger plot orchestrated by Oscar Paxton."

"Paxton's dead now."

"The Colemans and Marsden still committed crimes." Spright turned away. "Use that information as you will."

"Thank you. Honestly, I don't know how we'd deal with nutjobs like this without people like you."

Once, the statement would have filled Patrick with pride, but now he felt humbled that God had allowed him to be part of His plan in this way. He had given Patrick his powers for a reason. Patrick wouldn't waste them.

"Good night, Officer." Spright walked toward the street. "I'm sure I'll see you out there."

"Uh . . . sure thing."

Spright sped away, leaving the police officer and the precinct behind.

* * *

Alexa rubbed the gauze wrapped around her knuckles. She could feel the rough texture of the scabs beneath them. She deserved them—and more. If she had not snapped out of her rampage, she could have killed Paxton. Worse, she had been so distracted by the horror she felt that he had nearly caught her by surprise, which had forced Jarrett to kill Paxton. Now Joey was fatherless with no idea why, and Alexa felt saddled with the guilt of that, too.

She should have been more precise. She knew what her speed could do to Paxton's armor; she could have ripped every piece of it from his body without hurting him. Then, he would've been alive to be taken into custody and convicted. Joey would have realized the truth about his father and still had him in his life to deal with the fallout. Instead, Alexa was so blinded by rage that she had gone berserk, filled with a desire to hurt Paxton. As far as she was concerned, she carried the guilt of putting the arrow in his chest. She may not have pulled the crossbow's trigger, but she was responsible, right? She was everything Paxton had wanted her to be.

In the days that followed the fight on the football field, she tried to decide where to go from here. It was obvious to her, if not to anyone else on Patrick's team, that she was a liability. What would happen next time she lost her temper like that? What if it happened while she was fighting someone who didn't have a nearly invulnerable super suit like Paxton's? She could kill someone.

They didn't need her anymore. Now that Patrick had his speed back, he was more than capable of handling things on his own. She was just baggage to the team.

"Hey, Alexa!" Lucy called.

Alexa looked up. She had been sitting on her own in the cafeteria, at one of the corner tables at the back of the cafeteria where no one ever ate. She hoped to avoid interacting with her friends. But since they saw her, she smiled and waved them over.

"It's crazy that the cafeteria's even still open," Lucy said. "There's a big, gaping hole in the roof of the student center!"

"Well, the damage didn't spread this far." Patrick shrugged. "And they do have the rest of the building cordoned off."

Lucy shivered. "But it's so cold."

Alexa forced a smile as they sat down. She kept her attention on her food, scooping it into her mouth and fixing her gaze on her tray.

"It'll only get colder, too." Patrick set his tray down and picked up a roll. "Good thing we live in California, not the Midwest."

Bryce scooped a spoonful of vegetables. "You know, we got lucky. If Jan hadn't been able to cook all our stuff, we would've been found out down there."

"Could've been. But we're safe."

"You okay, Alexa?" Lucy asked. "Do your hands hurt?"

"No, I'm fine." Alexa finally looked up at her friends. "But . . . I've been doing some thinking. I'm not sure this city needs Friction anymore. I'm a liability."

Patrick, Lucy, and Bryce exchanged glances with one another and looked back to her as one. They all began speaking at once, their words forming a jumble as they protested her statement. She half-smiled—the closest she had come to genuine good humor since the fight—and held up a hand to quiet them.

"It's okay. The truth is, I'm not ready to be a hero. I need to be on my own for a while, figure things out for myself. I'm going to talk to my parents later today, and then I'm going to have myself administratively withdrawn from all my classes here at EBC. I don't know where I'm going to go yet . . . but I need to figure some things out."

"Alexa, what happened on the football field could happen to anyone," Patrick said. "It even happened to me! When Backfire threatened my parents, I almost killed him. Lucy was there. She could tell you. If not for her, I might not have stopped. But I grew from it. I didn't let it drive me away from my friends. We all make mistakes. That's what grace is for."

Alexa swallowed the lump forming in her throat.

That's what we're all about, isn't it?

Grace. She understood the concept, and Patrick was giving an excellent example of it now, but it felt so hard to make that truth a reality in her mind right now.

"I know. But I have to forgive myself, too. I'll come back someday, maybe. But I just need to figure all this out. Paxton really did a number on me. I don't know how long it will take to fix."

"You shouldn't have to do it alone," Lucy said.

"I'll be fine." Alexa stood and picked up her tray. "If you really want to support me, then let me go. It's not forever. It's just . . . for now."

She turned and left the table behind, not waiting for their response. Once she had dumped her tray and was outside the cafeteria, she turned, sped away, and let the wind dry the tears on her face.

CHAPTER 45

"What did you do?" Shannon asked coldly.

Asher swiveled his lab chair to face her as she approached. Her face was contorted in a mask of rage almost as furious as the one Anton Coleman had worn as a disguise. She was livid. He shuddered. Looking around to ensure no one was listening, he gestured for her to sit down in the empty seat next to him.

"What do you mean?"

"You know what I mean." Shannon sat down, her gaze boring into him. "I told you a secret about my father; and the same day, he gets held hostage by vigilantes and then arrested the day after. You told someone."

"Shannon . . ."

"Don't." She stood. "I thought I could trust you, Asher."

"You can."

She turned and stormed out of the classroom. Asher glanced at the clock on the wall. Class was about to start.

Guess I'm skipping.

He jumped up and followed her into the hallway. She was walking quickly; he had to jog to keep up with her.

"Shannon, wait! What's wrong? You told me you wanted to crack down on crime. That's why you wanted to become a politician, right? You want to take a stance against people like your father."

"Yes," she said. "But I wanted to be the one to see him put away. I wanted him to know that it was me who caused his downfall. I told you this stuff in confidence, and you betrayed me. After everything we've talked about . . . "

"Shannon." He grabbed her hand gently, pulling her to a stop. "I don't know what you want me to say."

"You clearly know some superhero or someone who does." She snorted. "Your friend Patrick? I should've guessed after all that superhero talk at dinner. And he went to Sojourn City for an internship. He must've met one of them while he was there."

At least, she didn't know the whole truth. Asher struggled to find a response. He had worked so hard to earn her trust. He couldn't destroy that now.

"Listen. I'm sorry I misunderstood. But be honest with me. That priest who hurt you—your father let him get away with it, didn't he? He knew. But because your priest knew he was the leader of the Seventy-Six, your father had to let it go; or the priest would've ratted on him."

Shannon clenched her jaw. "Congratulations. You figured it out."

"So, this is really just about revenge for you, isn't it? I saw what happened recently when someone became obsessed with revenge. It destroyed them." Asher realized he was still holding her hand. "I don't want it to destroy you, too. Shannon, I'm not asking you to forgive me right now. But I am asking that you still try to be my friend. I like you a lot, and I want to help you."

As he talked, some of the anger drained from her face. It was still there, welling behind her eyes; but she had contained it. Maybe . . . maybe he could get through to her. He said a quick prayer for God's help.

"That rage has to feel like a million pounds by now, doesn't it? You've gotten so used to carrying it that it just makes you numb. But if you let it go, you can feel free."

"I . . ." Tears rolled down Shannon's cheeks. "Why didn't he protect me, Asher? He's my dad, and he just swept it under the rug."

Asher pulled her into a hug. Her body convulsed with sobs. She pressed her head into his shoulder and cried. Asher gently rubbed her back. He didn't know how else to comfort her; his words could never be enough for what she'd had to endure. So he stayed with her, and he let her cry. It was the least he could do.

* * *

Airport security was nothing compared to what Jarrett and Jan had to go through getting back into CLOUD headquarters. Jarrett hadn't missed the constant suspicion and awareness that came from being a spy. It was nice to work with Patrick's team. They were young and inexperienced, but they were also trusting. He hadn't had to jump through hoops to help them.

He wished they could have stayed longer. Something sinister was clearly at play in New Echelon, something bigger than a feud between street gangs. Between Benjamin Weeks' ominous words about Paxton being an ancient enemy and the way Ty had crumpled when he saw Paxton dead, it was obvious that something very old and very dangerous was happening. Jarrett would have liked to figure out what. Unsolved mysteries bothered him.

There would be time for that later. For now, he had a job to do.

An agent stationed at the door finished checking Jarrett's belongings, nodded to him, and handed him his badge. Jarrett took it

and clipped it to his belt. Once he was inside the base, he waited for
Jan to finish her scan, as well. Finally, she walked in, too.

"You know, we never finished that conversation about kids."

Jan shook her head. "You don't give up, do you, Jarrett Mercer?"

"Not my style." He winked and fell in stride with her. "I know it's
not the best time for it. But I want to have that life before we get too
old for it. We're busy right now, and bringing a kid into the picture
could be tough. But I'm willing to make the sacrifice."

"That's sweet." Jan smiled and leaned over to kiss his cheek. "Let's see
what mission the Director has for us. Then, we can decide about kids."

It was a start—and at this point, Jarrett would take it. Reinvigorated
with hope, he walked toward his next task with a spring in his step.

* * *

"So," Lucy said. "She's really gone."

Patrick had seen the red form of Alexa's streak leading away
from campus earlier that afternoon, and Lucy confirmed that Alexa's
belongings had been cleared from their room. He would miss her, but
he couldn't say he blamed her, either. She would do what she had to do.

"What happens now?" Lucy asked. "We lost our brand-new lair. Do
things go back to the way they were before, you running off whenever
there's an emergency and me watching from my dorm room?"

"No way." Patrick wrapped his arm around her shoulder as they
crossed campus. "Well, some nights, probably. Sometimes, there will
be muggings and robberies—things I can handle in a few minutes. But
if this whole ordeal taught me anything, it's that I need you. There
are going to be cases where I can't handle everything on my own. I'll
need you to investigate things and Bryce to work his tech magic. Once

he gets a new computer, of course. We're a team—it's time we started acting like it. And that goes for me, most of all."

"You're a good man, Patrick Omer." Lucy smiled and kissed his cheek. "And that's why I love you."

Patrick felt more at ease now than he had in weeks. His youth ministry project had been turned in. Rick had been impressed with the level of study he had put into Christian opinion on superheroes. With Paxton dead and the Colemans and much of the Seventy-Six's leadership in jail, the streets were quiet. Carter's words hung in the back of his mind, warning of another threat on the horizon; but that was not a problem for today.

"What do you think Paxton meant about having plans for Alexa and the Colemans?" Lucy asked. "It seemed like more than just a casual statement."

Alexa had told them about Paxton's declaration after the fight ended. She had been as confused by it as they were; she had been working for Paxton for years, and she never felt he had plans for her outside of making her a superhero. Whatever it was, though, he wouldn't be able to follow through now.

"I don't know. But he's gone now. They're safe. And if he has any backup plans in place, we'll be ready for it."

Lucy squeezed his hand. "We will. Together."

CHAPTER 46

It was odd to think of a prison cell as home, but Ty was almost glad to be back inside Stone Gate Penitentiary. He was serving his sentence, once again moving toward the day when he could truly call himself a free man. Every day served here brought him closer to Emi and Joanie. Difficult as it was to sit in a concrete cube with his powers suppressed, he would endure it if it meant he could hold his daughter in his arms again.

With the evidence deposited at Sojourn PD by the Crusader and his team, the judge had been lenient on Ty. It was obvious that the "rescue" had not been his plan and that he had been taken against his own volition. No extra time was added to Ty's sentence.

Over the past few days, Joanie and Carter had both come to visit Ty. Joanie was relieved to the point of tears that Ty was safe. Carter reiterated his pride in Ty's decision to come home. Silas Rockwell, the man caring for Emi, even paid Ty a visit. He promised that Emi was doing well and that he and his family were eager for the day when Ty got out of prison and could have his daughter back.

Ty leaned against his cell wall and swallowed the lump in his throat. He had been shown so much grace over the past weeks. Shannon, the daughter of Ty's captor, had shown him grace. He hoped she was doing all right. Carter had shown him grace, as well—above and beyond what Ty deserved. Carter could have assumed the worst and dragged him back to Sojourn City in condemnation. He could have forced Ty to return to Sojourn City while he remained in New Echelon to help Spright. He could have refused to let Ty come along when he and Yeoman attacked the Seventy-Six. Instead, Carter had given Ty chance after chance to prove himself.

Tears welled in Ty's eyes. He looked up at the ceiling.

"Thank You, God. Thank You for Carter Jonson. Thank You for Shannon. Thank You for bringing me home."

Carter might never know how profoundly his actions had influenced Ty. Ty had never seen that level of grace from anyone—not since his father had died. Ty still had a lot of things to figure out—and he would always wonder about the Sicarans and McCrory's ominous words—but one thing was obvious. He had been given another chance at life. He needed to take it.

"God, I believe in You." Ty swallowed. "Please forgive me. Help me to be a man who shows the kind of grace Carter showed me—the kind of grace You show me. Amen."

* * *

Of all the punishments prison represented, Darius never would have expected boredom to be the worst of them. Lying on his cot and staring at the ceiling, he wondered how he would ever last through his entire sentence. He wanted to pull his hair out, and the fact that his powers were suppressed too much to use only made things worse. His cell was specialized, built with a dampener that kept him from using them. It was like knowing one of his limbs was there and being unable to use it.

He deserved to be here, though. Darius had had the power to stop everything his siblings had done. If only he had grown a spine and told Anton that he refused to go into crime with him—or even afterward, if he told Zee they wouldn't try to get revenge on Paxton. If he had stood firm, instead of cowing down to his siblings and going along with whatever they said, Anton might not be dead; and he and Zee might not be in prison.

The lights in Darius' cell flickered. For the briefest instant, he felt his powers again. He sat up on his cot and looked around.

Probably just a power surge.

He started to lie back down, and the fluctuation repeated. Darius got to his feet and walked to the barred cell door.

"What's happening? Guard?"

No response. Darius backed away from the bars. Whatever this was, it was temporary. He sat back down on his cot as the lights went out entirely. The murmurs of other prisoners rose, the only sound in the otherwise oppressively silent cell block. Darius felt his way along the wall to the window. The prison yard's floodlights were out, too. The only illumination came from distant city lights and the moon. A shiver crawled up Darius's spine to the back of his neck. He shuddered.

"Darius Coleman."

Darius jumped up and backed away from the cell doors. His ankle brushed the toilet, nearly causing him to fall; but his back bumped the rear wall of the cell. His breath came in short, choppy pants as he squinted to see where the voice had come from. It was useless; the darkness was all-encompassing.

"Who . . . who's there?"

"A messenger . . . with an offer."

The voice did not sound like it was coming from inside the cell. That was a relief. He relaxed slightly. What was this—some sort of gang scare tactic? Had one of the Seventy-Six bribed the guards to give him a few minutes alone with Darius? Maybe they wanted to make him an offer, since he'd been brazen enough to take a shot at Oscar Paxton's son.

"I'm not interested. I just want to serve out my sentence and try to return to some semblance of a normal life. Is that too much to ask?"

"You're not normal, Darius. That life is past."

"What do you want?"

"To give you a purpose. Oscar Paxton made mistakes because his interests were torn. He should have cultivated your talents, not murdered your brother. His allegiance to the Archdukes made him weak. You are not sullied by such weakness. You have power, and you want to make a difference."

"Well . . . yes."

"We can make that happen. Paxton was supposed to bring you to me, but he failed. Your talents would've been wasted with him. With me, you can prosper. I will take you away from this city, away from the crime that ruined your life. I will shape you into the world-changer that you want to be."

"What . . . what about Zee?"

"I have another agent speaking with her now. I am certain she will take us up on our offer." Darius could almost hear the smile in the man's voice. "Your sister is coming with us, Darius. Don't be left behind."

Darius took a step forward. "We'll be fugitives."

"You'll be beyond the reach of the law."

Darius' mind spun. *If I stay in prison, Anton died in vain.*

He remembered the conversation he'd had with Zee in the motel room, just after Anton's death. They had agreed that he wanted what was best for them. Anton would have been heartbroken to see them in prison. And if Zee was leaving . . . what good would it do for Darius to stay?

I'm not the one who did any of those things, anyway. I might have been an accessory, but I didn't commit their crimes.

"Lead the way."

* * *

Roland Demirci had spent long months on his mission to find amplified warriors to recruit to the Sicarans. It was a task he had not taken lightly, and he knew that not just any superhuman would fit his needs. Many of them would be ordinary people who had developed powers by chance. Given the opportunity, they would rid themselves of their gifts. He needed people who understood their powers gave them a purpose.

Oscar Paxton had already had a superhuman in mind when Roland approached him—a girl with superspeed, who he called Friction. Paxton had later discovered the Coleman triplets and attempted to recruit them, as well. But Paxton had been a failure. Roland should have known not to trust him. His focus on his business and on the Archdukes had distracted him from his loyalty to the Sicarans. The fact that he had already been training Friction long before Roland spoke with him indicated that he had personal plans for the girl.

Roland had agents tracking the girl, and he had retrieved Darius and Zoey Coleman himself. He was surprised that Darius had agreed to come along. Zoey's rage had been easy to stoke, and she had agreed to follow him readily. But Darius? He seemed too pacifistic. Roland was glad Darius had proved him wrong. With the two of them at his side, he could return to one of the Sicarans' training camps. He just had one more stop to make before he left New Echelon.

The sound of soft crying echoed down the opulent, wood-walled hallway. Roland kept one hand near the hilt of his dagger, ready to fight if a member of the mansion's security team saw him. But that was unlikely; Roland was skilled at being unseen. He crept closer to the warm light coming from the bedroom, and the cries grew more distinct.

Roland stepped into the room. Joey Paxton looked up at the sound of the squeaking door and jumped up from his bed, his eyes widening in panic. Roland extended his hands palms-out. He closed the door behind him. Paxton's mansion was large and nearly empty; sound would travel farther than normal in such a vast place. Roland reached up and removed his mask. Joey frowned.

"Who are you? What do you want with me?"

"I am an old acquaintance of your father's. My name is Roland Demirci, but he knew me as Keskin. I have come to give you my condolences on his death."

"You could've sent a card." Joey moved back to his bed and sat down. "Everyone else is."

"I can offer you more than a meaningless card, Joseph."

"Joey. It's Joey."

"Very well." Roland approached the boy. "I know how your father died, Joey."

"It was unfair." Joey scowled. "They got it wrong. Those superheroes—they were supposed to come and save me. But Dad wasn't the one hurting me—it was those two in the opera masks. But they just went and fought Dad, anyway. And they killed him. Some superheroes."

"Indeed. That's why I have come. I can offer you revenge."

"Revenge? How?"

"I come from a group, one your father has been part of for decades, which controls the ebb and flow of the world. We see when regimes need changing, when world powers need toppling, when new leaders need to be set up. We see imbalances, and we fix them. Superheroes are . . . an imbalance—one that we intend to fix."

Charybdis was the Sicarans' true enemy, but Joey did not need to know that now. The truth was, as long as superheroes stood against the Sicarans, it would be impossible to fight Charybdis effectively. Roland and the team he had been assigned by the Elite would take out superheroes first, and then they could focus on Charybdis. Joey was an important piece of that plan.

"What do you want from me?" Joey asked. "Money?"

"We don't need money. We need talent."

"What kind of talent can I possibly offer you?" Joey shook his head. "I don't even know what I want to do with my life."

"Perhaps now, you do."

Roland could practically see the gears of Joey's mind turning. He was intrigued. Roland only had to twist the knife a little further, and he would agree.

"I can give you the chance to take your revenge personally and at the same time become something more than you are now. You can be a tool for balancing the scales." Roland knelt next to Joey's bed. "If you want, you can even be the one to kill the superheroes who murdered your father."

"How . . . how would I do that?"

"Your father's armor. One of my agents recovered it, and we have the skill to repair it—even improve it. If you want to avenge your father, take up his title. Become Adranis."

Joey looked up, and Roland saw his father's fire in his eyes.

"When do we start?"

ABOUT THE AUTHOR

Jake Tyson, author of *The Vindicators* series of superhero novels, is a journalism graduate of Central Baptist College and has been writing creatively since nine years old. He is married to Jessica, with whom he has two beautiful daughters, Emma and Ophelia. He is a youth pastor at Oak Park Baptist Church in Little Rock, Arkansas.

For more information about
Jake Tyson
&
The Vindicators **Series**

please visit:

www.creatingforcreator.wordpress.com
www.facebook.com/jaketysonauthor96

For more information about
AMBASSADOR INTERNATIONAL
please visit:

www.ambassador-international.com
@AmbassadorIntl
www.facebook.com/AmbassadorIntl

*If you enjoyed this book, please consider leaving us a review on
Amazon, Goodreads, or our website.*

David al-Nassery is a man of renown. Hailing from distant Chaldea, he has made a name for himself in the United Kingdom as a philanthropist and an advocate for the political interests of the Middle East. Yet even as he surrounds himself with allies, enemies from his past await him. When confronted by a figure from his past on a cold, dark night, David is forced to reckon with the decisions he made in Chaldea—choices that cost thousands their lives.

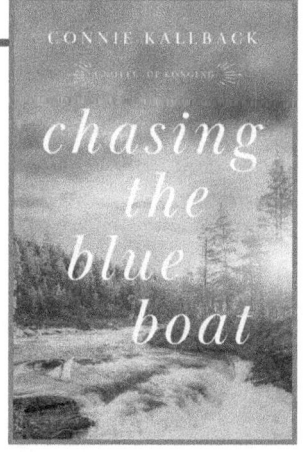

Nine-year old Dana Foster will follow her older brother, Luke, wherever he goes. But when tragedy strikes the Foster family, everything that Dana has ever known is suddenly turned upside down. In this coming-of-age story, discover the truths of God's grace in suffering, the blessing of forgiveness, and how to hold on to your faith when all hope seems lost.

When Sofia sets out from South America to start a new life in the States, she discovers evil is just as prevalent in her new country. Working at a hotel, Sofia sees numerous children she suspects are being held against their will. After Sofie meets Hector, they devise a plan to help the most vulnerable. But will she jeopardize her own citizenship status? And more importantly, if she and Hector don't rescue the children, then who will?